Mrs. Pollifax
Pursued

Mrs. Pollifax Pursued

Dorothy Gilman

WHEELER
PUBLISHING, INC.

★ AN AMERICAN COMPANY ★

Lg Pt
M

Copyright © 1985 by Dorothy Gilman.

Published in Large Print by arrangement with
Ballantine Books, a division of Random House,
Inc. in the United States and Canada.

Wheeler Large Print Book Series.

Set in 16 pt. Plantin.

Library of Congress Cataloging-in-Publication Data

Gilman, Dorothy, 1923–
    Mrs. Pollifax pursued / Dorothy Gilman.
      p.   cm.—(Wheeler large print book series)
    ISBN 1-56895-088-8 (softcover) : $22.95
    1. Pollifax, Emily (Fictitious character)—Fiction.   2. Intelligence
service—United States—Fiction.   3. Women spies—United
States—Fiction.   4. Large type books.   I. Title.   II. Series.
[PS3557.J433M73   1995]
813'.54—dc20   94-45327
                                                              CIP

Friday

PROLOGUE

Henry Bidwell was rich but this was of little consequence to him since he had always been rich. What mattered most to him was that he was successful in his work, his wealth increasing each day as a result of his own clear thinking, acute judgments, and calculations. He held a vital position in Claiborne-Osborne International, a conservative investment and holding company that prided itself on its global connections and was dedicated to making even more money smoothly, discreetly, and with well-concealed ruthlessness. He traveled abroad frequently to inspect these varied interests and to investigate new acquisitions, moving in a world made seamless by ease and convenience.

On this late Friday afternoon in April before departing from his desk he checked his calendar, noted that his wife was entertaining a dozen people for dinner that evening, and that he could anticipate a weekend of golf. As he nodded with satisfaction his phone rang and he frowned. His secretary had already left for the day and he did not appreciate phones that rang without Miss Ferguson's intervention. Nevertheless he picked up the receiver, said sharply, "Bidwell here," and listened to the voice at the other end, murmured, "I understand . . . you can't tell me when?" And then, "Of course, yes," and hung up. Following a glance at his gold Breitling watch he brushed a speck of lint from his Armani suit and picked up his briefcase, knowing that his chauffeur, Georges, would arrive punctually in five minutes. Walking to his private elevator he descended eighteen floors to the lobby, made his exit through the bank of glass doors, and walked out into the pleasant late afternoon sunlight. His limousine had not yet pulled into the NO PARKING space opposite the lobby doors; at the moment the space had been usurped by a dirty white van with a misspelled CHIGI SCAP METAL painted on its panel.

The driver of the van, giving him a sharp glance, looked a cheeky fellow in a ragged cap; his confederate had just walked around the van to its rear and was unlocking and opening the two rear doors. Bidwell stepped to the edge of the sidewalk and said sternly, "Look here, my good man, you can't stop here. Can't you read? No parking allowed."

The man gave him a mocking glance and said scornfully, "Put your head in a bucket, mister."

"The law is very strict," pointed out Mr. Bidwell. "On this street especially, the police—"

The man narrowed his eyes and moved toward him aggressively. "Yeah?"

Bidwell retreated a step from the curb but the man followed, thrusting his face close to Bidwell's. "Yeah?" he repeated, and lifted a dirty hand to shake a filthy rag in Bidwell's face.

It was at this moment that Bidwell realized he had misunderstood the situation, that this confrontation had been planned, it was premeditated, because something was certainly wrong: the rag shoved into his face had been saturated

2

with a chemical both unpleasant and penetrating, and his quick gasp only made worse the fumes searing his nostrils and throat. He was aware of the sidewalk beginning to move giddily up and down in front of him, ultimately coiling like a snake and then blurring fuzzily. As Mr. Bidwell slid down to join it he felt himself caught, lifted, carried away, and dumped on a hard metal surface. When the door slammed he was already unconscious on the floor of the Chigi Scap Metal van.

1

Wednesday

Mrs. Pollifax, relaxing for a few minutes over coffee at her kitchen table, dutifully scanned the headlines of the morning newspaper: OPEC MEETING ABORTIVE; FOOD RIOTS IN UBANGIBA; TORNADO HITS KANSAS; but she was far more interested in the abduction of Henry Bidwell four days ago, about which there was a long article, but with very little fresh news. His disappearance intrigued her; she enjoyed mysteries, having been involved in a number of them herself. Words like *snatched* appealed to her, and *no witnesses*—on such a busy street, too—fueled her curiosity. Reading further she discovered that "no witnesses" was not quite true: the police had now unearthed a fruit vendor on the next block who had noticed Bidwell standing on the curb because he'd seen him sway dizzily and be helped into a car. *Taken sick,* the vendor had thought, but since his view had been blocked by lines of parked cars, and he had been half a block away, his information was too scanty to be of help. Bidwell, however, remained missing and it was becoming more and more obvious that because of his position he'd been abducted for ransom.

If his situation intrigued Mrs. Pollifax, his importance did not, since planting basil in her greenhouse was the more vital to her this morning. Draining her cup of coffee, she picked up

4

her trowel and walked through the open door into the bright sunny greenhouse. Her geraniums were blossoming in colorful profusion but this year she was planting herbs, too, and she noted that both the mints and the sage were nearly ready to be transplanted into the garden. *This* was where she celebrated spring, planting and nurturing, adjusting vents and shade and drinking in the pungent smells of warm earth, lime, bone meal, and mint.

Glancing up from her work she was surprised to see a shabby white van once again drive past the house on its way up Maple Lane. She frowned because she had seen it pass the house three times yesterday, noticing it especially because of the sign on its side panel, which she had mentioned to Cyrus as he packed to attend the meeting of the American Bar Association.

"Lost art, spelling," he'd said. "Emily, where's the other blue tie I wear with this shirt?"

"You'll only be away until Monday," she'd reminded him.

"I spill," he pointed out. "Bound to spill if I don't carry spares."

She had laughed and restored the extra ties to his suitcase, but later the van had driven past for the third time and she had noticed how it slowed at the sight of Cyrus checking the tires of the car in the driveway. It was impossible to mistake it because it bore the same misspelled sign: CHIGI SCAP METAL.

Now it was passing the house again.

This, she told herself sternly, *is what comes of working for Carstairs and the Department; the antenna keeps working, there is too MUCH awareness, which is all very well on assignments fraught*

5

with danger but I am NOT on assignment, I'm in my own house and trying to plant basil.

On the other hand, she reflected thoughtfully, very few cars used Maple Lane; it was a shortcut to the highway that only neighbors used, and few people knew about, and its usual traffic was familiar to her: Mr. Gogan off to work each morning and returning; Mrs. Haycock driving to her job at the hospital; the young Abners delivering their son to day care, the mail truck, the carpenters building an addition at the Witkowskis.

She supposed that eventually there would be a reasonable explanation for this new vehicle going up and down the lane at such odd hours. What she did not understand was why its frequent appearances had begun to make her uneasy. *I need food,* she decided; of course she needed food after such an early breakfast, and with a glance at her wrist watch she put aside her trowel and returned to the kitchen. Opening the refrigerator door she inspected its contents critically: the chicken was for dinner, the salad—but she didn't want salad, she was too hungry after driving Cyrus to the airport at dawn. Her eyes fell on the package of Cyrus's favorite salami, and—*living dangerously,* she thought with a smile—she opened a fresh loaf of bread, unwrapped the salami, and made a sandwich. Pouring a glass of milk she carried her lunch on a tray to the patio where she could sit in the sun and admire the tulips and crocuses.

It was a pleasant scene; beyond the beds of flowers, at a distance, marched a row of birches that lined the unpaved road into the woods, but as her gaze moved from the tulips to the distant trees she saw that she was not as private as she had hoped: something white caught her eye. A car was parked on one side of the woods road, no doubt its occupant eating his or her lunch, too, she thought, and wondered why the discovery made her uncomfortable. With a sigh she stood up and carried her tray back into the house. Depositing it on the dining table, and scolding herself for doing this, she drew out Cyrus's bird-watching binoculars from the drawer of the buffet and walked to the window.

I'm being ridiculous, she thought.

They were very fine binoculars and, although a tree concealed the front of the car and its occupant, she could see that it was a shabby white van and she could make out five letters of the sign on the panel: SCAP M.

"I think," said Mrs. Pollifax aloud, very firmly, "that I will move the car out of the driveway and into the garage."

She had no idea why this was important, and as she walked out of the house and climbed into the car she asked herself why. *Because Cyrus is away?* she wondered, *and I'm alone here? But why move the car?*

Finding no ready answer she drove the car to the rear of the house; the garage doors obediently swung open and closed behind her, and for that moment she felt snug and relaxed. Reentering the house from the garage she walked down the hall past the living room and through the kitchen, and as she reached the greenhouse saw the white van drive past the house and disappear.

She sighed with relief.

Emily, she thought, *you've behaved very irrationally this past hour, and need I remind you that this*

7

is the route to paranoia? With grim resolve she resumed her planting of basil and presently found other matters to think about: the Garden Club meeting tomorrow, for instance, and the sandwiches she had volunteered that were already made and covered with a damp cloth in the refrigerator. Wondering if the men attending the meeting would be content with cucumber sandwiches, it occurred to her that she might add half a dozen sandwiches of salami. *Cholesterol be damned,* she thought, and abandoning the basil she walked into the kitchen to expand the refreshment menu.

The salami, however, was not in the refrigerator.

This seemed odd, since she had made a sandwich of it scarcely an hour ago; nevertheless the salami was not where it should have been in the refrigerator, nor was it on the counter or the kitchen table.

Puzzled, she emptied the refrigerator's top shelf of chicken, bread, salad, the platter of Garden Club sandwiches, and a carton of eggs, but the salami had not been hiding behind any of them; it was simply not there. With a sigh of exasperation she began the tiresome job of returning the food to the top shelf, but when she picked up the newly opened loaf of bread it struck her as surprisingly light; she examined it more carefully and felt a vague sense of disquiet because earlier she had extracted two slices from the top of the loaf and now there were at least five slices missing, as well as the crust.

Definitely uneasy now, Mrs. Pollifax walked to the cupboard in which she stored canned goods and ran a sharp eye over its contents. There had been eight tins of sardines yesterday and Cyrus had packed two of them for snacks; there should have been six left but there was now only one. Gone, too, were the screw-top jars of herring, and the six-pack of colas had been reduced to four.

The house suddenly felt oppressively silent. Mrs. Pollifax was no longer uneasy; a small chill was racing down her spine.

What this means, she thought, feeling her way gingerly toward an explanation, *is that while I drove Cyrus to the airport this morning someone broke into this house and stole some food.*

This was the rationale that she preferred, but of course it was entirely wrong because only an hour ago she had made a sandwich of the missing salami and bread.

Very reluctantly she approached the only viable explanation, and she did not like it at all. It meant that she was not alone here, there was someone else in this house with her. Now, at this moment. Hiding somewhere.

2

Mrs. Pollifax stood very still, listening, her senses heightened by the knowledge that someone else shared this silence that until a moment ago had been friendly and companionable and had now become threatening. Carefully she took stock of her resources: a flashlight for dark closets, the poker from the fireplace, and her training in karate. She dismissed the thought of calling the police because her call might be overheard in this silent house and bring the intruder out of hiding to confront her on his terms, not hers. *Too risky,* she thought, and armed with poker and flashlight she tiptoed up the stairs to begin at the top of the house.

Closets were opened in the master bedroom, in Cyrus's study, the guest room, and the hall. Mounting a ladder she slid open the hatch to the attic crawl space and shone her flashlight into each dark corner but found no one. Puzzled, she tiptoed down the stairs to continue her search but here too the closets yielded no one, and she was about to give up and call the police when she remembered the storage closet at the end of the hall next door to the garage, the repository of every miscalculated or outgrown object in the house. He had to be there, she realized, he had to be . . . Approaching it she hesitated, drew a deep breath, and flung open the door.

Her flashlight shone on the old lawn mower,

Cyrus's ancient trunk, a wicker birdcage, a pile of old draperies . . . and four empty tins of sardines.

"Oh please," whispered a frightened voice.

Mrs. Pollifax swung her flashlight toward the far corner, and the light shone on a girl huddled there staring at her with frightened eyes. "Please," she whispered again, shielding her eyes against the light.

Not an armed burglar . . . Mrs. Pollifax drew a deep breath and said, "What on earth . . . I mean what on earth are you *doing* here? In my *house*?"

"H-hiding," stammered the girl.

"Obviously," said Mrs. Pollifax dryly, "but who are you? You'd better come out and tell me what this is all about."

The girl shook her head. "Please, not yet, they might see me."

"See you? Who?"

She said, "When you left for the airport this morning—"

"Airport?" repeated Mrs. Pollifax, startled. "You were here this morning? *How long have you been hiding in this closet?*"

"T-two days, I think," the girl stammered. "At least it was Monday, you and your husband were both working in the garden and you'd left the side door open and so—I'm sorry—I just came in."

"All that time!" said Mrs. Pollifax in astonishment. "But who are you hiding from, parents? Police?"

"*Them,*" the girl said. "After you left for the airport this morning I heard a car drive in, I could hear the crunch of gravel. I think they looked in all the windows."

11

A car . . . the girl was afraid of a car . . . "Come out," Mrs. Pollifax said firmly. "It's quite tiresome standing here talking into a closet and there's no window here in this hallway. I want to know if this has anything to do with a rather dirty white van with a sign Chigi Scap—"

"You've seen it?" gasped the girl. "It's still here? They're still watching? How did you know?"

Mrs. Pollifax said calmly, "Because I watched it pass the house three times yesterday and again this morning, and while I was out on the patio—during which you removed the salami and bread—it was parked on the road into the woods."

The girl stared at her in surprise. "You notice things like that?"

Mrs. Pollifax smiled. "Definitely I do, yes, and now you will please come out of this closet."

The girl eyed her uncertainly, but she stiffly untangled herself and rose to her feet to climb over the birdcage and make her exit. Once in the hall Mrs. Pollifax looked her over frankly and with some surprise: the girl was smaller than she'd expected, only a shade over five feet in height, with a small pale face and disproportionately large eyes, a rounded chin, and brown hair cut very straight at her shoulder. *Not very prepossessing,* thought Mrs. Pollifax, noting the shabby tweed jacket, wrinkled skirt and stockings, yet the way she squared her shoulders and lifted a defiant chin showed courage, and the intelligence in her eyes suggested maturity: this was not a child but a young woman. In the light of the hallway her eyes looked green, and heavily lashed—really quite lovely in that small face—

12

with dark brows arched like commas above them. She wore no make-up, in fact she didn't look at all like the young girls Mrs. Pollifax saw in the shopping malls; there was something old-fashioned and waiflike about her.

Puzzled, she said, "If you're in danger I think we really must call the police."

"Please no," the girl said earnestly. "If that happens they'll harm Sammy, I know they will. If I could stay until it's dark, I'll go, I promise."

Mrs. Pollifax considered her thoughtfully. "You say you heard a car drive in this morning and the gravel crunching. Did they—whoever they are—try to get into the house?"

She shook her head. "I don't think so, but I could hear footsteps and it was about ten minutes before the gravel crunched again when they drove out. I had the feeling they were looking in all the windows. They couldn't have known how long you'd be away. You were gone a long time, it scared me."

Mrs. Pollifax nodded. "My husband's suitcase went into the trunk of the car last night, when it was dark and the car parked outside. I don't suppose they would have known I was taking him to the airport, they wouldn't have seen the luggage." She added thoughtfully, "But if they were watching the house this morning they would have seen two of us leave and only one return."

The girl's eyes widened. "You mean there are just the two of us now?"

"Yes. Do they know—absolutely—that you're here?"

"Probably," she said in a depressed voice. "Here or in the woods, but they've probably searched the woods. They saw me run into your garden, but you were both outside, so—so they didn't follow."

"I see," said Mrs. Pollifax, nodding, and added crisply, "Then of course they'll want to search the house and I really think we must give them every opportunity to do so while it's daylight because I should object very much to their breaking in at night. Yes, definitely we must encourage them to do it now."

"I don't understand," faltered the girl, "you'll let them find me?"

"Of course not. What I mean," explained Mrs. Pollifax, "is that you and I will both leave the house now and you'll come shopping with me for groceries. Well-hidden in the car, needless to say. The car is in the garage"—*thank heaven,* she thought—"and if I leave very publicly they ought to find it a perfect time to pick locks, enter, and look for you. And when it's dark I'll drive you—" She looked at the girl questioningly. "Drive you home? Or somewhere."

The girl flushed. "You're going to a great deal of trouble for me. I'm sorry. But how can you know if they've searched the house when we get back?"

There was a twinkle in Mrs. Pollifax's eye. "You might say that I am not a stranger to the criminal mind," she told her. "Just leave it to me. Now go and wash your face, you must already know there's a bathroom next to this closet. Wait for me in the hall."

While the girl was in the bathroom, Mrs. Pollifax busied herself inserting tiny slips of sticky tape to the door frames of the front and patio doors, after which she moved vases and pots of flowers to each windowsill downstairs, marking

14

with a pencil precisely where she had placed them. They moved into the garage where Mrs. Pollifax arranged her on the floor of the car with a blanket over her, and then artfully tossed a few empty cardboard cartons on top of her. Backing out of the garage she drove around to the front driveway and stopped by the front door. From this vantage point she made a great show of bringing out her grocery cart and inserting it into the back. She then locked the front door and drove up Maple Lane, where one quick glance told her the white van was parked on the woods road. From here she drove into town to the grocery store.

She was not followed. Parking at the supermarket she said over her shoulder, "No Chigi Scap Metal behind us, I'm locking the car, are you all right?" Hearing a muffled affirmative she added, "I won't be long."

She had shopped only two days ago and needed very little, but at the delicatessen counter she purchased several sandwiches and a bag of cookies for the girl. She was gone only ten minutes, scarcely long enough for a thorough search of her house, and so she continued on to the bank where she cashed a check. Following this she estimated that by the time she reached home she would have given Chigi Scap Metal thirty minutes and she saw no point in lingering. She realized, with some amusement, that anyone else would be appalled at her believing what a nameless girl had told her; anyone else would delight in pointing out to her that the child might be a front for an organized gang of thieves and that she would arrive home to find the house robbed of everything valuable. Anyone else would . . .

15

Mrs. Pollifax, however, was trusting her instincts, and since they had kept her alive in many a dangerous situation in some very exotic countries, she was not about to abandon them on home territory. Something was wrong and she was determined to find out what it was and who Sammy might be. After all, it had proven a rather dull winter, and a girl in trouble appealed far more to her sense of adventure than a Garden Club meeting.

The garage door opened soundlessly, she drove in, and the door closed behind them. "Wait here—don't move!" she told the girl, and entered the house with a feeling of intense curiosity and a great deal of hope that her scheme had worked.

She was pleased to find the cellophane strips at the front door broken, and proceeded to search the house again. Nothing had been taken. When she returned to the garage she said in a low voice, "You can come out now, they've been in the house and satisfied their curiosity."

"They actually came in?" gasped the girl, pushing aside blankets and cartons and climbing out. "Just as you predicted?"

"Yes, and now I think it's time you introduce yourself. After that I'll scramble some eggs for you and you can tell me where to drive you once it's dark. Where you live."

"The scrambled eggs sound lovely. My name is Kadi Hopkirk, and—"

"Katie?"

She shook her head. "No, K-a-d-i—and I have a room at the YWCA in Manhattan where I go to art school."

"I see . . . . and I'm Emily Pollifax. I suggest you crawl under the windows, and sit on the floor in the kitchen, keeping well out of sight, while I scramble the eggs . . . Chigi Scap Metal *must* have given up by now, but I feel it unwise to assume anything."

"Oh you do understand," the girl said eagerly. "Thank you."

Once ensconced in the kitchen Mrs. Pollifax pursued her inquiries as tactfully as possible. Breaking eggs into a bowl and whipping them she asked, "Were you followed *out* of New York City on Monday, or did this happen after you reached Connecticut?"

"I was in New Haven," explained Kadi. "I heard through the grapevine at school the New Haven police were looking for a quick-sketch artist, and I'm awfully good at remembering faces and drawing likenesses fast. It seems to be what I do best. And I need money. But they thought I was too young," she said with a sigh. "They said I might have to draw corpses—as if I haven't seen enough of them already."

"Oh?" said Mrs. Pollifax with interest, turning to look at her. "*Many* corpses?"

The girl said without expression, "Where I come from there have been—well, massacres, really, so I know what killed people look like."

"I see," said Mrs. Pollifax, and presented her with a platter of eggs. She did not ask the obvious question as to where that might be but she was determined to find out; there would be the long drive into Manhattan, and once the girl felt safer she would be less tense and guarded.

As she turned away from the girl, however, tray in hand, she glanced through the open greenhouse door and saw the white van pass the house again. *Blast them,* she thought indignantly, *they've*

17

searched the house, why are they still haunting Maple Lane?

She did not mention the reappearance of the van but looked instead at her wrist watch; it was two hours until darkness. Leaving the girl to her lunch she went off to hunt out her road maps and to trace the fastest route into Manhattan.

They left at seven, with Kadi in the back, but unblanketed, lying instead across the rear seat, her head cushioned and low. Mrs. Pollifax took care not to turn on the car's headlights until she had left the driveway behind, and turning left to avoid the woods road she took the shortcut to I-95 south. Traffic was surprisingly light at this hour. Once on the turnpike, aware that Chigi Scap Metal had not yet abandoned Maple Lane, she checked her rearview mirror occasionally while she considered how best to wring from her companion an explanation of what terrified her.

She had driven only seven or eight miles when it became impossible to overlook a dull green sedan at some distance behind them. She noticed it because no matter how many trucks or cars passed her, the sedan remained steadily there, keeping to the same 50 m.p.h. which she was driving. *Coincidence,* she told herself—after all, it was not a white van—but to reassure herself she lightened her foot on the accelerator and gradually slowed until the speedometer needle hovered around 30 m.p.h.

The driver of the green sedan did not pass, however; he, too, slowed to 30 m.p.h.

I don't believe this, thought Mrs. Pollifax in astonishment, *this is not only incredible but very tiresome.* Worse, she realized this implied Chigi

18

Scap Metal's having more resources than expected if they could also produce a green sedan. *If*, of course, it was following them. Seeing an exit sign ahead, and determined to find out, she turned off I-95 and drove down the exit ramp onto a secondary road illumined by the lights of a gas station. She headed into its bright lights and stopped, waiting, her eyes on the rearview mirror.

"What's wrong?" called Kadi from the rear.

"What's wrong," said Mrs. Pollifax grimly, "is that I slowed to a miserable thirty miles per hour and the car behind us *still* didn't pass, except now it's a green sedan, in which case—" She nodded as the dark green car drove down the exit ramp, and pressing her foot hard on the accelerator, tires screaming in outrage, she swerved out of the gas station and headed for the I-95 north ramp, reversing their direction.

"In which case what?" called Kadi.

"In which case we're being followed and I'm heading back north to try and lose them." And to her companion, "Why, Kadi? Who *are* these people?"

"I don't know, I don't know," cried Kadi. "You have to believe me, I don't *know*."

3

Wednesday

Carstairs was experiencing an unusually busy Wednesday when Bishop walked into his office and interrupted him. Carstairs gave him a baleful glance and growled, "Now what?"

"Mornajay's called from Upstairs," Bishop told him. "It's about the Bidwell abduction, the FBI's asked our help in a small matter."

"Like what?"

"Bidwell traveled abroad so often on business that for the moment they're working on the theory that some terrorist group or other in one of those countries might be involved in the kidnapping." He handed Carstairs two sheets of paper and a leather notebook. "He could have made enemies."

Carstairs leaned back in his chair. "They've had a ransom note?"

Bishop nodded. "Yes, but they're keeping it under wraps. It included a rather dim photo of a man bound and gagged whom they've identified as Bidwell, even with his face partially covered."

"Where was the ransom note posted?"

"Manhattan. A postbox near where they seized him but postmarked three days later."

"So what does the FBI want from us they don't already have?"

Bishop said dryly, "The security of certainty, I'd guess . . . the odd chance that we might have

20

one of these names in *our* files. Bidwell's company supplied the dates of each trip he made to Europe. It was Bidwell's secretary who proved a godsend; when they interviewed her she wondered if his personal engagement calendar might still be locked in the drawer of his desk. They picked the lock and have a record in detail of his appointments in Europe. Jed Addams at the FBI is asking us to run these names through our cross-reference files and see if we've picked up any information they don't have."

Carstairs shrugged. "Fair enough." He placed the package to one side with his other paperwork, at which point Bishop said tactfully, "They want it today."

Carstairs groaned. "Then preserve my sanity by bringing me a fresh cup of coffee, will you?"

"Coffee and a hair shirt coming up," said Bishop cheerfully, and presently placed a cup of steaming coffee on the desk.

Coffee in hand, Carstairs glanced quickly over the dates of travel supplied by Claiborne-Osborne International, and then turned to the more interesting private engagement book that had been locked in the man's desk. Making a note of the many dates when Bidwell had left for Europe, Carstairs turned to those pages in the engagement book to check the people he might have seen, and what projects he'd inspected.

This was now late April. In December Bidwell had flown to Paris and met with a Yule Romanovitch and an Achille Lecler, after which the three had joined a group from the Abercrombie Tin Company and spent the evening at a nightclub. There were various phone numbers scribbled on the pages but Carstairs assumed these had already been checked by the FBI. On Bidwell's second day in Paris he'd had an appointment with Lecler but also with a Rogere Desforges, followed by phone numbers and "flight 1192." The next three pages were blank. On the sixth day he was back in Paris to return to New York on the *Concorde*.

Three weeks later, still in December, he'd made another trip abroad, this time for a brief stop in Switzerland and then on to Paris for a number of appointments, and on the fifth day the scribbled numbers 1192 appeared again. Curious, Carstairs skipped ahead to the next trip abroad; this had occurred in mid-January, a flight to Paris and again the notation "flight 1192" followed by four blank pages. On March 3rd he'd flown to Paris, and again in early April, and on each of these trips his calendar included "flight 1192," with pages left blank for several days, before appointments resumed in Paris until his return to the United States. And of course he'd been abducted two weeks later.

The FBI, however, wanted names checked, and these Carstairs proceeded to list: Achille Lecler, Rogere Desforges, Yule Romanovitch, E. Buttersworth, J. Kriveleva, M. Teek Soo . . . He ran these through both computers and then their cross-reference files on terrorist groups, and came up with nothing suspicious about any of the men; they simply weren't listed as dangerous in any respect. They weren't listed at all. Straightforward businessmen, he guessed, and put in a call to Jed Addams at the FBI. "We've nothing on any of them," he told him.

"Damn," said Addams.

"Since we're on the subject of Bidwell," put

in Carstairs pleasantly, "what personal life did he happen to have? His marriage? Children?"

Addams said wearily, "No real personal life. His marriage? Seems to have been money marrying money. So-so, if you know what I mean. Two children in Ivy League colleges. His wife plays bridge and gives dinner parties. All image, you know how it is. Affairs? Not Bidwell, he's all business. Only recreation golf."

"You'd say his life is an open book then," concluded Carstairs.

"Well, if you insist on clichés, old chap, yes."

Carstairs frowned as he ended the phone call. They seemed to have missed or ignored the references to a flight 1192, it was names they were interested in. . . . People. As Bishop walked into his office he said absently, "I've reported to the FBI that we've nothing on any of Bidwell's acquaintances in Paris, apparently they all have clean hands and a clean heart."

Bishop nodded. "Sounded a bit crazy to me, anyway. Or desperate."

"But thorough," Carstairs reminded him. "There's one inquiry I'd like you to make for me personally, however, strictly private."

"What's that?"

Carstairs sighed. "My insatiable curiosity, Bishop. On each trip Bidwell made abroad there's a scribbled notation in his engagement book that reads 'flight 1192,' followed by three or four blank pages. See if you can find out from Paris where flight 1192 goes, will you?"

"Right. What airline?"

Carstairs said sheepishly, "None listed."

Startled, Bishop said, "Good God, that's like

looking for a needle in a haystack. Two airports in Paris, and how many flights a day?"

"Hundreds. But how many flights 1192?"

Bishop sighed. "Could take a couple of days."

"I'm not only curious, Bishop, but I'm patient. See what you can do."

Bishop said suspiciously, "Does this have anything to do with Bidwell's abduction?"

"Absolutely nothing at all," Carstairs assured him cheerfully.

The inquiry did not take days, however; by early evening Bishop was in his office beaming triumphantly. "Got it! Thank God for computers, Paris has found the needle in the haystack for you."

By now Carstairs had almost forgotten the attack of curiosity that had overtaken him in an earlier season of the day, but the word Paris rallied his memory. "Flight 1192?"

Bishop nodded. "Flight 1192 leaves Paris twice a week for Africa. To Ubangiba, to be exact. Leaves at 8 A.M. for the capital city of Languka."

Startled, Carstairs said, "*Africa* . . . what the hell was he doing *there*? And where on earth is Ubangiba? Have we any information on it?"

"Somewhere," said Bishop. "Actually I seem to remember it being in the newspapers recently but I can't recall why or when. Will the Department's abridged Africa notes do?"

"Anything," said Carstairs.

The file on Ubangiba, once on his desk, did not have much to say about the country. In the past two decades it had possessed two other names and seemed to be mostly known for its recurring coups. Otherwise it was just another small sub-Saharan country, half of its land fertile enough to grow crops, the rest sand, desert, and goat-herding nomads. Its exports were animal hides, sunflower seeds, and groundnuts. It had gained its independence in 1981; the first elected President had been assassinated; the second President had been ousted in a 1989 coup by a Daniel Simoko, who had proclaimed himself President-for-Life.

No industry, no oil, mused Carstairs. *No terrorist groups either.* Still, he couldn't help but wonder what had drawn Henry Bidwell to such a desolate country five times in the past four and a half months.

Unless Paris had been careless and there was another flight 1192 they'd missed.

With a sigh he returned to his paperwork, wished Bidwell a happy return from whatever nightmares he must be enduring in captivity, and promptly forgot about him.

4

"Sardines!" cried Mrs. Pollifax suddenly as they headed north on I-95, still followed by the green sedan.

"I beg your pardon?" said Kadi. She was seated boldly in the front seat now, but keeping a low profile.

"Sardines," repeated Mrs. Pollifax. "I've been trying and *trying* to puzzle out why these people searched the house and found nothing, but still seem to think you were hiding there." She added grimly, "Four empty sardine tins in the storage closet, two empty cola cans and no doubt bread crumbs as well. Idiotic of me to forget that, we never removed them."

"I forgot them, too," said Kadi sadly. "I can be quite intelligent when I'm not frightened but I never thought of them either. And I suspect you were quite distracted by finding me in your house. You really think they saw the empty tins and guessed?"

"In any thorough search they would definitely see them," said Mrs. Pollifax. "They're what I noticed in the closet even before I saw you and I can think of no other reason why they're still following us. Kadi, I think it's time you tell me what this is all about, and why I shouldn't take you to the nearest police station where you'd be safe."

"I'm not sure that I *would* be safe," said Kadi soberly. "And I don't really know what it's all

26

about except that Sammy's in trouble. Real trouble, I think, but I can't prove it and nobody would believe me."

"Try me," said Mrs. Pollifax, giving her a quick glance. "Who is Sammy?"

She said cautiously, "A boy I grew up with. In another country, which is why nobody here would find it important. I forgot Yale is in New Haven, and anyway I hadn't heard from Sammy since he came to the United States nearly four years ago, but suddenly there he was, walking toward me on the street in New Haven, and his eyes lighted up and he raced toward me and we hugged. And he was glad to see me. *Glad*," she repeated.

"Of course," murmured Mrs. Pollifax.

"But then the young man with him joined us, and Sammy changed," Kadi said. "Sammy introduced him as his roommate, Clarence Mulimo, and suddenly he was very formal. I said why didn't we have a cup of coffee and talk, because we were standing right next to a coffee shop. His roommate shook his head and said something to Sammy that I didn't hear, but Sammy insisted. And that's when it all happened."

"What happened?"

Kadi was silent, remembering the shabby coffee shop, nearly empty, and how Sammy and his friend had sat across from her, and how she'd asked Sammy how his mother was.

"He said 'She is very well, thank you, *and how are your parents, Kadi?*' "

She turned her face to Mrs. Pollifax and added quietly, "That really startled me, you see, because he knows very well that my parents are dead. He was trying to tell me something but I didn't know what, so I just asked how he liked college, and he asked me what had brought me to New Haven. A job interview, I said, but I didn't think I'd pleased them.

"And then his roommate said 'Excuse me' and headed for the men's room and I was so relieved, and I said 'Sammy'—"

She hesitated, her voice unsteady. "Right away Sammy placed a finger warningly to his lips, and then he reached under the table where Clarence had been sitting and brought out a tiny plastic object that had been attached there with a suction cup. Some kind of listening device."

"An electronic bug," said Mrs. Pollifax, extremely interested now.

Kadi nodded. "He put it back and then drew out a pencil and scrap of paper, and while I talked idiotically about the weather, and missing home, he wrote three words, and when he handed me the slip of paper it read NOT ROOMMATE— GUARD.

"I just gaped at him, I mean I was terribly alarmed and awfully puzzled, too, but I shoved the note in my pocket and asked what courses he was taking at Yale and then I told him, 'Your roommate's returning, Sammy, he seems very nice.'

"And then," she said shakily, "then Sammy reached inside his shirt and drew out—"

She stopped, and Mrs. Pollifax glanced at her. "Yes?" she prodded.

Steadying her voice Kadi said, "It was a ball of pink modeling clay, the kind you see in toy shops, the sort that children play with, or maybe an adult would use like worry beads. I didn't understand until he peeled away a tiny corner

28

of it—to show me what it concealed. It was so valuable it made me gasp. And then his hand went under the table with it, I reached under the table, too, he placed it in my hand and I dropped it quickly in my pocket."

Mrs. Pollifax said lightly, "And what was it he gave you?"

She shook her head. "That's Sammy's secret, so I can't tell you, but I knew I couldn't stay any longer, I said I'd have to catch my bus now, and—and I went out, very worried, knowing something was wrong, and outside there was parked this white van with those crazy misspelled words Chigi Scap Metal. I began to walk the four blocks to the bus station but I'd not gone far when I realized the van was slowly following me."

"Did they try to approach you?"

"No, because I started to run and I raced into the bus station, the New York bus was there and filling with passengers so I climbed on it right away. But one of the men must have left the van to see where I was going because when the bus started for New York the van was behind it."

"But you didn't go to New York," Mrs. Pollifax reminded her.

In the light of the dashboard Kadi looked miserable. "No, I panicked. I thought they wanted to find out where I live, and I knew they mustn't. The bus stopped in Bridgeport and I thought of leaving it there but I was too scared, so I didn't, but then later we began passing houses and gardens, and I thought of asking the bus driver to please stop—and he did—because I run very fast. I thought I could lose them easily on foot."

"Except you didn't."

"No, and they almost caught me, the two men.

One of them chased me through back yards, and if you hadn't been in your garden—'' Her voice broke. "Now they're still after me, Mrs. Pollifax, and what are we going to do?"

Mrs. Pollifax said calmly, "I don't know yet, but I have a full tank of gas, my car is very good on mileage, that green sedan looks quite old, a real 'gas guzzler,' and it's possible they may run out of gas before we do, and have to stop. I think we simply keep driving north and hope. But tell me, Kadi, in what country did you and Sammy grow up?"

"Most people have never heard of it," she explained soberly. "It's in Africa. My parents were missionary-doctors, you see. It's a small country. It's called Ubangiba now."

By half-past ten Mrs. Pollifax had grown tired of driving; Kadi had volunteered to help but she had no license, and in any case the green sedan remained resolutely behind them and Mrs. Pollifax did not care to risk the consequences if they stopped even for a moment. Noticing how tired Kadi looked by the light of the dashboard Mrs. Pollifax resisted making any more demands on her, and their conversation had become polite and desultory; she had learned how to say hello— *moni*—in the language of Ubangiba, and that Kadi was studying drawing and woodcarving at art school, but by now Mrs. Pollifax was definitely looking forward to a bed and some sleep after the day's rather disturbing encounters. She interrupted the silence to say firmly, "Obviously my theory about their running out of gas has been rapidly running out of possibility."

"Yes," Kadi said politely.

"And we need sleep."

"Oh yes," agreed Kadi.

Mrs. Pollifax nodded. "Somehow we've got to lose them, and it can't be done on a highway. A city is best, and I should have tried it miles ago." She pointed. "We're approaching Worcester, it could be risky. Are you game?"

Kadi said with spirit, "How can you ask? The word bed is right now the loveliest word I can think of, I haven't slept in one since Sunday."

Mrs. Pollifax gave her a quick glance and smiled. "Off we go then," she said, turning down the exit ramp. "I think we need a place for the night near the highway, in case a fast getaway becomes necessary. Nothing fancy, more like that," she said, pointing, as they passed a rundown motel with a bright neon sign proclaiming it the Bide-A-Wee. "We'll aim for that later."

Having found a goal she now applied herself to losing the green sedan by driving up one street and down another, always taking care to remain in the neighborhood of the Bide-A-Wee lest she not find it again. They spent twenty-five minutes racing traffic lights before they turned red, except the green sedan disdainfully ignored the red traffic lights anyway, and continued to tailgate them until abruptly a small miracle occurred. Kadi said exultantly, "They've stopped! They've stopped, Mrs. Pollifax! The light turned red for them but *this* time there's a police cruiser behind them waiting for the light to change, and they *had* to stop!"

Mrs. Pollifax sighed with relief. "Let's fervently hope we can find the Bide-A-Wee again, and quickly. I remember it having lots of parking space, too," she said, and several minutes later

31

she was pulling into the parking lot beside the motel and maneuvering her car between two small pick-up trucks. "We'll ask for a room overlooking the car," she said firmly. "I shall insist."

Presently they were ensconced in room 211, and while Kadi showered in the bathroom Mrs. Pollifax turned on the small television to a flickering screen and to a voice saying, "It has now been six days since Henry Bidwell was abducted, and if the police have any clues as to his abductors they are keeping them private. . . . Bidwell's wife is under a doctor's care, and his employers are offering a reward of fifty thousand dollars to anyone with information as to his whereabouts. . . . In Paris today, OPEC met again and the price of oil . . ."

Mrs. Pollifax snapped it off and sat down on the bed, longing for a toothbrush. Kadi came out of the bathroom and said, "It's your turn," and lay down on the opposite bed and promptly fell asleep. Mrs. Pollifax lay down on her own bed and then, perversely, found herself wide awake and not sleepy at all.

I'm uneasy, she thought, frowning, *but I've been uneasy all day, why can't I sleep now?* At last, long after eleven o'clock, she left her bed to stand at the window and gaze out at the lights of the city, her glance eventually moving to the street below, and finally to her car, and then across the street to the bright lights of a larger motel. She watched as a car drove into the entrance of the motel across the street, disappeared and soon emerged at the other side—circling it, realized Mrs. Pollifax, suddenly alert—and as the car drove toward the Bide-A-Wee it passed under a street light and it was a dark green sedan.

Chilled, Mrs. Pollifax realized that Kadi's pursuers were methodically checking every motel in the area for her red car.

There is something frighteningly important about this, she thought, *they're merciless, what will they ever do to Kadi if they overtake her, what do they want of her?*

"Kadi," she said in a low voice, "Kadi, wake up, they're about to find us."

The girl was on her feet at once. "Where?"

"We've got to leave," Mrs. Pollifax told her. "And *fast.*"

Kadi was beside her, shrugging into her tweed jacket. Mrs. Pollifax picked up the phone and called the desk clerk. "We need a taxi, please—quickly—it's an emergency."

"Emergency?" mumbled a sleepy voice.

"We need a hospital—*hurry*!"

The desk clerk, sufficiently aroused, said, "Cab—right, I'll call."

"How long?"

"Three to five minutes, I'd guess."

She fervently hoped he guessed right.

"What on earth," Kadi said, staring at her, open-mouthed.

"You're having an attack of appendicitis," Mrs. Pollifax told her crisply. "Fetch your knapsack, I'll carry it down. . . . Walk bent over and clutching your stomach."

"But why? What about your car?"

"Take a look out the window," Mrs. Pollifax told her. "They're going to find it in about two minutes. No, they've already found it, they're shining a flashlight on the license plate."

Kadi looked stricken. "Oh God."

Mrs. Pollifax opened the door. "Quickly—lean on me. Be *sick*, Kadi."

"I *feel* sick," gasped Kadi as they raced down the stairs.

5

It was half-past ten and Carstairs was working late in his office, quite alone; Bishop was presumably asleep or out nightclubbing. Carstairs had just completed the last of his work when the next day's Departmental bulletin could be heard arriving on his fax machine. He yawned and thought of ignoring it until morning, but after a moment's reflection he tore it from the machine and glanced through it. There was the usual review of progress—he skipped this—and with more interest turned to the Departmental FYI memos, which so often held juicy gossip and rumors from around the world. NOT FOR PUBLIC CONSUMPTION, he read: FBI reports first attempt at delivering Bidwell ransom failed, unidentifiable sources report 50 million demanded . . .

"Good old 'Unidentifiable Source,' " murmured Carstairs, but fifty million was a hell of a lot of money, in fact it had to set a record; *someone* found Bidwell of great value. His glance slid to Memo: MIDDLE EAST DEPT.: Iran. Two Europeans reported arriving Teheran private plane, met by top government limo, i.d.'d by "friendly parties" as Yule Romanovitch, A. Lecler.

Carstairs yawned again, put aside the bulletin and rose from his desk to go home when abruptly he sat down and picked up the Departmental bulletin again: the names Romanovitch and

Lecler had struck him as vaguely familiar and he wondered why. Frowning, he leaned back in his chair and attempted an emptying of his mind, hoping the answer might spring from his subconscious as so frequently happened; in fact he sometimes found his subconscious more reliable than Bishop's memos as he juggled three and four projects at a time.

Got it! he remembered: *the FBI inquiry on the kidnapped Bidwell.* Springing from his chair he went to the files and there they were, the same names scrawled in the engagement book that Bidwell had kept locked in an office drawer, the same two men, surely, that Bidwell had met several times in Paris: Lecler and Romanovitch, like a vaudeville team.

He wondered if Mornajay was still Upstairs in his office, and rang his number. Mornajay had left, however in Europe it was morning: he put in a call to Bernard at Interpol in Paris and was presently connected.

"Bernard," he said, "I'd like to know what you might have, if anything, on a Yule Romanovitch and one Achille Lecler." Glancing over the list he added, "Also, a Rogere Desforges."

"Hmmmm," murmured Bernard, "give me half an hour, will you? But I can tell you at once who Rogere Desforges is. You will find him easily enough in your *Who's Who*, he is one of our geophysicists, very well known."

"Geophysicist," repeated Carstairs, frowning. "Right—get back to me, will you?"

"Burning the candle?" suggested Bernard. "Or whatever the idiom is?"

"That's right, Bernard, at both ends."

Forty minutes later Carstairs received

Bernard's return call. "What we have on these two men," he said, "is limited and murky. The two are middle-men, involved in a number of questionable deals, and probably more that are unknown to us. Lecler has a New York office as well as an office in Paris. In New York he is Lecler Consultants, in Paris he is L-V Investment Company. They operate just inside the law, barely, so that we've never been able to pin anything on them but we'd love to."

"Interesting," said Carstairs. "Any known connection with terrorist groups?"

"I'd say absolutely out of character," replied Bernard. "They're very suave and subtle, these two, but strictly non-political. To my knowledge they've never been associated with violence of that sort. Dirty deals, yes, but that's another category."

Carstairs hesitated and then he said, "Would you hazard a guess as to why an American businessman would contact them separately, or together, a number of times on his visits to Paris?"

"My friend," said Bernard, "I do not like to be overly suspicious but I would take a close look at whatever company your American businessman represents, which is—?"

"A holding company," said Carstairs.

"Ah yes, my friend, but does one know what it 'holds'? Such a splendid word, 'holding,' and your American laws are a little loose, are they not? But please, I do not wish to be so negative, yet still—"

"I understand," Carstairs told him. "And thanks, Bernard."

"You'll share? As I said—"

"Definitely," Carstairs told him, "but for the

moment it's mere curiosity and speculation.'' He
hung up with a sigh. For all practical purposes
he had reached a dead end, but still it remained
odd, a man like Bidwell associating with two men
of such dubious reputations that their dossiers
were recorded at Interpol. He had learned little
that interested him except for the fact that Rogere
Desforges was a geophysicist.

Geophysicist, he repeated, and scowled. There
was something there. Not graspable yet, but
lurking.

He decided that it was time to learn more about
this Ubangiba that had so interested Bidwell that
he had made five trips there inside of four and a
half months. He had told Bernard that his inquiry
was mere curiosity and speculation but it was
more than that: those blank pages in Bidwell's
engagement calendar still bothered him, they did
not fit a man whose life Addams had called an
open book.

Switching off phones and computers, he extinguished the lights in both offices, and with his
coat under his arm headed for the Reference
Room. Here, surrounded by atlases, directories,
phone books, and updated files on every country
in the world, he placed his coat over a chair
and began by looking up Claiborne-Osborne
International. The words *syndicates* and *consor-
tiums* were prominent, and he ran his eyes down
the list: foreign banks, oil-drilling, hydro-electric
power, earth-moving machinery . . . active in
Tunisia, Algeria, Egypt, and Pakistan . . . offices
in Cairo and Paris, main office in New York.

He reflected dryly that rather a lot of terrorist
possibilities existed there, except that he had no

idea why anyone would single out Henry Bidwell to kidnap. No link there.

But there was one country missing from that list of Claiborne-Osborne's interests, and that was Ubangiba.

Pulling out more books he came at last to an in-depth history of the country and began to read attentively. It seemed the area, now called Ubangiba, was first mentioned in 1783 by one Ebu Taylor, lone survivor of a Sahara caravan wiped out by the Tuareg. Rescued by a tribe called the Shambi, he was taken to "a pastoral land where the Shambi and Soto tribes lived in peace under the benign rule of a King Zammat."

"Local myth," he read, "has it that centuries earlier a quarrel arose between Chief Mombolu of the Soto tribe, and Zammat, chief of the Shambi tribe. To avoid war it was decided by the wisemen of the country that both men should be bound together in a room into which two poisonous snakes would be released, and in that manner the gods would decide which man would survive to be ruler of both tribes. It was Chief Mombolu who died, and Zammat whom the gods favored."

Carstairs thought dryly, *Interesting way to run an election.*

"From that time on," he read, "the King's totem has been a pair of intertwined serpents, represented on both the sacred royal gold ring that only the King can wear, and later by the flag of the country, on which two serpents repose on a scarlet background."

Carstairs skipped ahead to World War I, where Britain, rather against its will, inherited the country by the Treaty of Versailles.

"The British effort to dethrone the King," he

read, "roused violent protests from the people. Ultimately, a Parliament was allowed under the King; a railroad was built but never used, an attempt made at a cement factory that went bankrupt, the country fell into decay. The British maintained a consulate and gave minimal financial aid but basically the country was considered unrewarding. It continued as a Kingdom until King Zammat VIII, educated at Oxford, negotiated independence from the British and prepared his country for free election of a President.

"At his death," it concluded, "the sacred royal gold ring disappeared, and because of this the tribes have since regarded with distrust the ensuing rulers, including King Zammat's popular son, who was the first and only elected President, but who died mysteriously five months later. According to the belief of the people, he was poisoned by two serpents angered by the loss of the sacred royal ring, and they have regarded this as the reason for their many misfortunes since then."

And a good many misfortunes there had been, concluded Carstairs, noting the riots, droughts, and coups that followed. One more restless African country; obviously it was time to forget Ubangiba, yet he continued to stare at the map of the small elongated country, impoverished, threatened by drought, overlooked and forgotten, scarcely worth invasion by ambitious neighbors. What had been Claiborne-Osborne's interest in Ubangiba? Had Bidwell made enemies there?

He decided that in the morning he would arrange for someone to interview Claiborne-Osborne International and learn just what they planned to develop there. Until he knew what lay behind those concealed trips to the country, there had to remain the suspicion that Bidwell's abduction was somehow tied to Ubangiba.

He knew better now than to question his curiosity; there was something about Bidwell's secret 1192 flights that troubled him, and he had no idea why.

Bishop, more knowledgeable, would have said it was what made him special, an almost psychic quality that led him to follow his instincts against all reason.

6

Descending at top speed into the tiny lobby of the Bide-A-Wee, Mrs. Pollifax flung bills and key at the desk clerk just as a cab drove up to the lighted entrance. "In you go," she told Kadi, and opening the taxi door, "Nearest hospital, please—in a hurry!"

The driver glanced at Kadi and said, "Right on, lady." As he headed out into the street Mrs. Pollifax glanced back and saw two shadowy men approach the lighted entrance. It was too dark to see their faces but she and Kadi had been seen entering the cab. She knew this because the two figures abruptly halted in surprise and, as the cab drove away, she saw them race back toward their own car . . . to follow.

Kadi said, "But Mrs. Pollifax, a *hospital?*"

"Trust me," she said.

The taxi drew up to the huge lighted entrance. "City Hospital, ma'am. Five bucks."

"Yes," she said, fumbling for bills. "Where are we, what corner is this, what streets?"

"Chandler and Park, ma'am."

They hurried up the steps to the admissions entrance and through the doors, where Mrs. Pollifax led Kadi to the long row of chairs along one wall and said firmly, "Sit."

"But where are you going?"

"To that public telephone over there."

She was quite familiar with the number by now. It might be midnight, but in the Baltimore offices of William Carstairs, attorney-at-law, the lights would be on all night, and someone always at the switchboard.

A bright voice answered almost at once. "Legal office," it chirped.

"Is this Betsey?" asked Mrs. Pollifax.

"Yes it is, but who—*Mrs. Pollifax?*"

"Yes, and I'm in trouble, Betsey, I need help, is there someone—*someone*—to talk to?"

"I'll put you through at once," she said efficiently, and a moment later a sleepy voice said, "Bishop here," and yawned into the receiver.

"Bishop, it's me—Emily Pollifax—and I need help," she told him. "Badly. I can't explain why because I don't know, but my house has been searched and I've been chased across Connecticut and they're still following. Do you have any safe place for us to go—what you call a 'safe house' for hiding?"

At the Department people did not ask unnecessary questions. Bishop merely said, "Where are you at this precise moment, Mrs. P.?"

"In Worcester, Massachusetts, at City Hospital, corner Chandler and Park, with a companion feigning appendicitis, but we came in a taxi and they may have followed us here, too."

Bishop said, "Give me the number you're calling from, I'll get back to you in five minutes. Can you hang on?"

"There are lights and people here," she told him, but her voice trembled a little from tiredness and the beginnings of a fear that she couldn't name.

"Five minutes," Bishop told her reassuringly.

She hung up and looked around her. Finding Kadi, she smiled as cheerfully as she could but

refused to relinquish her position by the telephone to join her. She thought it the longest five
minutes that she had lived through in a long time,
and when the phone rang she interrupted its first
ring.

"Bishop here," he said.

"Yes."

"Stay where you are, near people. Inside of
thirty minutes a young man named Pete will meet
you there, he has your description, and *he'll* be
wearing a black leather jacket and red sweater.
We've found a 'safe house' for you—a rather odd
one but safe."

"Bless you, Bishop," said Mrs. Pollifax, and
marveled at his asking no questions because she
had absolutely no idea what she could have said
in reply.

"But who did you call?" asked Kadi wonderingly as she joined her.

"A friend," said Mrs. Pollifax. "There'll be a
man coming for us in half an hour, wearing a
black leather jacket and red sweater, and Kadi,
I want to know—I *must* know about your friend
Sammy now. Can you believe him, can you trust
him, and all that he implied? That he's in *danger*?"

Kadi gave her a startled glance. "*Yes*, I believe
him, and *yes*, I trust him, and if you doubt me I
can tell you what my father said of him, and my
father taught him at the missionary school, and
loved him like a son. He said, 'Young Sammy
will be a *good* leader of his people, there's no
cruelty in him, and he is bright, very bright.' But
his eyes were no longer bright when I met him,"
she said sadly.

"Leader? What do you mean leader?" asked
Mrs. Pollifax.

"Well," explained Kadi earnestly, "Ubangiba used to be a kingdom, it was one of the last countries to gain its independence, which is when the King decreed that it would be a democracy, and he set the date for elections. But then he died, you see, he was very old but—" She frowned. "But also very wise, I think. His son was very popular and he was expected to be elected President, and he was, but five months later he died quite mysteriously—they think poisoned."

"Oh dear," said Mrs. Pollifax. "And then?"

"Then no more elections," Kadi said sadly. "Mr. Chinyata took over and made himself President-for-Life and nearly ruined what was left of the country. There were food riots, people were hungry, and after that there was another coup—which," said Kadi, her voice trembling a little, "was when my parents were shot. It was General Simoko who next made himself President-for-Life, except really he is a dictator."

"Your parents shot!" exclaimed Mrs. Pollifax, startled. "My dear, I'm terribly sorry to hear that—but Kadi, I have to ask you what connection this has with your friend Sammy."

Kadi sighed. "Well, you see, Sammy's grandfather was King Zammat VIII, back when there was a King, and it was Sammy's father who became the first and only elected President and then died. And Sammy dropped the Z to be *Sammat*."

Mrs. Pollifax sat very still, absorbing this startling fact so casually tossed at her. *Not Sammy but Sammat*, she thought, and felt glimmerings of understanding. She did not know what she understood yet—it all sounded very exotic and foreign to her—but vague possibilities occurred to her, unclear as yet, and convoluted, but spelling wickedness. "So he is not just Sammy," she murmured, "but Sammat, grandson of a King and son of a President. Who sent him to Yale, Kadi, do you know?"

"I don't know," Kadi said miserably. "But he is there, with a roommate who isn't a roommate."

Mrs. Pollifax nodded. "And who presumably has you followed," she added soberly. "It's a pity we couldn't have stopped in New Haven and kidnapped Sammy."

"Could we go back?" Kadi asked eagerly. "Could we rescue him?"

Mrs. Pollifax shook her head. "You've become dangerous to them, Kadi, presumably because you're a friend of Sammy's. Besides, it's too late," she told her, seeing a tanned young man in a black leather jacket and red sweater approach them. "We can only find safety for *you* just now."

Planting himself in front of her the young man said, "I'm Pete, any luggage?"

Mrs. Pollifax shook her head. "No luggage."

He glanced curiously at Kadi. "Car's just outside, slide fast into the back seat."

There was a driver already at the wheel, making their getaway very fast, the car in motion the moment the doors slammed. But looking back Kadi said, "They're there, Mrs. Pollifax, they must have found out from the cab driver where he took us."

"Being followed, are we?" said Pete, glancing back.

"Green sedan."

He nodded. "Okay . . . this is Tom, driving, we'll try to lose them but it doesn't matter now if we don't."

"Doesn't matter?" echoed Mrs. Pollifax. "Where are we going?"

"A small private airport. Orders are to tuck you away safe—you must have clout, lady."

Kadi gave her a quick, puzzled glance but said nothing.

They had left the city behind them when the car turned down a narrow road, its headlights picking out a field and several small planes grouped around a hangar. They were deposited next to a helicopter with its motor already idling. Mrs. Pollifax and Kadi were ushered out by Pete, the car turned and sped away.

"In you go," said Pete, boosting them up into the helicopter.

"You too?"

"I'm the pilot," he told her with a grin, and latching the door behind them he took his place at the controls. The rotoblades began to turn faster and faster, and suddenly they were being lifted from the earth into the night sky.

"Mrs. Pollifax," said Kadi in a small voice, "am I being kidnapped?"

Mrs. Pollifax glanced at her tired anxious face and said calmly, "I think we both are. I admit that I didn't expect this, either, but I trust my friend and you must, too. Difficult as it may be at this moment," she added dryly.

Kadi said wonderingly, "Your friend must be very powerful, Mrs. Pollifax."

"Well, you see," Mrs. Pollifax told her with a smile, "I send him a fruitcake every Christmas."

Kadi laughed shakily.

The earth lay below them like a patchwork quilt of flickering lights followed by great dark spaces of land. Presently Kadi fell asleep, which

Mrs. Pollifax thought a great blessing; she would have preferred to sleep, too, but it was night, which she had always found the least secure season of the day for confronting Unknowns, and she was too tired to sleep. She had to remind herself that she really could never, *never* have abandoned this girl to the thugs pursuing her, and that wherever they were going it had been arranged by Bishop, but it was necessary to hold firmly to this because it was taking a very long time to reach whatever safe place he'd found for them.

Too long a time, she thought, after a glance at her watch told her that it was past one o'clock in the morning of a new day, and that they were into their second hour of flight.

Responsibility, she sighed, naming it. . . . *I have made myself responsible for this Kadi who spent two days and nights huddled in our closet out of fear.*

Obviously she was not going to be present at the afternoon's Garden Club meeting.

She began to think of Kadi's Ubangiba and what it might be like. Africa was such a huge continent and she had seen only one African country, and that had been on the Zambezi River. She supposed there were similarities nevertheless: the attractive capital with its villas and its roads laid out by early colonialists, and beyond this elegance the shanty towns, and then the countryside where women, erect, barefooted, and proud, walked along the roadside carrying huge baskets on their heads filled with kindling or food, and there were glimpses through the trees of dirt paths leading to thatch-roofed villages. She wondered if Kadi's Ubangiba had baobab trees silver in the sunlight, and towering anthills as high as a man's waist.

She realized the helicopter was flying lower now and beginning its descent. Peering out of the window she saw a blaze of light ahead in the dark countryside and wondered what it could possibly be: *surely not another airport,* she thought with a sinking heart. She nudged Kadi and said, "We're landing, Kadi."

The helicopter banked and turned and she lost sight of the cloud of brightness until it reappeared in the window across the aisle, but at a distance; the helicopter was coming down now, making its uncanny horizontal drop to the earth. They landed with a slight jarring in the middle of a dark field.

"Where are we?" asked Kadi, rubbing her eyes.

"We're here," Pete told her. "Don't worry, you're expected." He crawled past them, unlatched the door, and jumped down to help them out.

With the opening of the hatch a flood of noise rushed at them: muted shouts and screams, and underlying these the sounds of rollicking music, while—emerging out of that distant brilliance—Mrs. Pollifax saw a man with a flashlight making his way toward them across the dark field.

She said in consternation, "But where are we?"

"Rural Maine," said Pete. "You'll have to move back, I'm taking off again now."

Bewildered, Mrs. Pollifax said, "But have you brought us to the right place? This surely can't be a safe house."

"Nothing beats it," Pete said.

"But that's merry-go-round music—it's a carnival!" shouted Mrs. Pollifax.

49

"You got it," grinned Pete, and with a flip of his hand he closed the hatch and, a moment later, at the controls again, he set the rotoblades turning. The helicopter rose in a gust of cold wind, leaving them standing in the middle of the dark field waiting for the man with the flashlight.

7

Thursday

A light was turned on each of their faces, and behind its blinding flash Mrs. Pollifax could see the shape of a burly man and the outline of a limp, wide-brimmed hat.

"Name's Willie," he said without preamble. "Watch your step, follow me."

He guided them across untilled earth toward the blaze of lights. Ahead of them, rising out of its brilliance like a great spider web, Mrs. Pollifax saw a towering ferris wheel that slowed and then stopped, its pause eliciting a fresh burst of screams from those at the top, but even these couldn't blot out the undercurrent of noise from below that sounded to Mrs. Pollifax like a buzzing swarm of angry bees in a hive. She could see nothing more of the carnival than the ferris wheel because a cluster of trailers intervened, and it was toward one of these that Willie led them. Emerging into the dimly lighted circle of trailers they paused and she saw Willie's face for the first time, and Mrs. Pollifax, in the act of yawning, promptly closed her mouth. She was startled: his was a broad Slavic face, high cheekboned, the muscles smooth and hard as the burl of a tree, and his skin dark as a gypsy's. Not a man to cross in an argument, she was thinking, and in no way did he resemble a manager in his faded jeans and shirt, yet the sign on the door of the trailer read

MANAGER. He opened it and stood back for them to enter.

They walked into a warm, over-furnished living room where Mrs. Pollifax counted two couches and a startling number of lamps and overstuffed chairs; on one wall hung a gaudy poster advertising Willie's Traveling Amusement Shows, and next to it a picture of Elvis Presley painted on black velvet. With a nod to a dazed-looking Kadi he said, "Your daughter can wait here, I'll ask you kindly to step into my office, I've a few words to say." He spoke with a faint accent that Mrs. Pollifax couldn't identify but struck her as familiar, if she could only think where she'd heard it before.

"Not my daughter," explained Mrs. Pollifax. "Her name is Kadi, spelled K-a-d-i."

He gave her a sharp glance. "African name, isn't it?"

"Yes," said Kadi, surprised.

Mrs. Pollifax was surprised, too, and looked at him with sudden respect.

He led her into an office where he pulled out a chair for her at one side of the large desk while he seated himself behind it and returned her frank stare with ironic interest. With a glance at the clock on the wall, he said, "I won't keep you long, it's nearly two o'clock, the carnival closes at two."

She said incredulously, "But—a carnival? Run by the Department?"

He looked pained. "Never say that, ever. When bankruptcy threatens it's Willie's Rich Uncle who rescues. No Department, no names. Willie's Rich Uncle. Remember that."

"Yes," she said meekly, and stifled another yawn. "But it's certainly inventive."

Studying her face he frowned. "They tell me you're experienced." He said bluntly, "You don't look experienced. They want you to help."

She said politely, "That was very kind of Bish—of Willie's Rich Uncle," and then, sharply, "What do you mean *'help'*?"

"We've had an accident here," he said. "A few minutes after midnight, too late to stop you coming, you were already on the way. I had to make a call to Baltimore—"

Poor Bishop, thought Mrs. Pollifax, twice interrupted in his sleep.

"—because of the accident."

"Accident," she repeated, stifling another yawn.

"A very suspicious one. It's been suggested you help while you're here."

Mrs. Pollifax was not so sleepy that she didn't understand the inference. She said quickly, "Oh, but I can't stay, it's Kadi who was in danger, we only met this morning—no, yesterday morning, and thanks to Bishop—"

"Willie's Rich Uncle," he pointed out.

"No, *BISHOP*," she said flatly, in revolt now. "Thanks to Bishop we were lifted completely out of a dangerous situation but I didn't expect *this*. My only interest is in seeing Kadi safe. I mean—" She stopped and fumbled for words, realizing that she'd not given a thought to anything but getting away from the Chigi Scap Metal people, and what *had* she expected? "I assumed I'd go home tomorrow," she told him. "Even Kadi could go back to her New York art school

53

now. At least," she added doubtfully, "they couldn't trace her there. I don't *think*."

"You don't think," he mocked.

"I'm tired," she admitted, "it's been a long day. I must get in touch with—all right, Willie's Rich Uncle tomorrow about some help for Kadi. You do have a phone?"

"A temporary link-up, yes," he told her. "Of course—we're a business."

"You were saying there was an *accident*?"

He nodded. His skin had a luster to it in the light of the desk lamp like highly polished wood, and there was a gap between his two front teeth when he spoke. These details she noted from habit, just as he too, she knew, was taking pains to read her face and learn who and what she was. "Yes," he said. "To Lazlo, sent here for protection—like you and the girl."

"That's a calculated hit," she told him.

He suddenly smiled, and she realized that she might eventually like him.

He leaned forward across the desk to emphasize his words. "So I'll tell you. . . . Sometime after midnight there was a shout of 'Hey Rube,' which—" he explained, seeing her look blank, "is the signal in any carnival for trouble. Like everybody else Lazlo picked up a tent stake and joined the others down by the gate. And that," he said heavily, "is where somebody in the crowd stuck a knife in his back."

"Stuck a—was he killed? Is he alive?"

"Barely. He's in the hospital, in critical condition—and he was sent by Willie's Rich Uncle, you understand?"

She understood; strange as it might seem to find such a person in this bizarre environment he meant that Lazlo was an intelligence agent who had withstood dangers she could only imagine, and he had been sent here to be safe. And tonight someone had tried to kill him.

She said, frowning, "But you called it an accident!"

He leaned back in his chair, eyes narrowed. "I'm keeping this short because you'll see I've work to do, but what's important—and suspicious—is that after the ambulance took Lazlo away I couldn't find anyone who had shouted 'Hey Rube,' and not a single carnie reported having had any trouble to need one."

Startled by this she said, "But would they tell you?"

He glanced at his watch. "Most I can vouch for, they're back every season and they'd tell me, yes. I run a clean carnival, no fly-by-nighter gets in unless he can prove he's not parking his car behind his tent for a quick getaway after robbing the tip blind. A couple of the acts in the Ten-in-One are new—had to be, I have to take what I can get—and a couple of concessions are new to me. Those I can't vouch for."

"Perhaps there'd been a quarrel?" she hazarded.

His gaze was scornful. "Why should there be a quarrel? A good man, very quiet. Once he'd rested I put him to work collecting tickets for the merry-go-round. He bunked alone, I never saw him talk to anyone."

Mrs. Pollifax fought back another yawn, longing for sleep, and with the feeling that she'd already sustained enough shocks during the past hours, she struggled to make sense of everything he had told her. She said, "What sort of trouble usually produces this 'Hey Rube' you spoke of?"

He shrugged. "A townie who feels he's been cheated, a drunk trying to pick a fight. The whiz mob causing trouble—pickpockets that would be. One of the grifters playing too strong and taking a mark for everything he's got. Doesn't happen often."

"So you actually think," began Mrs. Pollifax, but he stopped her by rising from his chair.

"What I think I've got no proof of," he said flatly. "If it was someone from outside who traced him here they could be gone by now, *but how did they find him*? If there's a leak at Willie's Rich Uncle, that's something else. But if there's a rotten apple in my show, if somebody got planted here—" His eyes glittered. "*Somebody* knew enough about us to shout 'Hey Rube.' I can't be everywhere at once and they've told me you have good eyes and good instincts."

As she stood up, too, he said roughly, "You can surely spare a few days in spite of the danger?"

"Danger?" she repeated.

"Of course—to you and the girl. If Lazlo's cover got blown, somebody may know too much about a certain connection with Willie's Rich Uncle and blow this cover, too. The plane may have been heard landing, and God knows you don't look like a carnie, you'll stand out like a dog in a duck pond."

"Yes," she said, and realized that her jaws had begun to ache from yawning.

He looked her over critically. "But Willie's Uncle says you'll do. I'll see Gertie gets you some old clothes to wear. Any good at fortune telling?"

Startled, Mrs. Pollifax said, "I've never done any."

He nodded. "We'll think of something. The girl's small, the Professor's magic show can use a small girl to saw in half." With his hand on the door he paused. "That's for tomorrow, now I'll show you where to sleep, but what's your name?"

"Mrs. Pollifax, Emily Pollifax."

He shook his head. "Not here. Better be called Emmy something. Emmy Smith? Jones?"

Since she was married to Cyrus Reed she said dryly, "Reed?"

"Okay, Emmy Reed." He opened the door to the living room where Kadi sat patiently waiting. She jumped up at the sight of Mrs. Pollifax and said, "Is everything all right?"

She nodded. "Everything's all right, Kadi, we'll stay here for just a few days, if you agree. Just to be sure."

With a shiver Kadi said, "Oh, I'd like to be sure, yes."

Outside, the buzz of sounds from the midway had diminished, the ferris wheel had stilled, and the merry-go-round was silent. Willie led them past two brightly-lighted trailers to a small and shabby dark one, and taking a key from his pocket he unlocked the door and pushed it open. "You'll have a quiet sleep, nobody wakes up here before ten or eleven," he told them. "We're here one more night and then it's tear-down and we move on to the next town. Give you time to get acquainted." He walked around Kadi, reached inside and turned on a light that shone garishly on shabby walls and broken venetian blinds.

"Beds," said Kadi, pointing, as Willie left.

Mrs. Pollifax saw them: a pair of narrow bunk

beds, each with a blanket folded at one end and a pillow lying at the other. She thought, *Well, if I've exchanged a frying pan for a fire, at least I'll face it rested tomorrow.* She stepped inside, sat down on the bed to test it, abruptly stretched out, turned over, and immediately fell asleep.

Kadi, surprised, looked down at her, and then with a smile she covered her with a blanket and gave Mrs. Pollifax a shy kiss on the cheek.

"*Zikomo*, friend," she whispered.

8

Thursday

When Carstairs arrived in his office the next morning he found Bishop at his desk drinking what was apparently his fourth cup of coffee, given the empties lined up beside the In and Out baskets. "Late night?" said Carstairs tactfully.

"Not the kind you think," Bishop told him gloomily. "I was called twice by Betsey during the night. In my bed, sound asleep. Now I'm trying to wake up. The first call was Mrs. Pollifax, who I sent to Willie's—"

"Mrs. Pollifax!" exclaimed Carstairs. "To Willie's? What happened? What on earth—"

"The second call," went on Bishop, interrupting him, "was from Willie himself, reporting an attempt made on one of our men there sometime after midnight. He's in the hospital, stabbed in the back and in critical condition."

Carstairs whistled through his teeth. "I don't like the sound of *that*. Who was it?"

"Lazlo, a.k.a. Aziz Kalad."

Carstairs looked stunned. "We smuggled him out of Iran four months ago, what the devil is he doing in hiding at Willie's?"

"We turned him over to Farnesworth, remember?" said Bishop. "Lazlo refused a leave, said after four years of undercover work in Iran he was too edgy to lie in the Caribbean sun or take any sort of vacation, said it would drive him crazy.

He asked for quieter work to get back the taste of being free again. Farnesworth put him to work in Boston. Simple surveillance jobs, I believe."

Carstairs said angrily, "Couldn't have been very simple if he's ended up in a safe house. Damn it, he's invaluable to us. What does Willie think, a random knifing or did 'they' find him? In which case—"

"Willie finds it pretty suspicious," Bishop said. "It seems a call of 'Hey Rube' went out around midnight that sent everyone running to the gate, which is where Aziz—Lazlo, that is—was stabbed in the crowd, except that later Willie couldn't find anyone who had shouted this 'Hey Rube,' and what's more couldn't find anyone in the entire show who'd run into any trouble that demanded it."

"Damn," said Carstairs. "Willie's always been snug harbor, a perfect back-up place. Does Farnesworth know about this?"

Bishop shook his head. "Not yet, I figured Willie's strictly our business."

"And so is Lazlo. Bishop, contact Farnesworth's office and tell them we need to know—top priority—why and how Lazlo happened to be at Willie's—to be knifed like a sitting duck. Details, Bishop, I want details."

As he rose from his desk Carstairs added with a frown, "And Mrs. Pollifax, what the devil's happened to her? She's not on assignment."

"There wasn't time to ask," Bishop told him. "Her call came through at half-past eleven, before Willie's call. She sounded at the end of her tether, said she'd been chased from Connecticut to Massachusetts and was calling from Worcester's

City Hospital where she'd taken refuge for the moment. She was asking for help."

"Alone?"

Bishop frowned. "I don't think so. . . . No, she mentioned a companion feigning appendicitis, that's how she put it. Not Cyrus, or she'd have said so."

Carstairs sighed. "Well, give her a call and find out. If it's fallout from one of her past assignments, and someone is tracking *her* down, too—"

Bishop shook his head. "Show people sleep until noon. A thought that turns me green with envy," he added. "Willie said she needed sleep pretty badly."

"Well, contact her later when you've time," growled Carstairs. "You've notified Upstairs about Lazlo?"

Bishop nodded. "They're setting things in motion, there's a guard posted now at the hospital in Ellsworth, Lazlo's in intensive care but they're checking everyone with access to the hospital."

"Good. Now, I've got a job for you," Carstairs told him. "If you can stay awake to do it. I want you to fly to New York—Helga can take over your desk for you—because I've set up an 11 A.M. appointment for you with the acting CEO at Claiborne-Osborne International." He dropped a file on Bishop's desk. "Reading material for you en route so you can ask intelligent questions."

Surprised, Bishop said, "Has the FBI cleared this visit, or are we being *sub rosa*?"

Carstairs said silkily, "When did the FBI ask us to check our files? We set our clocks back a day, Bishop, it's today they approached us. Or late yesterday. We're only following up their que-

61

ries in regard to Bidwell versus terrorist groups in Europe."

Bishop gave him a long hard look. "All of which is camouflage for what specific question?"

Carstairs smiled at him benevolently. "Why, to learn what their interest is in Ubangiba, of course. Without revealing *our* interest."

"You mean *your* interest," Bishop told him accusingly. "I don't get it, I really don't. What is it you suspect?"

Carstairs' face sobered. "I honestly don't know, Bishop, but those blank pages in Bidwell's engagement book bother me, I can't get them out of my head . . . a book locked away in his drawer and therefore not for public consumption, or so one presumes, it troubles me, yes. And the man's been kidnapped, is being held for some incredible ransom, and why Bidwell, of all people?"

"He was featured in *Fortune* magazine last year," pointed out Bishop. "It was made clear enough then how rich he is. A billionaire, if I remember correctly. Enough to entice any nefarious schemer."

"Then why didn't they abduct him last year? Nobody's found any secrets in his life, yet he wrote no names on those blank pages, no record of appointments, left no clues—and now he's been kidnapped. I'm hoping your trip to New York will explain everything so that I can put it out of my head once and for all." He glanced at his wrist watch. "You'll miss your plane. Ah— here's Helga," he murmured as Bishop's secretary appeared in the doorway. "Get moving," he told his assistant. "Be subtle, be tactful. Take over, Helga—all hell's been breaking loose today."

"So I've heard," she said demurely, and seated herself at Bishop's desk and began gathering up the empty coffee cups.

Carstairs moved on to his office, where Departmental reports and data had begun collecting on his desk. The hospital to which Lazlo had been rushed in Ellsworth, Maine, reported him out of intensive care but not in stable enough condition yet to be flown to Boston to a specialist; the guards posted in the building reported no attempts to infiltrate, and no suspicious approaches. It was still possible, thought Carstairs, that Lazlo had simply been the victim of a random incident, some young local punk on drugs or out to prove his manhood. . . . With some relief he turned to the paperwork that was always waiting for him, and called in Helga to dictate further memos and reports.

He had finished lunch at his desk when Bishop phoned him from New York.

"Well?" growled Carstairs. "Has Claiborne-Osborne found plutonium in Ubangiba? A rich lode of gold, or possibly oil?"

Bishop did not immediately reply, and Carstairs stiffened. "Well?" he said sharply.

"Claiborne-Osborne International," Bishop said at last, "has never heard of Ubangiba. I had to show the acting CEO where the blasted place was on the map."

Carstairs said quickly, "Do you believe him?"

"He'd have to be a candidate for an Academy Award if he was lying," said Bishop. "He seemed honestly and genuinely puzzled by my query.

63

When I pressed him, he called in a few other people who seemed just as blank on the subject."

"And?"

"I stopped on my way out to query Bidwell's secretary. She too had never heard Bidwell or anyone in the company refer to Ubangiba, but at least she reads the newspapers and knew the country existed."

"I see," murmured Carstairs. "Curiouser and curiouser . . . Good work, Bishop, I'd like to tell you to stay and sample a few fleshpots in the Big City but you're needed. Come home."

"Yes, sir. Incidentally, I'm calling from a bar where the TV news is turned on, and Bidwell's wife was just making a plea to her husband's kidnappers to release him."

"What's she like?" Carstairs asked idly.

"Very groomed, very top-drawer. Finishing school accent. I'd say nothing in her life's prepared her for this sort of thing."

"How's she taking it?"

"I detect a mix of shock and embarrassment, the embarrassment at having to be seen on television making such a public plea, and the shock as expected."

"Right. See you." After wishing him a good flight back Carstairs sat for some moments thinking about what Bishop had told him. If Bishop was right, then Bidwell's flights on 1192 had been strictly his own business, but what had taken him there so mysteriously?

One of Bidwell's appointments in Paris had been with a Rogere Desforges whom Bernard had identified as a geophysicist. Perhaps there was something graspable there: it was possible that

Desforges had been more than a casual luncheon guest, but certainly it was time to find out.

Switching on his intercom he said, "Helga, bring me a *Who's Who*, will you? American, British, and French."

It would have taken Bishop three minutes to secure these; Carstairs could not help but notice that Helga needed twelve minutes to find them.

"Stand by," he told her, opening each one to D. "I'm looking up one Rogere Desforges, geophysicist, and if I've any luck you can put a call through to France for me and see if he's out geophysicing or reachable. I'd like to speak to him today. What time is it in Paris?"

"Seven o'clock in the evening, sir," Helga said crisply.

"Damn," swore Carstairs. "I see that his office is in Paris, his residence in Rouen. Try both, and keep your fingers crossed."

9

Kadi, waking in the morning, was not particularly startled at finding herself in a strange bed. She had slept under a number of roofs when she was being smuggled out of Ubangiba, after the coup that had cost her parents their lives, and from there she had gone to Ohio to live with an aunt and then to New York City to art school. She liked to think this was what Emerson called 'revolutions' in a life that accustomed one to change. Her father had been very partial to Emerson.

There was a stirring in the bed across the narrow aisle, and seeing Mrs. Pollifax, Kadi abruptly remembered the last few days, and the fear that she'd lived with, and she felt a wave of gratitude toward this woman. This was followed by a frown because she found it very mysterious, Mrs. Pollifax summoning a pilot, a plane, and an escape from Chigi Scap Metal with such dispatch, rather like a genie producing a miracle.

She thought, *There is more to this than she's told me, and she is certainly not the person I first thought; there are dimensions here that interest me very much.*

But what a relief it was to feel safe!

She sat up as the door opened and a woman in jeans and a baseball cap walked in. "Hello, dearies," she said cheerfully, "I've some clothes for you, Willie's orders."

Mrs. Pollifax, waking, gave the woman a puzzled glance, saw Kadi, looked around the trailer and sat up, too. "Obviously I wasn't dreaming—

I'm still here," she announced. "Hello, Kadi . . . And you?"

"I'm Gertie, Pogo's wife." She had a weathered midlife face under the baseball cap, and now she began to sort the clothes that she carried over one arm. "For you—jeans, socks, and T-shirt," she told Kadi, blithely tossing them at her. "And for the lady—Emmy Reed, isn't it? Nothing yet, but we're looking for a shirt and if you're cold tonight here's a sweater. A bit moth-eaten, but what the heck it's warm."

"Thank you very much," said Mrs. Pollifax, accepting her largesse. "And is there food in that little refrigerator?"

"Bless you no . . . Turn left when you leave and head out into the midway, breakfast's at the grab-joint. Cook-house," she explained. "Can't miss it, sign says BIGGEST HOT-DOGS IN USA, and only place open." To Kadi she said, "You'll find the Professor there, you'll have to learn the ropes by six o'clock."

"For what?" asked Kadi.

"Why, to be sawed in half," she said in surprise, and went out, closing the door behind her.

Kadi looked at Mrs. Pollifax in astonishment. "I'm to be sawed in half and she called you Emmy Reed?"

"I'll explain later," Mrs. Pollifax told her, "but just now we need breakfast. And," she added with a smile, "after I've seen you sawed in half I must speak with Willie about certain matters, having been *quite* blurred last night. Let's go!"

"But—*sawed in half?*"

Mrs. Pollifax nodded. "It seems we must both sing for our supper while we're here, and join the carnival."

"Oh," said Kadi, brightening, "what *fun!*"

Mrs. Pollifax wasn't at all certain that it was going to prove fun, not if there was a murderer hiding among these people, but she could admire Kadi's attitude. They walked out onto the midway, past the transformer and the Loop-o-Plane and found the Professor waiting for them outside the tent that housed the portable kitchen. He strode toward them at once, happily measuring Kadi's smallness.

"She'll do, she'll do," he said triumphantly, and to Kadi, with a bow, "I'm the Professor, purveyor of magic and wizardry, enchantments and all the wonders of illusion. And you?"

"Kadi Hopkirk," she said eagerly.

Mrs. Pollifax, obviously of no importance to him in his world of wonders, looked at him with amusement. His most distinguishing feature was a bright yellow goatee trimmed to a knife-edged point; otherwise he was a rather pale and plainfaced middle-aged man with a dyed goatee and what looked to be a toupee dyed to match it. There was, however, an earring in his left ear, and his fingers glittered with rings and she found this satisfying: he was clearly a man who did the best with what he'd been given. He led them under the canvas to the counter and introduced them to Mickey. "Coffee and breakfast for them, Mick," he said. "On the double, we've work to do."

A few other carnies sat on stools, staring into space, not quite awake yet and not speaking. It was early for them, explained the Professor, and he bade them hurry through their eggs and fried potatoes so Kadi could be rehearsed. "Tatiana," he called to a glorious redhead, "this is the new girl. Come!"

The shapely redhead yawned, muttered words under her breath, and abandoned her coffee to follow them as the Professor led them out of the cook-house, past the ferris wheel, and down the midway. "By daylight," he said, "it's a bleak and empty piece of earth but just wait 'til six P.M., this place will light up like the 4th of July . . . crowds, music, lights, glamour . . . !"

It did look bleak in the pale sunshine, conceded Mrs. Pollifax, its concession booths shuttered by canvas shades, the sawdust still damp underfoot with dew, and not a soul in sight. The Professor strode ahead of them toward the largest tent on the midway and stopped for them to admire it.

"This here's the Ten-in-One," he said. "Ten side-shows under one canvas, except we got only eight this month. And the platform's called the bally platform and I'll bet you never saw grander pictures anywhere."

"No indeed," admitted Mrs. Pollifax, almost assaulted by the gaudy canvases that hung over the platform: THE SNAKEWOMAN OF BORNEO depicted a dark and wild-haired woman wearing snakes on her lap and around her neck; EL FLAMO, FEARLESS FIRE-EATER, had faded somewhat in color but he stood regally in profile, very erect, with flames curling out of his mouth; JASNA THE KNIFE-THROWER ("one miss and he dies") stood poised in tights, knife in hand, while the man at whom she threw them was already framed by knives. The pictures marched side by side in a long line and for just a moment Mrs. Pollifax felt that stir of excitement she'd known as a child when she'd visited a carnival, and looking at Kadi, seeing her eyes wide with wonder, she smiled.

The Professor led them past the ticket booth and inside. "You believe in magic?" he asked Kadi.

"Of course I believe in magic," she said earnestly, "but it's impossible to saw a lady in half."

"Why?" asked the Professor, regarding her with amusement.

"Because you would no longer have a lady to saw in half for the next performance."

"Alas, she has the logical mind, but such an innocent! Have you visited a carnival before, young lady?"

Kadi shook her head. "I grew up in a country without them."

"What a sad country, I cry for it," he said dismissingly. "Now we practice. Precision is everything! Practice, practice!"

The space inside the big tent held a line of closed booths, but the main focal point was a stage at one end with several rows of bleachers facing it. The Professor switched on lights and from behind the stage's backdrop he pushed out a platform on wheels. "Who is Kadi replacing?" Mrs. Pollifax called to him.

"Shirley," he said. "She eats too much. Too big, very uncomfortable for her."

"Then why do you need Tatiana?" she asked.

"Ah, the disillusionment," he rued. "Sit—you will be the audience, we will perform for you. Kadi, Tatiana, come. As you see," he announced to Mrs. Pollifax from the stage, "we have two boxes resting on this platform, I slide them apart—they move, you see?" He slid them together. "Note also there are no trapdoors below, no mirrors. Now, Kadi, you will please climb into this box on the top and slide down into the platform under the boxes. See? In you go."

"That platform's too narrow," protested Kadi.

"You will go there, it is *not* too narrow. It only *looks* too narrow to contain a person, it was *designed* to look too narrow—all magic is illusion here! Climb in, please, when the act begins you will already be hidden inside."

Looking doubtful Kadi climbed into the gaudy box on top of the platform and apparently found a space in which to insert herself because she vanished from sight.

"Now we begin." He and Tatiana bowed and dramatically unhinged the fronts of each box, dropping them to prove they were empty and without mirrors. With fluttering gestures Tatiana was helped up and into the boxes atop the base where she lay down, after which the Professor closed the hinged sides, leaving only her hands and feet extended at each end.

"Now, Kadi," he called, "you can hear me?"

There came a muffled reply.

"I will commence. I have closed the hinged sides—dramatically, of course—so only Tatiana's head and feet can now be seen. Pay attention, young Kadi, you are hearing me? Good. Now I will turn the platform around—in a big circle—you feel this?—to show the audience no tricks, no trapdoors, there is only Tatiana, and it is now, as I turn you on the wheels, and while Tatiana's feet are out of view of the audience, this is the signal for you to slide your feet up through the opening in the base and push them out, you understand? At the same moment, as the apparatus turns, Tatiana withdraws her feet, hugging her knees tight in her box, and you become Tatiana's feet, except—*mon Dieu*—it is good I have many sizes of the same shoes to match. Excellent, your feet have emerged. . . . Now we are back to our original position; now I pick up my saw and Tatiana screams, and you, Kadi, wriggle your feet—so—and with cries of terror I begin sawing."

Fiercely he sawed the boxes in two, accompanied by screams, until he slid the two boxes apart and the illusion was perfect: Tatiana's head remained at one end, presumably her feet wriggled at the opposite end, and between them there was only empty space.

Mrs. Pollifax laughed and applauded. "Bravo!"

"It is good? You see now?" asked the Professor, beaming.

"I see, yes. Tell Kadi I must go now," she called to him, and still chuckling she left them to their rehearsing and went out to find Willie.

Once again she sat across from Willie at his desk, this time to deliver her ultimatum. "I was tired last night," she told him, "and my thinking blurred but it is *not* blurred now. My husband will be returning to Connecticut on Monday from a meeting of the American Bar Association and I have every intention of being there when he comes home. If I'm to be of any help to you for a few days I need a great deal more information, for instance when your carnival opened and when this man Lazlo arrived here, and who might have come after he did, on the assumption that possibly he was followed here."

Willie leaned back in his chair and stared at her

with distaste. "The police have just arrived to ask questions, and now you come to ask questions and speak of Bar Associations and such nonsense?"

"Yes," she said pleasantly. "Are you a Rom?"

"*What?*"

"Gypsy?"

His eyes glittered dangerously. "You ask—why?"

She shrugged. "You have the look. . . . I thought so last night, sleepy as I was," she said dryly. "I traveled once with gypsies in Europe."

"*You?*"

She nodded.

"Such a one as you?"

She smiled forgivingly. "Such a one as I, yes, and owe them my life."

He said scornfully, "This is hard to believe. What were the names of these people you profess to know—you, a *gajo?*"

"It was in Turkey. . . . There was Goru, and there was Sebastien and Orega, but most of all there was their Queen, a wonderful Zingari by the name of Anyeta Inglescu."

He stared at her, silent and frowning, and then with a nod he said brusquely, "I will get out my record book." Bringing it from a drawer of his desk he said, "We opened on March 1st in western Massachusetts, in the town of Lanesborough. We winter in Florida, do a few still dates in the South, strictly for Willie's Rich Uncle, you understand, but it's in the East they want us, and the carnival season always opens March 1st." He opened his record book. "Lazlo reached us in Vermont the second week of March, I was told to expect him. He came by bus, walking out to us from town."

"Not by plane?"

He looked amused. "We are not often so near such a big field to provide a quiet landing, and public airports are conspicuous, often watched, it can be difficult. I don't know why he came by bus, there must have been a reason because he walked in exhausted, with a broken arm."

"With a *what?*"

"A broken arm. We set it for him here, I've done it before. Gus and Pogo helped, and one of the roustabouts had been a paramedic." Consulting his book again he said, "But I remember we were not fully booked in the Ten-in-One when he came."

"You book everyone ahead of time?"

"Most," he said, nodding. "Most are regulars, very loyal, they come every season, the same three foremen and most of the acts and the roustabouts. Pogo and Gertie are the concession managers, I see they added a Spin the Wheel and a Cat-Rack game after Lazlo came. Those two, plus Jasna and her father and the Snake Woman came late. Lubo runs the Spin the Wheel, and Pie-Eye the Cat-Rack."

Mrs. Pollifax, fascinated by these names, said, "Then four arrived after Lazlo. But if Lazlo was followed here, surely it would be impossible for whoever located him to suddenly set up an act for a carnival?"

"Not so hard to set up a concession joint," he told her. "Anybody can do that, but harder for one of the Ten-in-One acts, they need talent. But," he added, "you're being naive, because anyone sent to me by Willie's Rich Uncle is big-time, and whoever hunts him or her is big-time, too, and they need only snap a finger to find a killer."

"Even to find a killer who's a Snake Woman or knife-thrower?" she said dryly.

He smiled. "You'd be surprised, I'd be willing to bet the man who arranged your coming here—I name no names—could do the same." He returned to his list. "But it would need twenty-four hours at least to set something up, and all of these qualify. I had an ad running in Gibtown," he explained. "We lacked a couple more concessions and I had only six acts for the Ten-in-One. We take the leftovers, you see, the big Expositions get the class acts. You take the Contortionist—his name's Norbert—he's a real class act but you'll notice he's too fond of the booze to make it anywhere but a gilly show like this."

"And the Snake Woman, and the Jasna act?"

He sighed. "Jasna's damn good with her knives but somebody may have realized her father's blind and figured it a bit nasty, her throwing knives at a blind man."

"Blind?"

Willie nodded. "Lost his sight some years ago," she said. "Takes guts standing there and having knives thrown at him, and not even able to duck. As for the Snake Woman, I don't know."

"At least you've given me four names," Mrs. Pollifax said. "Anyone else?"

He shook his head, and leaning back in his chair looked her over thoughtfully. "You'll need good cover for asking questions I can't ask, and have no time to ask, anyway. A couple of years back in Vermont we had a feature writer from some newspaper spend a day with us—wrote a nice piece about how a carnival works. What about being here for the same purpose?"

"Oh, *much* better than fortune-telling," she

agreed. "How soon can you get word around that last night's plane brought a newspaper writer to do interviews?"

He grinned. "If I tell Boozy Tim, word will get around fast enough. Incidentally, if anyone questions you at the gate tell them you're 'with it,' meaning with the carnie."

Mrs. Pollifax nodded and looked at her list:

> *Lubo/Spin the Wheel*
> *Pie-Eye/Cat-Rack game*
> *Jasna the Knife-Thrower*
> *The Snake Woman*

"But if one of them had been planted here to kill Lazlo," she said with a frown, "wouldn't they have made a quick getaway?"

"Not *too* quick," he said. "With the police circulating it would have been conspicuous, not to mention suspicious. This would have been a clever killer, a pro, who chose just the right time—a crowd, nobody noticing. He or she would sit it out until the police leave."

She nodded and rose, and with a faint smile said, "You changed your attitude toward me very suddenly, Willie, may I ask—?"

He grinned. "Oh, that." Showing her to the door he opened it for her. "I will tell you one day, but I will say now that the name of Inglescu is not unknown to me. Do you know the words in Rom *'ja develesa'*?"

She smiled. "Go with God?"

He nodded. "*Ja develesa*, then. And be careful."

10

The report on Lazlo had been sent down to Carstairs from Farnesworth's office, and it lay now on his desk in a neat little package that told him the conversation had been taped, for which he was grateful. Helga had put in her calls to France for him and had reached Desforges's residence successfully—he was having dinner with friends and was expected home by nine o'clock, European time. There was other work to do while Carstairs waited but he yielded to temptation and inserted the Lazlo tape on his machine, at the same time scanning Farnesworth's accompanying note: he had scrawled *What's up? Herewith Lazlo's phone call to me March 10, from Boston, where tailing a cash courier named Kopcha.*

The tape began.

"Yes, Lazlo here, calling from downtown, I may have been followed, I'm not sure. As scheduled, I had Kopcha under surveillance when he drove to a shell of a building half boarded up on a mean street, climbed the stairs and entered and after a minute I followed. He went into a third room, the only one with a door, and closed it behind him but there was a small foyer between the hallway and the door and I hid behind a pile of bricks to listen, God knows it looked safe enough with bricks to hide behind."

His voice, very controlled until now, trembled slightly. "What I heard was three men, two rough-talking but also a voice that spoke with authority, you know? Very smooth, with a French accent, I'm sure of this. They'd been expecting Kopcha and asked if he was interested in making some money on a big job, a cash pick-up—a ransom, they called it—in about a month's time. In April. They needed another man."

Farnesworth's voice, "Go on."

"Kopcha treated them with contempt, he was really arrogant. Wasn't interested in any small-time job, he told them scornfully, or working for a foreigner, and he walked out and left, followed by the others, which is when they found me behind the bricks, dragged me back into the room—the man with the French voice had disappeared—and they beat me up. Wanted to know how much, and what I'd heard, and who I was. I got away but one of them, for a couple of blocks, was behind me. Of course I lost Kopcha."

His voice broke. "I'm not feeling so well, I think my arm's broken."

The operator's voice broke in asking for more dimes and there was the sound of coins dropping into the slot.

Farnesworth said, "I'm hearing you, Lazlo. Two questions, fast. Any idea what you stumbled into?"

"Not a clue."

"What were these two men like, the two that beat you?"

"Nasty types. Looked just what Kopcha thought them, small fish with a small job. Shabby."

"And what do *you* think?"

There was hesitation before Lazlo spoke. "Not so sure of that, could be camouflage."

Again hesitation, and a sound of retching.

"Sorry, I got hit in the gut, too. I thought maybe—I was at Willie's some years ago, would he be anywhere near Boston?"

"Best place for you," Farnesworth said, "Let's see where he is. . . . Hold on a minute. . . . Here we are, he's this week in Pownal, Vermont. But you sound in bad shape, Lazlo; if you can make it there fine, but go to a doctor first. I'll notify Willie to expect you."

"Yes."

And that was the end of the tape that had been recorded in March, one week after the carnival opened; now it was April and Willie was in Maine. *Poor devil,* thought Carstairs, *he escaped from that situation with a broken arm, only to have a knife plunged into his back weeks later.* It *could* be assumed that he was careless in making his way to Vermont in March, but Carstairs fervently hoped this wasn't the case because he didn't want to consider the possibility of losing Willie's Traveling Show as a safe house.

On the other hand, he reflected, leaning back in his chair and frowning, if Lazlo had been followed that craftily, that successfully, and for such a distance, it implied that what he had stumbled into on March 10th—what Kopcha had dismissed so casually, and Lazlo, too—was a hell of a lot more important than either of them realized.

Judiciously he considered Lazlo, born Aziz Kalad, a very experienced and dedicated agent who had spent four years undercover in Iran, risking his life to survive and to smuggle out information. Hard to believe that he wouldn't cover his tracks, and then Carstairs amended this as he recalled the sound of retching and of nerves gone hellishly ragged. *Burn-out,* he mused; a broken

79

arm, probably a high temperature—yes, they should have insisted he take a vacation. He *could* have become careless in the route he'd chosen two months ago to reach Willie in Vermont.

He switched on the machine and played the tape again, this time curious about the job Kopcha had been offered. The word ransom interested him, as did the reference to "next month. In April." It was next month now, and the word ransom loomed very large in the news.

Helga's voice interrupted his thoughts and brought him back to the present moment. "Your call to France has come through, sir, Mr. Desforges is on line three."

With an effort, Carstairs removed his thoughts from Lazlo to concentrate them on the country of Ubangiba and a geophysicist named Rogere Desforges.

"Monsieur Desforges?" he began.

The man had a pleasant voice, and once Carstairs had introduced himself Desforges shifted easily into English with only a faint accent.

Carstairs drew a deep breath. He had the advantage of the man at the opposite end of the line: he knew precisely what he wanted to ask, and he knew the skill with which he must question him, but it held all the elements of a surgical operation with the risk of hitting a wrong nerve and killing communication. "You're aware," he said gently, "that Henry Bidwell has been abducted in the United States?"

"Yes, I've seen something of it in the newspapers here. Most tragic!"

Carstairs said carefully, "In our attempts to find out if he had provoked interest from some foreign group we'd be interested in learning of your visit to Ubangiba with him." He waited, poised for disappointment, braced for word that Desforges's only connection with Bidwell had occurred in Paris, and that he'd never seen Ubangiba.

With infinite relief and a sense of triumph he heard Desforges say easily, "Oh yes, that was certainly interesting. I must say, those African potentates live well. *Most* interesting."

Carstairs, in an attempt to decipher just what this meant, hazarded an amused, "Well entertained, were you?"

"*Mon Dieu*, yes! Champagne, pheasant, caviar, all the good things of life."

Carstairs, hopes rising, continued, "You would say, then, that Bidwell had established a congenial relationship with the President?"

"Definitely, yes. Old friends, one might say. We stayed at the palace two of the nights, and when we went out into the field we had escorts and guards. Very well taken care of. Of course the people are starving," he added ruefully, "while the President is designing a third palace and having all his caviar flown in from Europe. One regrets this sort of thing but business was business in Bidwell's case."

"Of course," Carstairs said, and, "What *was* the nature of his business, M. Desforges?"

"That, I am not at liberty to tell you, of course, without Bidwell's consent."

"As you know," Carstairs said crisply, "this is Central Intelligence calling. Perhaps if your Sûreté asked the question?"

Desforges hesitated. "I would have to say the same to them, you know. Client confidentiality and all that." He added cautiously, "It is perhaps permissible to say that Monsieur Bidwell and his company now own exclusive mineral rights to the country."

"Oh yes," Carstairs murmured noncommittally. "Do you happen to recall the name of the company?"

"Offhand, no, I only glimpsed it on documents."

"Would it be Claiborne-Osborne International?"

"No, no, quite different, Something-Something Mining Company of Ubangiba, but I don't recall the attached name."

Aha, thought Carstairs, and risked another wild guess. "With Lecler and Romanovitch involved, of course."

"Yes, their names were mentioned."

Better and better, thought Carstairs, there was beginning to be a shape to this. "Thank you, M. Desforges," he said, and as if just thinking of this he added, "Oh—one last question, if I may ask it without endangering your—uh—client confidentiality. Would you say that from a business point of view their acquiring the mineral rights will prove profitable?"

"Hmmmm," murmured Desforges thoughtfully. "Of course oil or natural gas would be far more profitable but I suppose any form of energy in that region . . . With cheap labor, and it would have to be *very* cheap labor—a bit Leopoldish, of course—but with cheap labor profitable, yes."

Carstairs felt a rush of excitement; Bidwell might not have struck oil but he felt that he had struck it. "Thank you, M. Desforges," he said with conviction.

Energy, he reflected, and rang the Africa section; it was time to find out what, if anything, Bidwell planned for Ubangiba. "Allan?" he said. "Carstairs here. I want to learn what your geology department can find out from the various strata—what I think are called the metamorphic and sedimentary rock formations?—of the country of Ubangiba. I want to know just what minerals could possibly be unearthed there. Not known, you understand, but potential."

"What do you mean, not known?" asked Allan.

"Just that. So far as the usual descriptions of the country go, there are no minerals at all. On the other hand, someone seems to have discovered something that's made it worth tying up exclusive mineral rights over there and I gather it's neither oil nor natural gas."

"Hmmm," murmured Allan. "Tin, gold, iron-ore, wolfram . . ."

Carstairs shook his head. "It's been referred to as energy-producing but not oil."

"That'll take a few days," said Allan. "We'll have to start from scratch with an analysis, and do some real research."

"That's expected," Carstairs told him. "As soon as possible, though, and with my thanks."

He glanced up as Bishop walked into his office.

"I'm back," said Bishop gloomily. "Raining in New York and my trip was a wild goose chase, wasn't it? A total waste?"

"Not at all," Carstairs assured him smoothly, and with a glance at his watch, "Nearly four o'clock, you've not had time to connect with Mrs. Pollifax, I suppose?"

"No rest for the weary," sighed Bishop. "I'll try right now but Willie seldom inhabits his office afternoons. He does, however, have an answering

83

machine so I'll just keep calling and leaving messages. That should annoy him."

"Do that," said Carstairs, turning to the work on his desk. "She's safe, which is what matters, but I'd like to know why on earth she needed a safe house here in the United States when not on any assignment. Keep trying."

11

Kadi was having the time of her life. After all, she had never been sawed in half before, and in concentrating on the Professor's instructions and listening for the key words that would tell her the moment when she and Tatiana would be spun dizzily in a wide circle, she completely forgot her two days in a closet, Chigi Scap Metal, and her anxieties about Sammy. She had entered a world of magic and drama, and after a very sobering adolescence she was experiencing playtime. It was surprising how restful it felt, and how liberating.

By two o'clock the Professor announced that she had mastered the timing of her role in the act and that she could be released to investigate her startling new environment. Before she left he delved into a trunk in the rear and handed her a pair of black stockings and a pair of size 5 shoes that matched Tatiana's. "Take 'em along and be back here six o'clock sharp."

Kadi went at once to the trailer to rummage through her knapsack for the sketchbooks she'd taken to New Haven in what felt now an eternity ago. A carnival, she thought, would be a wonderful opportunity for sketching faces.

She found Mrs. Pollifax already in the trailer with a notepad in her lap. "I'm to be a feature writer for a newspaper and interview some of the carnies," she told Kadi. "I have narrowly escaped being a fortune-teller."

Abruptly Kadi sat down, knapsack on her lap. "Mrs. Pollifax—"

"It's Mrs. Reed," she reminded her pleasantly.

"Reed . . . Reed," said Kadi, "but why? And—you said you would explain, didn't you? To be here of all places, and suddenly you're not Mrs. Polli—I mean, suddenly you're Mrs. *Reed*."

Mrs. Pollifax nodded. "Yes, I suppose you have to know. . . ." Leaving her bunk to sit beside Kadi she said, "You understand this is *very* confidential."

"Yes," Kadi said, watching her face.

Keeping her voice low, "You've heard of the Central Intelligence Agency in this country, the CIA?" Kadi nodded. "Some years ago, during a difficult time in my life"—she smiled, remembering—"I applied for work with them, quite outrageously, of course, but also out of desperation because I'd come to a dead end in my life. The man who interviewed me—I can't describe how shocked he was—wanted to get rid of me as fast as possible, but by chance I was seen by a man who was looking for someone just like me and thought I'd be an excellent courier. An Innocent Tourist, he called me.

"I barely survived *that* mission," she told Kadi dryly, "but it ended successfully and since then I've been given other assignments abroad. So you see, when I found you in my closet I was—well, somewhat experienced in surprises, and when I made my phone call from the hospital it was to someone I know in the—the *Department*."

Kadi, watching her wide-eyed, said shakily, "You mean I picked just the perfect person to help me."

"Not perfect," Mrs. Pollifax said modestly,

"but not un-initiated. The surprise for me is that this carnival is semi-supported by my—er—friends, as a place where people in danger are occasionally sent by the Department for safekeeping. Willie told me this last night. It's assumed that Willie's Rich Uncle bails out the carnival when it can't pay its bills, which I have to say is tremendously inventive and clever. But one of the men sent by Willie's Rich Uncle was knifed last night while we were flying here and I've been asked to help. *Only* for a few days," she added firmly.

"Wow," said Kadi admiringly. "Can I help, too?"

Mrs. Pollifax smiled. "You can help by remembering to call me Emmy, or Mrs. Reed, and by noticing anything odd here. Except," she added reasonably, "I expect that *everything* will seem rather odd to us. For instance—" She glanced at her list, "I am now going to try and locate a Snake Woman. What do you plan to do?"

"Sketch people," said Kadi. "For practice."

Mrs. Pollifax looked at her thoughtfully. "A very good idea. Of course a few here may object to being sketched. . . . Perhaps you could explain that Willie's trying you out for a concession of your own. Sketching people."

Kadi leaned over and kissed her on the cheek. "I do admire the way your mind works."

"And if anyone questions you, say you're 'with it,' " added Mrs. Pollifax.

"With what?"

"I suppose with the carnival; it's what one says, or so Willie told me. To tell them you belong."

"Belong," said Kadi wistfully. "What a nice word," and opening the door she walked out, sketchbook and pen in hand, to explore the midway.

Mrs. Pollifax found a match and burned her small list of carnival suspects and then ventured out herself. It was past three o'clock and as she left the circle of trailers and entered the midway she saw a police car parked near the big tent called the Ten-in-One. A policeman was standing beside it. Mrs. Pollifax's glance veered to the right as a second policeman ushered out of the tent an extremely odd-looking young person carrying, in outstretched arms like a libation, a gleaming mahogany box. Mrs. Pollifax slowed her pace, not sure whether the policeman was escorting a young woman or a young boy: he or she was thin as a reed, and tall, with a shock of orange hair clipped in the style referred to as punk, wearing a pink halter tight as a Band-Aid across the chest, and tight black slacks. Only when her eyes fell to the high-heeled shoes, and at last noted two small bulges under the halter did she realize it was a young woman. Her face was no less startling than her tall thin body: thin sharp features and a bright slash of scarlet lips.

"She's got her knives, Lieutenant," the policeman called to his companion. "Very different ones, no similarity."

"Let's see," the lieutenant said. "You're Jasna?"

The young woman nodded and placed the mahogany box on the hood of the car. Opening it, she said in a lightly accented voice, "These I work with. The case stays locked. It is locked *always* until my act begins."

Mrs. Pollifax, lingering in the shadow of a booth, watched the lieutenant bring out a tape measure, pluck one of the long pointed knives from the box and measure it. "You throw these? At a man?"

She nodded indifferently. "Yes."

"You never miss? He doesn't mind?"

"He taught me," she said with a shrug. "Before that it was I who stood on the platform and he who threw the knives."

From between two concession booths a bearded man appeared, wearing a long cape, his head tilted up, eyes concealed by dark glasses. "Jasna?" he called. "Jasna?"

"Over here, Papa," she called out to him.

As he took a few steps forward he prodded the earth with a cane, and Mrs. Pollifax realized that he was the blind man that Willie had mentioned last night. The two policemen watching his progress looked shocked. "Good God, blind," murmured the lieutenant.

"If you must know, yes," the girl said coldly, "but once, in Europe, he was famous before he lost his sight." To the old man she said, "It's all right, Papa, they only wanted to see the knives, see if one had been stolen, or if I—" She gave the two men an amused glance, "If I went about trying to kill people."

Her father's cane found the car and he stopped, his cane as alive as fingers searching for Jasna. "Over here, Papa," she said softly. "Now—you have seen the knives, we can go?"

The lieutenant brought a photograph from his pocket. "From the depth and width of the wound it would have been a knife like this," he said, handing the photograph to her. "Ever seen one of *these* knives?"

She said scornfully, "It looks like a kitchen

knife, you would do better to ask in the cook-house."

"I'd call it a dagger," the lieutenant said.

She said with a shrug, "Not one of mine."

Mrs. Pollifax decided to move along before she was seen, and slipping through the space from which Jasna's father had entered the midway she walked around the back of the Ten-in-One and came out farther down the midway. Several of the booths were open now and occupied, with their flaps rolled up; at one of them a man on a ladder was touching up a sign with a paint brush while Kadi was standing at another booth arguing with the man behind the counter. As Mrs. Pollifax neared her she heard Kadi say, "I told you I'm 'with it' but I'll pay, I will if you want. All you have to do is start the ducks moving, I don't even want a prize."

She was facing a ruddy-faced man with a stubborn mouth who glared at her angrily. "You nag worse than my wife . . . nag nag nag," he growled. "To get rid of you—okay once, just once, you hear? Then *scram*."

Mrs. Pollifax stopped behind her. It was a shooting gallery that had caught Kadi's attention, a few rifles in a row on the counter and a line of yellow ducks in suspension along the back wall. With a martyred sigh the man pressed a button and the ducks began moving; he continued to glare at Kadi, who picked up one of the B-B guns, aimed, fired rapidly and knocked over all eight of the moving ducks.

Beaming, Kadi thanked him. "That was great fun, thanks, really."

Mrs. Pollifax, staring at her in surprise, was not alone in her reaction.

"Hey girlie," shouted the man, "come back."

Kadi turned.

"Can you do that again?"

"Well, I suppose so," Kadi said, considering this.

"Even faster? Show me." He pressed the button and the ducks flew upright again and began moving across the back panel, but faster now. Kadi lifted a rifle, aimed, fired, and seven of the eight fell over. He stared at her. "Look, kid," he said, "you wanna work for me tonight? You be my stick and I'll pay you, it'll bring in the marks like bees to honey."

"What's a stick?" asked Kadi.

"The come-on . . . the tip sees how easy a kid like you shoots down the ducks, they can't wait to get out their wallets." He winked. "At least until they win too much." He didn't explain what he did if they won too much.

Kadi said politely, "Thank you very much but I've got a job with the Professor, I'm being sawed in half."

He leaned forward eagerly. "Look, any time you're between acts, you come here, I'd appreciate that, young lady. Name's Pogo." He thrust out a calloused hand to shake, and Kadi politely extended hers, shook it and said, "I'll see, Pogo. Thanks."

Turning and seeing Mrs. Pollifax, she grinned. "Hello, Emmy Reed!"

"Kadi," said Mrs. Pollifax in awe, "where on earth did you learn to shoot like that?"

"Oh, at home in Ubangiba," she said, joining her. "Sand grouse and scorpions and snakes—Sammy and Rabi and Duma and me. I had only a B-B gun but Sammy and Duma had real pistols."

91

"You certainly won Pogo's heart." Mrs. Pollifax glanced down at the sketchbook Kadi carried tucked under her arm. "I see you've already sketched him."

Kadi laughed. "Well, it's mostly a caricature, there wasn't much time."

"But I recognize him at once," said Mrs. Pollifax, studying the quick sketch. "That protruding underlip—and that's a very witty line suggesting his broken nose. Have you done others?"

Kadi stopped and turned a page. "Just this."

"Jasna!" exclaimed Mrs. Pollifax. "Perfect! I've just seen her." Smiling, she said, "I'll have to write the New Haven police department and tell them what a terrible mistake they made, not hiring you."

"I wish you would," Kadi said wistfully. "I really need a job."

"You just had an offer," pointed out Mrs. Pollifax with a twinkle.

Kadi laughed. "I did, didn't I."

Willie was striding down the midway, looking harassed, but seeing them he stopped. "Go all right with the Professor?" he asked Kadi.

"Oh yes," she said eagerly, "but Mr. Willie, how did you know my name was African?"

He grinned. "Rule one in a carnival: never ask personal questions. So I'll ask you one: what country you from?"

"Ubangiba."

He nodded. "Know any pidgin English?"

She laughed. "A little. *Gut ifnin, ha yu de?*"

"*A de wel,*" he said, laughing with her. "*A de fayn.*"

"*Gut,*" she told him. "*Waka fayn.*"

MORE dimensions to this man, thought Mrs. Pollifax; *it suggests a good many adventures for the CIA in his youth.* She said, "I'm sorry to interrupt, but where will I find the Snake Woman, Willie?"

He glanced at his watch. "Still in her trailer. Dark brown mobile home, red curtains," and to Kadi, with a smile, *"Waka fayn,"* and strode away.

She left Kadi staring after Willie with a look of amazement and pleasure on her face, and made her exit from the midway, giving the police car a surreptitious glance and noting that it was empty. Reaching the circle of trailers she located the dark brown mobile home, as long and luxurious as Willie's. An extremely voluptuous young woman was sunning herself in a lawn chair near it, and seeing Mrs. Pollifax she called out with a friendly smile, "Come say hello, you're the lady going to get us in the newspaper, right?"

Startled, Mrs. Pollifax said, "But how did you know?"

The girl laughed. "Boozy Tim told me, Boozy Tim knows all the gossip, he knows *everything* that goes on here. Have a seat." A hand with brilliant red nails indicated the chair next to her.

Mrs. Pollifax made a mental note to look up this Boozy Tim who "knew everything," but she resisted the invitation. "I'm looking for the Snake Woman, are you—?"

"Oh, her ... she's feeding her snakes just now." The hand was casually waved toward the trailer behind her. "I'd advise waiting, it's a messy business."

Mrs. Pollifax eyed the mass of brown hair in the girl's lap. "Is that alive?"

"Lord no," she said, laughing. "It's my wig,

honey, I was brushing it." She held it up to her head to display long corkscrew curls that reached to her waist. "I'm half the girlie show, me and Zilka. Shannon Summer's the name. Sit."

Mrs. Pollifax sat. She also stared, for there was a great deal of Shannon Summer at which to stare, six feet of her at least, with long legs and curves that appeared to defy every law of nature, topped off with a saucy round face and wide smile. "Girlie show?" she said.

"Yeah, just bumps and grinds, they're real strict in this state. Anywhere these days, mostly."

"With that figure," said Mrs. Pollifax frankly, "I should think you'd be in show business. Broadway, I mean. Aren't you wasted on a carnival?"

Shannon Summer laughed contentedly. "Oh, this is the life for me, I like to move. . . . Move move move is my motto. I got booked once in a revue in New York, and staying in one place drove me crazy. Besides, I got lonesome. This is like family."

Struck by what she said, Mrs. Pollifax realized that she ought to be writing it down, and brought out notebook and pen.

"Do I get my picture in the papers?" asked Shannon.

Mrs. Pollifax found herself embarrassed at telling a blatant untruth but she said smoothly, "Probably, yes, but not until the last day I'm here; he can't be spared until then."

"Here only one day?" pouted Shannon. "Honey, you can bet your aunt's fanny it'll rain. Is he good looking?"

"I'm sure of it," Mrs. Pollifax told her, fingers crossed.

"Good. Are the fuzz—police—still poking around?"

"Their car's still parked on the midway."

Shannon's eyes turned mournful. "Pretty tough on that guy Lazlo. Frankly I never seen him until he was on that stretcher. Hi, Boozy Tim," she called.

Mrs. Pollifax turned to meet Boozy Tim and couldn't help but smile. He was a toothless, wizened, joyful little man wearing a baseball cap set at a jaunty angle. He grinned and tipped his cap to her.

"Boozy Tim," said Shannon with authority, "has met God."

"I beg your pardon?" said Mrs. Pollifax.

"Yes ma'am," said Boozy Tim, twinkling at her. "Met with God. He come to me—me, Boozy Tim. Talked to me, too."

"Tell her," Shannon said. "Tell her."

Boozy Tim nudged his way onto the arm of Shannon's chair and lifted his arms dramatically. "He come to me all gold, a gold cloud, like how things look on a misty day, fuzzy, you know? and shimmering all over. And he lifted his arms to me—" He nodded eagerly. "Like this. And he told me things."

"Private things," Shannon announced, nodding.

"Yes ma'am. And I never took a drop of liquor again, no need for it after *that*."

"No," whispered Mrs. Pollifax, mesmerized by the radiance of him as he spoke. "Not after *that*."

He pointed a finger at her. "You're Emmy Reed," he said, and winked at her. "Come to make a story about us."

She admitted to this, wondering what his wink

meant, and if he knew very well that she was an impostor. Shannon had said "he knows everything" and perhaps he did, but she could only return his delighted smile without skepticism: how else, she wondered, could one respond to such a happy little man? "I'd better be about my business," she said, rising, "but I feel very privileged to have met you, Boozy Tim, and perhaps—perhaps we can talk again later?"

"Yes ma'am," he said, beaming at her. "Pleased to meet you." He tipped his hat again as she left them to head for the Snake Woman's trailer, hoping the snakes had now been fed their rats or mice, or whatever it was that gave snakes pleasure. She had lifted her hand to knock on the closed door when a buzz of electronic static interrupted the calm of the afternoon and a loudspeaker sprang into life.

A harsh voice battled the static to say, "This is Willie here. . . . No tear-down tonight, the police won't let us go. Not anybody, not until they finish their investigation. A hell of a bad show for us, but there it is. . . ."

A smoother voice followed: "This is Detective-Lieutenant Allbright to say we are sorry for this inconvenience. However," he explained firmly, "we can't allow you to move on to a town sixty miles away until our investigation into the near-murder of one of your people has been completed. Anybody leaving will be stopped and arrested. Thank you."

Behind her Mrs. Pollifax heard Shannon say, "What the hell's going on? A roustabout gets hurt and the fuzz never care, and what about Willie? Posters out, the next lot rented and pegged, the squeeze fixed by the patch . . ."

96

Mrs. Pollifax shook her head with a smile at this new vocabulary and knocked on the door facing her. She could hear voices arguing; she knocked again.

The door was flung open by an angry, dark young man with black hair and mustache. Behind him Mrs. Pollifax glimpsed a faded blonde woman who shouted at him, "I *told* you we should have left last night, I *told* you—"

Mrs. Pollifax said politely, "How do you do, I'm—"

She was not allowed to finish. The man said, "Sorry, lady, we're leaving. . . . Throw me the keys, Elda—*keys.*"

A set of keys flew through the air, and gripping them he slammed the door behind him and raced to the cab that pulled the trailer. Mrs. Pollifax retreated as the motor roared, the trailer backed a few feet, moved out of the circle and tore off across the field, bouncing over ruts and hillocks.

Obviously it was the police announcement that had sent the Snake Woman and her companion in full flight, which in itself, thought Mrs. Pollifax, was certainly very interesting. She wondered if they would succeed in making their escape over the fields or if the police had anticipated just such a move before the announcement. In any case the Snake Woman had just earned an asterisk beside her name on the list that Willie had given her, and Mrs. Pollifax set out to find the Spin the Wheel booth and to see whether its proprietor Lubo would earn an asterisk, too, or just a plain check beside his name.

12

Crossing the midway, Mrs. Pollifax noticed Willie talking sternly to Boozy Tim next to the transformer; when she glanced back the two men were just disappearing into Willie's trailer. More booths—or joints, as Willie called them—had begun opening up as the afternoon progressed; the man painting his sign was climbing down from his ladder, and she was relieved to see that farther down the midway Lubo's Spin the Wheel was unshuttered and occupied. The booth was difficult to miss: a flashy banner shouted SPIN THE ARROW! VALUABLE PRIZES VALUABLE! and in somewhat smaller but no less garish colors: Win a TV! Win a VCR! FUN FUN FUN!

The man behind the counter didn't look fun at all; she guessed him to be in his thirties, with a face as still as a pool of unruffled water. Not expressionless, she decided, but guarded and watchful, and the dark eyes that lifted as she neared him were so piercing they produced the effect of an electrical shock: she felt measured, analyzed, X-rayed, categorized, and all this with a riveting stillness that was unnerving. She wondered if they were the eyes of a Mephistopheles, a mystic, or a murderer.

"You must be Lubo," she said cheerfully. "Willie's given me permission to spend a few days with the carnival, I'm doing a feature story for my newspaper."

"What paper?" he asked abruptly.

"Portland *Gazette*," she fired back.

"Never heard of it."

Nor had she, but to match his machine-gun style of shooting out words she said crisply, "It's new."

A tight perfunctory smile twitched the corners of his mouth; she doubted that he believed her. "So?"

Notebook in hand she said, "So I'd like to ask how long you've been working in carnivals, Mr. Lubo, and has it always been with Spin the Wheel? And do you enjoy the life?"

He shrugged. "Don't know yet."

"That new?"

"That new."

She smiled politely. "What made you decide to join Willie's Traveling Show?"

"Needed work." His eyes were studying her with an intensity that made her uncomfortable.

She scribbled a few words, nodding. "Interesting . . . May I ask what line of work you were in before?"

Without expression he said, "No."

"You're not exactly giving me feature-story material," she told him frankly, meeting his eyes, and with a pleasant smile added, "Not exactly forthcoming, are you?"

"No," he said.

She nodded. "Thanks anyway," and walked away, still scribbling on her notepad but adding now: Lubo, cultured voice, intelligent, expensive-looking Rolex watch, new at carnivals, not precisely hostile but definitely neither communicative nor friendly. Eyes a bit scary.

The Cat-Rack booth was still closed. As she

returned to her trailer she saw that the Snake Woman's long brown mobile home was in place again, ignominiously turned back by the police, apparently, and its red curtains tightly drawn as if to close out the world. *Not* an auspicious moment for an interview, decided Mrs. Pollifax, and continued on to the trailer that she and Kadi shared.

She found Kadi crouched on her bunk trying on the black stockings and shoes for the six o'clock opening. "They pinch," she said, taking a few steps in the shoes. "But aren't they pretty?"

"Yes indeed, and at least you needn't walk in them," pointed out Mrs. Pollifax. "Do more sketching? I was wondering if you remember enough of Sammy's roommate to sketch him for me, and Sammy, too."

Kadi smiled. "I don't have to sketch Sammy, I've a snapshot of him." Reaching into her knapsack she pulled out a wallet and then a photograph. "Here's Sammy."

It was a group snapshot, taken under a hot sun: three black faces, three white. Kadi said, "That's my mother and father—and Rakia, the head nurse, and Tiamoko, my dad's assistant— and me—and that's Sammy at the far end."

Obviously it had been taken some years ago; Kadi looked fourteen or fifteen at most, and very small next to Sammy, who was a sturdy and attractive teenager with a broad smile on his face, but she found herself more interested in Kadi's parents. They stood in front of a shadeless cement-block building with a sign that read: MANKHWALA NYUMBA. "What does that mean?" she asked, pointing.

"Medicine house."

"Why were they shot, Kadi?" she asked gently.

Her face totally without expression, Kadi said, "Because someone betrayed them, they were accused of helping too much the people wanting change, they were shot as spies."

Yes, they would have helped, thought Mrs. Pollifax, studying the two of them: Mrs. Hopkirk with her plain strong face, Dr. Hopkirk erect, reserved, with eyes and brows that matched Kadi's. Never for them the easy life or the easy choice, by the look of them and their surroundings, but it was Kadi who must be protected now.

When she handed back the photograph she noticed that Kadi didn't look at it again—or dared not. "Thank you," she told her with a smile. "And now it's surely time for early dinner, isn't it? I intend to try one of those 'biggest hotdogs in the USA'—how about it?"

"Oh, *yes*," Kadi said, and they headed companionably to the grab-joint.

At six o'clock Mrs. Pollifax stood in the field outside the entrance and watched the carnival spring into life. Over the ticket booth loomed a proscenium on which spotlights played across giant words proclaiming WILLIE'S TRAVELING SHOW OF FUN AND MIRTH, Games! Prizes! Rides! Shows! Behind her the field was filling with cars and trucks, and people—*townies,* she remembered—were pouring in, abandoning for this night their televisions and VCRs to see live entertainment. On the platform next to the entrance the talker was shouting, "Hully, hully, hully . . . a world of treats for you tonight, folks. Two lush and beautiful gals straight from Paris France do the Dance of the

Seven Veils that'll knock your eyes out, I can tell you! And Elda the Snake Woman with her ten live and dangerous snakes you won't see anywhere but here at Willie's . . . and don't miss Jasna the Knife-Thrower—she might miss tonight, ladies and gentlemen, she might miss!"

His booming voice was supplanted by others as Mrs. Pollifax walked past the ticket booth, confiding that she was 'with it' and proceeded onto the midway, braced against the waves of sound that had blossomed all at once to transform the midway into a promise of adventure and excitement. The ferris wheel had begun turning, the thumping music of the merry-go-round formed a backdrop to lighten the heart, and passing the concessions the voices competed in mounting volume for attention . . . "Hey, mister . . . Hey, pretty girl! . . . Hey, tall guy . . . step right up, ladies, try your luck! Cotton candy here, cotton candy here . . . !"

And somewhere among these people, she reminded herself, was a murderer, unless Lazlo's attacker had walked through those same gates, cleverly drawn a crowd and dashed away as soon as the deed was done. A possibility, conceded Mrs. Pollifax, but surely with so many carnies at work it would have needed more than one visit to the carnival to locate this Lazlo who had quietly collected tickets at the merry-go-round. Willie, encountered earlier on the midway, reported the police had already checked the three motels in the area and had found one traveling salesman who had not left his motel at night, and three families with small children. In these small towns strangers were noticed, and motels had few guests in April. If Lazlo was important enough to have been tucked away here by the Department, she thought it more likely the carnival had been infiltrated—there was that "Hey Rube," for instance—and whoever "they" were, they would not have been careless; there would have been a plan worked out to precisely fit the circumstances.

And the circumstances at a carnival, she thought wryly, were exotic and surely daunting.

What she refused to consider was the carnival's cover being blown as a safe house; she couldn't bear to think of all these people losing their jobs and Willie his traveling show.

I'm becoming hooked, she thought with a smile.

Pogo's shooting gallery already had a cluster of young men and boys around it. As she passed Lubo and his Spin the Wheel she slowed, and then stopped to admire his technique: he was still the same Lubo, speaking with rapid-fire crispness into his microphone but softly, in a low voice, and so confidentially that passersby stopped to hear what he was saying. "The odds are eight to one," he was almost whispering into his mike. "Try the wheel, beat the odds, I dare you . . . Mathematically you'll find this game is . . ."

She walked on, wondering if Lubo could be the one. She would do what she could for Willie, at least until Cyrus came home and until Kadi was safe, but she saw no likelihood of unearthing a suspect in only a few days. She could readily understand that Willie had no time to prowl about and investigate, whereas she was free to wander and observe, but she was also a stranger to these people. She might, of course, be less threatening to them than the police, who had been circulating all day; they were still here, but less obtrusively; she had noticed one of their cars parked behind the trailers not far from where the plane had landed and she supposed a few plainclothesmen might be roaming the midway.

The Ten-in-One was just opening and a tall thin man was testing the microphone on the bally platform. She stopped, eager to see Kadi's performance no matter how invisibly she performed. The talker cleared his throat, called out, "Over here, friends, step this way, folks!" and began describing the delights awaiting them in the side-show tent. To emphasize this, Shannon and Zilka made their entrance on the platform to a flurry of shrill whistles; they were all legs and long hair, with everything in between scanty, sequined, and glittering. El Flamo joined them brandishing a flaming torch, followed by the Professor and Tatiana, her red hair set off by black tights. Last of all came the Snake Woman, so ignominiously returned to Willie's by the police. She was introduced with one huge snake in her arms and another wrapped around her neck. *Brave woman,* thought Mrs. Pollifax, looking at her closely, but not a happy one, she decided: not even the heavy eye make-up could quite distract from the anxious, haunted expression in her eyes. *Going on forty,* summed up Mrs. Pollifax: faded blonde hair badly curled and lips too red. Only when she held up one of the snakes did her face change, become tender and younger as if the snake in her hands gave her more contentment than any human.

Mrs. Pollifax walked inside, and for the ensuing thirty-five minutes she watched as Jasna coolly aimed and threw her long and deadly knives at her father standing against a distant backboard;

saw the Snake Woman talk to her snakes, play with them, give a running commentary about them, heard them hiss alarmingly, and appreciated her finale when she draped all ten snakes around her. She watched the Professor draw eggs out of a hat and rainbow-colored scarves out of his ear, and she was pleased to see that he successfully sawed Tatiana and Kadi in half.

It was following this that she found Boozy Tim standing beside her. He said, "Willie tole me I should talk to you now."

"Oh, good," she said, "I've been wanting to talk to you, too, you know so much and I so little."

"Yes'm," he said, beaming at her. "Happen to know why you're here, and mum's the word."

Leaving the midway they moved into the shadows back of one of the booths, where she turned to face him. "Boozy Tim, can you tell me anything about last night? Were you in the crowd when the man was knifed?"

"Yes'm," he said, nodding.

"Anywhere near?"

"Yes'm."

"Did you notice anything? See any of it? See anyone *near* Lazlo when it happened?"

Boozy Tim sighed. "Well, like I tole Willie— he had me in his office this afternoon—I didn't see anything *really*, except—"

She said quickly, "Except?"

He made a face. "Just a man with a white beard, like I tole Willie. Wouldn't have noticed him at all except he stepped on my foot. Never saw his face but—" He frowned, puzzled. "Something familiar about him. *Something.*"

"Like what?" she asked.

He hesitated. "Don't rightly know, Emmy. Just saw the beard as he turned sideways, away from me. Didn't see his *face*. Maybe the way he held his shoulders. Or his nose. Or his head, maybe."

"What was he wearing?"

He shook his head. "Wasn't much light down there, all those people squeezed in a huddle. Dressed like a townie, I'd say, black sweater, black windbreaker. Only saw him quick—sideways, and then his back."

"He didn't apologize for stepping on your foot?"

Boozy Tim shook his head. "In a hurry. No."

In a hurry . . . "You told Willie this?"

"Yep, except I didn't think of it right away."

"Did you notice anyone else near Lazlo?"

Again he shook his head. "Didn't even know Lazlo was up ahead of me 'til he just sunk to the ground and somebody screamed."

"Who screamed?" she asked.

"Lady who runs the hanky panky near the gate—she come over to see what the 'Hey Rube' was all about, excepting there warn't no reason for any 'Hey Rube' at all, it turned out."

"And Willie knows this? You've told him?"

"Oh yes, ma'am. But there's nobody here in Willie's show with a white beard. White as Santa Claus's beard, pure white like snow. Nobody here like that."

"I see," she said, frowning. "How old would you have guessed the man to be, the one who was in a hurry to leave, and stepped on your foot?"

Boozy Tim considered this judiciously. "Can't say, but he moved pretty damn fast for a man with a white beard."

"Do you think the beard was false?" she asked. "A disguise?"

This had apparently not occurred to him and he looked troubled. "Only saw it fast," he said. "Real fast, and never thought about it anyway 'til Willie asked and *asked* if I'd noticed anybody up near Lazlo. Hear he's still alive, is that right?"

"So far as I know," said Mrs. Pollifax, frowning over his story.

"Willie really grilled me," Boozy Tim said. "He tole me 'Boozy Tim, if you was there you *seen* things' and I said 'no, Willie, didn't see a thing.' But then my foot was hurtin' and all that— still hurts a little—so I remembered *that*, and tole him."

"Thank you," she said gravely, and smiled at him. "You must be a great help to Willie, do you run a concession?"

"Me?" He grinned his broad toothless smile. "Oh no, ma'am, I repair what breaks down. Not much I don't know about the pig-iron—rides, that is—when they stop runnin'. Mechanic, that's me," he said with pride.

Mrs. Pollifax smiled back at him. "I like you, Boozy Tim."

"Like you, too," he said in a pleased voice. "Gotta check the merry-go-round, want a ride?"

"*Love* one."

"I give 'em all names," he confided. "You ride on Cynthia, she's my favorite."

In this manner Mrs. Pollifax ended her first carnival evening riding dreamily up and down on Cynthia, lights flashing, the calliope playing "In the Good Old Summertime." She would have preferred to imagine herself riding to the rescue of the cavalry, or across a great desert to meet a sheikh who would definitely resemble Cyrus, but her mind remained fixed on a man who had stepped on Boozy Tim's foot in his hurry to leave the crowd last night, when people usually moved closer to learn what had caused a woman to scream.

13

Friday

On Friday morning Bishop arrived in his office fifteen minutes late. "Sorry," he apologized, "but I ran into the FBI at the café where I eat breakfast every morning . . . you know, Jed Addams. Want to hear the latest news on the Bidwell abduction?"

"Is anyone immune?" said Carstairs dryly. "What's been happening?"

"Strictly hush-hush, of course, but Jed says there have been three aborted attempts at delivering the ransom—three, no less, in the one week. They put together the fifty million in unmarked bills—no mean feat—and they followed instructions to the letter but nothing happened. The next attempt at delivery is to be late this morning, but in the meantime—" He stopped.

"In the meantime what?"

Bishop grinned. "I'm only trying to milk the one slice of drama on a dull Friday, but in the meantime a video's been found in a Manhattan post office, left on a counter yesterday, with Bidwell pleading for his life. They've decided to air it publicly today on the twelve o'clock news."

"Bidwell, himself? Not his wife?"

Bishop nodded. "Bidwell himself, speaking from captivity. Incidentally, Jed says his wife is still under a doctor's care but one of the chaps at the house is of the opinion that it wouldn't matter all that much to Mrs. Bidwell if the abductors *did* kill her husband. Portrait of a happy marriage, what?"

"Only one amateur's opinion," Carstairs reminded him.

"Right, only one man's opinion," Bishop agreed with a smile.

Carstairs pointed to the small television set in the corner. "I'd like to hear that, I'll be interested in how Bidwell's been enduring his captivity. The noon news, you said? Remind me."

"You bet," said Bishop, and went back to his desk where at ten o'clock he made his sixth attempt to reach Willie and his Traveling Show in Maine, and again connected with his answering machine. "Foxy so-and-so," murmured Bishop, "I'll wager he's switched off his phone completely so he can sleep." He made a note to try again in an hour or so, and seeing the day's newspaper tucked in his OUT basket he scanned the headlines, then turned to the second page for a quick glance. At the bottom of the page he found a small headline: RENEWED VIOLENCE IN UBANGIBA.

Carstairs's Ubangiba, he thought, and picking up a pair of scissors he cut it out for his attention, half humorously because of the strange interest Carstairs had been developing in the country these past few days. Before putting it aside he noted the words *rioting* and *two deaths,* and the fact that the Ubangiban *gwar,* once worth seventy-five cents to the U.S. dollar, was now worth only eight cents.

Poor Ubangiba, he thought.

Carstairs, in his office next door, had just completed the signing of three reports when a call came through from Allan in the Africa section.

"About Ubangiba," he reminded Carstairs. "The soil analysis has been done for you post-haste, and we'll be faxing the report to you in a few minutes."

Carstairs said, "Fine, but can you tell me now, briefly, the conclusion? Did they find possibilities?"

"Only one," said Allan. "There's a mountain running along the southern section of Ubangiba, not high—a line of hills, actually—and from his analysis, which you can struggle with once the report reaches you, the only possibility would be coal."

"Coal!" exclaimed Carstairs. "In Africa?"

"Yes, our geologist points out that by mid-century Algeria was operating four or five mines they'd found in the Sahara desert. At Kenadsa to the west of Columb Bechar there was a vein of coal that produced 350,000 tons a year, for instance. Not pit mines, the seam runs through the hills in what he calls 'galleries.' About forty miles farther south they discovered a seam of coal of even better quality, and coal was later found at Ksi, Ksou, and Mazarif. If there's coal in Ubangiba it could be a remnant of the same primeval forest or marsh that ran through the area aeons ago. He doubts these mines are still in operation. They've probably closed down since the discovery of natural gas in the north, but coal there is, or was."

"Not much anyone can do with coal in the middle of nowhere," growled Carstairs. "No way to export it in a landlocked country, and the yield sounds damn small."

"Oh, I don't know," said Allan. "I would think in a country with no natural source of power except the sun it could do *something*. Heat and light a city or two, dig artesian wells, not to mention run a railroad or a few factories."

"Hmmm," murmured Carstairs. "Well, send the report along."

Coal, he thought as he hung up, and he admitted to disappointment. Oil and natural gas had pretty much supplanted coal, and coal scarcely seemed worth those concealed trips to Ubangiba to capture its mineral rights. What had Desforges said? Something to the effect that with cheap labor it could be modestly profitable. He'd said something else that Carstairs couldn't recall, something to do with cheap labor that nagged at his memory for a moment but without result; fortunately he had his conversation with Desforges on tape, when he had time to review it. For now, however, he could only feel baffled, and—he had to admit—a sense of let-down. He couldn't imagine a modest profit exciting a man like Bidwell with his ability to amass millions . . . or billions, according to Bishop.

He glanced at the news clipping that Bishop had left on his desk about the country, crumpled it up, and tossed it away. *I'm losing interest in this—thank God,* he thought, *and it was never my business, anyway.*

At half-past noon Bishop returned from a quick lunch in the cafeteria and picked up his phone to once again dial Willie's 207 number. This time the phone was answered on its seventh ring.

"Sorry old chap," he told Willie, "but I'm tired of leaving my cheery voice on your machine, it's time I talk with Pete's cargo the other night, no matter how busy you are."

"It's time, yes," agreed Willie. "Incidentally,

we'll be here one more night, the police insist on it. It will cost."

"Our problem, not yours," Bishop assured him. "We don't appreciate our people getting stabbed in the back."

"Right. Hold on, I'll fetch her."

A door opened and closed, and Bishop waited; presently faint voices were heard and at last that of Mrs. Pollifax, somewhat breathless. "Hello, I'm here," she said.

Bishop grinned. "So I notice, and it's been damn hard finding the right time to reach you. Carstairs, not to mention yours truly, want to know what the devil happened to you two nights ago."

She said warmly, "And I want to thank you for rescuing us, Bishop."

"Yes, but from what?" he asked. "And who was chasing you, and who is the 'us'? Talk, for pete's sake."

He heard her take a deep breath. "Give me a minute to put it all together or it'll take hours." After a brief hesitation: "Alright, it started with Kadi Hopkirk," she began, "who needed help and is here with me: age nineteen, grew up in Africa, now studying art in New York. She was interviewing for a job in New Haven when she ran into a boy she'd grown up with, a student now at Yale. They met on the street. This childhood friend of hers introduced the young man with him as his roommate, and then over coffee slipped her a note saying, *'Not roommate—guard.'*"

"I'm listening," Bishop told her.

"She left puzzled and rather alarmed. A van parked outside the coffee shop began following her—to the bus station—and then followed her bus down the turnpike. At some point after Bridgeport, in a panic, she asked the bus driver to stop, jumped out, and ran through a neighborhood of houses and gardens, unfortunately pursued by the two men on foot, and ended up hiding in my house for two days without Cyrus and me knowing it. And I might add," she said, "that during those two days the same van drove past my house often enough for me to notice it even before I found her hiding in a closet."

"Same one?" asked Bishop skeptically. "How could you tell?"

She said tartly, "No one could *help* but notice it was the van she described, because of the crazy sign on its panel, Chigi Scap Metal."

"You mean Chigi *Scrap* Metal, don't you?"

"No, scap—they'd left out the 'r.' *Not* scrap."

"Okay, scap," he murmured. "And this girl. You found her in your house, but what sort is she? Believable?"

"A quite delightful missionary's child," said Mrs. Pollifax, "and as to believable I can testify to the fact that my house was entered and searched, after which we were followed up and down the Connecticut Turnpike for hours. We lost them in Worcester just long enough to register at a motel, but they found us there an hour later. My car's still there, we got away by taxi—to the hospital, where I called you."

Bishop was silent for a moment, puzzled by what he'd heard. He said at last, "Well, we can do something about your car, anyway. What motel? I'll send Pete for it."

"Bide-A-Wee," she told him. "It's near the highway exit, or in that area. But I'm very curious

114

about Kadi's friend Sammy and I know she's worried about him."

"All very strange," admitted Bishop. "One wonders—but I've got this on tape for Carstairs, he'll want to get back to you—he's at a meeting Upstairs just now. Any progress on you-know-what?"

"No, but the police are here questioning everyone," she told him. "And so am I." She added brightly, "It was Willie's idea that I be a feature writer for a newspaper, I'm about to interview the Snake Woman."

"Snake Woman," repeated Bishop blankly. "Yes, of *course*, the Snake Woman."

"And Kadi is being sawed in half," she added blithely, and hung up.

Bishop grinned. He decided that Mrs. Pollifax was thoroughly enjoying herself in spite of those earlier protests about being "stuck" that Willie had described.

An hour later when Carstairs returned from his conference Upstairs Bishop told him, "I've finally connected with Mrs. Pollifax at Willie's; I've got it all on tape."

Carstairs nodded absently. "Good," he said in that voice that meant his thoughts were elsewhere.

"I *said*—" began Bishop again.

"Yes yes, I heard you," Carstairs said impatiently. "They've been able to question Lazlo at last, he's been patched up enough for an interview."

"Does he know who attacked him at Willie's?"

Carstairs looked at him blankly. "At the carnival? No, I wanted him questioned in more detail about what sent him to Willie's in the first place,

115

on March 10th. They just faxed the results to Mornajay."

Thoroughly puzzled, Bishop said, "But so long ago. That's important?"

Carstairs glanced down at the sheaf of notes he carried. "We think he might have been followed from Boston to the carnival, which at least would prevent our closing down Willie as a safe house, and could possibly give us a clue as to who stabbed him a month later. Lazlo had been given a surveillance job in Boston, where he tailed a man named Kopcha into a tenement building. There he overheard scraps of conversation about a ransom pick-up in April."

Bishop whistled faintly. "A ransom pick-up in *April?*"

Carstairs nodded. "When Lazlo came out of that building he'd been beaten up and his arm was broken. That's when he went to Willie's."

"Bidwell was kidnapped in April, do you think possibly—?"

"I think *possibly*, yes," said Carstairs, but added sternly, "*Only* a possibility, however. If by chance it was Bidwell's abduction they were discussing, that tenement building could be where they planned to hold Bidwell, and where he may be hidden away now. I'd wanted more, but I'm not sure I have more."

Carstairs frowned, scanning the faxed sheets. "He'd already described the size of the building: it was tall, vacant, brick, most of its windows boarded up. . . . Asked to describe any possible identifying details on the street he remembered a fire hydrant at the vacant lot next to the building—not much help—and a van parked in front of the tenement, rather grubby, he says, with a sign on it 'Chigi Scap Metal—' " His frown deepened. "A type error here, they must mean Chigi Scrap Metal—"

Bishop leaped out of his chair in excitement. "No, no, let me look!"

"What on earth," protested Carstairs. "All I said was . . ."

"I know, I know, you said Chigi *SCAP* Metal—and so did Mrs. Pollifax, it's on her tape, I tell you it's on her tape, she described just such a van and I said just what you said, 'you mean scrap, don't you?' and she said no, Chigi SCAP Metal, they'd left out the *R*."

"Are you mad? How can Mrs. Pollifax—" Carstairs stopped and stared at Bishop in astonishment. "It has to be a mistake, what possible connection—" With an effort he rallied, to say quietly, "I think you'd better give me that tape, Bishop, and no calls for the next half an hour."

Carstairs retired to his office, and when he had listened to the tape of Mrs. Pollifax's conversation with Bishop he sat for a long time considering what he had heard. With a sudden glance at his watch he picked up the phone and prayed that Willie was in his trailer.

A woman's voice answered. Carstairs said, "Emergency call to Willie, his Uncle speaking."

The voice said, "This is Gertie. Just a minute, I see him talking outside the trailer."

Carstairs waited, but impatiently, and once connected he said, "Willie, this girl who arrived with Pete the other night. You know her at all? Name of Kadi?"

Willie said, "Nice kid, really knows how to handle a B-B gun."

"She's from Africa?"

"Yep."

"Happen to know what country, Willie?"

"Yep."

"So?"

"Ubangiba."

Carstairs felt a flick of excitement. He said quietly, "Thanks, Willie," and rang off to sit and scowl at his desk as if he could find an answer there. *Ubangiba again,* he thought . . . an abduction . . . a stabbing . . . a man in Boston who spoke of a ransom pick-up in April . . . Lecler and Romanovitch . . . a safe house, and a girl pursued by a Chigi Scap Metal van . . . and Desforges's report.

What *had* Desforges said that he wished he could recall? He picked Desforges's tape out of the rack and inserted it into his machine and listened with concentration to every word. He had said, "with cheap labor, and it would have to be *VERY* cheap labor—a bit Leopoldish, of course—but with cheap labor profitable, yes."

"Leopoldish" was the word he'd sought.

Carstairs reached for his dictionary and turned to Biographical Names. There were several Leopolds listed but if he understood Desforges correctly he had been referring to Leopold II, King of Belgium from 1865 to 1909.

Leopold and the Congo.

Carstairs replaced the dictionary and frowned; it was like a jigsaw puzzle, he thought, for which he held in his hand only a few pieces, none of them fitting yet and most of them missing, but there began to be a single intelligible thread. He sat for a long time over his puzzle, dropping one piece into place only to remove it and try another.

At last he ran Desforges's tape again through the machine, and when the tape ended he said aloud to himself, "I have to be mad to think what I'm thinking—utterly mad—and yet I'm thinking it."

But it would certainly explain the huge ransom demanded for Bidwell's release.

He had reached one decision, however: in the morning, Saturday, he would send Bishop personally to Willie's in Maine. It was time to interview Kadi Hopkirk.

14

Mrs. Pollifax, on her way to visit the Snake Woman, saw Boozy Tim slumped on a wooden crate next to the transformer. "Hello, Boozy Tim," she called out to him but he only mumbled a greeting and returned to scowling at the ground; without a smile on his face he looked shrunken and tired, all radiance gone.

Meeting Shannon in the trailer compound she asked, "What's wrong with Boozy Tim? He looks as if he's lost his last friend, he scarcely spoke to me."

"Off his feed," Shannon said, nodding. "One of those viruses, for sure. Sat next to him at breakfast, he stared at his food and left without touching it."

"What do you do here for a doctor?" asked Mrs. Pollifax.

Shannon chuckled. "I guess go see the girl who came with you, she's been telling me all about how medicine men cure things in Africa."

"Kadi has?"

Shannon grinned. "Yeah, her doctor-father was real interested, he knew a couple of them. Honey, would you believe that once, when a guy had gone crazy over there, some medicine man buried him alive in a pit for an hour—with a *goat*—then said a lot of incantations and when they dug him up the goat was dead and the madman alive? Cured, too, because her father checked him out."

"Sounds a reasonable equivalent of shock treatment," said Mrs. Pollifax, "but I doubt its use for Boozy Tim just now."

Shannon giggled. "No, we don't have a goat or a medicine man." With a glance at the sky, she frowned. "Don't like the look of those clouds."

"Rain?"

"A wipe-out night it if rains, honey. Where you off to now?"

Displaying her notebook and pen Mrs. Pollifax confided that she was on her way to the Snake Woman's long sleek trailer. "To interview her," she said, and aware that she was even more interested now in the man who lived with her, she added, "*And* her companion."

"Oh, Jock." Shannon made a face. "Funny. I know his type and believe me, his sort usually has an eye for the girls but he's too busy managing *her*." With a shrug she added, "Maybe that's why she lets him call the shots, to hold onto him, but he can sure be nasty. So good luck, honey."

It was Jock who opened the door to Mrs. Pollifax: lean, handsome, impatient, his eyes cold until he registered the fact that she was the woman from a newspaper, at which point he smiled, flashing perfect white teeth against his tanned skin. "Hey, Elda," he shouted. "Publicity. The interview lady." With exquisite politeness Mrs. Pollifax was ushered inside. "Have a seat—no, not that one, take this."

The Snake Woman walked out of an inner room saying doubtfully, "Publicity?"

Mrs. Pollifax scarcely recognized her this morning: there was no slash of scarlet across her lips, the curls had been sleeked back and she wore

121

a pair of horn-rimmed glasses. "Oh dear," she said, "I was feeding Herman."

"I'll do it," her companion told her, "but take off your glasses, will you?"

"You know I can't see much without them."

"Take them *off*," he said. "You want your picture in the papers with them?"

Mrs. Pollifax politely intruded to say, "No camera yet, that comes later."

At this Jock gave her an indignant glance but rallied to say, "Well, tell her how you grew up in Borneo, Elda." He walked out, presumably to feed Herman.

The Snake Woman smiled faintly. "I wasn't born in Borneo, of course, I grew up in farm country out West, Nebraska, and then Montana. Would you like coffee?"

Mrs. Pollifax had seen enough of her surroundings by now to refuse, once her gaze had fallen upon the large glass cages that lined one wall of the room, each one occupied by what had looked like giant coils of rope until one of the ropes had drowsily stirred. Nor was she unaware of the white mouse that suddenly scampered across the room. Bringing out her notepad she said, "I see you really live with your snakes . . . let's begin with your name."

The Snake Woman sat down at the other end of the coffee table and said, "Okay, I'm Elda Higgins."

"And Jock, he's Higgins, too?"

"Oh no, we're not married. Not yet anyway," she said comfortably. "He's the one who talked me into this. I was teaching, you see, at a small midwestern college—teaching herpetology." Her voice sharpened, for a second became almost sarcastic as she added, "He told me what a lot of fun it would be, and lots of money, too, if I showed off my snakes at big expositions, seeing I had so many as pets." She rose and went to one of the cages and Mrs. Pollifax winced as she drew out a six-foot-long snake with brown stripes. "He likes to be held," she said, carrying him back to the chair. "He's a boa, isn't he beautiful? His name is Jimmy."

"Boa *constrictor*?" Mrs. Pollifax said weakly.

"Yes."

Recovering, Mrs. Pollifax asked if she was finding her new career fun and profitable.

Elda sighed. "Profitable? Well, it should be, it's just—" She hesitated. "No, not yet. We started the season with a big exposition in New York State and it looked great, but then Jock quarreled with the management, so we came here. We came late." She said with a wry smile, "So I can't say there's much money yet, no, this being so small a carnival."

Mrs. Pollifax smiled sympathetically. "I couldn't help but overhear yesterday—I was about to knock on your door—that you'd wanted to leave earlier."

Startled, Elda said, "Oh, Jock—Jock doesn't like the police." Aware that she'd been indiscreet she added quickly, "Really it was me, it just seemed as if we could do better somewhere else, it's not *that* late in the season. It's the money, you see, it costs to keep the place warm enough— nearly eighty degrees—for the snakes, and feeding them's expensive, and there's the travel, and the trailer payments, and I've got a daughter back in Nebraska . . ." Her voice trailed away as if she might cry if she continued.

"I'll write that down, it's very interesting," said Mrs. Pollifax, scribbling a few lines. "Have you known Jock long?"

"No, not long," she said and then, brightening, "but he knows carnivals and that sort of thing, he used to be a barker in the Strates Shows, and—"

"And sold you on the idea," said Mrs. Pollifax. "And the snakes, are they still highly dangerous?"

"No, not now," Elda said with a flash of anger.

"Not poisonous?"

The anger faded and she said without expression, "Jock refused to live with me unless their venom ducts were cut." She gave an abrupt laugh that sounded false. "Well, he probably was right, because they don't like him, but I'll tell you this." She leaned forward, with passion in her voice, "No rattlesnake or python or boa ever, *ever*, bit me, I've raised them since I was a kid of seven or eight years old, and never, *never* did they hurt me."

"How do you do it?" asked Mrs. Pollifax, marveling.

Elda leaned back, relaxed again, to say easily, "Well, they *know* me, you see, we're friends. I talk to them, pet them, feed them, tame them. There aren't many deaths in the United States from snakes, you know, it's mostly from the diamond-back rattlers, and I don't fool with them. King-snakes, boas, pythons, and sidewinders are what I have. *Three* gorgeous pythons." She nodded toward the cages along the wall. "Want to see them?"

"Uh—not just now. Would you call yourself a snake-charmer?"

Elda laughed. "Oh, there aren't any snake-charmers, just strong-minded people."

Strong-minded Elda might be, thought Mrs. Pollifax, but not where Jock was concerned. With an uneasy glance at the boa that was slithering out of Elda's lap she rose, saying, "I think this gives me enough material for the moment, I want to talk to some of the concessionaires I've not spoken with yet."

"Oh, them." Casually picking the boa up from the floor, Elda opened the door for Mrs. Pollifax and blinked at the sun outside.

Mrs. Pollifax said, "Do you know any of your neighbors? Mingle at all?"

Elda said eagerly, "Oh I'd love—" She stopped and glanced back toward the kitchen. "No," she said. "No, I don't know any of them."

Jock again, thought Mrs. Pollifax, and left, feeling that she was not going to be of any help to Willie; any talents she might possess for ferreting out skullduggery had become sidetracked by the novelty of her surroundings. Considering Elda the Snake Woman, for instance, she thought her as caged as any of her pythons but this could, of course, be only a cover; she might instead be a consummate actress and not a professor of herpetology at all. The police had certainly made her companion Jock nervous but it was quite possible this was for reasons other than international espionage. . . . She had overheard the police interviewing Jasna and her father yesterday, and if his blindness was what had reduced them to bringing a class act to Willie's small carnival she thought they concealed his blindness very well. At the Ten-in-One last night she had witnessed their performance with much interest. In his white satin robe and with his full black beard he had resembled a Russian patriarch, the dark glasses quite understandable due to the brilliance of the spotlight trained on him. She noted that he had already been placed in position before the curtain was raised: the two worked hard at concealing his handicap. There was also Lubo, stubbornly and relentlessly secretive—even Kadi hadn't been able to pry any information from him—yet carnies, she realized, were not the usual run of people; in any normal society she supposed they would be called misfits: voluptuous Shannon, for instance, who scorned Broadway to move, move, move . . . Boozy Tim whose eccentricities were regarded here with pride and even awe; where else would he find so amiable and responsive an audience?

The sun had emerged again from behind the clouds, and its heat flavored the air with the scent of sawdust. She decided to see if Pie-Eye had opened up his Cat-Rack booth yet, and headed for the midway. The man called Jake was fussing with the transformer and gave her a nod as she passed. She had not yet met Pie-Eye but she had glimpsed him at his stall the night before and had noted the bright pink turban he wore around his head, setting off a lean and swarthy face with a pencil-line mustache that punctuated thin lips. Now she saw that his booth was open and that he was talking to—of all people—Kadi, which she thought would definitely make her questions easier. She strolled across the midway to join them.

"He's not pie-eyed," Kadi told her, "but nobody can pronounce his name so he's called

that, but he doesn't like it. His name's really—"
She looked at him questioningly.

"Pyrrhus," he announced. "The name of a king," he reminded her firmly.

"Yes indeed, and how do you do," said Mrs. Pollifax. "And you run the Cat-Rack game?"

He shrugged. "This year, this season, yes." He smiled at her benevolently.

"And other seasons?" she asked, returning his smile.

Again he shrugged. "Anything, everything! Mental telepathy, fortune-telling, Spin the Wheel, the penny-pitching board, I can do anything. I am a psychic and also," he admitted charmingly, "a genius."

"That's a great deal of talent," she told him, and added mischievously, "I wonder that you're here and not at one of the big expositions."

His charm at once vanished. He stared at her with suspicion, saying coldly, "I go where I choose—where my destiny points—I move with the wind."

"It's a southeast wind today," Kadi said ingenuously. "A hot one, too." She winked at Mrs. Pollifax and turned to leave. "Let's go find Boozy Tim, Emmy." Once out of hearing she whispered, "Nobody likes Pie-Eye, Gertie says they think he's a bit light-fingered and on the lam. Maybe he's the one."

"I'll make a note of that—and of your expanding vocabulary," teased Mrs. Pollifax. "Any more sketching?"

Kadi glanced down at her sketchbook. "Only of the two men in the Chigi Scap Metal van who chased me. At least I tried, except of course I never saw them close-up."

Glancing at the two faces Mrs. Pollifax murmured, "Older than I thought. Asian, perhaps? Rough and tough as well, from the look of them, not at all the sort anyone would appreciate being pursued by."

"No," said Kadi. "I just thought, if I tried to get them on paper, I might get them out of my dreams. They chased me into your garden last night, too, when I was asleep." Having stated this in a matter-of-fact voice she added with a smile, "Did you know Boozy Tim's sailed all around the world on cargo ships? Except that when Willie found him he was homeless and living on the streets."

"I didn't know that."

Kadi nodded. "There's more news I haven't told you: I've been offered three jobs already—three! Pogo, the Professor, and—don't faint—Willie. For the summer."

"Willie!"

Kadi nodded happily. "He wants me to make a sketch of him for his livingroom—although *not* to replace Elvis Presley—and to design new carnival posters and touch up the Ten-in-One canvases, especially El Flamo and the Dancing Girls."

Amused, Mrs. Pollifax said, "And have you said yes?"

Kadi looked troubled. "I told Willie I had to find out first about Sammy." Glancing up and down the midway she added, "Where can Boozy Tim be? Jake," she called to the ride foreman, "have you seen Boozy Tim?"

Jake gave her a shy smile; everyone smiled at Kadi, noticed Mrs. Pollifax; it was impossible not to, for she was blossoming like a girl at her first prom, her eyes shining, cheeks pink, dark hair blown into tangles.

"Boozy Tim?" repeated Jake. "Gone into town. Walked."

Surprised, Mrs. Pollifax said, "On such a hot day? Shannon said he wasn't feeling well this morning."

Jake frowned. "She offered him a ride but he said he wanted to walk." He shook his head. "Hardly ever leaves the show, guess he needed something really bad." He added consolingly, "He'll be okay, it's only three miles and Shannon said she'd keep an eye out for him to give him a ride back."

Mrs. Pollifax was considerably relieved to hear this.

She and Kadi approached their trailer together and Mrs. Pollifax unlocked the door, an act that proved more difficult than usual. "Stubborn," she said, inserting the key a second time and frowning.

"Maybe needs oiling," said Kadi.

"Certainly needs *something*." Once again Mrs. Pollifax withdrew and inserted the key in the lock and this time it turned hard but unlocked the door.

They walked in and Mrs. Pollifax said, "Oh-oh."

"What?" asked Kadi.

"You'd better find Willie, we've been searched," she told her. "Carelessly, too. I left my purse under the pillow, totally concealed but now half of it's visible, and where's your knapsack?"

Startled, Kadi glanced quickly around the

129

small trailer. "It's on the seat by the table but I know I left it on my bunk. Emmy—"

"Find Willie, you can see if anything's missing when you get back. The side window's open and the screen knocked out. Whoever it was must have left in a hurry when they heard us outside."

With Kadi gone Mrs. Pollifax looked through her purse, finding its contents disarranged but nothing missing, not even the seventy dollars in her wallet. Whoever had searched it, however, would know now, from her checkbook and credit card, that her name was not plain Emmy Reed. She wondered how important this was.

When Willie at last arrived he looked grim. "Someone checking you out I do not *like*. What's missing?"

"I don't like it either," she responded, "and nothing at all has been stolen."

"Worse yet," said Willie, looking grimmer.

Kadi was groping through her knapsack, finally spilling its contents across the bunk: two chocolate bars, four sketchbooks, a change purse, wallet, a book, pens and pencils, a passport, three lipsticks, a brush and comb, and a small folder neatly lettered: *Résumé, Kadi Hopkirk.*

Mrs. Pollifax smiled a little at the collection. "All there?"

Kadi nodded.

"I don't like this at all," repeated Willie. "In broad daylight, too, and nothing missing. It makes me think whoever knifed Lazlo really *must* be here still and is getting nervous. Or curious. If you'd been robbed it would have been one thing, but with nothing taken—"

"Do you think my so-called interviews are making someone edgy?"

Willie considered this. "No," he said thoughtfully, "it's more likely someone feels watched."

"Certainly not by me," she said indignantly. "The only person I've consistently watched each evening is the Professor, when he saws Kadi in half." Glancing past Willie to the window she saw Boozy Tim trudging past the trailer with a large white paper bag in one hand, and she gave a sigh of relief. "Thank heaven! There's Boozy Tim at last, we've been worried about him."

Willie looked grim again. "Just the person I want to see." Striding to the open door he called out to him, and stepped down from the trailer. The two met just outside the window. "Boozy Tim, what the hell's wrong with you, you been sick?" he demanded. "Everybody comes to me and wants to know what the hell's wrong with you today."

Boozy Tim said earnestly, "Just trying to *think*, Willie. Honest, Willie, if I could think *hard* enough I just know I could help with that Santa Claus fellow that stepped on my foot."

Willie's voice turned gentle. "Not sick, then?"

"No, Willie, just trying hard to *think*."

"Well, don't try anymore, Boozy Tim—*don't*," Willie told him. "We're all missing your smiles."

"You are, Willie? Really? Okay, Willie, I'll stop if you say so."

"I do say so. C'mon, let's hit Mick for a cup of coffee at the grab-joint, you look tired."

So that's it, thought Mrs. Pollifax; Boozy Tim had wanted desperately to please Willie, and it was no wonder if he had lived on the streets before being embraced by the carnies. Shannon had described the carnival as a family, and for the

131

regulars who joined the show every year she could see that it must be exactly that.

Kadi, re-packing her knapsack, said, "Guess I'll take a shower now, it'll be show-time soon enough."

Mrs. Pollifax nodded. The incident had ended, she would presently restore the window screen to its frame, join the crowd for an early dinner at the cook-house and at six the carnival would open, but she knew that it would not be quite the same, for something had changed: Lazlo's attacker was no longer a mysterious possibility but was becoming a presence.

At six o'clock Mrs. Pollifax moved against the influx of townies streaming through the gate to head for the Ten-in-One. She walked to the sound of the merry-go-round playing the lilting strains of the "Blue Danube," and by the time she entered the big tent the music had changed to a jolly "Ciribiribin." It was ritual now to watch Kadi's first performance of the evening, after which she would accompany Kadi as she hurried over to Pogo's shooting gallery to become his stick for fifteen or twenty minutes. Once inside the tent she paused beside the Talking Sphinx— *Ask Any Question, the Sphinx Will Answer You!*— and wished she could ask if it was a murderer who had searched their trailer this afternoon, but the young ventriloquist behind the sphinx would only think her quite mad.

It was a warm night, even warmer under the Ten-in-One canvas. She took her place in the bleachers and watched Norbert the Contortionist wrap his legs around his neck, marveled at El Flamo the Fire-Eater; and then as the Professor arrived on the stage she turned her head to see what sort of business the carnival was pulling in this night. It was now that she saw Boozy Tim standing in the shadow of the bleachers watching, his eyes narrowed and as intent as laser beams. He had said, *Honest, Willie, if I could think hard enough I just know I could help with that Santa Claus fellow,* and Willie had said, *Don't try anymore, Boozy Tim, don't.*

Obviously Boozy Tim was still trying; he was studying every move the Snake Woman made, his face clouded and somber. The Snake Woman retired and the Professor appeared on stage, and Boozy Tim watched him closely, too. After the Professor, thought Mrs. Pollifax, there would come Jasna and her father, and then El Flamo the Fire-Eater, and she began to admit a feeling of deep uneasiness. *He shouldn't, he really shouldn't,* she thought, because in his attempt to identify the person who had stepped on his foot two nights ago he would soon become conspicuous; and with a shock she recalled Willie saying, "It's more likely someone feels watched."

She wanted to say to him, "Stop watching like that, it's dangerous," but her decision was distracted by the ending of the Professor's act and Kadi appearing at her side. Nevertheless as they passed Boozy Tim, Mrs. Pollifax stopped. "Boozy Tim," she said in a low voice, "come outside with us, won't you? Kadi and I are off to Pogo's and you can keep me company. Do come!"

"Yes'm," he said politely, not removing his eyes from the stage. "In a little while. Not yet."

He was still watching as they left the Ten-in-One.

133

15

Bishop did not receive kindly the news that on Saturday morning he was to fly to Maine and interview Kadi Hopkirk. "Damn it," he protested, "I've a date tomorrow to lunch and play golf, I've only just met this blonde, she's stunning and she *likes* me."

"I like you, too," said Carstairs dryly. "So does Mrs. Pollifax. Even Kadi Hopkirk may like you."

Bishop sniffed indignantly. "I might point out that none of you are blonde, with sylphlike figures, work for the Treasury Department, and can talk in depth about the Federal Reserve."

Carstairs raised an eyebrow. "Talk about the Federal Reserve? Oh, please, Bishop."

"Oh well." Bishop grinned sheepishly. "If I've expressed my disappointment clearly enough I'll stop, but there are times—"

"What we're paid for," Carstairs reminded him. "However, you'll be at Willie's by two in the afternoon and should be back by evening, I promise you a free Sunday and you're the only person I trust for the job."

Having admitted this he returned to his usual brisk self. "Now I want two things done: I want inquiries sent out to the state police in New York, Connecticut, and New Jersey regarding a white van with the name Chigi Scap Metal on its panels, license unknown. Mrs. Pollifax didn't happen to notice the *color* of the plate, did she?"

Bishop shook his head. "It could very well have

been neatly muddied and obscured for daytime, and unlit for night driving, but since it was always behind them it's not too surprising if they didn't notice." He glanced at his watch. "I'll get to work on the police calls, but what was that second job?"

Carstairs smiled. "Whenever it feels right for you—at the proper time this afternoon—you might give Jed Addams a call at the FBI and learn whether this morning's ransom drop-off met with any success. Now let me get back to work, you know how Fridays are."

"On my way." At the door Bishop hesitated, turning to say with a grin, "I admit there are compensations in regard to the trip to Maine. When I spoke with Mrs. Pollifax she was about to happily interview a Snake Woman. I'll be interested in how she deals with a carnival, it should be quite a change from her Garden Club."

"Even more interesting if she's learning who knifed Lazlo," pointed out Carstairs, but Bishop had already closed the door behind him and didn't hear.

Promptly at 11:57 the television was turned on; a soap opera was just ending and Bishop watched a voluptuous blonde actress with enormous interest. After two commercials came the excited announcement that Henry Bidwell had at last been heard from, and was presumably still alive, and the film was flashed on the screen. It had been filmed by an amateur, the lighting was poor, the background blurred, but Bidwell's face was close to the camera and clear enough for a bruise on one cheek to be seen, and smudges under his eyes. His voice was tired. He said that he was

George Bidwell, that he was not being ill-treated but the ransom had still not been paid, he had been told that the police had fouled up several attempts and he was begging them to expedite the payment because he was now in fear of his life. "I beg of you," he pleaded, "for God's sake return me to my family before they kill me, *these are not patient people.*"

Abruptly it ended.

"Dramatic," said Carstairs, nodding.

"Dramatic!" exploded Bishop. "Not ill-treated, but did you see the bruise on his cheek? The FBI had jolly well better stop fooling around or they'll have blood on their hands."

Carstairs gently pointed out that pick-ups were not so easily arranged.

Bishop sniffed. "Jed Addams said the last attempt was out on a country road in New Jersey, no doubt with an agent up every tree and a helicopter circling."

Amused, Carstairs said, "And just how would you plan delivery and pick-up, then?"

Bishop scowled. "Well, I'd—" He stopped. "A busy street corner in New York? Drop it maybe in a litter basket, one of those wire things?"

"You'd leave fifty million in unmarked bills in a litter basket on a street corner, and hope no vagabond would get to it first?"

Bishop said irritably, "Well, I don't know, but it's their job to come up with something creative, isn't it?"

"Yes," agreed Carstairs, "but not so creative they scare off the kidnappers who want to be certain they're not being watched, photographed, or followed." He glanced at the clock. "Now 12:07 . . . well, we've seen Bidwell. Don't get so bogged down in paperwork you forget to check with Jed Addams about the latest attempt."

"How could I forget? I thought about 2:30?"

"Sounds good."

Once alone Carstairs attacked his own paperwork, was called Upstairs for a conference with Mornajay and returned at three o'clock to find Bishop looking pleased. "It's finally happened," he said. "The ransom. I don't know how, but at first light—at 5 o'clock this morning—the Bidwell son proved useful after all. He accomplished the delivery on a motorcycle or bicycle somewhere near the estate, and before he even reached home the kidnappers confirmed by a pre-arranged signal that the pick-up was successful. Now all they have to do is wait in suspense for Bidwell to be delivered safely, too."

"Not bad for a week's work," said Carstairs. "And somebody had a good head on his shoulders—not too light, not too dark at 5 A.M. Good show!"

At half-past five in the afternoon Carstairs was dictating notes to Bishop and finishing up the last work of the day when the buzzing of the phone interrupted them. "Carstairs here," he said and a minute later, placing his hand over the receiver, he told Bishop, "It's the New York police, they've found the Chigi Scap Metal van." He returned to the phone, said, *"Where?"* in a startled voice, and then, "Empty? And how long?" He made a face. "Right. I appreciate your help, we'll be in touch." He hung up, looking sober and a little sad, until Bishop forced himself to ask, "So where did they find the van?"

Carstairs sighed. "It's just been pulled out of the East River. Someone on the docks heard a big splash over an hour ago and saw the last of it go down and called the police."

Bishop whistled through his teeth. "Anyone in it?"

"One body. That of the driver, but they say the window and door on the passenger side were open so there may have been two of them. Poor devils, no matter what their crimes."

Bishop stared at him, appalled. "Does any of this make sense?"

"It could," said Carstairs noncommittally. "It might. It may." Turning his attention to Bishop he said, "It's getting late, you'd better go home and pack your bag, you've a plane to catch in the morning to Maine."

"Yes, but if anything else is going to happen—"

"Nothing else is going to happen," Carstairs told him, "I'll be leaving shortly, too."

With a wry smile Bishop said, "But not immediately? What's left to do?"

"Think," said Carstairs wearily.

"Oh," said Bishop, and went out.

When he had gone Carstairs switched off his phones to sit quietly at his desk and go over the same old puzzle again, updating it by rote: an abduction, a stabbing . . . a man in Boston who spoke of a ransom pick-up in April . . . Lecler and Romanovitch . . . Desforges's report . . . a girl from Ubangiba pursued by a Chigi Scap Metal van, and to this he could now add Bidwell's $50 million ransom paid and one Chigi Scap Metal van hauled out of New York's East River.

"Their usefulness over—they knew too much," he said aloud. "Very well thought out and engineered. Very!"

But there were still several pieces of the puzzle missing—important ones—and he frowned over these for a long time until he glanced at his watch, realized he was hungry, and decided that he might think better if he had some food.

In the table-service room he ordered a lamb chop, spinach, and a baked potato and tried to remember if he'd had any lunch. He doubted it, and congratulated himself on his decision to inject nourishment into his thought processes. He was trying to decide whether to order apple pie or ice cream for dessert when he saw Allan from the Africa Department heading toward him, a lanky young man with a head of bright red hair whose last name he couldn't remember.

It was possible, he thought, that he'd never known it.

"Hi," Allan said. "I was just leaving and spotted you. Didn't realize you were still in the building or I'd have called you."

"Called me?"

Allan nodded amiably. "Yeah. Don't know whether it would interest you or not, but you did ask for that geological report on Ubangiba, right?"

"Yes indeed," said Carstairs.

"The news was on the BBC an hour ago that their President's dead."

Carstairs looked at him in surprise. "Are we talking about Ubangiba?"

"Right."

"*And President-for-Life Simoko is dead?*"

Allan nodded. "Just thought I'd tell you in case it's of any interest," he said, and with a smile and a nod he continued on his way toward the exit.

Carstairs sat very still, thinking how very much this did interest him, so much so that he forgot dessert and returned at once to his office to begin a series of phone calls, several of them to Europe, and one of them to Bishop.

16

Saturdays

On Saturdays the life of the carnival changed drastically because it was matinee day, the gates opened at two in the afternoon, the acts in the Ten-in-One were reversed—the last one seen first—and the take was the biggest of the week, barring rain. Whether there would be crowds today was a matter of speculation, since under normal circumstances the carnival would have left during the night to establish itself sixty miles to the north. Now it remained to be seen whether their attractions had been exhausted; over lunch in the cook-house there was still a fair amount of grumbling over no tear-down during the night, and their being trapped here for an additional day. A Saturday, too.

Any worry about the weather had dissipated: it was June-hot with a small breeze distributing the usual smells of the carnival: hot popcorn, grease, sawdust, and the freshly cut grass in the field beyond. As Mrs. Pollifax and Kadi left the grab-joint they were accosted by Willie with an odd expression on his face. "I don't get it," he told them, "I can't find Boozy Tim. Jake hasn't seen him, Shannon hasn't seen him today, nobody knows where he is. Do you? Have you seen him?"

Mrs. Pollifax stiffened. "You're sure he's not in his trailer?"

141

Willie shook his head. "It's locked up tight. I looked through the back window and nobody's inside. What's the matter?"

"What's the matter," said Mrs. Pollifax slowly, "is that last night in the Ten-in-One, waiting for Kadi, Boozy Tim was there studying each of the acts and watching *intently*, apparently still looking for the person who stepped on his foot. I tried to stop him, but—"

Willie, staring at her in astonishment, said, "You mean he kept at it, when damn it he promised me?" And then, assimilating the reality of it, "Where was he standing, was he conspicuous?"

"Anybody in the aisles is conspicuous from the stage," pointed out Mrs. Pollifax, "but at least when Kadi and I left he was pretty much in shadow. I don't know how obvious he became after that."

Willie said grimly, "And here I thought he was sleeping late because of his damnfool walk into town yesterday. He's frail, you know. I think we've got to call in the *gavver* on this."

"Gavver?"

"Police. They're still guarding the exits but there's one of them in my trailer now making a phone call, the sandy-haired one called Bix."

Kadi said earnestly, "I can help look, *everybody* can help, Willie. You think he had a heart attack or something?"

Mrs. Pollifax caught Willie's eye and held it. "Are you thinking what I'm thinking?"

His lips thinned. "You're damn right, but let's keep this quiet, we open in forty minutes. No panic. Wait here. No, come along with me."

"What is it?" asked Kadi, hurrying behind Willie with Mrs. Pollifax.

She said, "You remember my telling you what Boozy Tim saw on Wednesday night, the man with a white beard hurrying away from the crowd. He thought—felt—there was something familiar about him; now we're afraid Boozy Tim may have discovered who it was."

"You mean he's been trying to find—and maybe did?" gasped Kadi. "Oh God, if anything's happened to him!"

They were close behind Willie when he flung open the door to his trailer, and they followed him inside. The officer he'd called Bix was sitting at his desk, phone in hand. Willie said, "Trouble, Bix, Boozy Tim's missing. Nobody's seen him since last night."

Startled, Bix said, "The little guy, the one who saw—"

"Yeah." Willie was leaning over his desk and opening a drawer and Mrs. Pollifax's eyes widened as she saw him draw out a small, snub-nosed black gun, load it, and tuck it into his belt.

Bix returned to the phone to say, "Trouble, Chief, better call in a few state police. Got to hang up." At once he was on his feet. "Where do we look? Going to announce this over the loudspeaker?"

Willie shook his head. "The exits are still guarded, so he has to still be here. It's best we don't broadcast this, or whoever's fooling with Boozy Tim might—might—" He didn't finish, saying instead, "Let's you and me do the empty warehouse trucks—the trailers can wait until they're empty—and Emmy here, and Kadi, you check the booths. Under, over, and behind. Damn it, we open in thirty minutes and the place will be full of people—impossible!" Handing

143

both Mrs. Pollifax and Kadi flashlights he added, "Let's meet in fifteen minutes at Boozy Tim's trailer."

They separated quickly, Mrs. Pollifax and Kadi heading out into the midway. Most of the booths were already open and at Lubo's their reception was hostile. "Why the hell should I let you prowl around my counter?" he demanded.

"Because Boozy Tim's missing," Mrs. Pollifax told him crossly.

"What—that nice little guy?"

"Just get out of our way and don't waste our time."

To Mrs. Pollifax's surprise he immediately stepped back and allowed them to open a coat locker in the rear and inspect every dark corner.

Up and down the midway the two of them went: the fortune teller's tent, Wheel of Fortune, the slum skillo joints, the Milk-bottle and Spindle games, the Bingo tent, Penny arcade, the merry-go-round, Whip, ferris wheel, and Dodge-'em cars. . . . There was no Boozy Tim, and their search consumed twenty minutes of precious time, so that it was only ten minutes before opening-time when they rushed back to Boozy Tim's trailer to find that Willie and Bix were late, too.

Waiting outside, Mrs. Pollifax peered into Boozy Tim's trailer through the only window at her level and found her glance meeting an opposite wall inside, on which movie-star cut-outs occupied nearly every inch, running the gamut from Janet Gaynor to Madonna. She could see a tiny sink piled high with unwashed dishes, and a corner of his dining table on which lay the white paper bag that Boozy Tim had carried with him on his return from town yesterday. But there were other objects on the table as well, puzzling shapes she couldn't identify from this vantage point, and half of them cut off from view.

"You're frowning," said Kadi, "what is it? Is Boozy Tim there?"

"No, but I'm seeing the paper bag he brought from town yesterday, and something strange on the—go find Willie, Kadi—*fast!*"

"I see them on the midway talking to Jake."

"Then get them here quickly!" commanded Mrs. Pollifax.

After one look at Mrs. Pollifax's face Kadi raced toward the two men, shouting, and returned with them. "You didn't go inside earlier?" Mrs. Pollifax demanded of Willie. "I think it's terribly important."

"I'll get the skeleton key," said Willie.

"No—break down the door," she told him. *"Now."*

"Break down—but why?"

"I don't *know* why," she cried in frustration, "it's a *feeling* I have. *Please.*"

The door resisted, splintered and opened, and Mrs. Pollifax led them to Boozy Tim's dining table.

There was an open tin of white paint, a tin of talcum powder, a smear of ketchup, a paint brush, and two dark false beards, one of them half-painted white, the other one pure white with talcum dust surrounding it, as if the entire tin of talcum had been emptied over it.

This, thought Mrs. Pollifax, was what he'd walked into town to buy: Boozy Tim, deeply troubled, doubting himself, and afraid of what he suspected, had wanted to be sure.

145

Kadi, leaning over the small splash of red, said, "This isn't ketchup, it's blood."

They stared in shock at the splotch of red.

Willie said, "It must have happened last night, then, his trailer lighted, someone at the window seeing what he was experimenting with—"

"—and walked in on him," finished Bix.

"Oh dear God," whispered Kadi.

In a stunned voice Mrs. Pollifax said, "But there's only one person working in this carnival with a full beard."

"That's true," gasped Kadi. "It's true, she's right."

With a glance at his watch Willie said grimly, "It's 2:03 and we're open now. *And the acts are reversed in the afternoon shows.*"

They stared at one another in shock, and then Willie shouted, "RUN! And Bix—call in your police!"

It was proving a profitable afternoon for the Ten-in-One; the bleachers were full, the Snake Woman was just completing her act, and as the audience applauded and she left the stage Jasna took her place, strolling in casually, all silver in a sequined jumpsuit, very tall and very calm. With a curt bow to the audience she placed her case of knives on a tall stool, opened the case and displayed the knives that glittered in the spotlight. The audience settled into silence, watching intently. Selecting one of the knives she gestured toward the curtain, which slowly rose to reveal the backboard and her father standing against it, but in a strikingly different costume this afternoon: a long black robe and a hood that concealed half of his face.

146

Except the figure was smaller than Jasna's father, and did not stand up straight but sagged, head lowered until it rested on his chest, *and there was no beard.*

"It's Boozy Tim" gasped Mrs. Pollifax. "Willie—Kadi—it's Boozy Tim up there, she's going to kill him and call it an accident!"

"Not in *my* carnival," said Willie grimly. Eyes narrowed, he said, "We've got about one minute, she won't dare kill him on the first throw, I'd guess the second or third, but we can't crowd her, if she sees us she'll kill him right away."

Mrs. Pollifax said desperately, "I know karate but I'd never be able to get near her, not close *enough.*"

"And I'm wearing a gun," Willie said furiously, "and at that distance—I'm not that good."

"Give the gun to Kadi," she told him quickly. "Kadi, she doesn't know you . . . walk fast to the other side of the bleachers and pray you can shoot the knife out of her—" She faltered as Jasna aimed and threw the first knife, and the audience gasped as it pierced the backboard next to Boozy Tim's left shoulder. "—out of her hand. Hurry," she whispered as Willie handed her the small snub-nosed gun. Kadi tucked it into her belt and vanished behind the bleachers.

Slowly Mrs. Pollifax began to move down the aisle as if looking for a seat, her mind running over possible karate strikes, all of them impossible with Jasna on a stage several feet above the ground, and too far from the edge of the stage to be reached with a blow to an ankle. She was aware of Willie following behind her, doubled over so that he'd not be seen, and she fervently hoped this sudden activity in both of the aisles

147

would not catch the eye of the woman on the stage.

Jasna reached for her second knife, aimed it and sent it flying to a point an inch from Boozy Tim's right shoulder, where it hung, quivering; and now, picking up speed, she reached for the third knife, and—

A shot rang out. A woman screamed. The knife fell from Jasna's hand and for just a second she stood frozen, staring incredulously at the knife on the floor and then Mrs. Pollifax reached the stage, rushed across it and thrust Jasna off-balance with a blow across her shoulders. As she staggered, Willie grabbed both of Jasna's arms and held them tightly behind her as the Ten-in-One was suddenly full of police in uniform rushing down the aisles.

Mrs. Pollifax hurried to the figure slumped against the backboard and pushed back the hood. "Hand me one of the knives," she shouted to Willie. "He's unconscious and tied here with a rope."

Willie thrust a struggling Jasna into the arms of a policeman, handed Mrs. Pollifax a knife, and turned to the audience. "Sorry, folks," he said, "a little trouble here but the show goes on." To someone behind the curtain he shouted, "For God's sake bring on Shannon and Zilka," and then he joined Mrs. Pollifax in sawing the thick rope that had kept Boozy Tim barely upright. Released, Tim fell into their arms and they carried him off the stage.

"Is he alive?" whispered Mrs. Pollifax as they laid him on the floor behind the curtain.

Kadi, rushing in to join them, gasped, "Is he alive? Will he be alright?"

"He still has a pulse but it's weak," said Willie, on his knees beside him. "Heavily drugged, I'd guess. Damn them anyway . . . Kadi, call an ambulance, the phone's in my office and—ah, there you are, Bix, we need an ambulance on the double. Did you find Jasna's father?"

"Did you think I would?" His voice was bitter. "I'll phone in his description as soon as I've called the ambulance, he can't have gotten far if he's blind." He stopped, looking shocked. "But he can't be blind."

"No, not blind," said Mrs. Pollifax. "Call the ambulance. Take Kadi with you, she's seen enough for one day."

"Right," said Bix. "Come on, Kadi, let's *go*."

When she hesitated Willie looked up and said, "And give her a shot of brandy, bottom drawer my desk."

As they hurried away Mrs. Pollifax whispered, "He looks—almost dead. Are you finding a heartbeat?"

"That too is faint," said Willie. "If you're into praying, pray."

"I feel more like crying," said Mrs. Pollifax shakily.

"Then you cry and I'll pray," Willie told her and they sat with Boozy Tim between them while on the other side of the curtain Shannon and Zilka performed their bumps and grinds to the music of "Toot Toot Tootsie."

Twenty minutes later Boozy Tim was carried out of the Ten-in-One on a stretcher, and with sirens screaming the ambulance made its exit, Pogo and Jake following in Shannon's car. A shaken Mrs. Pollifax and Willie left the scene to walk back to his trailer and wait for news from the hospital. Even among carnies the show had to go on, and an equally shaken Kadi had returned to the Ten-in-One to join the Professor and Tatiana and be sawed in half. Crossing the compound, Mrs. Pollifax found it utterly unreal to hear in daylight the beat of the merry-go-round music and the usual screams from the ferris wheel. She thought it unreal, too, when Willie said, "I guess we move on tonight if the police are satisfied. A busy night ahead!" Abruptly he came to a halt. "What the devil!"

Mrs. Pollifax jumped. "What? *What*, Willie?"

He pointed. "Helicopter landing in the field."

"Police?"

"No—no, it looks like Pete."

They stood beside Willie's trailer staring out at the field where the helicopter had come to a rest like a glittering insect in the bright sunlight; the hatch opened and two men jumped down, followed by Pete. The three of them began walking toward them across the newly clipped field: Pete in a scarlet zip-up jacket; a stocky gray-haired man in a business suit; and a younger man with sandy hair and an agreeable face that Mrs. Pollifax recognized at once. "It's Bishop!" she exclaimed. "It's actually Bishop, but what can he possibly be doing here?"

A moment later, nearing them, Bishop called out a hello to Willie, and to Mrs. Pollifax, "I've come to take you and Kadi Hopkirk back to Carstairs. . . . No time to waste, you've fifteen minutes to collect your gear."

Mrs. Pollifax stared at him blankly: two worlds were suddenly in collision here on this sunny field, and Bishop's world had nothing to do with the merry-go-round music behind her, or with Boozy Tim, or with Jasna, or the tide of voices from the midway. She said indignantly, "I can't possibly leave now, Bishop, we've just learned who knifed Lazlo, the police have taken Jasna away but nobody's found her father yet, Boozy Tim's been drugged and taken to the hospital and they may have killed him, and—"

It was Bishop's turn to look blank. Pulling himself together he interrupted to say, "But Carstairs needs you. I brought Charlie to replace you but now he can stay and find out what the hell you're talking about. Right now Carstairs wants to know about Chigi Scap Metal."

"Chigi Scap Metal?" she faltered.

"Fifteen minutes," he reminded her.

After the events of this day even the Chigi Scap Metal van felt distant to her. With a sigh of exasperation Mrs. Pollifax turned back to the midway and made her way toward the Ten-in-One to find Kadi, thinking stormily that it was obvious neither Carstairs nor Bishop understood carnivals, or that by summoning Kadi they were depriving Pogo of his stick and the Professor of Tatiana's feet . . . and of herself, she admitted, and was furious.

17

Mrs. Pollifax was still nursing a distinct feeling of anger when Bishop ushered her and Kadi into Carstairs's office. It was nearly seven o'clock but not even two and a half hours on a plane had diminished her indignation at being forcibly removed from Willie's. She was sure that absolutely nothing Carstairs had to say could make up for her being torn away from the carnival before she could learn whether Boozy Tim would survive, who Jasna was, and whether her father had been found yet.

After only one glance at her Carstairs said, "You're angry."

"Very," she snapped.

"And no doubt hungry, too," he added. "There are trays on the way up from the cafeteria with dinner for the three of you . . . and you're Kadi Hopkirk," he said, smiling at her. "Are you angry, too?"

She grinned. "Mostly hungry. But very curious, of course, it's certainly been a strenuous few days."

He nodded. "Chigi Scap Metal."

Mrs. Pollifax forgot her anger to say, "But how did *you* hear about Chigi Scap Metal?"

"Obliquely," he told her. "It looks as if it or they may be linked to a case I've become interested in, and in which I've been pursuing a few tenuous leads. For instance, the men in the van may have been involved with whoever attacked

Lazlo on Wednesday night at Willie's. A month ago the van was noted by Lazlo in Boston, parked outside a tenement house where he was also attacked, his arm broken, after possibly overhearing something of importance."

Mrs. Pollifax said eagerly, "Willie said Lazlo arrived at the carnival with a broken arm."

Carstairs nodded. "Yes, and we feel pretty sure the men he overheard in the tenement suspected that he'd heard too much and someone decided he was dangerous. Actually Lazlo had overheard very little but they didn't know that. Ah, but here comes your dinner. Bishop, bring in tray tables, will you, and then I want to hear about what I dragged you away from at Willie's this afternoon."

A bowl of hot chili was set before them, with corn muffins and butter, and a carafe of coffee for the three of them. Mrs. Pollifax, picking up a spoon, explained, "You have to understand first about Boozy Tim."

"I beg your pardon?"

"Boozy Tim was *nice*," Kadi said at once. "And he'd met God, you know."

Once this had been explained Mrs. Pollifax added, "He finally realized that the man who stepped on his foot after the 'Hey Rube'—the man with the Santa Claus beard—had to be Jasna's father. Perhaps the way he walked when he thought no one was watching—"

Kadi interrupted to say, "Except I wouldn't have put it past Boozy Tim to sneak under Jasna's trailer and listen, or peek in windows, and if once he guessed that Jasna's father couldn't be blind—"

"But his beard wasn't white," put in Mrs.

153

Pollifax. "Once it was suggested to him that the man might have used a disguise, Boozy Tim walked into town, bought two false beards, and came back to experiment with what might change an authentic black beard for only an hour or so. Except unfortunately he confided in no one, and obviously the man was precisely the one we looked for. . . . We think Jasna and her father gagged him—there was blood on the table—and carried him back during the night to their trailer to decide what to do with him. He had to be killed, but it had to look like an accident, as if he'd taken the place of Jasna's father that night, and her aim—"

"Would have *killed* him," finished Kadi in an astonished voice, "Which I must say has left Jasna holding the bag once her father got away. Somehow . . . I drew a sketch of Jasna," she told Carstairs.

"Yes and she's extremely good," put in Mrs. Pollifax, "it might help to identify her."

"Help we can use," Carstairs told her. "Otherwise someone merely named Jasna—"

Kadi dug into her knapsack for her sketchpad and turned the pages to her sketch. "Here she is."

Carstairs studied the drawing and frowned. Handing it to his assistant he said, "Bishop, get the files on Olga Broniewski; the Broniewskis were in show business in Europe, and except for the butchered hair, damned if this doesn't look like her." As Bishop abandoned his chili to search the files, Carstairs added, "If that's who Jasna is, that bearded blind 'father' of hers would have been her husband Tamas."

"Husband?" echoed Mrs. Pollifax.

He nodded. "In his mid-thirties, and a ruthless chap—a dangerous pair, they usually travel with a circus." After a quick glance at the two photos that Bishop handed him he nodded. "Take a look."

Mrs. Pollifax looked, and sat back satisfied. "That's certainly Jasna, but with longer hair."

Kadi, staring at the photograph of the man, stammered "B-but that's her blind father? He's young and incredibly handsome!"

Amused, Carstairs said, "A lesson for you in what disguise can do. It certainly explains how he got away. I'd guess that once he helped his wife dress and drug your Boozy Tim, and roped him to the backboard, he simply trimmed his beard and strolled through the gates when the carnival opened. A handsome young man returning to his car, or looking for his girl-friend . . ."

"But where's the connection?" asked Mrs. Pollifax.

Carstairs ignored this. "Any other sketches, Kadi?"

"I've a snapshot of Sammy," she told him, reaching into her knapsack and bringing out her wallet.

Carstairs reached out for the photo but his glance lingered a moment on Kadi's face, and Mrs. Pollifax decided that he didn't often see anyone so fresh and young in his office. Leaning over, Kadi pointed. "There's Sammy."

"Sammat, grandson of a king," murmured Carstairs. "Nice face."

"A *good* face," Kadi said firmly. "Can you, *will* you, help him?"

"Oh yes," he said.

Surprised, Mrs. Pollifax said, "It's important?"

"Very. Let me consider for a moment," said Carstairs, "because there's a great deal to do."

They sat and waited while he stared at the ceiling, glanced at Kadi, smiled vaguely at Mrs. Pollifax, and at last said crisply, "Kadi, I need the full name of your friend Sammy: how he would be registered at Yale."

"Sammat Yusufu."

"And his roommate's name?"

"He was introduced as Clarence Mulimo."

Carstairs wrote the names on a memo and said to Bishop, "Put through a call to the New Haven police department, will you, Bishop? Tell them I'll be there—" He glanced at his watch. "By nine o'clock at the latest, but first I want to speak to the chief on the phone."

"New Haven police?" gasped Kadi. "Oh, but please, that will—"

"Steady," counseled Carstairs. "I want two officers sent to the University to bring your Sammy to the police station for questioning about a stolen car."

"But Sammy would never, *never* steal a car," protested Kadi.

Carstairs smiled at her forgivingly. "He can explain that to the police at the station. It's the only way we can separate him from that roommate of his."

"Ah," murmured Mrs. Pollifax, intrigued by such beautiful deviousness.

"And you will be going with me to New Haven," Carstairs told them. "You, Mrs. Pollifax, and Kadi, too. Order a plane for us, Bishop, and after you've done that I want the passenger lists checked on every plane flying to

Paris this weekend—names, Bishop, names. Who does wigs?"

"W-wigs?" stammered Bishop.

"Wigs."

"That would be Hazard's department."

"Good. Take Kadi with you and fit her out with a blonde wig, find some colorful touristy clothes for her, and above all a pair of dark glasses. Large ones. Mrs. Pollifax, I don't know what your plans may have been before this interruption in your life, or how much you care to tell that husband of yours, but I'm preempting you for a few days; you can use Helga's phone to call him. You and Kadi are accompanying me to Ubangiba."

"Ubangiba!" cried Kadi happily.

"Ubangiba?" repeated Mrs. Pollifax. "Accompanying you? *YOU* are going to Ubangiba?"

Bishop laughed. "You really are planning skullduggery—and going yourself?"

With a grin Carstairs said, "High time, Bishop . . . living behind a desk grows tiresome, and what I have in mind is going to need enormous tact, duplicity, diplomacy, and a great deal of bluffing, or the State Department will have my head. You'll take over for me, Bishop, I've cleared it with Mornajay." To the others he said, "Now carry those trays of food somewhere else—go away, out!—while I put in a call to the New Haven police, and to Paris. And while we're in New Haven, Bishop, have passports issued for Mrs. Pollifax and daughter Kadi—no, make it Katherine."

"Right, sir," said Bishop, added this to his list, and ushered Kadi and Mrs. Pollifax into his office, and Mrs. Pollifax into Helga's cubicle where she could call Cyrus.

The phone number of the hotel at which Cyrus was spending his last night was duly found, and she asked to speak with Cyrus Reed, present for the American Bar Association meetings. The desk clerk rang his room, and rang and rang. He said at last, "If he's with the Bar Association, ma'am, most of them are out celebrating the appointment of one of their members to a federal judgeship."

"That would be Gilbert Montano?" she asked.

"Yes, ma'am, care to leave a message?"

Mrs. Pollifax sought wildly for a message that might sum up her past several days. "Tell him," she said carefully, "that his wife has been—has been called *away*. And that Mr. Carstairs—that's C-a-r-s-t-a-i-r-s—needs her a few days longer. Did I say that too fast for you?"

"No, ma'am, I've got it all down, shall I read it back?"

"Please do."

Once this had been accomplished she hung up and swallowed her disappointment at not reaching Cyrus. On the other hand, she reflected, he would probably have tried to reach *her* during the past several days and suffered the same disappointment, so it was only fair that she experience it, too. He would come home to an empty house—a house with bread crumbs and sardine tins in a closet, no wife, and possibly no car yet if Pete had not had time to retrieve it. She could only remind herself that in the refrigerator he would find salami and a chicken as well as the Garden Club sandwiches artistically arranged on a platter.

The Garden Club left a very long time ago.

She stopped Bishop as he rushed through the

office and asked for Willie's phone number in Maine and dialed it. He must have been sitting by his phone waiting for news, because he answered on the first ring. "Willie, it's Emmy Reed," she said. "How is Boozy Tim?"

Willie took his time answering. "I've been in touch, Emmy, he's coming out of it okay, but a real close call, believe me. Those two *bengs* nearly killed him with all that dope, and he's still pretty confused, but the doc's with him and he's had his stomach pumped out, poor guy. Jake and Pogo are with him, too."

"That's good news. It's tear-down night after you close, isn't it?"

"Yep—sorry you're missing it. By the way, you were suspicious about Lubo. The police made him talk. Insisted." Willie chuckled. "Seems he's a math whiz who started a computer company in the '80s—very big with Wall Street—and then Japanese competition drove him into bankruptcy and closed him up. The crazy guy decided to make a clean break and have some fun for a change."

"How very creative!" said Mrs. Pollifax.

"No, crazy." He laughed. "But I promised to tell you something, didn't I. About Anyeta Inglescu?"

"Yes—you *do* know of her?"

"Know of her? She's my grandmother. *Ja develesa*, Emmy," he said, and hung up.

On the flight to New Haven Mrs. Pollifax found herself once again yawning, and once again seated next to this engaging child whom she'd discovered in her closet, and she could not help but experience a slight sense of *déjà vu*. It seemed

159

very strange to be traveling with Carstairs; he had not been exactly forthcoming, and she had no idea what had triggered this whole-hearted commitment to helping Kadi and her friend, not to mention his interest in Ubangiba; Bishop had said something about his being obsessed with the country for the past few days, but she had no idea why. Certainly *something* must be happening there, or else Carstairs had gone berserk but she was confident that Carstairs never went berserk.

At the police station Carstairs insisted upon a room in the rear of the building, well out of sight, and they were given one lined with lockers and with cartons piled high in one corner. Chairs were carried in, and Mrs. Pollifax and Kadi sat in a silence permeated by tension while Carstairs was summoned to the telephone a number of times, to return looking pleased.

He was with them again when there came sounds in the corridor of a voice protesting, other voices muffling the protest, the door was opened, and two policemen ushered in Sammat Yusufu. As the officers released him, Sammy's mouth dropped open at the sight of the three people waiting for him, and as Kadi rose from her chair he gasped, *"Kadi?"*

"Hi, Sammy," she said, beaming at him. "I think I've brought help."

Mrs. Pollifax decided that the snapshot she had seen of Sammy had not done him justice: he was full grown and mature now, the rich dark color of his skin set off by a white shirt open at the throat; his eyes were thoughtful under a slash of black brows, his features strong and well-cut . . . *the face of a poet or a prince,* thought Mrs. Pollifax, or, from the look of his broad shoulders, a boxer.

But if her first impression was of a wary young man this had changed when he saw Kadi: his face lit up with pleasure, even joy, and he exuded warmth.

"But what can this mean?" he asked, his eyes moving from Kadi to Carstairs to Mrs. Pollifax.

Carstairs said, "It means, from what Kadi has told us, that we've needed a serious talk with you alone, and definitely without your roommate."

Sammat's face relaxed. "Without Clarence . . . I see. But this is very clever of you, those two policemen will tell you that Clarence insisted he come with me, it was necessary for them to physically push him away. Which was astonishing," he added frankly.

"Exactly, and we mustn't keep you long from him."

"Kadi did all this?" Sammat asked, turning to her.

"Well, you see, after seeing you on Monday I was followed," she explained, "and this is Mrs. Pollifax in whose house I hid for two days—to get away from them—and this is Mr. Carstairs, who is—"

Carstairs interrupted her curtly. "Who is a friend. Sammy, we'd like to know who sent you to the United States four years ago, and with Clarence Mulimo as a guard. Do sit!"

"I will stand, sir, because Clarence, he is under very strict orders and—"

"From whom?" snapped Carstairs.

"This I don't know, sir, and there has been no way to find out. I felt at first that when they assassinated my father they would have killed me, too, if I didn't have some value for them in the future. I think they sent me here to get me out

161

of the way, but lately this has changed. From what I've learned, eavesdropping on Clarence's phone calls—the phone is in the hall but near our room—I think something is going to happen soon in my country, a coup perhaps, I don't know, but I do think that soon I will be taken back to Ubangiba, possibly to be killed, or if there is a coup then to become—what is the word, sir, a puppet?"

"That will do," nodded Carstairs.

"Yes, puppet. To be shown to the people as their leader, because they respect the royal line, but with someone behind me pulling the strings."

"You don't know who that would be?"

He shook his head. "No, sir, but Clarence has had his suitcase packed for a week, and there have been phone calls to him every night, like never before. I thought he might have been told to—but this is the United States, he could not as easily kill me here. Sir, I really must return to my dorm or Clarence will become suspicious."

Carstairs said in a hard voice, "I can tell you why Clarence has had his bags packed for a week. The news has come over the wire services tonight that President Simoko is dead."

"Dead?" cried Kadi.

"*Heya*," gasped Sammat, and then, "But he has been in good health, surely this means—"

Carstairs nodded. "Yes, of course. His death has to have been planned."

"Poison or a bullet?" asked Mrs. Pollifax with interest.

Carstairs gave her an amused glance. "We don't know yet, but since arriving in this room my assistant Bishop has telephoned to report that Sammat and Clarence Mulimo, and a Mr. Achille

162

Lecler, are booked to fly to Paris tomorrow morning, and presumably from there to Ubangiba on the Monday morning flight 1192."

Sammat felt for a chair and sat down.

"Would you be a good leader?" asked Carstairs softly. "Would the people accept you?"

Kadi made a move to speak but Mrs. Pollifax shook her head.

"I have studied hard to be one—always hoping," Sammat said gravely, and suddenly looked much older. "I have majored in economics, I have studied the many agricultural experiments taking place in Africa, I have studied democratic systems, and banking. I believe the people would accept me, which would be most unfortunate if I cannot speak truth to them or make the changes needed to bring prosperity to my country."

"But you feel sure the people would accept you?" repeated Carstairs.

It was a question asked again but in a different voice, and Mrs. Pollifax gave him a quick, curious glance. Definitely there were undercurrents here of which she could only guess.

Kadi said, "Even if uncertain of who he is at first they would accept him because of—"

"You have it?" asked Sammat. When she nodded he smiled, and to Carstairs he said, "When my grandfather was dying, sir, he summoned the royal diviners—those he trusted to speak truth—and they threw the cowrie shells and told him they saw only evil for ten harvests, and that he must have his son—my father—bury the sacred royal gold ring and let no one see it for ten years, and no one know of this but my father. When my father became President, just before he was

163

killed—as if he knew it would happen—he showed me where it was hidden."

Mrs. Pollifax looked at Kadi and smiled. "So that's what Sammy gave you in the coffee house. Under the table."

Kadi flushed.

Startled, Carstairs murmured, "I have read something of that sacred gold ring, yes. You mean you have it? Is it known that you have it?"

Sammat said gravely, "It is not known, sir, no. I have kept it carefully concealed."

Carstairs glanced at his watch and made a face. "You *must* be delivered back to your dormitory. The police will have found it a case of mistaken identity and will apologize formally in front of Clarence for bringing you here at such an hour. It also looks obvious that you will be flying to Paris tomorrow and then to Ubangiba."

Sammat stood and waited, his face expressionless. "It seems unbelievable, sir, but I don't see how—"

"You will not be alone," Carstairs told him. "In Paris when you board flight 1192 you will see me—my name is Carstairs—traveling with a Mrs. Reed and her daughter, who will be Kadi, as well as with two other gentlemen who will join us in Paris. Since Kadi is known to Clarence you will find her somewhat disguised but in any case you will give no sign of recognition or take any notice of us, you understand? *Not until we arrive in Ubangiba.*"

Puzzled, Sammat said, "I recognize you then, sir? But how could this be explained?"

"We need a connection." Carstairs turned to Kadi, "I understand that your father was a missionary in the country?"

She nodded warily.

"We'll use that," he said. "I will have visited her father some years ago<AF..8>—Kadi can fill me in on details. You were introduced to me then, and having suddenly recognized me you will introduce yourself and invite us all to go with you."

Sammat said dryly, "Even to prison if that is what they plan for me? I have, after all, been something of a prisoner already these past few years."

Carstairs smiled. "I would think it more likely the President's palace, but let's just say that I want to be certain no one disposes of you as they did the late President Simoko."

It was very warm in the room but Mrs. Pollifax shivered at this.

"So—off you go," Carstairs said abruptly, and opened the door to the hall. To the two men outside he said, "You can return him now."

Kadi said, "The ring's in my knapsack, Sammy, would you like it now?"

"No, Kadi," he said, smiling. "Keep it for me—until we reach home."

Sammy walked out, joined at once by the pair of men who had brought him there, and Carstairs glanced again at his watch. "You were right, Kadi, your young friend's in considerable danger. Back to headquarters now, to wrap things up and get a few hours' sleep—Bishop will have booked rooms for you—and then—"

"And then?" asked Mrs. Pollifax.

"At eight tomorrow morning we fly to Paris— on another airline, of course—to await Monday morning's flight to Ubangiba."

18

Sunday

It was in Paris that Mrs. Pollifax at last reached Cyrus in Connecticut. "You're home!" she exclaimed. "I was afraid I'd miss you."

"I'm home but the house is damn empty," he growled. "What the devil are you doing in Paris?"

"I'm quite safe, I'm with Carstairs."

"Carstairs! Thought he never left his desk."

"He said it was high time he did."

"How long have you been in Paris? When did he call you in?"

"He didn't, this time I called *him*. Or Bishop," she amended. "On Wednesday night. Possibly you haven't been home long enough to notice the empty sardine tins and crumbs in the closet, and the car missing?"

"So that's it," Cyrus said. "Car's not missing. Struck me as damn odd, though. Just paid off the taxi on arrival when a man drives our car up the driveway here, hands me the keys and goes off in the taxi I came in. Didn't *look* like a mechanic."

"I doubt that he was," Mrs. Pollifax told him frankly, "since I had to abandon the car in Worcester, Massachusetts."

"Worcester! Emily, what in the world—"

"Cyrus, I'll explain later, it's nearly time for the plane. I expect truly to be home in two or three days and—I must run—see you soon!"

She hung up quickly before he could ask what

plane she was about to board. This was a pity, she thought, because Cyrus was probably the one person in fifty who would have heard of Ubangiba and who would know precisely where it was located on the continent of Africa. Replacing the phone in its cradle she glanced toward Gate 12, where a line was already gathering for the twice-weekly departure for Languka, Ubangiba. Seeing Kadi she smiled; *poor Kadi,* she thought, masquerading in a blonde wig with corkscrew curls like Shannon's and inhabiting a noisy yellow dress, her eyes concealed behind huge purple-rimmed dark glasses. Carstairs stood behind her with the stranger who had joined them at the hotel after breakfast, and who had been introduced as John Stover.

This is Carstairs's ballgame now, she thought, and admitted that at first she had minded very much his being so secretive about his intentions. She found that it no longer mattered now what he was up to, he was giving her the opportunity to observe a real professional at work, a man who had been OSS-trained in World War II and had operated in the Paris underground and later in Libya. She had admired his original bent of mind ever since she'd met him, and now she intended to watch and learn. *Watch closely,* she resolved, and as she observed Carstairs from this distance she already noticed something strange take place: Carstairs had brought with him on the flight to Paris a brown leather attaché case; now she saw a man at the rear of the line move up to Carstairs, stand beside him for a moment, and without looking at him place a black alligator-hide attaché case on the floor next to Carstairs, and carry away Carstairs's brown one.

So now Carstairs had a black attaché case, and a very elegant one, too, which must be important. *Beautifully done,* she thought admiringly, *but certainly mysterious.*

Moving her gaze to the head of the line she caught a glimpse of Sammat, now wearing a bright *dashiki,* and she wondered which of the men near him was the Mr. Lecler with whom he was to travel, and whether he was really named Lecler at all, and if he was as French as his name sounded. *An extremely interesting trip,* she mused, and leaving the bank of phones she walked over to join Carstairs, Kadi, and Mr. Stover.

Once on the plane she sat next to Kadi, with Carstairs in a seat behind them; when she turned to speak to him she saw that his seat companion was the man who had traded attaché cases with him. They were introducing themselves now, as if they were strangers to each other, the man explaining that his name was Devereaux, he was a Parisien, and then he and Carstairs began speaking in French and she could no longer eavesdrop—which of course was why they were speaking French, she reminded herself. Definitely, she thought, the attaché case needed keeping an eye on, in case any more conjuring tricks took place in Languka.

The plane was only half-filled: Sammat's party had vanished into first class; Kadi explained that the groups of businessmen on the plane would probably stay just the night and one day in Languka, because on the following day a local plane from Agadez would land in Languka on its way to Dakar. Kadi thought the two stewardesses were Hausa and Fulani, and the steward Ethiopian but she couldn't speak to them because she was traveling incognito. This she mentioned regretfully before she drew out a book from her knapsack: Camus's *The Plague*. Mrs. Pollifax, who had left home on Wednesday with only a purse, was reduced to magazines bought in Paris.

Four hours later they began their descent over Ubangiba and Mrs. Pollifax looked down at a desert that was dotted with small moving objects that she guessed to be goats or cattle; soon the desert changed into green fields, and then brown fields threaded by a single dirt road, with occasional villages of conical huts. These were followed by clusters of shanties, then a suburb of square white concrete houses, and then a broad tree-lined boulevard marking Languka itself, which was a dusty-looking, crowded city of flat low buildings, except for two colonial-style white buildings with sloping roofs. "Palaces," said Kadi scornfully, looking over Mrs. Pollifax's shoulder as the plane swept low over the city and continued beyond it to the airport. "President Daniel Simoko Airport," announced the pilot, and they landed bumpily.

And so, thought Mrs. Pollifax, *we are here, and I have no idea why, unless it's to be sure that Sammat isn't murdered or sent to prison, but I can't believe the CIA to be THAT altruistic.* She rose and followed Kadi down the aisle, with Carstairs and Devereaux behind her. A platform was wheeled up to the door of the plane and they descended into an almost suffocating heat and sun to walk toward a gleaming white terminal building with a photograph of the President over the entrance. Mr. Devereaux hurried past her and she saw that it was he who now carried the black attaché case that he had presented to Carstairs in Paris. He

169

passed Sammat and Clarence and the man at their side who had to be Mr. Achille Lecler. In one quick glance of appraisal Mrs. Pollifax received the impression that Mr. Lecler was a man of great efficiency, this from the manner in which he herded his two charges along, his lips thinned with impatience, but a man who also enjoyed his luxuries and was somewhat vain, as witness the strip of mustache punctuating his pale face, the cream-colored silk suit that he wore, and the black-and-white shoes with pointed toes. Except for the air of arrogance that he'd culti-vated, she thought he looked simply a nonde-script middle-aged white man struggling against a growing paunch from too rich a diet, and given to inappropriate clothes. Certainly he looked out of place in Ubangiba.

Mr. Devereaux, leading the crowd to Passport Control, moved through it quickly with a nod to the cluster of uniformed policemen, slowed, and then reached Customs only a little ahead of Sammat's group. Both his carry-on bag and his attaché case were opened and Mrs. Pollifax observed their contents: pajamas, shirts, toilet articles, and books. Mr. Lecler was next in line, and it appeared that he too carried a black attaché case fashioned out of the hide of an alligator, a fact that she'd not noticed as he disembarked. His case, however, was not opened. Instead he was greeted with a polite nod by the Customs officer and his attaché case was merely placed on the conveyor belt to be carried through the metal detector.

They know him here, realized Mrs. Pollifax, and having promised herself that she would keep an eye on all such attachés she was now rewarded, although it remained difficult to believe what she saw: for just one second Mr. Devereaux's and Mr. Lecler's matching cases lay on the Customs counter, and having diligently kept Mr. Devereaux's—or Carstairs's—in view, she was stunned to note—could her eyes be deceiving her?—that Mr. Devereaux walked away with Mr. Lecler's black attaché case. *More* sleight of hand! She hastily dropped her gaze, and with both men gone she deposited her purse on the counter.

"This is all?" said the man.

"It's a large purse," she pointed out as he drew from it the pajamas she'd had to buy in Paris, followed by brush, comb, lipstick, toothbrush, and wallet.

He gave her a disapproving glance and allowed her to move toward the exit.

It was now that she heard Sammat say, "But—excuse me, sir, are you not the Mr. Carstairs who once visited Mr. Hopkirk, the mission doctor here?"

She turned to see Carstairs react warmly. "You're not—you can't be—Kadi's friend Sammy? We met, yes—how many years ago? But this is astonishing!"

"Isn't it?" said Sammat, glowing securely now as he shook hands with him. "I return, sir, from university in the United States after four years away from my country."

"No!" cried Carstairs in surprise. "Four years! But I must introduce you to my sister Mrs. Reed-Pollifax and her daughter Katherine, and this is my friend John Stover, an anthropologist, and there is one more to our party but I see he has gone ahead. My dear Sammy, we simply *cannot* part now, after all these years. I remember so well what a good time we had!"

"Indeed we mustn't, no," Sammy said, looking suddenly mischievous. "We are heading for the palace, which I'm sure you would enjoy very much seeing. It is quite new and most lavish, I hear. May I introduce Clarence Mulimo and Mr. Achille Lecler with whom I traveled? I'm sure they would like you to see the palace, too." He darted a quick glance at Mr. Lecler, whose lips had contracted into such a thin line that he appeared almost lipless; definitely he did not appreciate Sammat's offer of hospitality. "And you must also be in need of refreshment after the long flight."

Kadi said in a gushing voice, "Oh, I would *love* to see a palace. A real palace? Mums, did you hear what he said? A real palace, wouldn't it be *thrilling*?"

Carstairs gave her a startled glance, smiled faintly, and returned his gaze to Sammat, saying politely, "If it's not an intrusion—?"

Mr. Lecler said with equal politeness, "It is a most *inconvenient* time, perhaps tomorrow? There is a reception committee waiting outside, and Sammat is to be presented to the people in only an hour—"

"Which I'm sure Mr. Carstairs would enjoy seeing, too," said Sammy firmly, and to Mrs. Pollifax, not looking at Kadi, he explained, "It seems that my homecoming has been known for some hours, and the people told that I am returning, our President having died only yesterday."

Carstairs said in surprise, "But I had forgotten, Sammy, you are King Sammat's grandson!" and to Mrs. Pollifax, "This will be exciting indeed, Sammy being a member of royalty."

"Royalty!" squealed Kadi, clapping her hands girlishly. "Oh just wait 'til I tell all the kids at home!"

Sammat smothered a laugh. "Quite so," he said, and ignoring Mr. Lecler he said regally, "You have a car outside? We will leave together."

"But Sammat—"

"We go together," Sammy told Mr. Lecler sternly. "He is a *friend*, you wish me to be miserly? One *shares* with a friend."

"I do not like this," said Mr. Lecler warningly, and Mrs. Pollifax observed from the expression on his face that Mr. Lecler could also be ruthless as well as arrogant.

Sammat turned his back on him to walk beside Carstairs, saying, "How many years has it been, sir?"

"Too many! Ah, Devereaux, here you are. . . . We've been invited to the palace, and this is the old friend of the Hopkirks' about whom I was telling you. Sammy, this is Monsieur Devereaux."

Clarence Mulimo had disappeared; Mr. Lecler was clearly outnumbered. They moved in a group toward the brilliant sunshine just beyond the arched entrance, over which hung still another huge photograph with SIMOKO in blazing red letters. Mrs. Pollifax noted that Mr. Lecler gave Carstairs several quick, puzzled glances. Perhaps there was suspicion in his gaze, too, as there very well might be, she reflected, should this man have had anything to do with Chigi Scap Metal and its pursuit of Kadi. Certainly he had taken charge of Sammy and Clarence, there was no doubt about that.

The reception committee of which he had spoken was waiting outside, although Mrs. Pollifax had never before seen such a sullen-looking group of people, kept firmly in place by scarlet-coated policemen; it seemed obvious they had been rounded up unwillingly for this event.

Sammat, scrutinizing the faces behind the ropes, gave a cry of "Laraba!" He broke away to stride toward a thin, barefooted woman wearing a red T-shirt, long black skirt, and polka-dotted kerchief. Her closed dark face came to life, she laughed, and they embraced.

With a sigh Kadi said, "Damn, I'd like to hug her, too, that's Laraba and here I am all gussied up as a blonde in weird clothes."

"A good friend?"

"A *very* good friend, it was she and Rakia, my father's nurse, who hid me and smuggled me out of Ubangiba."

The sullen faces in the crowd became less sullen; a few men broke ranks to crowd around Sammat and shake his hand, and then Mr. Lecler irritably pointed out that a limousine was waiting. He missed one detail, however: as Sammat returned to them he grinned at Kadi, and in passing said to her softly, "Laraba says hello and welcome, she wasn't fooled for a minute."

Kadi laughed.

The grass surrounding the terminal looked a hectic green, like Astro-turf, and the long white limousine incongruous among the battered cars and taxis parked near the entrance. *What a curious group we are,* thought Mrs. Pollifax; Stover and Devereaux poker-faced, Lecler furious, Kadi and

Sammat beaming at each other, and who knew what Carstairs was thinking or feeling? Reaching the limousine it proved difficult to arrange the seating: eventually Mr. Stover volunteered to sit beside the driver but Mr. Lecler was forced to employ a jump seat, obviously resenting this very much.

As they left the airport behind, Mrs. Pollifax thought that once there must have been a grand design for the approach to the city, because this was the tree-lined boulevard that she had seen from the plane, running in a straight line from airport to palace; unfortunately, years of neglect, coups, and riots had dissipated any grandeur. The parade of dusty trees barely screened the hovels behind them, and the walls of once-prosperous villas were pocked with bullet holes. When the walls ended there was an eruption of colorful, less private life: a crowded marketplace with signs in startling neon shades proclaiming FODIA! COLA! MKATE! MAKALA! CAFE!—at which point it became necessary to stop and allow a herd of goats to cross the boulevard.

"Now as to the program for the rest of the day," said Mr. Lecler, leaning forward in his jump seat to claim Sammat's attention. "Within the hour there will be a spontaneous gathering of the people outside the palace to welcome you, and you will speak to them graciously from the balcony. There is then the President's funeral already being planned, elaborate, of course, and as impressive as our President Simoko's years of rule have been. Later there will be a meeting with the chiefs of the Shambi and Soto tribes to discuss the next government." With a small tight smile he added, "And I have already assured you that we will find *something* for you to do in that government, after which there will be a state dinner in the Gold Room.''

Mrs. Pollifax, seated beside Sammat, heard him mutter words in a low voice. Silent until now he said, *"Troɔbul de taym in nɔ dé."*

Only Kadi, seated on the other side of him, understood that in pidgin English he was saying there was a lot of trouble here.

Mrs. Pollifax only heard her murmur, ''That's for sure, *bo.*''

19

The approach to the palace was lined with bougainvillea, and then the limousine swept up to an entrance that would surely equal the most luxurious of European hotels, its doors manned by guards in uniform.

Sammat said calmly, "As you will recall, Mr. Carstairs, my grandfather did not live in a palace but in a house made of earth in the royal compound."

Carstairs said quickly, "I remember, yes."

The guards snapped to attention as the limousine stopped, and one of them came forward to open the car's doors. "Ah, Mr. Lecler," he said, and saluted.

So he really is well known, thought Mrs. Pollifax, making note of this, *and perhaps even lives here?*

They were escorted through heavy glass doors into a vast entrance hall of marble, at the end of which hung a gold relief of President Simoko's smiling face. Carstairs, looking around, murmured, "The President did himself well."

"It would make an excellent hospital or school," pointed out Sammat.

Lecler, overhearing this, laughed. "I don't think we'd agree on *that*." To the guard he said, "Joseph, take these people to the Ceremonial Hall," and to Sammat, "And you—you will come to my office, please."

Sammat smiled politely. "I will first see my friends to the hall you speak of," and to Joseph,

"I am Sammat Yusufu, and do not know where the Ceremonial Hall is, will you show us? And bring my guests some cold drinks to refresh them."

The guard's eyes widened. "You—*you* are Zammat—of *Zammat zisanu ndi zitato*?" He bowed low.

Sammy placed a hand on his arm. "Only the grandchild—*mdzukulu*—of a king, Joseph. No need to bow, just show us the way."

"Yes, *sir!*"

Mr. Lecler looked very nearly apoplectic, but hid it by abruptly turning away to stride toward a gilt door on the left; he opened it and vanished, presumably into an office.

Joseph led the way up the broad marble staircase, speaking with animation to Sammat in their own language; as Mrs. Pollifax climbed the stairs, Carstairs caught up with her to say pleasantly, sotto voce, "No way to bring weapons into the country, Mrs. P, we may have to rely on Stover's judo, and you and your brown belt you-know-what. *Be vigilant.*" Having said this he accelerated his pace and moved ahead to join John Stover.

So, thought Mrs. Pollifax, *something is going to happen,* and she felt reinvigorated.

Reaching the second floor, they followed Joseph across a wide corridor to a pair of gleaming brass doors that Joseph dramatically swung open for them. Here Mrs. Pollifax stopped, frankly awed by what she saw: a huge room with polished mahogany floors, the right wall lined with french windows opening onto a balcony, and a ceiling that glittered with crystal chandeliers. . . . A few steps into the room and her gaze included clusters of gilt chairs with scarlet upholstered seats, and at the far end what looked like a throne. Certainly it was the focal point of the room, a heavy golden stool—surely gold, not gilt—placed squarely against a scarlet tapestry on which two serpents were prominent. On either side of the throne hung matching scarlet curtains on long rods, and Mrs. Pollifax watched with interest as John Stover immediately crossed the room to the curtain on the right and flung it open to reveal a narrow hallway beyond; with a nod to Carstairs he closed the curtain, walked to the other side of the throne and repeated his performance before joining them again.

Seeing Mrs. Pollifax watch him, he smiled and said lightly, "Just curiosity."

Amused, Mrs. Pollifax thought, *Oh really?*

No one spoke. Devereaux strolled over to the french doors, opened one, and stepped out on the balcony to return, saying, "Already a crowd of people milling around."

"Herded here by the police?" said Sammat dryly.

Devereaux shook his head. "Saw no police."

They turned as the brass doors opened and Joseph arrived carrying a tray holding glasses and a pitcher; an aide followed with a table on which Joseph placed the tray, and then Lecler walked in; at once Mrs. Pollifax felt the change and knew this was what they'd been waiting for. Lecler still carried his black attaché case but now in his other hand he held a sheaf of papers.

"So," he said almost benevolently, "you have refreshments and the people are gathering below. Sammat, it is nearly time."

"A beautiful room," Mrs. Pollifax told him. "That lovely gold bench or stool, for instance—"

She turned to point, but her glance abruptly slid instead to the scarlet curtain on the right of the throne: it lacked several inches in length so that it did not quite meet the floor and she saw that someone was now standing behind it, listening.

"—solid gold," Lecler was saying. "It has belonged to the Kings of Ubangiba for centuries."

No one else had turned to look toward the throne. "Surely 18-carat gold?" she suggested, and inched her way toward Carstairs to nudge him. Without moving her lips she murmured, "Someone's hiding behind the curtain."

"Eighteen carat?" scoffed Lecler. "Absolutely not, it is 25-carat gold."

Her nudge and her words produced in Carstairs no glance toward the curtained alcove; he merely looked amused and nodded.

"So," repeated Mr. Lecler, ending his attempt at hostlike graciousness, "it grows time now, Sammat." To Carstairs he said, "You comprehend, he has a speech to make? He must studiously read it to be sure that he does not stumble over any words."

Carstairs said, "Yes, it sounds as if they're eager to see and hear you, Sammat, you mustn't keep them waiting."

"No, no," Lecler said quickly, "you do not understand. He does not speak *yet*, he has not seen the speech written for him. Joseph, escort these guests to the Green Room . . . Sammat," he said, handing him the sheaf of papers, "read over your speech now to be sure it goes smoothly."

Carstairs stepped forward, took the papers from Sammat, and tore them into shreds. As they floated to the floor like confetti he said curtly, "I think Sammat knows what he wishes to say without needing someone else's words put into his mouth."

Lecler stared at him incredulously. "You dare?" he gasped. "You *dare*? Sir, you have just destroyed the speech that Sammat, a king's grandson, is to make to his people! Such impertinence, such interference, is intolerable. One call to the guards, Mr. Carstairs, and you will find our prisons very unpleasant!"

"I'm sure they are," agreed Carstairs, "but you might first like to know what brings me here to this country."

"*Not* a tourist?" scoffed Lecler angrily.

"*Not* a tourist, no," said Carstairs, and added casually, "I have merely been following to Ubangiba $50 million in ransom money picked up two mornings ago in Westchester County in the United States."

A stunned silence followed until Carstairs broke it to add pleasantly, "Of course Ubangiba will be very grateful for the $50 million in unmarked bills that you've brought into the country, and which you no doubt *believe* you have in that black attaché case on the floor beside you." As Lecler looked down at his case in horror Carstairs said in a kind voice, "I don't think you'll find the $50 million there, Lecler. You will note that I, too, have a black attaché case, and my friend Devereaux, a most gifted practitioner of sleight of hand, produced miracles as you both passed through Customs. I will not tell you anything more about him but I will add that Mr. Stover is not an anthropologist but a member of the United States FBI."

Wonderful, thought Mrs. Pollifax.

Lecler gaped at Carstairs and then with trembling hands tried to open the catch on his attaché case, forgetting that it was locked.

Mrs. Pollifax, daring to speak, asked, "Does this have something to do with—"

Carstairs interrupted her to say, "Sammat, go to the balcony now, the crowds sound restive, they want you."

"But sir—"

"It's best you go, Sammat."

"But sir—"

"Now," Carstairs told him flatly.

Sammat walked to the french doors, opened them, turned once to look back at them all, then walked out onto the balcony to a roar of sound that was deafening. Kadi walked to the doors and closed them.

"Open your attaché case," Carstairs told Lecler.

"No," snapped Lecler, "and I don't know what you're talking about." He drew himself erect. "In the meantime," he said harshly, accusingly, "you provoke an international incident with such insolence, you have come here—an *American*—to illegally and illicitly disrupt the affairs of the sovereign government of Ubangiba. The police must be called. Joseph—at once!"

"On the contrary," Carstairs told him, "I didn't come for that purpose at all. I followed a ransom, it's true, but that's not what personally brought me here. What I came for—" He turned toward the curtained alcove and said, "You can come out now, Bidwell." And to Lecler he said, "Bidwell is what I came for."

"Bidwell?" faltered Mrs. Pollifax. "Henry Bidwell?"

From the other side of the room Kadi gasped, "The man held hostage in New York? The kidnapped man?"

"Neither hostage nor kidnapped," said Carstairs. "Well, Bidwell?"

The curtain trembled a little but did not open. It was Mrs. Pollifax who walked the few paces across the room to pull the curtain aside and stand there staring at the same thin, autocratic face she had seen pictured in newspapers and on television, but now drained of color, bloodless and stricken. Turning to Carstairs she said, bewildered, "But how—and *here*?"

"Don't move, any of you," Lecler said in a deadly calm voice. "Don't move, I have a gun. Mr. Carstairs, you will kindly slide your attaché case across the floor to me, *now*, at once!"

Carstairs hesitated and then, with one foot, pushed his attaché case several feet across the polished floor as Lecler drew from his cream-colored silk suit a gun that Mrs. Pollifax automatically identified as a 9mm Smith and Wesson.

"None of you," said Lecler, "will leave this room alive."

Oh dear God, thought Mrs. Pollifax, *I was counted on to help and now I'm too far away, and that means Stover—Stover, if you know judo, use it now.*

But it was Joseph in his scarlet uniform who moved up behind Lecler as soundlessly as a cat and sent the man stumbling forward, grabbed him before he fell, turned him around and hit him hard and furiously across his jaw, knocking him to the floor with his fists. *"Udiyo,"* he cried passionately. *"Udiyo, udiyo . . . Be ku-bada udiyo."*

From the other side of the room Kadi called, "He is calling him evil—*evil*—born to be evil."

Joseph stood defiantly, breathing hard. Carstairs said gravely, "And we thank you, Joseph, for our lives." Leaning over he picked up Lecler's gun and training it on the man framed by the scarlet curtains he said, "Well, Bidwell? What do you have to say for yourself, and to the millions of people—not to mention your wife and children—who have pictured you kidnapped, bound and gagged and abused in some basement cellar for nine days, doubtless even praying for you? You have demeaned and insulted every hostage that's ever been taken captive and who has lived with *real* terror."

Bidwell stammered, "I . . . I . . ." and he fainted, sinking to the floor with one of his outflung arms resting on Mrs. Pollifax's shoe. With distaste she withdrew her foot and walked around him. *"Not* a hostage?" she said.

"As pretty a disappearing act as you'll see in your lifetime," said Carstairs.

Kadi had opened the door to the balcony and Mrs. Pollifax could hear Sammat's voice clearly and confidently speaking to the people in their language. "But how did you know?" Mrs. Pollifax asked Carstairs.

From the crowds outside came a roar of laughter and then a cheer, and Kadi turned to them, smiling. "Sammy has told them *everything*," she said "and they are *with* him, they understand what nearly happened, and he makes a promise to them of *makasi*—a new path. You heard, Joseph? *Makasi!"*

20

It was evening in the palace. Sammat had met with the Chiefs of the Shambi and the Soto, and had gravely accepted their plea that he take over the *ufumo*—the chieftainship—of their sorrowing country and restore its heart, or *mtima*. Stover and Devereaux had vanished to make a number of phone calls, Devereaux to Paris and Stover to Washington—a laborious and time-consuming process—while Achille Lecler was under guard in a clinic awaiting a doctor to wire his jaw. Following a brilliant sunset, night had fallen like a curtain, but the darkness was filled with the muted sound of beating drums—talking drums, Sammy had told them, spreading news of the events of this day across the fields and the desert—*and now I know I really am in Africa*, thought Mrs. Pollifax.

She glowed with contentment: there had been a bath in a real tub—she had missed that at Willie's—and she had been loaned a *dashiki* while her clothes were being laundered and pressed. She was in Africa, of all places, witnessing the unmasking of a clever and unscrupulous billionaire; during the past several days she and Kadi had inadvertently arrived on the periphery of Carstairs's suspicions about Bidwell and the two of them had supplied him with the dimensions needed to confirm his suspicions. Two paths had converged: Carstairs had found his man and,

185

what was most important to her young friend Kadi, they had brought Sammy safely home.

Yet only seven days ago, she remembered, she had neither heard of Sammy, nor of Ubangiba, nor of Kadi Hopkirk, who had been hiding for a day and a night in her hall closet. *Really,* she thought, *it has been QUITE an astonishing week!*

Now she presided over a long and candle-lit refectory table in the shadowy dining hall of the palace, Sammy and Kadi on either side of her, and Carstairs seated next to Bidwell, whose left hand was handcuffed to his chair.

"Well?" she said, addressing Carstairs across the table.

Carstairs gave her a faint smile and nodded. "Yes," he said, and turning to Bidwell, "You understand that we are your first judge and jury."

Bidwell licked dry lips and whispered, "But how did you know? How did you ever guess? It was so carefully, so *very* carefully—"

"Planned, yes," agreed Carstairs. "For years, I'm sure."

"But—how? We made no mistakes, I *swear.*"

Carstairs considered this judiciously. "I'd say that your worst miscalculation was insisting that you not know when or how your abduction was to take place, or by whom, leaving it entirely up to your two confederates, Lecler and Romanovitch, to arrange. Due, no doubt—I can only guess—to your fear of the abduction being witnessed. They were to do the dirty work, and you were to play the part of innocent victim, it had to look absolutely authentic should anyone chance to notice the abduction taking place. And so—not knowing precisely when or how—you left behind your engagement calendar locked in a drawer, a fact known only to your secretary who spoke of it to the FBI."

"Damn it," whispered Bidwell. "Damn *her.*"

"And in that engagement calender were those five mysterious flight 1192's," continued Carstairs, ignoring this crude dismissal of a loyal secretary. "There were also, of course, your appointments with Desforges, Lecler, and Romanovitch, but it was the 1192's that piqued my curiosity. You were a man whose life appeared to be an open book and yet you made five mysterious and concealed trips to Ubangiba, and I might add that your Claiborne-Osborne people, when questioned, scarcely knew of the country's existence. Initially I felt those trips might hold the key to your abduction: a terrorist group, perhaps, or a band of Ubangiban nationalists who objected to your presence. I thought you might have been snatched by a group like that."

"But this scarcely—"

"Very true," agreed Carstairs. "Actually it was something that Desforges said—oh yes, I spoke with him in Rouen, he was very discreet, very proper, he refused to tell me anything except that you'd bought the mineral rights to the country. He did concede, however, that what had been discovered would be only modestly profitable, and he used a curious word: only with cheap, very cheap labor, he said. Very Leopoldish."

"Leopold?" repeated Sammat, startled.

"Yes, a name that I overlooked at the time; I was too disillusioned when our Geology Department reported that coal was the only possibility in Ubangiba, given the terrain. I had expected gold, or natural gas. . . . Perhaps it began when I asked myself why this passionate interest in coal? From you, a man accustomed to million-dollar deals, a man believed to be a billionaire; I very nearly lost interest."

"But you didn't," said Mrs. Pollifax, smiling.

He smiled back at her. "No, because at that point Bishop handed over to me his taped phone interview with you, Mrs. P, where you spoke of being chased through Connecticut and into Massachusetts by a van with 'Chigi Scap Metal' on its panels, and only an hour earlier that same van had been described to us by one of our men named Lazlo—but I won't bore you with that detail just now."

"Later?" urged Mrs. Pollifax, the name Lazlo being all too familiar to her.

"Later, yes. Suffice to say, it was at this point that Kadi and Mrs. Pollifax entered the picture. This Kadi," he said, smiling at her, "who grew up in Ubangiba, met a good friend in New Haven named Sammy who was also from Ubangiba, and who appeared to be in trouble. That's when political possibilities entered this puzzle to enhance matters, and of course very soon a most intriguing connection was made."

He met Bidwell's glance and held it. "Stop me if I'm wrong but I assume—having seen and heard your impassioned plea on video only Saturday—that as soon as the abduction took place you were rushed somewhere to film several dramatic appeals to be issued at suitable intervals, and then—even before a ransom note was sent out—you were on your way to Ubangiba with a new passport. Of course you left Lecler in charge of the two Chigi Scap Metal chaps, and as you must know by now they were killed on Friday by Lecler, about the same time that President

Simoko here in Ubangiba was murdered by Romanovitch."

"Who is still missing," Kadi reminded him.

"Not for long," said Carstairs. "Joseph has taken a few trusted friends in the police to look for him."

Sammat interrupted to say, "Joseph has also taken me to the room where President Simoko slept, sir, and has shown me the trunks of gold bullion hidden there . . . so much! It will certainly serve to back our currency, the *gwar* that has lost so much value. But how greedy Simoko was!"

"Bidwell was greedy, too," said Carstairs looking at him. "Fifty million ransom, Bidwell? *That* was rather suspicious. . . . My last-minute inquiries uncovered the fact that you'd never kept all your money in the United States—doubtless it was stashed away in Swiss banks—but it wasn't enough, you also wanted everything that remained in the United States, you wanted it *very* much, and what better way to get it moved out of the country than to be abducted and the ransom collected by Lecler and brought to Ubangiba."

Mrs. Pollifax, puzzled, said, "But why and for what?"

"Ah," said Carstairs, "that's where Leopold comes in. Look at Sammat, he knows what I mean."

Sammat nodded. "King Leopold and the Congo."

"Your question, Mrs. P, is the same question that I asked of myself: why and for what? A modest vein of coal certainly couldn't explain Bidwell's interest in the country. What then, I wondered, could it be? Having made billions and become sated with money, what did he still lack?"

They waited expectantly.

"I realized I was thinking too small. What he wanted was to own a country. His *own* country."

"Nobody can own a country," said Kadi flatly.

"No? King Leopold II did, and I'm sure Bidwell had him in mind. . . . But let me tell you about King Leopold the Second of Belgium, who died in 1909. I've read and reread the story these past two days until I believe I can quote from memory." Leaning back in his chair he closed his eyes, and as if the pages had become engraved there he recited, " 'Failing to interest his country in acquiring the Congo during the "great scramble" for Africa during the late eighteen hundreds, the King used his own personal fortune to further his personal ambitions . . .' "

He opened his eyes to say in a harsh voice, "So he employed Henry Morton Stanley—you could almost substitute Lecler and Romanovitch here—to explore the Congo, to make treaties with the chiefs, and to map its rivers. Eventually Leopold established a trading monopoly in rubber from which he alone—not Belgium—made enormous profits under a system of abusive forced labor and sickening atrocities.

"And not until 1905," he continued, "did Europe wake up to the fact that a single individual owned an entire country—think of it, an entire country owned by one man—who ruled it as the most absolute of absolute monarchs."

"Owned a country!" whispered Kadi.

"Fair and square," nodded Carstairs. "And even when Europe learned of it—Conrad's *Heart of Darkness* brought it clearly to the world—Europe did nothing, nothing at all, being too occupied with its own small wars and conflicts."

"Wow," Kadi said, "I didn't know *that*."

"I did," Sammat said. "It was a bloody and brutal story in Africa's history."

"Well, Bidwell, am I right?" Carstairs asked, turning to him. "You intended to become the missing Judge Crater of this continent and rule a country using young Sammat as a decoration and ruling him as well, isn't this true? A new hobby, right? A toy to play with? A little fun for you in your later years?"

"Stop—stop," groaned Bidwell. "Tell me, I beg of you, what will happen to me now."

" 'Beg of' me?" mocked Carstairs. "Well, there are certain possibilities I can think of. . . . I admit, much to my sorrow, that at the moment I can think of no laws you've broken, unless as an accessory to the murder of President Simoko. Definitely, however, the $50 million dollars in ransom that you went to so much trouble to bring here—" He reached down for his attaché case and slid it across the table to Sammat. "I think it only fair and just that it remain in Ubangiba for the development of the country, since it was for that purpose it came here."

Bidwell made a strangled sound of protest.

"After all," pointed out Carstairs, "it's Bidwell money, originally a ransom to be paid to return you to the family that you've abandoned. That *could* be your future. Stover is conferring about that."

"Returned?" Bidwell said in a shocked voice. "To my family?"

Carstairs shrugged. "Why not? The ransom has been paid and will never be traced—those unmarked bills—and it's possible our government may think the most creative punishment is

191

that you be found gagged and bound in New York and quietly returned to that family. With the stipulation, of course, that you immediately retire from Claiborne-Osborne International and never leave the United States or be involved in any business again."

"That fifty million is *mine*," Bidwell said desperately. "And you can't arrest me, you have no legal rights, we're on foreign soil!"

"Ah, but we're not arresting you," said Carstairs smoothly, "the FBI is only carrying out its assigned job of rescuing a kidnapped American citizen. We will merely be returning a captured American to the United States, where you may or may not be arrested. However, I would like to remind you that recently the Supreme Court ruled that in the case of 'hot pursuit' the FBI may enter a foreign country to recover a person wanted for criminal activities."

"I won't go," stormed Bidwell.

"Or," pointed out Carstairs, "the whole story can be told. The newspapers will love it, your family will be crushed, and I'm sure you can be sent to prison for *something*, I'm not sure for what, not being an expert on the subtleties of the law. If not as an accessory to murder, then surely Ubangiba can try you for the attempt to overthrow its government."

Bidwell attempted to rise from his chair but was held back by his handcuffs. "That's blackmail!" he shouted.

Carstairs laughed in his face.

They were silent, each of them staring at Bidwell and realizing how very nearly he had succeeded in his scheme. It was only Carstairs, thought Mrs. Pollifax, who had been intuitive enough to weave together dissimilar and fragile threads to make a whole out of a crazy, outrageous pattern, and she marveled at him again.

The silence ended with a sigh as Carstairs said, "Enough . . . Stover is arranging a special plane for us in the morning—no rest for the weary!—to return Bidwell to the United States. Devereaux is going to stay on for a week, though, Sammat, and help in any way he can. I hope none of you feel we're deserting Sammat?"

"I'm a little tired," admitted Mrs. Pollifax. "Before I'm overwhelmed by jet lag I think I'd like to go home and see Cyrus."

"Kadi?"

Kadi said shyly, "Would it be possible for me to stay until the Thursday flight back to Paris and New York? I'd like to find my parents' graves—Laraba will know where. And visit with old friends."

"By all means," said Carstairs. "And Sammy? You'll be very busy, I'm thinking."

"I certainly will," he said earnestly. "We must restore the old legal system, once surviving lawyers can be released from prison. Banks and credit unions have to be opened again, and the Simoko army disbanded and new people trained. I'd like to turn half of this palace into an Agricultural Center, and half into a high school; but first I must bring in two experts whose books I have studied, they are agricultural experts on what can best be grown in Africa, and what experiments have been successful."

"And the $50 million?" asked Mrs. Pollifax with a smile.

"Food," he said quickly. "Grain at *once* to fill the shops for the people to buy, and seeds—but the seeds will be given away. And yes, perhaps some equipment to mine that coal you spoke of, sir, so that it can fuel the digging of new wells— but I must go slowly and not make mistakes, sir."

"And elections?" asked Carstairs.

Sammat shook his head. "Not until the people have full bellies and a taste of what it feels like to be free. They would only vote for me now, you see, and that would be very bad."

Kadi grinned. "Well, if I learn you've made yourself President-for-Life, Sammy, I'll come over with my B-B gun and—"

"*Heya*, Kadi," he said, grinning, "you remember the time Duma shot wild by accident and—"

She giggled. "—and my father took six pellets out of me, and I couldn't sit down for a week."

Carstairs, watching them, smiled. "There is this, too, young lady. When you tire of art school—and if the CIA still exists," he added dryly, "we could use someone with your gift for sketching faces and remembering them."

"Well, thank you," she said, and to Mrs. Pollifax, "*Another* job offer, Emmy Reed!"

But Mrs. Pollifax was watching Carstairs, who was looking intently at each of their faces around the table. "It's extraordinary," he said. "We have here in this room, however briefly, all the characters who played out this drama. For me it's extraordinary."

"I don't suppose it happens often for you," conceded Mrs. Pollifax, "but this one you've seen through to the very end."

"No," said Sammat firmly, "he has seen it through to a *beginning*."

epilogue

This week Willie's Traveling Amusement Shows was encamped not far from the ocean in northernmost Maine, so that on this early June morning the fragrance of salt air mingled companionably with the smell of the fresh sawdust that Jake was shoveling out of the truck being driven slowly around the midway. A morning breeze from the sea played with the seats of the ferris wheel and sent them swinging gently, while two seagulls observed the scene from the ridge-pole of the Ten-in-One. The bright sun had not yet extinguished the shadows cast by the stalls but it picked out Shannon as she emerged from her trailer in a not-too-clean robe and made her way to the grab-joint. Down at his Spin the Wheel, Lubo had set up a lap-top computer on the counter and was making calculations. In the trailer compound Gertie was hanging her washing out to dry, while three trailers beyond her the Snake Woman opened her door and sat down in the sun cradling a python in her arms.

It was an otherwise tranquil morning until its silence was suddenly invaded by the sound of the merry-go-round coming to life, its horses slowly rising and falling, its carousel bursting out with the lively rhythms of "Who Stole My Heart Away."

"Faster, Boozy Tim, or you'll rock us to sleep," called Cyrus, astride a black horse with a scarlet saddle.

195

"Yes, faster," called Mrs. Pollifax, and fluttered a hand at Kadi, who laughed up at them, paintbrush in one hand, a bucket of paint in the other, and who watched them as they rode side by side in perfect contentment, round and round, dreamily, and then the rollicking music paused, clicked and changed to "In the Good Old Summertime."

Kadi thought, *I have a family again. . . .*

Willie, striding onto the midway, came to an abrupt halt, startled by the sound of the carousel at such an early hour. He looked at Boozy Tim, and then at Cyrus and Mrs. Pollifax, and he shook his head and grinned. "Not *again!*" he said, and chuckled as he headed into the cook-house for coffee.

About the Author

DOROTHY GILMAN has written books for adults and children. She is the author of ten Mrs. Pollifax novels, including *Mrs. Pollifax and the Second Thief*, *The Unexpected Mrs. Pollifax*, *Mrs. Pollifax and the Golden Triangle*, *Mrs. Pollifax and the Whirling Dervish*, and *The Amazing Mrs. Pollifax*—as well as eight other novels.

She divides her time between Norwalk, Connecticut, and Albuquerque, New Mexico.

IF YOU HAVE ENJOYED READING THIS
LARGE PRINT BOOK AND YOU
WOULD LIKE MORE INFORMATION
ON HOW TO ORDER A WHEELER
LARGE PRINT BOOK, PLEASE WRITE
TO:

WHEELER PUBLISHING, INC.
P.O. BOX 531-ACCORD STATION
HINGHAM, MA 02018-0531

CHITTY CHITTY BANG BANG

and the
Race Against Time

CHITTY CHITTY BANG BANG

and the
Race Against Time

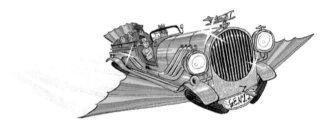

Frank Cottrell Boyce

illustrated by Joe Berger

CANDLEWICK PRESS

Text by Frank Cottrell Boyce copyright © 2012 by The Ian Fleming Estate
Illustrations by Joe Berger copyright © 2012 by The Ian Fleming Estate

First U.S. paperback edition 2014

Library of Congress Catalog Card Number 2012952070
ISBN 978-0-7636-5982-0 (hardcover)
ISBN 978-0-7636-6931-7 (paperback)

13 14 15 16 17 18 BVG 10 9 8 7 6 5 4 3 2 1

Printed in Berryville, VA, U.S.A.

This book was typeset in Stone Serif.
The illustrations were created digitally.

Candlewick Press
99 Dover Street
Somerville, Massachusetts 02144

visit us at www.candlewick.com

For Mr. Patrick Roose—
our very own El Dorado
F. C. B.

1

Most cars are just cars. Four wheels. An engine. Some seats. They take you to work or to school. Then they bring you home again. The Tooting family car was not one of these. The Tooting family car was different. The Tooting family car was a beautiful, green, perfectly restored 1921 Paragon Panther, the only one ever built. Her wheels flashed in the sunshine. Her long, majestic bonnet gleamed. Her seats were as soft as silk, and the instruments on her walnut dashboard sparkled like summer. The glossy ebony handle of her Chronojuster glowed invitingly. Most cars don't have a Chronojuster. It's a special handle that allows you to drive backward and forward in time. That's how special Chitty Chitty Bang Bang is—time travel is fitted as standard.

If an ordinary car breaks down, it might end up in a lay-by with steam coming out of the engine. When the Tooting family car broke down, it ended up in an ancient steaming jungle being eyed by a hungry dinosaur.

"Dinosaur!" yelled Little Harry. He seemed to think that the rest of his family might not have noticed the gigantic head swaying over the treetops, drooling spit, and bellowing its hunger.

"Dinosaur!" yelled Little Harry again.

None of them had ever seen such a creature before. No living being has ever seen such a creature. But all of them—even Little Harry—knew what it was.

Tyrannosaurus rex.

"Hang on, everyone," yelled Dad. "Jem, watch the back. We're going to reverse."

Dad pushed hard on the accelerator and yanked the gears around. Black smoke billowed from the exhaust. Sludge splattered into the air. Chitty Chitty Bang Bang moved. Six inches. Down into the mud.

Then her engine stopped.

"Why has the engine stopped?" asked Mum.

"It's just stalled," said Dad.

No one said a word. They were all thinking the same thing. To start the engine, someone would

have to get out of the car and turn the crank handle.

"If we just sit tight, maybe it won't see us and we'll be safe."

"Or maybe it will see the car and think, *Oh, tinned Tootings!*" muttered Mum.

"Or maybe it will crush us underfoot," said Lucy, "burying us in mud so that over the years we turn into fossils, and in millions of years, we will be one of the great mysteries of science—a family of humans that somehow managed to get themselves fossilized in the age of dinosaurs. We'll be the Great Tooting Conundrum. Except they won't know our name was Tooting."

The head loomed closer. It was so vast that Jem felt like he was staring at something through a microscope. He could see the bits of mud and twigs caught in the folds of its pebbly skin; the stains of blood on its white dagger teeth. Its tongue was as rough as a gravel path. Its nostrils were a pair of wet, grungy bin lids; its eye, a tiny, twitchy rivet.

Maybe it won't see us, thought Jem.

But just as he thought that, those bin-lid nostrils twitched. They closed up. They opened again. The tyrannosaur had sniffed, and its sniff was so powerful that every leaf and branch rattled and Lucy's hair went flying round her head. It was sniffing for food. It had definitely sniffed out the Tootings.

"Fascinating," said Lucy. "For years now, there has been a debate about whether *Tyrannosaurus rex* was a true predator—able to move fast and catch and kill its prey—or whether it was just a very big scavenger, eating only animals that were already dead."

"Why is that interesting?" said Jem.

"Because if it is a scavenger, it will leave us alone; but if it is a predator, it will kill us."

"Actually, that *is* quite interesting."

There was a sound like the sound that a house might make if someone picked it up and dropped it from a great height. It was the creature's foot, landing a few yards

in front of them. Its curved, cruel claws dug into the earth as it steadied itself. Its toes stretched like leathery bridges. Its leg was a tower of meat. Under the skin, chains of muscle shifted like the gears of a terrible machine.

"On balance," said Lucy, "I'm going to say predator."

Everyone leaped out of the car and into the undergrowth.

No one looked up.

No one looked back.

No one stopped running. Until they were all standing, breathless, inside what felt like a big green bus shelter. It was a single giant leaf, bent toward the ground by a raindrop the size of a melon. Jem found himself staring at

the changing patterns on its surface. He could hear his father and mother discussing what to do, but for some reason he couldn't tear his attention away from those patterns.

"We need to get far away from that tyrannosaur as quickly as possible," said Dad. Not a sentence he'd ever expected to have to say.

"But what if there's another tyrannosaur round the corner?" said Mum. "What if there's a HERD of them?"

"Opinion is divided," said Lucy, "but it's definitely possible that they moved in herds."

Suddenly Jem realized what the fascinating pattern on the surface of the raindrop was. "Little Harry!" he gasped. For the pattern was the reflection of Little Harry's bottom as he crawled back into danger.

"Dinosaur!" giggled Little Harry—correctly—as he toddled through the undergrowth.

Without pausing to think, Jem ran after him. Surely he would catch him in no time. But it was amazing how quickly his little brother could move on his hands and knees. Unlike Jem, Little Harry did not have to push leaves and branches out of the way or clamber over roots and stones. He just kept shuffling forward, singing, "Dino-saur. Dino-saur . . ." until he crawled out into the sunlight where the

huge, savage, drooling creature was now examining the bonnet of the car with its nose.

"Dinosaur!" yelled Little Harry, and waved at it merrily.

The dinosaur turned its mighty head toward him as Jem burst through the undergrowth and swept his little brother into his arms. He was about to turn and run back to safety when something stopped him. The eye. That tiny, dark eye was staring straight at Jem. The tyrannosaur was looking at Jem, and Jem could not look away. Not even when that wide mouth opened, not even when that fence of cutlass teeth flashed in the sun, not even when that giant foot unhooked itself from the ground and swung into the air.

Then there came a terrible noise, an earsplitting, tree-shaking noise, a noise that made Jem jump, a noise that went . . . *Ga gooo ga!*

Ga gooo ga? thought Jem. *That's not a very dinosaury noise.*

"*Ga gooo ga!*"

"That sounds like . . ."

"*Ga gooo ga!*"

It was Chitty Chitty Bang Bang sounding her unbelievably loud original 1921 motor Klaxon.

"*Ga gooo ga!*"

*

There was only one thing that the tyrannosaur wanted to know about Chitty Chitty Bang Bang: namely, could you eat her? She put her mighty foot down and turned to look at the Thing That Went Ga Gooo Ga.

The standard Tyrannosaurus Test for Whether You Can Eat a Thing or Not is: Does it try to run away? If it doesn't try to run away, it's probably not fresh. The Thing That Went Ga Gooo Ga didn't try to run away. On the other hand, it didn't smell off. It smelled sort of interesting. This tyrannosaur was not a fussy eater. "Interesting" was nearly as good as "fresh" in her book. Another standard Tyranno-saurus Test for Whether You Can Eat a Thing or Not is: Does it beg for mercy? Does it scream, "Please, don't eat me!" or "Run, children, run!"? The Thing That Went Ga Gooo Ga hadn't said a word until now, but here it was saying, "Ga gooo ga!" This did not sound like a plea for mercy. It sounded more like a warning or even — but this was impossible — a *threat*?! No one had ever threatened the tyrannosaur before. She wasn't sure how she felt about it. It gave her an unusual feeling in her tummy. It might well have been the beginning of a laugh, but because she'd never laughed before, she didn't recognize it.

So she was already slightly uneasy when the next thing happened.

The Thing That Went Ga Gooo Ga threw a bolt of lightning at her. Every shadow in the glade shifted as though the whole forest were whirling. It felt like the sun had come up and gone down again in an instant. What was it?

Chitty Chitty Bang Bang had switched her headlights on full beam and switched them off again. The tyrannosaur had never seen light so sudden or so bright come from anywhere and definitely not from food.

That was it. She decided to give up on the whole idea of eating Chitty Chitty Bang Bang and concentrate instead on eating those little creatures that were running around. Namely, the Tooting family.

By now Mum was happily hugging Little Harry in the safety of the bus-shelter leaf.

"How could you do such a thing?" she said, covering him with kisses. "Don't ever run away again."

"We have to stick together," said Dad. "Oh!"

Dad said "Oh" because the melon-size raindrop had finally fallen off the end of the bus-shelter leaf and exploded around his feet like a water bomb. Without the water to hold it down, the leaf sprang back into place on its branch.

"Amazing." Lucy sighed. With the leaf gone, they could see the whole forest rising around them. Wisps of mist drifted between the tree trunks. A dragonfly the size of a bicycle flitted among the ferns, its million-colour wings whirring in and out of visibility. Beyond all that, the huge, oily back of the tyrannosaur moved away.

"Now, that," Lucy sighed, "is a predator." She took out her phone—which was shaped like a big jelly baby—and began to film.

She was right about this. *Tyrannosaurus rex* was

a predator, and like all predators it noticed every single little thing. This tyrannosaur, for instance, even noticed the tiny flash of light that sparked from the tiny lens of the camera of Lucy's phone. It turned its head around to get a better look.

The moment it saw the Tooting family, the tyrannosaur felt more relaxed. They were definitely food. They were doing all the things that food was supposed to do—running around in a confused way and screaming their heads off. The screams in particular really got the tyrannosaur's juices going. She swung around. She would be over them in a single stride.

"Run!" yelled Dad.

"But keep together!" yelled Mum.

"Hold hands!" yelled Dad.

They held hands and ran into the undergrowth, hoping that the ferns would hide them. The ferns didn't hide them. In fact, their every move made the fern tops shake in a way that said "Dinner's here." The tyrannosaur carefully lined herself up with the Tooting family's escape route. Her colossal tail swept through the glade as she steadied herself.

The Tootings followed Dad between the thick stalks of the primeval fern. With Little Harry perched on his shoulders, Dad dodged left and then right. He thought that maybe if the tyrannosaur

was watching them, this would make her dizzy or confuse her tiny brain.

Sadly he was wrong. All the dodging just made the food look fresher and more tasty.

It also made Jem anxious. He was thinking, *What if we get lost? It was Chitty that brought us here. Only Chitty can take us back. If we lose track of where she is, we'll be stuck here, dodging hungry tyrannosaurs for the rest of our lives.*

Then Jem stopped running.

And so did Mum.

And so did Dad.

And so did Lucy.

They stopped dead in their tracks.

They stared in horror into the undergrowth.

Something was coming toward them. Scything through the leaves and stalks and branches at amazing speed.

It wasn't the tyrannosaur.

It was too fast, too low, and much, much too unstoppable.

"Duck!" yelled Dad.

They threw themselves onto the ground just in time as the something crashed out of the undergrowth and hurtled through the air above their heads.

It smacked into the ground behind them.

"*Ga gooo ga!*"

It was Chitty Chitty Bang Bang. When the tyrannosaur swung around, she had swiped the car with her tail and sent her spinning through the air, right into the path of the Tootings.

"Well, at least that got her out of the mud," said Dad. "Thanks, tyrannosaur."

The tyrannosaur probably heard him say this, because by now she was towering directly over the Tootings, with her mouth wide open, ready to swallow them.

Then she saw that thing. That Thing That Went Ga Gooo Ga went "*Ga gooo ga*" again. Then it did its lightning again. Then the food that she was about to eat climbed inside it. This really worried the tyrannosaur. To a tyrannosaur, if food—for instance, a family—climbs inside something, that means that the something has eaten the food. The something was eating her food, right in front of her. How unbelievably cheeky! The tyrannosaur decided to think this over and possibly discuss it with some other tyrannosaurs.

The Tooting family settled down happily into the lovely soft leather of Chitty Chitty Bang Bang's seats and breathed deep, contented sighs.

"In all my long life," said Mum, "I have never seen anything so relaxing and reassuring as the

sight of a tyrannosaur walking in the opposite direction from me and my family."

"Let's see if we can get this Chronojuster to take us home," said Dad.

"What?" said Mum. "We've come all the way to the Cretaceous period, we've just escaped an attack by a *Tyrannosaurus rex,* and you want to go HOME? Surely we're going to take a look around first?"

"Take a look around?" said Dad. "I honestly think from a health-and-safety point of view that the idea of taking a look around a fetid swamp full of flesh-eating monsters—"

"Not in a swamp full of monsters," said Mum. "In a luxurious flying car."

"Oh," said Dad.

Jem cranked the handle. Chitty's engine purred. Her wheels sliced through the soft ground, and when she was going just fast enough, Dad pulled the ebony flight button, and Chitty flicked out her wide, elegant wings. The wings caught the breeze, and soon the car was soaring up through the shreds of mist, slaloming through the giant conifers. When Chitty's undercarriage brushed the tops of the tree

ferns, dozens of giant dragonflies came skittering out, their wings a hurry of rainbows. A butterfly floated by—so big they could see the feathers on its antennae. From the top branches of a gigantic magnolia, a family of what looked like stripy mice watched them intently.

"Strange to think," said Lucy, "that we're related. They must be like our second cousins nine million times removed."

She took a photo for the family album.

Then all of a sudden, they were above the treetops.

"Look at those weird branches sticking out of the treetops," said Jem. "They look like gargoyles."

The moment he said this, the gargoyle branches leaned forward and flopped into the air, opening up their leathery wings and stretching out their leathery necks.

"Pterodactyls," said Lucy, taking out her jelly-baby camera again. "They seem to be interested in us, and the feeling is mutual."

Jem dug out Chitty's manual and started to flick through the pages frantically to see if she had any form of onboard anti-pterodactyl defences. But

when he looked up, he saw that the creatures were surprisingly small and unthreatening. They were following the beautiful car through the clear blue sky, the way children at home might follow it along the pavement. Even pterodactyls could appreciate the loveliness of Chitty Chitty Bang Bang.

"Do you think they like chocolate?" asked Mum, pulling out a bag of chocolates that she'd bought in a shop in Basildon. She threw one to the nearest pterodactyl. It folded its wings, caught it, and threw back its neck to swallow it.

"The word today," said Dad, "is surely *unbelievable photo opportunity*."

"Oh. Yes," said Lucy. "Do it again. I didn't catch it."

They flew over the forest, tossing chocolate to pterodactyls, without a care in the world. Until Lucy asked if she could have one.

"Do you think they'll be all right?" said Dad. "You don't think time travel might have affected them?"

"Of course they're all right," said Mum. "Their sell-by date is sixty-six million years in the future. Youngest first . . ."

She held the packet out to Little Harry.

That was the first time anyone noticed.

Little Harry wasn't there.

2

Most scientists agree that *Tyrannosaurus rex* liked to hunt alone, like tigers. But most scientists are wrong. *Tyrannosaurus rex* liked to hunt in packs, like wolves. There was nothing a tyrannosaur liked better than running around in a tyrannosaurus gang, knocking trees over, frightening smaller dinosaurs. The tyrannosaur's idea of a really great night was settling down with a dozen or so tyrannosaurus friends around the body of a large herbivore, ripping it to shreds while discussing favourite tyrannosaurus subjects. For instance:

"Mammals—will they ever catch on?"

"Feathers—are they just a passing fad?"

"Comets—reality or myth?"

"Extinction—it'll never happen," etc.

So when Chitty Chitty Bang Bang scared her,

the first thing the tyrannosaur did was hurry off to talk things over with the rest of her pack. When she told them she had seen something that looked like food but that flashed light and made warning noises, some of them were intrigued—maybe this was a comet? Maybe it was the End of the World? Others just said she was a fussy eater. But all of them wanted to know more. The whole pack trooped back to the glade where the tyrannosaur had had her strange encounter.

The ground shook. Trees crashed. Everything in their path that could run ran. Thirteen fully grown tyrannosaurs thrashed through the forest to the very spot where Little Harry was waiting.

The moment before Chitty took off on her flight across the treetops, Little Harry had slipped out of his seat and clambered over the door. He had waited all his life to see real dinosaurs, and he couldn't understand why his family wanted to get away from them. When the whole mud-churning, tree-barging, tail-thrashing, cutlass-toothed pack of tyrannosaurs burst roaring back into the glade, Little Harry clapped his hands and cheered, as though Santa and his reindeer had just dropped in to offer him his own personal Christmas.

The tyrannosaurs, on the other hand, were disappointed. They'd come to see flashing lights

and hear terrifying Klaxons, not just another obviously-edible-but-not-very-meaty mammal. *Oh, well,* thought thirteen tyrannosaurs at the same time, *at least I get a snack out of it.* And thirteen tyrannosaurus heads bent down to swallow Little Harry.

The thing that saved him was that—unlike any other creature that has ever lived—he ran *toward* the tyrannosaurs. No one runs *toward* a hungry tyrannosaur. Even baby tyrannosaurs do not run toward Mummy when Mummy is hungry, because—horrible but true—family loyalty means very little when a tyrannosaur is hungry.

Little Harry, however, ran forward. He ran right under the tyrannosaurs' heads, hoping to get a better view of their funny little arms. Tyrannosaurs have many talents, but backing up is not one of them. When Little Harry ran out of reach of their mouths, some of them tried to turn to the right; some tried to turn to the left; some tried to go right round; some just stood there, bewildered. The result was a lot of tyrannosaurs banging heads. And the result of that was a lot of angry tyrannosaurs. Little Harry loved this more than anything. As giant killer lizards bit huge bloody chunks out of one another and clawed and bellowed in pain and fury, Little Harry clapped his hands and yelled, "Again!"

This behaviour did slightly refocus the tyranno-saurs' attention on Little Harry. The cleverer ones managed to get themselves into a good position to snatch him up in their jaws. But just then . . .

"*Ga gooo ga!*"

Chitty Chitty Bang Bang flew back into the clearing. Lights flashing. Klaxon sounding. No one had mentioned before that the mysterious object could fly. The only thing they'd ever heard of that could fly and flash light at the same time was a comet. And all they knew about comets was that they made you extinct. With all the grace and pre-cision of a troupe of seven-ton ballerinas, the tyran-nosaurs spun on their three-toed feet and fled from the scene.

"Dinosaurs!" yelled Little Harry, as his mother swept him into her arms.

"Yes," she said, "we noticed them."

"Let's get out of here and go home." Dad grabbed the handle of the Chronojuster.

"Whoa!" said Jem. "Not so fast! We don't want to end up in some distant future where the whole world is flooded and everyone's got gills."

"Good thinking, Jem," said Dad. "That was a narrow escape. Gently does it."

"Although," said Lucy, "a post-apocalyptic sub-marine future does sound quite interesting."

"Not as interesting as getting safely back to Basildon," said Dad, moving the lever gently forward.

The Tootings' first time-trip had been so sudden and unexpected, they hadn't really noticed what it felt like. This time, though, as the giant ferns around them trembled, blurred, and then vanished, they were able to enjoy the strange tingly sensation that time travel gives you. It's like a cool breeze that seems to pass straight through your body, filtering through all your cells. A wide red desert unrolled beneath them like a carpet. The sky filled up with unexpected colours and towers of red and purple clouds. Lightning flickered, illuminating great piles of bleached bones.

"I think we just passed through the mass extinction at the end of the Cretaceous," said Lucy.

"So nearly at Basildon, then?" said Dad.

"Just another sixty-six million years," said Lucy. "Oh!"

Everyone said "Oh!" at the same time because all across the sky, the menacing clouds turned white and fluffy, and the dark sky turned bright blue. Blades of tall grass popped up from the sand like quick green fireworks, until the whole desert became a rippling savanna where the long necks of

big birds rose up like feathery periscopes. Then, as if an invisible hand were wiping the whole landscape clean with a cloth, a strange blankness began to spread from east to west. The land was turning white, the sky grey.

"The Ice Age is coming," said Jem. "Do we have any antifreeze?"

"I'm not sure," said Dad. "Maybe the best thing is to speed up."

So the whole Ice Age rolled over them quick as a spring shower, leaving just a powdered-sugar dusting of frost on the bonnet. As soon as the glaciers had gone by, Dad slowed down again so that they could watch the mighty new rivers pouring over the land. A brown bubbling torrent ran by just a few hundred yards in front of the car, cutting deep into the soil. They watched as the river carved a steep valley around them.

"The word today," said Dad, "is *highly informative and completely memorable geography lesson.*" He pressed harder on the Chronojuster, speeding time up just a little. Soft round hills rose up as though someone were inflating huge balloons beneath the soil.

Dad pulled the Chronojuster back, and time slowed down. Meadows spread out around them.

A massive creature with a shaggy golden pelt shambled by without looking at them.

"Doggy! Doggy!" yelled Little Harry.

"In fact, it's *Megatherium*," said Lucy. "We're in the age of the mammals, the Cenozoic. We're back in our own era."

"Not far from home, then," said Dad.

"About another million years," said Lucy.

Time flies when you're enjoying yourself, and the Tootings certainly enjoyed watching the river snuggle down among the new-made hills, and the thick deciduous forest gathering on their slopes. Herds of deer and buffalo thundered back and forth as the seasons flew by.

"I have to admit," said Dad, "I'm seeing a very different side to Basildon. Whoa! What was that?"

Somewhere above the forest, he had glimpsed something amazing. He brought Chitty to a halt. Immediately everyone covered their ears. While

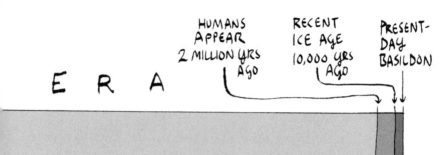

they had been travelling through time, everything was silent. Once they were still, they were bombarded with clattering, twittering birdsong.

"Look," shouted Dad, "I just spotted it out of the corner of my eye."

A thin column of smoke was rising from a clearing somewhere down the valley.

"That's not a forest fire—that must be someone's bonfire. That's humans."

"We can't be more than a couple of hundred thousand years from home," said Lucy.

"We should go and say hello," said Mum. "It's only polite. After all, they are relatives."

"No!" said Lucy. "Think about it. What if we accidentally left a penknife or a box of matches behind? That could alter the course of human history. We might come home and find that the whole world had changed. Basildon might be full of people performing human sacrifice."

"Or talking newts," said Dad.

"What?"

"Newts that talk. It could happen. Anything could happen."

Lucy's phone rang, playing an annoyingly perky tune.

"How can the phone be ringing?" gasped Lucy. "Phones won't be invented for a couple hundred thousand years. Electricity hasn't been invented yet. I'm not even sure that *talking*'s been invented."

But the phone kept ringing. Louder and louder.

"Hello?" said Lucy.

"Helllllllooooooo," purred a female voice. "We seem to have missed you in traffic. But we don't want you to worry."

Lucy froze. It was the voice of Nanny. The Nanny of notorious international supervillain Tiny

Jack. The Nanny who just a few days ago had tried to steal Chitty and feed the children to Tiny Jack's hungry piranhas.

"Nanny?" said Lucy, trying to be polite but almost choking in the process. "How on earth—"

"These jelly phones—aren't they just marvellous?" cooed Nanny. "You can call them wherever and whenever."

"We're a couple hundred thousand years in the past," said Lucy, amazed, putting her on speaker phone.

"Are you really? Well, don't worry. We can wait. We're quite comfortable where we are. Your front door very kindly put the kettle on the moment we opened it." (Dad had done some DIY that caused the front door to greet guests and boil the kettle for tea.)

"Our front door?" hissed Mum. "Where is she?"

"Thirteen Zborowski Terrace," purred Nanny. "It's soooo cosy. Jem, can you hear me? Tiny Jack is utterly delighted by your Scalextric race track. Oh, and Mr. Tooting, I must say I'm very impressed by your collection of punctuality certificates . . ."

"My punctuality certificates were in my special box," gasped Dad, "under the bed."

"That's right," cooed Nanny. "You're too modest. We're going to put them all on the wall for

you, aren't we, Tiny Jack? We're going to decorate your room for you too, Lucy. It's so gloomy! We're going to brighten it up, aren't we, Tiny Jack?" She lowered her voice. "The poor mite. He's so bored. I'm trying to keep him cheerful, but what he really needs is someone to play with. Come home soon! We'll make sure the kettle is on!"

She hung up.

The Tootings looked at one another. The thought of Nanny and Tiny Jack poking around their house made them feel ill and angry and frightened all at the same time.

"The evil supervillain Tiny Jack!" exclaimed Mum. "I was so busy escaping from stampeding dinosaurs, I forgot all about the evil supervillain Tiny Jack!"

"And now he's got my punctuality certificates," said Dad.

"My perfectly matte-very-black wallpaper." Lucy sighed. "Just when I'd got the room exactly how I like it."

"Let's go straight home and throw them out," said Mum.

"We can't just throw them out," said Jem. "They're evil supervillains. We're just an ordinary family from Basildon."

"Ordinary family from Basildon!" snorted Mum.

"We just defeated a herd of ravenous dinosaurs. We are the Mighty Tootings. And this is Chitty Chitty Bang Bang."

"Exactly," said Lucy. "We've got Chitty Chitty Bang Bang. Imagine what will happen if Tiny Jack gets her again, now that he knows she has a Chronojuster? If Tiny Jack had a time machine, he could . . ."

"Steal all the gold in El Dorado," said Mum.

"El Dorado is a myth," said Lucy.

"The Crown jewels, then," said Jem, "or the secret plans for the atomic bomb, or moon rockets, or fighter planes or . . . anything. If he gets Chitty, he could travel back and forth through time doing anything he wants. Nobody would be safe. He could change the course of history. In the wrong hands, Chitty Chitty Bang Bang is not just a fantastic car—she's a superweapon. Maybe we should stay here in the Stone Age."

"We haven't packed for the Stone Age, though," said Dad. "We've got no toothpaste. No soap. We'd probably need spears to catch our food . . ." He sighed. "The word today is *it's all my fault*. If only I'd been content with the standard air-cooled flat-four 1.5-litre camper van. Why couldn't I have left Chitty's twenty-three-litre Maybach aero engine in the tree where I found it?"

"But then we wouldn't have had all this fun," said Mum. "Don't worry about it. Tiny Jack is just a little boy. All we have to do is go back to our time, and I'll give him a good talking-to."

"Will that really work?" asked Lucy. "Last time we met, he tried to feed us to piranhas."

"Everyone has their off days," said Mum.

"Maybe we could travel through time," said Jem, "and gather a band of heroes—Sherlock Holmes and Superman and maybe Sir Lancelot—and come back and defeat him."

Lucy pointed out the one small problem with this plan. "All of those people are fictional. Tiny Jack is real."

"OK. What about Winston Churchill and Mahatma Gandhi?"

"Both so busy. Also, they didn't really get on."

"Plus the Chronojuster is quite sticky and hard to control. You might set out for 1945 and end up in 1845. Or we might set out to get Winston Churchill and end up with Hitler."

"Surely you can fix that," said Mum. "You're so good at fixing things."

"I don't know anything about how Chrono-justers work. I'm not sure anyone does."

"The Potts!" cried Jem. "That's it. All we have to do is find the Potts."

"What Potts?" said Mum.

"The Pott family. Commander Pott," said Jem. "Look, it's all here . . . in the logbook."

The logbook of Chitty Chitty Bang Bang was 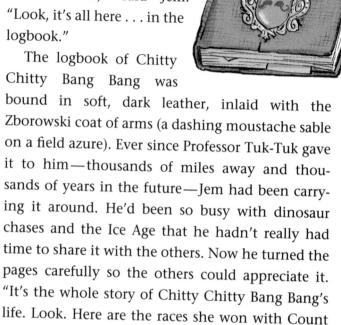 bound in soft, dark leather, inlaid with the Zborowski coat of arms (a dashing moustache sable on a field azure). Ever since Professor Tuk-Tuk gave it to him—thousands of miles away and thousands of years in the future—Jem had been carrying it around. He'd been so busy with dinosaur chases and the Ice Age that he hadn't really had time to share it with the others. Now he turned the pages carefully so the others could appreciate it. "It's the whole story of Chitty Chitty Bang Bang's life. Look. Here are the races she won with Count Zborowski—the 1921 Lightning Short Handicap at Brooklands, the 1922 Lightning Short Handicap . . . then there's a burnt page. The book must have been in the car when she crashed. Then there's a gap. All these pages are damp and mouldy. That must be when she was left in the scrapyard. Then look. New people. The Pott family. The dad—Commander Pott of the Royal Navy. His wife, Mimsie. Their children, Jeremy and Jemima. And these pages are

full of postcards and stamps from their travels—Calais, Egypt, South America, India. And look—in the back, all these drawings and diagrams. These are the plans for what they did to Chitty. Look, here's how the wings work. This one must be the time machine. This—'Monsieur Bon Bon's Secret Fooj Formula'—that must be to do with fuel. 'Fooj' must be some kind of fuel."

"Actually that's a recipe for fudge," said Mum, reading over his shoulder. "They just spelled it wrong."

"The point is, it was the Potts who changed Chitty from a racing car into a submarine time machine that flies. They're geniuses. If anyone can help us defeat Tiny Jack, it's them."

"This makes everything very simple," said Lucy. "Let's go."

"Go where?" said Dad.

"Isn't it obvious?" said Lucy. "We have to do three things. Number One: Find the Pott family. Jem, when was their last reported whereabouts?"

"1966."

"1966," mused Mum. "The year that England won the football World Cup. Your dad would love to go there. Let's go."

"Number Two: Explain to Mr. Pott—"

"*Commander* Pott," put in Jem. "He was in the Navy."

"We explain to Commander Pott that his great invention—Chitty Chitty Bang Bang—is in danger of falling into the hands of an evil supervillain who could use it to destroy the whole world."

"Oh, he'll be so annoyed about that."

"Number Three: Ask him to give us one last ride in Chitty—back to our own time and our own house. And Number Four: Make him promise to go back to 1966 and uninvent Chitty."

"*Uninvent Chitty?* You mean, let him take her away and never bring her back?" gasped Mum. "But that means we can't have any more adventures! I was hoping to meet Marie Antoinette and the Queen of Sheba."

"We should probably prioritize saving the world."

"Wait a minute," said Jem. "If Commander Pott goes back to 1966 and uninvents Chitty, won't that mean Chitty never existed? And if she never existed, won't that mean that we don't just not have any more adventures, but we won't have had the ones that we've had?"

"Say that again," said Dad.

"If we get back to our own time and he goes back

to 1966 and uninvents Chitty, it will be impossible for us to have had our adventures, because we had them in Chitty and she will never have existed."

"Interesting thought," said Lucy.

"You're making my brain hurt," said Dad.

"For instance, will Lucy still have video of the tyrannosaurs on her jelly-baby phone?"

"Please stop," said Dad.

"Are you saying we'll forget all about Chitty?" said Mum. "Because I don't think I could stand that. With Chitty we're the Mighty Tootings, but without her we're just some people from Basildon."

"Some people from Basildon who saved the world," said Dad. "Ready, Tootings?"

"Ready, Dad," said Lucy and Jem.

"I suppose." Mum shrugged.

"Setting the course for 1966! Time for the Tootings to save the world."

3

Dad slid the Chronojuster forward. The wind of time breeze whistled through the Tootings' bodies as they hurtled through history.

Dad's thought was: *Will we have time to see the World Cup before we go off and save the world?*

Mum's thought was: *It'll be really interesting to see all those 1960s fashions—the short skirts, the long legs, the bright colours.*

Lucy's thought was: *It'll be really horrible looking at those 1960s fashions—the short skirts, the long legs, the bright colours.*

Little Harry's thought was: *Dinosaurs?*

Jem's thought was: *You can set a course for 1966, Dad, but in the end Chitty will take us wherever she wants to go. She's up to something, and we need to know what.*

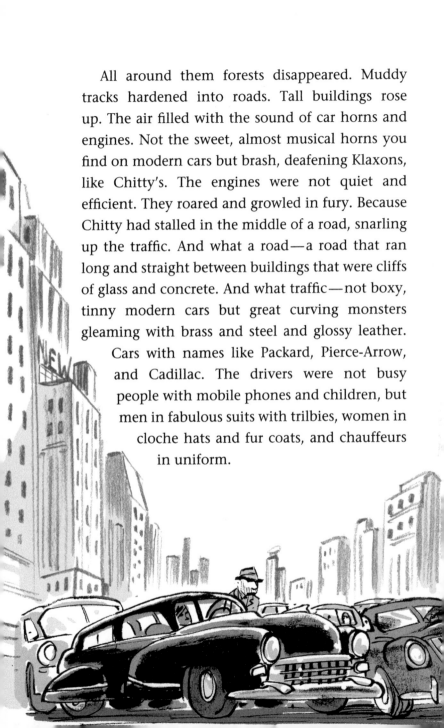

All around them forests disappeared. Muddy tracks hardened into roads. Tall buildings rose up. The air filled with the sound of car horns and engines. Not the sweet, almost musical horns you find on modern cars but brash, deafening Klaxons, like Chitty's. The engines were not quiet and efficient. They roared and growled in fury. Because Chitty had stalled in the middle of a road, snarling up the traffic. And what a road—a road that ran long and straight between buildings that were cliffs of glass and concrete. And what traffic—not boxy, tinny modern cars but great curving monsters gleaming with brass and steel and glossy leather.

Cars with names like Packard, Pierce-Arrow, and Cadillac. The drivers were not busy people with mobile phones and children, but men in fabulous suits with trilbies, women in cloche hats and fur coats, and chauffeurs in uniform.

"Basildon has got so congested." Mum sighed.

"I get the feeling that this is not Basildon," said Jem.

"I get the feeling that this is not the twenty-first century," said Lucy. "Judging by the hats and cars, I'd say this was in the 1920s. Judging by the fact that the sign says 'Broadway,' I'd say we were in New York."

"I'll get us out of here," said Dad, jumping out and tugging at the crank handle.

"Why would you want to get out of New York in the 1920s?" said Mum, looking around in wonder at the shops, the coats, the architecture, the faces. "Can't we stay awhile?"

"I suppose going through the Ice Age has damaged the starter motor," said Dad. "And look at this . . . no wonder she won't start." Great skeins of Cretaceous spider's web had got themselves wrapped around the crank shaft, and now it wouldn't budge. Car horns honked louder. Drivers yelled more furiously. Dad got stressed.

"Don't get stressed," said Mum.

Jem tried to help. He held the spanner, fetched the oil, apologized to the other drivers as he tried to unravel the prehistoric spider's web. It was surprisingly strong and sticky. It was just beginning to come loose when two immaculate leather shoes walked past him. A dashing young man with a curly moustache and a long silk scarf leaped gracefully onto Chitty's bonnet and put his hands in the air. "Ladies and gentlemen of this New York," he called in a rich, commanding English accent, "do calm down. Yes, you are stuck in traffic. But is that such a terrible thing? You are at least stuck outside my house"—he waved his hand at a magnificent brick building with a flight of steps rising up to the front door; in front of the door was a ridiculously tall butler in white tie and tails—"which makes you my guests. Crackitt, crack it open!"

Crackitt must have been the name of the ridiculously tall butler. And what he cracked open was champagne. Gallons of it. From inside the magnifi-

cent house, a dozen or more neatly dressed young ladies came tap dancing, all carrying bottles and glasses. In and out of the traffic they danced, pouring champagne for the motorists and passengers. But it wasn't the dancers or the champagne that interested Jem. It was the young man in the scarf. He had seen him before somewhere, or at least a picture of him. "Don't look on this as a traffic jam!" he was crying. "Think of it as an unexpected party." Then he looked down at Jem and at the hank of sticky white stuff he was holding. "I say," he said. "What on earth is that?"

"It's prehistoric spider's web," explained Jem. "Amazingly strong and quite sticky. Chitty got caught up in one this morning—or sixty-six million years ago, depending on how you look at it. Our car can travel back in time."

"Can she really? Extraordinary. No use to me, of course. I'm more interested in going forward in time— toward the finishing line."

Suddenly Jem knew where he had seen the man.

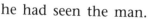

"Are you," he asked, "by any chance, are you . . . Count Zborowski?"

"The very same." The Count smiled, bowing his head. "My compliments on your rather magnificent car. A Paragon Panther, if I'm not mistaken."

"That's right," said Jem. He patted Chitty's gleaming wheel arch and thought, *I don't know why you brought us here, Chitty, but I do know it's not a coincidence that you stalled outside the house of your first owner.*

"I had a Panther myself," said the Count. "I was reliably informed she was the only one of her kind. But perhaps my informer was not as reliable as I thought."

"No, no," said Jem. "This is her. This is your car. This is Chitty Chitty Bang Bang."

"That can't be quite right, you know," said the Count. "I was racing my Chitty at Brooklands—Lightning Short Handicap, 1922—and I'm afraid the dear old thing went stark-staring bonkers, drove straight through the timing hut, dashed near killed me. Completely wrecked herself."

"That's her," said Mum. "The very same Chitty Chitty Bang Bang."

"Dad restored her to her former beauty," said Jem proudly.

"Even though I'm talking," said the Count, "I'm speechless. Really. I have no idea what to say. She looks even more beautiful now than she did when she was new. Sir, you must surely be the finest mechanic in the world."

"Well," said Dad, "if I were really that good, we wouldn't be having all this trouble getting her started."

"Step aside," said the Count. "I have a wrinkle for Chitty's engine that works on even the coldest morning. Crackitt!"

Crackitt passed the Count a short sword and a bottle of champagne. The Count took the bottle in one hand and the sword in the other, and with a single sweeping gesture, he sliced through the neck of the bottle, as easily as if it had been made of butter. Champagne gurgled out, bubbling over Chitty's bonnet.

"Oh!" gasped Mum, impressed. Lucy and Jem applauded, but, more importantly, Chitty's engine spluttered.

"Give the starter a shove, Jem," said Dad.

Jem jumped into the driver's seat and tried Chitty's starter motor. Her splutter turned into a roar. The Count placed his hand on the bonnet. The roar turned to a purr, as if Chitty recognized

the touch of her favourite hand in all the world.

"Hear that?" yelled Dad. "The word today is *we are back on the road again*."

"Champagne," said the Count. "An infallible cure for engine trouble. Has to be a good year, of course. This is the '98. Chitty was always very particular about her champagne. Chin-chin, by the way . . ." He took a gulp of the champagne and then offered the bottle first to Mum and then to Lucy.

A strange sound like a mouse being strangled came from somewhere inside Lucy. Jem, Mum, and even Little Harry stared at her. She'd never made a sound like this before.

"Lucy," said Mum, "I know this sounds unlikely, but . . . Did you just giggle?"

"I have never giggled in my life," said Lucy, narrowing her eyes, "and you know that."

"Oh, but what a shame! You do it so dashed nicely." The Count smiled and took another gulp of champagne.

The strangled-mouse sound came from inside Lucy once more.

"You just did it again!" said Mum. "You are definitely giggling."

"I'm not giggling," growled Lucy. "I'm thinking. For instance, I'm thinking . . . if this is New York in 1926, then alcohol is illegal."

"Oh," said the Count, "dash it. I always forget champagne is alcohol."

A little way farther up Broadway, the yowl of sirens split the air. It was the sound of the New York City Police Department coming to arrest someone for distributing gallons of hooch. Up and down Broadway, the other motorists threw away their glasses, leaped into their cars, chewed mints, and tried to act like they'd never touched a drop.

"What a dashed nuisance," said the Count. "I'm going to be carted off to jail for the rest of my natural, just as I was going to drive the most important race of my life."

Then, *"Chitty, chitty,"* said Chitty's engine.

And, *"Bang, bang,"* said her exhaust.

Chitty Chitty Bang Bang was ready to go.

The Count leaped in next to Jem. "How are you at getaway driving?" he said.

The sirens were louder now, but they were almost drowned out by the revving of the other cars' engines, the sounding of their horns, and the yelling of their drivers, all desperate for Chitty to move so that they could get away from the police.

Before Jem could explain that Dad was the driver and that he was only in the driving seat in order to press the starter button, Chitty barged away from the kerb and roared off down Broadway.

"Wait!" called Dad, who was still on the pavement. Chitty, of course, did not wait, but she *did* swerve to miss a fire hydrant, giving Dad just enough time to jump aboard as she swung around the corner into West Thirty-first Street.

"Smooth work," said the Count, ruffling Jem's hair.

"It's not me; it's the car," said Jem, clinging on to Chitty's steering wheel, hypnotized with fear as pedestrians and red lights whizzed past. But Chitty's engine drowned out everything he said.

"Bang! Bang!" yelled Little Harry.

"Yes," cooed Mum. "Chitty Chitty Bang Bang."

"Bang! Bang! Bang!" insisted Little Harry.

He's not talking about the car, thought Jem. *I wonder what he is talking about.*

"Bang! Bang! Bang! Bang!" yelled Little Harry, and just then a swarm of bullets buzzed past Jem's head like furious wasps.

"Trouble ahead!" called the Count. Two police cars were powering toward them, lights flashing. "By the way, they seem to be shooting at us."

Jem tried to keep hold of the wheel, but it spun out of his hands as the car swung left and then right.

"What a nuisance." The Count sighed. He poked his head up and shouted at the police, "I say! Be careful, can't you! You've burst our back tyre!"

Then he turned to Jem and said, "Would you mind driving her on two wheels? You know, sort of tip her on the side and keep her steady as she goes?"

Before Jem could speak, Chitty lurched over to one side, brakes screaming for mercy as she shimmied onto Fifth Avenue, on her two left wheels, her two right wheels up in the air.

"Perfect." The Count smiled, clambering out onto the side of the car, crawling along her bodywork toward the rear wheel.

"What are you doing?" yelled Mum.

The Count balanced on the running-board, bullets whistling round his head. "It's not too sticky once you get the hang of it," he yelled back. "Just like surfing. Except for the bullets, of course. Keep her up on two wheels, old chap, while I change the tyre."

The Tooting family watched in awe as the Count removed Chitty's back tyre while hurtling along Fifth Avenue at full speed. "Did it all the time at Brooklands," he said. "Can't afford to stop to change tyres when you're in a race, you know. Have to do it while you're on the move. There she goes." He pulled the flat tyre off and hurled it from the back of Chitty, toward the police cars. Swerving to miss it, the police cars rammed into one another. "That'll teach them to shoot at a chap while he's

doing his car maintenance. Now, where's the spare?" Within a few seconds, the Count had the new tyre fitted and was back on the passenger seat next to Jem. "Drive on all fours wheels now," he said. "Faster that way."

Just as he said this, a pair of police motorcycles flew out of the side streets, sirens blasting. They raced along, one on each side of Chitty.

"Couldn't we just stop and explain?" said Mum.

"Explain what?" said Dad.

"That we didn't know about their alcohol laws because we have come from the future via the late Cretaceous period."

The riders crouched over their engines, gripping their handlebars with massive leather gauntlets, staring into Chitty with their goggled eyes. They didn't look like they were interested in explanations.

"Trouble is," said the Count, "this is not the first time I've forgotten about the No Champagne law. Last time, I believe the electric chair was mentioned as a distinct possibility. Best head for the river."

"Why?" said Dad.

"The river is absolutely the only place to go when you're in lumber with the law," said the Count. "Head for the river, I always say. Not sure why, but it has a ring to it, don't you think?"

"What river?" said Jem.

"Not sure what they call it," said the Count. "But it's a jolly fine river. Just at the bottom of West Seventy-ninth."

"That's the Hudson River," said Lucy. "The official border between New York City and New Jersey."

Chitty was already spinning on her back wheels, skidding into West Seventy-ninth, rushing toward the Hudson River. Jem could see the funnel of a ferry boat and the dazzle of wide, cold water.

"You might want to brake now," said the Count. "River's coming toward us a little bit quickly . . ."

Jem could see an esplanade. An old man was feeding the seagulls. A family was looking over the metal railing, waving at passing boats. He tried to press the brake, but the brake seemed to press back.

"I honestly would brake now," said the Count, leaning back in his seat. "If you drive into fences too quickly, they break. I know because I've done it."

"Jem! Brake!" yelled Dad.

"Fasten your seat belts!" yelled Jem. No matter what Jem did, he couldn't make Chitty turn left or right. She was heading straight for the railings. "We're just going to have to trust Chitty."

"*Bang!*" banged Chitty as one of the police motorcycles tore ahead and dodged in front of her, trying to force her to slow down.

"*Bang!*" banged Chitty as she stopped as suddenly as if she had hit a brick wall. The police

motorcycle in front tore into the distance without noticing that Chitty wasn't following. The police motorcycle behind tried to swerve but too late, and hit Chitty's huge chrome bumper side-on. It spun round and round on its back wheel, blue smoke billowing from its tyres. Finally it toppled gently onto its side. The rider tried to stand up, but all that spinning had made him too dizzy.

The Count turned to Lucy. "What ho," he said.

"What ho," said Lucy, who wasn't sure what the polite response to "What ho" was.

"What ho, ho," said the Count.

"What?" said Lucy.

"Conversation is not my strong point, I'm afraid," said the Count. "Especially with ladies of the opposite sex. I'm all right as far as 'What ho,' but then I tend to get stuck."

"Very nice to meet you," said Lucy.

"Corking great coincidence strolling into you on Broadway like that."

A coincidence, thought Jem, *is exactly what this is not. Chitty wants to be here for some reason.*

Before he had time to think about that reason, a storm of blue lights flickered across the esplanade. Police cars. A fleet of them. Lined up across the bottom of the street, like a troop of cavalry, ready to charge.

"Well, toodle-oo," said the Count. "Perhaps I'll run." He tried to undo his seat belt, but it seemed to be stuck, and when he tried to slide out from under it, he seemed to get only more stuck.

Without even noticing himself doing it, Jem found that he had placed his foot on the accelerator. Such a nice, comfortable accelerator, so perfectly designed to fit your foot. You just had to press it. The hand brake, too, the way its ebony handle fitted so snugly and warmly into your hand, you just wanted to lift it up and let it . . . It was as though Chitty were whispering to him, persuading him to let her go. She was so difficult to say no to. Jem let slip the hand brake. Jem pressed the accelerator. Chitty rushed toward the blockade of police cars.

"Brake!" yelled the Count.

Chitty barged the police cars aside and tore across the esplanade.

"Brake! Brake!" yelled Dad.

The Count covered his eyes as the metal barrier splintered all around them.

"Actually . . ." said Lucy, as the car tumbled off the quay.

"In fact . . ." she said, as the freezing water rushed up to meet them.

"I think . . ." she went on, as Chitty rushed through the cold air. "I think you're going to like this."

4

Detective Finbar O'Shaunessy had joined the New York City Police Department in 1901 when he was sixteen years old. For twenty-five years, he had walked the streets of Manhattan, upholding the law. He'd dealt with robbers and riots, gangsters and gangs. He'd arrested a man who claimed he could saw the island of Manhattan in half. He'd seen Houdini escape from a straitjacket while dangling from a crane high above the river. He'd seen a man jump off the Brooklyn Bridge and survive. He'd met Charlie Chaplin and Babe Ruth. But in all that time, he'd never seen anything as surprising as what he saw on the esplanade that afternoon. A big jalopy of a racing car with a little kid at the wheel had smashed through the barrier and belly flopped into the cold black waters of the

Hudson. Detective O'Shaunessy had taken off his hat. He believed it was important to show respect when people died—even if they were bootleggers and joyriders. But the car didn't sink! It rocked unsteadily for a moment on the waves, then swung its bonnet round in the direction of Liberty Island and began to chug across the river and out of his jurisdiction.

"What in the name of Liberty . . . ?" said Detective O'Shaunessy, who did not know that under the waves, the wheels of Chitty Chitty Bang Bang were realigning themselves until they were all pointing backward. They turned, churning the water like propellers. Too confused to think, the detective waved his hat at them.

"What an absolute corker of a car!" said the Count. "I must say I had no idea she could float."

As if she had heard him, Chitty's engine went from churning to spinning as quick as a heart can leap, and the car sped through the water, shooting spray from her prow. The Tootings waved merrily from the backseat as she carved a great bow wave through the bay.

"I say," said the Count. "You really have done a marvellous job on her, Mr. Tooting."

"I don't know about that," said Dad modestly. "The fact is we've been having a bit of trouble with

the Chronojuster. It seems to be stuck. You don't have any handy hints about that, do you? Would champagne work, maybe?"

"What's a Chronojuster?"

"The Chronojuster is the thing that makes her travel through time."

"Never heard of it. She didn't travel through time in my day. You couldn't sail her, either. All I knew was that she went really fast. I seem to have underestimated the dear old girl. I couldn't take a turn behind the wheel, I don't suppose? For old times' sake?"

The sound of Chitty's engine deepened from chugging to purring. Instead of bouncing over the waves, she cut smoothly through them, as though inviting the Count into the driving seat. Jem shuffled out from behind the wheel. The Count stood up.

"Do you have a new car now?" asked Lucy. "A safer one?"

"I don't know about safer. She's certainly faster," said the Count, as he clambered over Jem. "Guess what I named her? Pretty clever actually. I called her Chitty Chitty Bang Bang . . . the Second. There. What d'you think? Got a bit of a ring to it, wouldn't you say?"

The moment he said this, Chitty's engine stopped purring and started roaring, and Chitty went from

gliding back to bouncing through the waves. Lucy grabbed the Count's hand as he struggled to keep his balance. Dad tried to reach the brakes, but it was no good. With a terrible splash, the Count tumbled into the dark, freezing water.

"Quick! A rope!" called Lucy, afraid that the Count might be left to drown as the car sped away. But as soon as the Count hit the water, Chitty's engine cut out. She rocked idly on the waves, making a low, watery, stuttering noise that sounded for all the world like a chuckle.

"See?" said the Count as, shivering and dripping, he struggled back on board. "She does have a temper."

They wrapped the Count in towels and blankets and used the heat from the pistons to brew him a mug of hot chocolate, while Chitty sailed upriver.

"Ice cream! Ice cream!" yelled Little Harry, pointing ahead.

"Too cold for ice cream, darling," said Mum.

"Ice cream! Ice cream!" insisted Little Harry.

"Too cold," said Mum, but Jem thought, *Little Harry is always right.* He looked where his brother was pointing—and there, pale and cloudy against the sunset, rising up from the waters, was the colossal figure of a woman; on her head was a crown and

in her hand—raised above her head—was what seemed to be a gigantic ice-cream cone.

"That's actually the Torch of Freedom," explained Lucy, "not an ice cream. We are looking at the Statue of Liberty."

As they watched, a fat full moon ballooned up behind the statue's head, like a silver speech bubble, flushing the giant face with moonlight. Music drifted toward them over the water, as though Liberty herself were singing. Someone was having a party at the base of the statue. Chitty puttered up to the Liberty Island landing stage, and the Count led them all ashore, saying, "Say what you like about Chitty—she could always sniff out a good party!"

At the base of the Statue of Liberty is a kind of fort. That night it was covered in fairy lights and pulsing with piano music. The shadows of dancers flickered across every window. A couple of elegant young men in beautiful suits were chatting in the doorway. They seemed delighted to see the Count.

"Count Zborowski!"

"Count Basie!" said the Count. "Tootings, this gentleman is the finest piano player in New York."

"In fact, I'm not even the finest piano player in this doorway," said Count Basie. "Allow me to introduce Duke Ellington."

"Count Zborowski," said the Duke.

"Duke," said the Count.

"I hope you are in good shape for the big race tomorrow," said 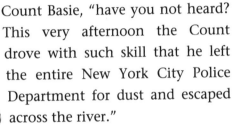 the Duke, "as I have a large bundle of dough riding on your victory."

"Duke," said Count Basie, "have you not heard? This very afternoon the Count drove with such skill that he left the entire New York City Police Department for dust and escaped across the river."

"With a driver of such skill, my money is safe," said the Duke.

"As a matter of fact," said the Count, "I wasn't driving. It was my young friend Jem Tooting here. Finest getaway driver in the business."

"Well, friends, here we have an excellent reason to celebrate," said Count Basie. "Let us step inside and dance."

"Oh! Yes!" said Lucy. All the other Tootings stared at her.

"But you hate dancing," said Dad.

"And it's been an unusually long day," said Mum.

"Sixty-six million years long, to be precise," said Dad. "I think we're too tired for music."

"You know," said the Duke, "everything is music. Out here in the cold, we have the music of the waves, the music of the gulls, the music of the sea breezes, and, if you listen closely, the music of the spheres. Indoors we have the music of Duke Ellington. Just another music. Only my music is indoors and warm, and accompanied by fine food."

"We *are* hungry," said Mum.

"Just for five minutes, then," said Dad.

As they walked through the doors, a lady with hair like candyfloss and lips the colour of raspberry sauce came at them with a silver tray. "Ice cream, anyone?" she said.

Little Harry really is always right, thought Jem.

Ripples of melody and thrills of rhythm filled the air. Champagne corks popped. Girls giggled. Cigarette smoked drifted and candlelight blushed. There were men in loud check jackets with scars on their faces. Girls in dresses covered in beads and feathers, with bobbed hair and sparkly shoes. And the strangest thing to Jem and Lucy was that everyone knew how to dance. There was no embarrassing

shuffling or stomping. People turned and spun and clapped in time to the music and in perfect tune with each other. This was the first time Lucy had ever been to a party that didn't involve pass-the-parcel and cake. It was the most fabulously beautiful event she'd ever seen. Up on the stage, Count Zborowski was speaking into a microphone.

"Ladies, gentlemen, and especially Tootings," he said. "Tomorrow I shall be racing in the greatest motor race in the world—the Prix d'Esmerelda's Birthday Cake. I had a new car built specially for the race, and a jolly fine car she is, too, with a jolly fine name for her—Chitty Chitty Bang Bang the Second. Until now, I have not had a mechanic. Tonight that has changed. Tonight I have found the greatest motor mechanic in the history of the world . . . not just a great mechanic, but a great inventor . . . Mr. Tooting."

All the lights went out apart from one big spotlight that was trained on Dad. The crowd cheered. Applauded. Slapped him on the back. Dad looked uncomfortable.

"Speech!" cried everyone.

"The word today," mumbled Dad, "is *I can't think of a word to say*."

"I'll pay you heaps of money," promised the Count. "And there'll be heaps of food."

"Thing is," said Dad, thinking sadly of the day he lost his job at Very Small Parts for Very Big Machines, "I've got these fat fingers . . ."

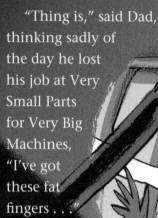

But no one heard him over the cheers and applause.

"You'll be marvellous," said Mum, pinching Dad's cheek. "I've always thought Grand Prix racing would suit you. Let's dance."

Jem and Lucy watched in horror as their parents moved toward the dance floor. Surely they weren't going to dance?

"What are we doing here?" groaned Lucy.

"I was just wondering that myself," said Jem. "Think about it. All the time we thought we were driving Chitty, it turned out she was driving us. Taking us all over the world to collect her old spare parts. She took us to the Cretaceous period to escape

from Tiny Jack. Now she's brought us here. There must be a reason."

"The reason," said Lucy, "is obvious." She was watching the dancers closely, wondering if she could learn the steps. "Or it will be when you're older."

"Lucy, what are you talking about?"

"Chitty is in love with the Count."

"What? Why would she be in love with the Count?"

"Because he's handsome and dashing. He hands out champagne to strangers, and he knows all these other counts and dukes, and he takes us to parties."

"She's a car. Why would a car be in love with a man? Why would a car want to go to parties? Wouldn't a car be in love with another car?"

"Cars don't fall in love with cars. They fall in love with drivers. The Count drove Chitty to all her greatest triumphs. They won cups and prizes together. People poured champagne on her bonnet. She misses him. She loves him. She wants him back. It's not easy to find a man as brave and stylish as the Count . . ."

"Hem, hem," said Jem, nodding his head meaningfully at Lucy. She looked behind her, and there was the Count, standing right at her shoulder. Had he heard all the things she'd said about him being

handsome and dashing and brave? Lucy felt hot and embarrassed.

"What ho," said the Count, glancing at the dance floor and taking a deep breath. *Oh, no,* thought Lucy, *he's going to ask me to dance, and I don't know how to dance, but I really would like to dance.* "What . . ." said Lucy, "oh . . ."

The "ho" came out as an "oh" because she had just seen the Worst Thing She Had Seen All Day. Worse than rampaging dinosaurs threatening her baby brother, worse than the New York City Police Department shooting at her, worse than plunging into the Hudson River—she saw . . . her parents dancing.

Why? Why? *Why?* Why were they dancing? They didn't have a clue! They tried to copy the other dancers, but they kept bumping heads and stepping on each other's toes. Somehow, instead of this making them want to die of embarrassment, it was making them laugh and . . . Oh, no. They had their arms around each other. They were going to smooch.

"I wonder," said the Count, "if I could interest you in a little . . ."

"Sorry," said Lucy. "Got to put Little Harry to bed." She grabbed Little Harry and headed for the exit.

"Me, too," said Jem.

"What," said the Count, as they vanished into the crowd, "ho."

Jem and Lucy didn't like Mum and Dad's dancing, but all the other guests were crazy about it. In New York in 1926, no one had seen anyone twist and shake like Dad before. Everyone wanted to copy it. An amazingly beautiful woman called Josephine Baker was the first to learn. She called the dance "the Toot" in honour of the Tootings. Seven minutes later, everyone on Liberty Island was doing the Toot. Seven days later, everyone in Manhattan was doing it. Seven weeks later, everyone in America was Tooting. And seven months later, they were Tooting in Brisbane and Belfast and Bali.

On the dance floor, Mum and Dad were surrounded by young people asking them to show them the steps.

"No, no," said Mum. "He has to go and lie down. After all, he's in the big race tomorrow."

"But I'm having such a good time," said Dad.

"Me, too." Mum smiled.

*

Jem was just about to step outside when a hairy hand with manicured nails and a big diamond ring grabbed him. At the end of the hand was a muscular arm. At the end of the arm was a broad, solid shoulder, and on top of the shoulder was a head with carefully brushed hair and a smile wide enough to hang washing from. The smile was unusually twinkly . . . *How could any smile be that twinkly?* thought Jem.

"If it is no bother," said the owner of the smile, "I would like you to make my acquaintance. I am known hereabouts as Mr. Lenny Man-Mountain."

"Diamonds!" said Jem, who had finally worked out what made the smile so twinkly: every one of Lenny Man-Mountain's teeth had a diamond in the middle.

"Well, Mr. Diamonds, I hear about how you leave the New York City Police Department for dust today in your amphibious automobile, and, I admit, I am most impressed."

"Thanks," said Jem. He was about to explain that his name was not Diamonds but Tooting,

when Mr. Man-Mountain turned to the beautiful young woman with the candyfloss hair and the tangfastic lips.

"This," he said, pointing to Jem, "is Mr. Diamonds, the celebrated getaway driver."

"Oh," squealed the beautiful woman, "let me give him a big lipsticky kiss!" As she peeled her lipsticky lips from his cheek, Jem found he suddenly no longer felt the need to say his name wasn't Diamonds, or that he was just a little boy from Basildon and not a New York getaway driver.

"I am most surprised by the youngness of his age," said the beautiful young woman. "It is impressive that he achieves so much in such a short life."

"This is true," said Mr. Man-Mountain. "Mr. Diamonds, if ever you wish to make a large amount of money by using your getaway driving skills to help me avoid the unwelcome attentions of the police, I will most certainly hire you."

"Sure," muttered Jem in a voice that he thought suggested that he was getting offers like this all the time. "Why not?"

Down at the jetty, Lucy was putting Little Harry to bed on Chitty's backseat. She wrapped him in a thick, fleecy tartan rug and made a pillow of his

little red backpack. It felt heavier than usual and was so full it wouldn't zip up properly.

"What have you got in there?" asked Lucy.

"Dinosaur," said Little Harry, stuffing it under the blanket.

"So that's where you're keeping your remote-control dinosaur? OK. You keep it nice and warm under there. And you can use my coat for a pillow."

Just as Little Harry was nodding off to sleep, a voice said, "What ho!" The Count leaned over the running-board and smiled at Lucy.

"Oh. Don't you like the party?" Lucy asked.

"It's an absolute corker of a party. I just thought I'd volunteer to do a spot of lookout duty."

"Lookout duty?"

"The party is stuffed to the rafters with criminal types and illegal hooch. Someone has to look out for the police. I tend to do that because everyone else likes to talk. I like to talk, too, of course, but I tend to get a bit stuck once I've said, 'What ho!'"

"I see."

"What ho, by the way."

"What ho to you, too. Are Mum and Dad coming out soon?"

"Gracious, no," said the Count. "They're the toast of New York. They seem to have invented this new dance. Would you like me to teach it to you?"

"Not now," said Lucy. "Or ever."

"Just looking out, then," said the Count. "Perhaps you'd like to look out, too?"

Lucy and the Count sat in comfortable silence on Chitty's long, warm bonnet. A faraway ferry sounded its hooter. The great cliff of the Statue of Liberty towered above them. Cascades of moonlight flowed down the folds of her skirts.

"Makes you wonder," said the Count.

"Wonder what?"

"Who she is. How she got there. Who built her."

"Who built who?"

"The Statue of Liberty. Look at her. She's dashed enigmatic, isn't she? Keeping the jolly old secrets of her origin and her significance to herself. She is a mystery mankind will never really solve."

"The Statue of Liberty," said Lucy, "was designed by the sculptor Frédéric Bartholdi. It was a gift from the people of France to the people of America on the occasion of the centenary of American Independence. Made in France, it was shipped in pieces and assembled here on Liberty Island. When the pieces arrived, they were driven through New York and given a ticker-tape parade. Bartholdi originally wanted the statue to be covered in gold, but it was too expensive. The finished statue is a hundred and fifty-one feet high."

"Gosh. Well, that's cleared up that mystery, then. It must be terrific being clever."

"You're clever. You can change a tyre while the car is driving."

"Ah, cars are different. You know where you are with a car. It's girls that confuse me. Take the Statue of Liberty—she's a girl—and gosh was I confused about her. Until you came along. Thanks a mill."

"Anything else I can help you with?"

"Do you happen to know anything about girls that aren't a hundred and fifty-one feet high and made of copper?"

"I am a girl."

"So you are. Now if you were a different girl—for instance, the one with the red lips and the candyfloss hair—speaking as a girl, what would you say to her if you were a chap?"

"I might say, 'Nice to meet you,' but I prefer someone dark and intelligent and a little mysterious and not so obvious."

LUCY
&
COUNT Z
↓

"Really? And you think she'll like that?"

"Why don't you just say, 'Hello, would you like to dance?'"

"I can't really dance."

"Then just say, 'Hello.'"

"What if she laughs in my face?"

"Why would she do that? You know, she might be in there right now thinking, *That Count Zborowski, he's so dashing and brave and handsome, why doesn't he ever talk to me?*"

"Do girls have thoughts like that?"

"Of course they do."

"Extraordinary. That's exactly the type of thoughts that chaps have."

"Girls or boys—everyone is just people."

"You know, I think I'll jolly well give it a shot."

The Count went back to the party. Thirty seconds later, he left the party with the girl with the candyfloss hair holding on to his arm. "Jolly excellent advice, Lucy," he called. "You'll never guess what . . ."

But the girl with the candyfloss hair didn't give her time to guess. She just blurted it out: "Count Louis and me are gonna be married!"

"*Married?*"

"I'm so excited. I am never married before in all my long life. Except that one time. But that was

in Arkansas. Also that was months ago. And who remembers that far back?"

"Not me, certainly," said the Count.

"OK," said the bride-to-be. "Let's go to church!"

"You're going now?" gasped Lucy. "But I thought you were about to drive in the Greatest Motor Race in the World."

"Crikey, the Prix d'Esmerelda's Birthday Cake! I completely forgot," gasped the Count. "I say, you wouldn't care to get married after the race, I don't suppose?"

"But, Louis! We've already told all these people . . ." People were pouring out of the party: Duke Ellington, Count Basie, Josephine Baker, Mum, Dad, Mr. Man-Mountain. They were all standing on the jetty, waiting to wave off the happy couple. "I want to go now. I'm going crazy waiting here," said the bride-to-be.

"There's no ferry until morning," said Lucy.

"That's exactly why it's so fortunate that your car is amphibious. Where's Diamonds? Diamonds is going to drive us."

"Who is Diamonds?" asked Dad, surprised to hear that someone else was going to drive his car.

"That would be me," muttered Jem, blushing as he stepped out from behind Dad.

"Oh, no," said Dad. "You're too young to drive. This is a big city."

"But Diamonds is the finest getaway driver in New York!" wailed the bride-to-be. "Please say yes. This is my happy day."

"Why would anyone need a getaway driver for a wedding?" asked Lucy.

"So we can 'get away' on our honeymoon, of course."

"But you can't just get married," said Mum. "What about all the nice things—a wedding dress, confetti, bridesmaids . . ."

"My mother told me, 'Always be ready for anything, especially anything romantic,'" said the bride-to-be, producing from her huge handbag a gorgeous silk-damask wedding dress. "If you'll all just look away for a moment, I'll wriggle into this. Especially you, Louis. It's bad luck to see the bride before the wedding."

Within seconds she was transformed into the perfect bride, complete with cloud-coloured dress, ivory veil, and a bouquet of snowdrops. "And look what I found!" she gasped, brandishing a fistful of very, very pink cloth at Lucy. "The perfect bridesmaid dress for the little lady."

"Oh, no," said Lucy. "Oh, no, no, no, no, no, no. No!"

"Oh, but, Lucy," pleaded Mum, "it's lovely."

"Mum, I've seen the back end of a pterodactyl and the front end of a *Megatherium*. But I have never seen anything half as horrible as that dress."

The bride-to-be began to cry big, mascara-smudging tears. "Ever since I am a little girl in Little Rock, all I want is pretty bridesmaids on my wedding day. That is all I ask."

The Count began to panic. "Lucy," he said, "help. You know all about girls. This one is crying. I don't know what to do. Can you make it stop?"

"I'll wear the dress," groaned Lucy.

"Really?" cooed the bride-to-be. "I do believe my mother will be so proud when she sees how prepared I am. Why, here I even have ribbons to decorate the car. And . . . all sorts of other things that may be useful."

As she said this last sentence, Jem saw her wink at Man-Mountain.

Dad would agree to let Jem drive only if he could sit in the front passenger seat alongside him. They set off into the bay, with Chitty's ribbons flying and Lucy's ribbons stuck firmly in her mouth as she sucked them angrily while Mum tied her hair into tight, tiny braids, each one fastened with a little gemstone butterfly.

"What do you think?" asked Mum, showing her herself in a mirror.

"You made my hair look like spaghetti infested with insects."

Out in the bay, the wind and seagulls were louder. Jem whispered to his dad, "There's something very strange here."

"Yes, what is it? It's very sticky," said Dad, who had put his foot on the roll of prehistoric spider's web.

"I'm not talking about that," hissed Jem. "That's prehistoric spider's web. I'm talking about this so-called wedding."

Dad bundled up the spider's web and tossed it onto the backseat.

"Sticky!" yelled Little Harry, patting it enthusiastically.

"Oh, Little Harry! Now I'll have to untangle you." Dad sighed.

"Dad, listen. Why would they get married if they've only just met?"

"Haven't you heard of love at first sight?"

"Why is Man-Mountain carrying a violin case?"

"Because he plays the violin?" said Dad.

"How can he play the violin? He's got big fat fingers."

"Are you saying," growled Dad, "that there is something wrong with fat fingers?"

"No, no," said Jem quickly. "I'm saying there's something strange going on here."

By now they had crossed the bay and trundled onto the jetty and into the streets of Little Italy. It was early morning. Street sweepers were cleaning the pavement, and traders were piling their stalls with fresh fruit and vegetables. Seeing a beautiful car with a bride in the back, the sweepers waved their brushes in the air. Whenever Jem had to stop at a traffic light or a road junction, the stallholders came with bags of sugared almonds for the bride and the children. One of them even sang to her.

"*Che bella sposa,*" he sang.

"How romantic," said the bride-to-be, then singing along.

Determined to find out exactly what was going on, Jem looked at her in the rearview mirror and said, "I was just wondering . . . What's your name?"

"That's exactly what I was wondering!" gasped the Count. "Darling, what's your name?"

The bride-to-be's eyes narrowed.

Lenny Man-Mountain growled, "What? You didn't hear what the stallholder guy said? Her name is Bella Sposa."

Lucy pointed out that "Bella Sposa" was just Italian for "Beautiful Bride."

"Well, *quelle* coincidence," said Bella Sposa.

"Bella Sposa is what I am called, and Bella Sposa is exactly what I am."

"How charmingly uncomplicated," said the Count with a smile.

"Thank you," said Bella. "I think you're uncomplicated, too."

The Count looked happier than ever when she said this. Even Mum said, "Aaaah!" and Bella Sposa kept singing that song. "After all," the bride-to-be said, "not everyone has a song named after them." Jem, though, was more suspicious than ever.

"Mr. Man-Mountain," he said, as they drove into Brooklyn, "I bet Bella would love it if you accompanied her on the violin."

"Bet?" said Man-Mountain. "How big a bet? I don't bet on anything under two g's."

"I didn't mean actual money. I was just using a figure of speech."

"When it comes to figures, cash is better than speech," said Man-Mountain. "Every time."

The Brooklyn streets were full of schoolchildren. They ran after Chitty, daring one another to jump up on her running-board.

"Look at the beautiful car!" they cried.

"Ga gooo ga!" answered Chitty.

"Look at the beautiful bride!"

Bella Sposa waved at them all.

A boy with very bright red hair jumped up on Chitty's running-board, right beside the Count. "Hey, mister! New York's finest shoe shine for your big day—ten cents?"

"Oh, my!" gasped Bella. "Look at his hair. It goes so well with the bridesmaid's dress. What's your name, kid?"

"Red," said the kid. "Like my hair."

"Such decorative hair. Climb in and you can be my page boy."

"OK, lady. It'll cost you a dollar, though."

"Wait," said Mum. "Hasn't your mother told you never to get into a car with strangers?"

"Sure, but my grandma told me there was no such thing as strangers, only friends we haven't met yet. Dollar, lady?"

"Yes, yes." Bella opened her big bag again and pulled out a white sailor suit and offered it to the boy. "Put this on. You'll look so dinky."

"You never mentioned no sailor suit before, lady," he said. "That's gonna be another dollar."

"Louis, darling, would you give this sweet little boy five dollars just for me."

The Count handed Red five dollars.

"Five dollars! Gosh, thanks, lady. I bet you're going to be the prettiest bride in the whole state."

"When you say 'bet,'" said Man-Mountain, "how big a bet exactly?"

"Do not bet with Lenny Man-Mountain, honey," said Bella. "Lenny Man-Mountain never lost a bet yet. Take a left, please," she added, as they reached the edge of town.

They turned down a narrow street. At the end, set back from the road, was an abandoned house, its windows shuttered and dark. Hunched over it, like a giant hippopotamus about to swallow it whole, was a vast, shadowy barn.

"Here we are!" shouted Bella. "I think the page boy should open the doors."

"Wait," said Jem. "This isn't a church."

"Excellent observational skills," said the bride-to-be, patting Jem on the head as she climbed out of the car. "I suppose that's important if you're a getaway driver."

"But if it's not a church . . ." pressed Jem.

". . . then it's a surprise. In we go. I am most excited. Groom first. Then our guests, Red and the

Tooting family, then my bridesmaid . . . and finally Mr. Lenny Man-Mountain . . ."

When Jem tried to follow the others in, Bella put her hand on his chest and said, "Stay in the car. Keep the engine running. We won't be long."

"But . . ."

As he tried to protest, Red came running out. "Rope," he said. "The big guy says he needs some rope."

"Why would you need rope for a wedding?"

"Does the phrase 'tying the knot' mean nothing to you?" snapped Bella. "Get some rope."

"We don't have any rope. Just that pile of pre-historic spider's web . . ."

Red picked up the hunk of spider's web and ran back inside. One second later, he was outside again, wiping strands of spider's web from his hands.

"Violin," he said.

"On the backseat of the car."

"You know, no one mentioned all this running and fetching. It could cost you another dollar."

"Just hurry it up, kid. Some of us are waiting to get married."

Red dashed back inside the barn.

There was a flash of flame.

A burst of gunfire.

A yell. A scream.

Man-Mountain strode out of the barn, followed by Red. He slammed the door behind them. "That concludes our business for today," he said. "OK, Diamonds, move it."

"What?" screamed Jem. "What did you just do to my family?"

Man-Mountain reassured Jem that his family wasn't dead. "At least, not yet they ain't. If you want to keep it that way, drive and drive fast."

"But what have you done with them?"

"Kid, you're the getaway driver, not a talk-show host," snarled Man-Mountain. "Just drive."

"I won't!" yelled Jem. "You can't make me!"

"Now we both know that that isn't true." Bella Sposa smiled.

"Say what you like," said Jem. "Chitty Chitty Bang Bang won't go anywhere without the Tooting family. She probably won't even start without them."

"Like a bet on that?" asked Man-Mountain.

"He hasn't lost a bet yet," warned Bella Sposa.

"I bet my life on it."

Man-Mountain cranked the engine, then leaned into the car and pressed the starter motor. Chitty started the first time.

"You lose." Man-Mountain smiled. "Now drive. We'll sort out the life you bet later."

5

As soon as the Tootings and the Count were inside the barn, Man-Mountain had opened the violin case Red had brought him and said, "Put your hands in the air."

"Oh, marvellous! Another new dance craze!" cried the Count.

"This is not a dance. This is a stickup. Put your hands up or I'll shoot." Man-Mountain took out a machine gun and fired into the air, frightening a lot of pigeons and making jagged holes in the roof of the barn.

"Here, kid," said Man-Mountain, throwing Red the ball of prehistoric spider's web. "Help me tie these good folks to that wooden pole there."

"OK, but it'll cost you. Another dollar at least," said Red.

*

The barn smelled of damp and hay. The only light came from the handful of sunbeams that stabbed through the holes in the roof made by Man-Mountain's machine gun.

"Weddings are so much more complicated than I imagined," said the Count. "I honestly thought there was going to be a bit of confetti, some prayers, and a cake. This is masses more interesting. What happens next?"

"Hmm," said Dad. "I'm trying to think."

Dad felt something tugging at his wrist. He tried to look around, but he was tied so tightly all he could see when he moved his head was Lucy's butterfly-infested hair.

"I suppose she did say we would be tying the knot," said the Count.

Now Lucy felt a tug on her arm. At first she thought it was her phone vibrating, but then Dad said, "What is that tugging?" so he could feel it, too. He tugged back. Something was on the other end of the spider's web.

"Little Harry?" said Lucy. "Where is he?"

"Little Harry?" called Mum.

A happy little voice answered from the dark. "Sticky!" it said.

Yes! Man-Mountain had forgotten to tie up Little

Harry. But the toddler had somehow managed to get himself stuck to the loose end of the spider's web. Gently Dad tugged at the rope, pulling Little Harry nearer and nearer.

"Sticky!" he cried.

"Yes, Little Harry, sticky," said Dad. If he could just get him near enough, then his youngest son might be able to help them free themselves.

"Bang! Bang!" cried Little Harry.

"Yes, Chitty Chitty Bang Bang is gone," said Dad. "But we'll get her back . . ."

"Bang! Bang!" insisted Little Harry.

If Jem had been there, he might have figured out exactly what Little Harry was trying to say. But he wasn't, so everyone just assumed that Little Harry was talking about Chitty Chitty Bang Bang.

That's why everyone was so surprised when Little Harry toddled out of the shadows saying, "Bang! Bang!" and carrying a machine gun.

"Now, Little Harry," said Mum, with all the quiet and calm she could muster, "put the gun down. Put it down very gently."

"Bang! Bang!" said Little Harry.

"Exactly," said Mum. "We'll all go bang-bang, and we don't want that, do we?"

"Please put it down, Little Harry," begged Dad.

"Nothing to worry about, everyone," said the Count. "I'm wearing my lucky cuff links. Nothing ever goes wrong when I'm wearing my luck—"

Little Harry had dropped the machine gun. The moment it hit the floor, it erupted, spraying bullets, thunder, noise, and smoke all around the barn. Wood splintered above their heads. Earth flew up from the floor. Wisps of hay swarmed through the air.

When the shooting stopped, the air was full of smoke and gunpowder, and Little Harry was sitting on the floor with a big grin on his fat little face. He clapped his hands and said, "Bang! Bang!" one more time.

"No one hurt?" said the Count. "Thank you, lucky cuff links. Oh, I say! What was that?"

The huge wooden pole to which Man-Mountain had tied them creaked, swayed, creaked again. It had been cut in half by a rain of bullets. Now it was falling over.

"If we all lean the same way," said Dad, straining. "Yes, that's it . . ." They guided the pole to the ground, and with a bit of wriggling and some lifting, they were able to slide the spider's web rope off the end of it and free themselves.

"That's better," said the Count, dusting himself down. "Now, where can my bride have possibly got to?"

"This is just a guess," said Lucy, "but Man-Mountain is a professional gambler. You are favourite to win the Greatest Motor Race in the World, which is just about to start. Man-Mountain has kidnapped you and left you here so that you can't enter the race. Meanwhile, he's bet on another car to win . . ."

"Of course!" cried Mum. "Chitty Chitty Bang Bang! He's bet a fortune on her, and since the Count can't enter, he's bound to win."

"But who would drive her?" asked the Count.

"Isn't it obvious? The best getaway driver in New York: Jem."

"My poor Jem!" sobbed Mum. "He'll be killed. Dad! Stop them."

"How can I stop them?" said Dad. "They've got a car that can fly and sail and travel in time."

"The finest getaway car in the world."

"What can I do? What can any of us do?" Dad sighed.

Bang! The barn doors burst into splinters.

Bang! A bomb of sunlight exploded around them.

"Chitty!" stuttered an engine. A massive machine, gleaming with chrome and smelling of petrol, rammed through the shattered door.

"Chitty!" it said again as it screeched to a halt in front of them.

"Sorry if I frightened you," said Jem, putting on the hand brake. "Going a bit faster than I meant to."

"What happened?" asked Mum.

"Well, Count Louis is the favourite for the Greatest Motor Race in the World, which is just about to start. Lenny Man-Mountain thought that if he captured the Count and held him prisoner here on Long Island, he could bet on Chitty Chitty Bang Bang to win instead. He was bound to win with me driving because I'm the greatest getaway driver in New York. Then he would pick up the prize and win a huge bet."

"That's exactly what Lucy said," gasped the Count, looking at her with disbelief. "How did you know?"

"It was obvious." Lucy blushed.

"How did you get away from them?" asked Mum.

"It wasn't me," admitted Jem. "It was Chitty. About a mile from here, there's a hill. She raced up it, and just as we were coming to the summit, this little blue light started flashing on the dashboard. I know better than to ignore Chitty, so I pressed it. Turned out to be an ejector seat. Just as we hit the top of the hill, the backseat flipped up and threw the two of them into the air. I saw them come down in a field. Then Chitty turned around and came to the rescue."

"Good old Chitty," said Mum, patting her bonnet.

"Let's see if we can get this seat back into place," said Dad. The backseat had flipped over onto Chitty's boot when it ejected Bella and Lenny.

They wound its muscular springs back into place and pulled it up again. As soon as it started to move, they realized that something, or someone, was trapped underneath.

"Am I dead?" came a boy's voice as a mop of red hair flashed in the bullet-hole sunlight.

"No, no, Red," said Lucy in a soothing voice. "You're not dead. You're just wearing ridiculous clothes."

"You got wedged under the seat when Chitty ejected Bella and Lenny," said Jem. "Chitty must like you, or she would've ejected you, too."

"Well," said Lucy. "At least we can change out of these silly outfits."

"Let me get this clear," said the Count. "Am I married yet?"

"No."

"Gosh, weddings take a dashed long time, what with all the tying people up and firing machine guns and so on. Or am I being impatient just because I'm excited?"

"No," agreed Mum, "it *is* more complicated than most weddings."

The Tootings looked at one another uncomfortably. None of them wanted to explain that a bride-to-be who ties you up in a barn, fires a machine gun at you, and then drives off in your car is probably not the bride-to-be for you.

"I have half a mind," said the Count, "to skip the whole thing and go straight to the Prix d'Esmerelda's Birthday Cake."

"Great idea!" said Dad, a bit too quickly. "Isn't that a great idea, everyone?"

"Of course, I could never do it really." The Count sighed. "It would disappoint the lady, and a gentleman never disappoints a lady."

"Speaking as a girl, . . ." said Lucy.

"Which is exactly what you are," said the Count.

". . . I think she won't be disappointed."

"Gosh, that would be terrific. But I say, why wouldn't she be disappointed?"

"Hard to explain. It's a girl thing. Girls change their minds a lot."

"I see. So . . ."

"Go and race. It's what you're good at. Chitty will get you to the starting line, won't you, Chitty?"

"Ga gooo ga!" sang Chitty.

6

The first person ever to own a car in America was a young man from New York by the name of D. Runyon Van Mellon. The car was a Renault Voiturette, which he had imported from Paris. The day it rolled off the boat, he had a quick read of the manual, cranked up the engine, and set out for his mother's house in Connecticut. It was her birthday, and the car was going to be her birthday present. D. Runyon Van Mellon hadn't read the bit in the manual about filling up the tank, so he just kept going until he ran out of petrol. The people in the small town where he came to a stop had never seen a car before. They were excited and generous. Some of them had their photo taken with it, while others went to fetch petrol. But when D. Runyon asked for directions to Connecticut, they had no idea how to get there. D. Runyon

made a guess and carried on until he ran out of petrol again. In that town, people had never even heard of Connecticut. Anxious not to miss his mother's birthday, D. Runyon drove on and on, increasingly worried, because whenever he stopped to fill up with petrol, nobody seemed to have heard of Connecticut. Even so, it was still quite a shock when the sun came up one morning on sand and cacti and men on horses driving cattle through clouds of dust. Hungry, thirsty, and very much in need of a change of underwear, D. Runyon Van Mellon had arrived in New Mexico. Three thousand miles off target.

D. Runyon was a proud young man. He pretended to have done it all on purpose, took a right, and headed back toward New York. It made him the first man to drive completely round the United States—an amazing feat of endurance. Anyone who cared to trace his circular tour on a map could see it was the shape of a gigantic birthday cake—a cake the size of America—which he had driven in honour of his mother. So the Greatest Motor Race in the World—the Prix d'Esmerelda's Birthday Cake—was born. It took place on the birthday of Mrs. Esmerelda Van Mellon. Every year thousands gathered to watch the start. A brass band blew a

bright blast, and, in an earthquake of engines, the Esmerelda Van Mellon Birthday Trophy—the longest, toughest, most dangerous, noisiest, most polluting motor race the world has ever seen—got under way.

It was always a magical and amazing day.

The Tootings missed it.

Due to the morning's kidnapping and carjacking activities, they missed the start of the race and had to chug slowly up to the field through crowds of people who were heading happily home.

"Better luck next year," said the race steward, rolling up his chequered flag and putting it back in his chequered-flag box.

"Oh, dash it all," said the Count with a sigh.

"Nice meeting you, Count," said Dad. "Sorry about the wedding. And the race."

"Shall we have a group photo?" asked Lucy, taking out her jelly-baby phone. "Just for the record. Oh!"

The "oh!" was because she found that she had a voice-mail message. The Tootings all gathered round to listen to it. It began with a blast of music and laughter. Then they heard Nanny shouting over the racket: *"Hey! Tootings! Your neighbours are*

*such fun! Poor Tiny Jack needed someone to play with,
so I invited a few people round and guess what? The
whole street came! Tiny Jack says it's his favourite party
ever. Come back soon. It makes me sad that you're
missing all the fun! I suppose you're all tied up."*

"Those people," wailed Lucy, "are having a party
in our house!"

"To the car, everyone," said Dad. "We're going
home right now."

"I thought we were going to 1966 first," said
Jem. "We won't be able to defeat Tiny Jack on our
own. If we go back on our own, he might get Chitty
off us. We have to get the Potts to help us first."

"Whatever we're doing," said Mum, "we need to
start. I want those people out of my house."

But when they went to get back into Chitty, the
Count was sitting in the driving seat. "I don't suppose I could take her for one last spin? I *have* missed
the old girl."

"Not really," said Jem. "We're in the middle of
trying to save the world from an evil supervillain."

"Jem!" snapped Mum. "After the Count has been
so nice—taking us to parties, inviting us to his wedding—it's the least we can do. Get in, everyone."

"But you said . . ." objected Jem, as they settled
into their seats and Dad cranked the engine.

"A lap of the park can't do any harm," he said

incorrectly, as he clambered aboard. Very, very incorrectly.

The moment the Count touched the starter, Chitty's exhaust backfired twice—*Bang! Bang!*—like an artillery salute. All over the meadow, people shrieked and ducked. *"Chitty-chitty-chitty-chitty,"* muttered her engine. The Count let slip the hand brake. She leaped forward, bouncing down the cinder track, throwing up dust, belching smoke, racing after the other cars.

"Count, it's been an honour and a pleasure," yelled Dad. "But if you could just turn her round . . ."

"The wheel won't turn. Also the accelerator seems to keep—well—accelerating."

Dad watched in horror as the needle on the speedometer crept toward a hundred miles an hour. A hundred and five. A hundred and ten. Fifteen. Twenty. Twenty-five . . . Every rivet in Chitty's body rattled. Her engine whined. Her passengers screamed.

"We're never going to make it!" yelled Mum, as they hurtled toward a sharp left bend.

For the briefest moment, Chitty slowed down into the bend, but then she powered out of it at a hundred and thirty . . .

"She always was good on the corners," yelled the Count.

"That's a comfort," said Lucy, "because there's another one right ahead."

"What?" gasped the Count.

"The road is bending back on itself as it descends an incredibly steep hill . . ."

"I see, but . . ."

It was too late. Chitty smashed through the fence that marked the side of the road and leaped into the air.

Jem was almost relieved when he felt Chitty leave the ground. *Surely now her wings will open,* he thought, *and we'll fly gently and happily above the trouble.* But no . . . There was a terrifying crunch as Chitty smacked into the rocky ground, barged through undergrowth, skittered over scree.

Below them they could see the next bend in the road and a convoy of cars speeding along the highway, jostling and dodging around one another.

"That's the race!" yelled the Count triumphantly. "We're in with a chance after all."

"No, we're not in with a chance," said Dad. "Because we're not in the race. The word today is *stop the car, we have a world to save!*"

"Are you sure that's all one word, old sport? It sounds like quite a mouthful to me."

Chitty swung onto the highway.

*

Motor racing is a dangerous and demanding sport. The great skill of it is to get your car into a good position, wait for the driver in front to take a corner a little bit wide, or come out of a turn just a bit too slowly, or fail to accelerate decisively enough down the straight, then grab your opportunity and roar into the lead. Most drivers like to do it with a mixture of cunning and courage. Chitty Chitty Bang Bang didn't bother with the courage or the cunning. She preferred force and fear. She didn't slide through the gap. She blazed up to the bumper, headlights glaring, Klaxon blaring. She shunted the cars in front of her, barged the cars alongside her, shovelled smoke at anyone who tried to sneak up behind. Drivers slowed down, pulled over, let her pass, afraid that she was some terrible mechanical demon.

Soon there was just one single car ahead of them. Unlike the other cars, it made hardly any noise. No clouds of smoke came shovelling from its exhaust. Quick, quiet, and creamy white, it threaded through the chicanes and slid round bends like a high-speed ghost.

"We'll never catch that," said Dad. "Unless it wants to be caught."

It seemed that the ghost car did want to be caught.

They squealed around a tight bend and saw

a long stretch of flat, straight road rolling out in front of them. There was the white car—half a mile ahead, dawdling along, as if it were waiting for them to catch up.

"Tinkety-tonk!" whooped the Count. "They want a proper race!"

He crunched down on the accelerator. Chitty shot forward and was sliding into place right alongside the ghost car. She really was a beauty—streamlined and glossy. Her silvery wheels rolled effortlessly over the rough road. Her windscreen gleamed. Her fenders shone. Her engine purred. At the wheel was the composed and immaculate figure of Crackitt the butler.

"Great gallons of gasoline!" exclaimed the Count. "That's Chitty the Second! That's my new car! Crackitt! What are you doing?"

Crackitt gave the Count a deep, respectful nod.

"It's no good. He can't hear me over Chitty's engine."

Crackitt, however, had thought of that. He produced a brilliantly shiny silver megaphone and addressed the Count through it. "When you were late for the start, m'lord," he bellowed, "I took the liberty of driving the car myself. I formed the view that a man of your brilliance and resource would very soon catch up with me, even if I was doing a

hundred and forty-five miles per hour. And that you would prefer to win the race if at all possible. If you're ready, sir, I'll leave the rest of the race to you."

Crackitt opened the door of Chitty the Second and shuffled over into the passenger seat. What he did not do was slow down. Both cars were moving at something close to a hundred miles per hour.

This didn't seem to bother the Count. He climbed right over Dad and opened Chitty's door. With no one in charge of her, Chitty careened all over the road, until Dad dived into the driver's seat and grabbed her wheel. The Count stood for a moment with a foot on both cars. "So you'll be doing the race with me, Crackitt. That'll be cosy."

"I'm afraid not, sir. I have ironing and dusting to do at the house. I made arrangements for my return there, the moment you were available." He nodded down the road. Speeding toward them, just a few feet above the ground, was a small yellow biplane.

"Propellers!" yelled Jem. "Duck!" The plane's propellers—like the blades of a giant unseeing food blender—were heading straight for them. "They're going to dice us like human pesto. And car pesto. Car-and-human pesto . . ."

"Louis!" yelled Lucy. "Duck!"

"What? Oh! Ah. Excellent suggestion," said the Count, bobbing his head just as the plane thundered over it.

"If you'll excuse me, sir," yelled Crackitt. The butler leaped up and grabbed the plane's axle as it soared away with him into the wild blue sky.

"*Au revoir*, Crackitt!"

"Indeed, sir, I'll have the kettle on for when you return."

The Count was still standing with one foot on each car, but now that there was no one in Chitty the Second's driving seat, this position was becoming more difficult to maintain. He clambered into the other car, then, just as he was sitting down, looked back at the Original and Best Chitty Chitty Bang Bang and at Lucy.

"What ho!" he called. "Care for a spin?"

"Oh!" said Lucy. "Yes. Please."

"No, Lucy," warned Dad as Lucy steadied herself at Chitty's door, ready to leap into the other car. "What have we told you about jumping back and forth between speeding racing cars?"

"Nothing," said Lucy. "The subject never really came up."

The Count held out his hand to her. She stood there with the freezing wind blasting through her hair, about to make the leap from one car to the other. She tingled with a sense of how fantastically, brilliantly wonderful life had been since Chitty came along. Before Chitty came, she would go for weeks—years, even—without seeing giant squid or rampaging dinosaurs or a gun-crazy gambler. The reason Dad had never given her advice about leaping between speeding racing cars is that it wasn't something she'd ever had to do. He'd given her advice on not squeezing the toothpaste in the middle and making her bed before leaving for school, because until Chitty came along, brushing her teeth might well be the highlight of her day. Now here she was speeding along, about to jump into the arms of the dashing young Count and roar off into the lead in the world-famous Prix d'Esmerelda's Birthday Cake! She was suddenly

filled with love for Chitty, for Dad, for Jem, Mum, and Little Harry, for taking her on this fantastic adventure.

"Jump, Lucy! Don't be scared!" called the Count.

What was he on about? She wasn't scared!

"Come and see how the new, improved Chitty runs!"

Those were probably not the best words to use around the Original and Best Chitty Chitty Bang Bang. The roar of her engine dropped to a growl. *"Bang!"* went her exhaust and, inevitably, *"Bang!"* again. These bangs were so loud that the whole car shuddered, and Lucy was flung into the back-seat of the Original and Best Chitty, which then thundered past her "new, improved" version and swung in front, waggling her triumphant fender from side to side, honking her defiant horn, and showering the immaculate white car with dust and fumes.

"Whoa! We're going to win this race!" shrieked Red.

But the new, improved Chitty slid easily past the Original and Best, with barely a sound. She did not waggle her triumphant fender or honk her defiant horn. She just got smaller and smaller as she sped into the distance. Chitty slowed down, as if she had given up hope, as if she didn't care anymore.

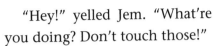

"Hey!" yelled Jem. "What're you doing? Don't touch those!"

Red had clambered over into the front seat. He was fiddling with Chitty's dials and buttons. "Man-Mountain gave me twenty-five dollars to make sure the Count doesn't win this race. We gotta beat him. Come on. I thought you were a great driver. Give me a hand here. Is this the thing to make it go faster?"

"Don't touch that!" warned Dad, trying to shove Red aside.

"Really, don't touch it!" shouted Jem, trying to pull Red away.

As they struggled, Chitty hit the verge. Then she hit the other verge.

"Don't touch that handle. Please don't touch that—"

It was too late. Red had grabbed the Chronojuster and was jerking it up and down in its slot when Chitty hit the bend and somersaulted into the air with every Tooting screaming.

She slipped the hand brake. Chitty turned an elegant loop in the air, came the right way up, spread her wings, and began a long, lazy glide toward the ground. Of course, when her engine started up, so did the Chronojuster, and once again they felt the bubbles of time breezing through their bodies.

"What's going on? It tickles," said Red, as he sank back into the safety of his seat. "It tickles! And . . . whoa . . . what is that?"

Far below them, as far as any of them could see, stretched a forest. Long, wispy clouds flew like banners over the vast army of trees.

"That's rain forest," said Lucy.

"I'm setting a course for 1966," said Dad.

"Which way would that be?" asked Lucy.

"Well . . . forward . . . about forty years forward."

"We've moved in time since then," said Lucy. "And we don't know in which direction. Red just bashed the Chronojuster up and down. That forest could be a thousand years in the past. Or it could be in some strange future. We need to go down there and find out before we move."

"Where would we land?" said Jem. "There's no space."

"Yes, there is," said Red. "Over there. See that gap between the trees? It has to be a landing site."

instance, and it will drop like a stone and smash into the ground. Chitty's brakes were different. When Dad pressed on them, she stopped and parked elegantly in the middle of the air.

"Shall we go back down, then?" asked Mum.

"Not sure," muttered Dad.

"Not sure what?"

"My foot is still on the brake. What if I take it off the brake and she starts falling? What if I take the hand brake off and the wings go in? What if—"

"Honestly," said Mum, "I think we should just trust Chitty."

Honestly, thought Jem, *I'm not sure we can.*

"We can't stay up here forever," said Mum, and reached across Dad for the hand brake.

"Wait!" said Dad. "Just let me think."

"Better not to," said Mum. "Whenever you think, it all goes wrong."

are sitting completely still, upside down in midair, breaking all the laws of physics."

"I never broke no law!" yelled Red. "You can't put that on me. Let me go!"

"Go when you like." Lucy shrugged. "All you have to do is let go of the wheel. But unless you've got a parachute, you'll probably find yourself splattered like jam a thousand feet below."

This is what had happened. When Chitty somersaulted off the road and then over a cliff, Dad had pressed on her brakes. Most brakes don't work in midair. Slam on an aeroplane's brakes, for

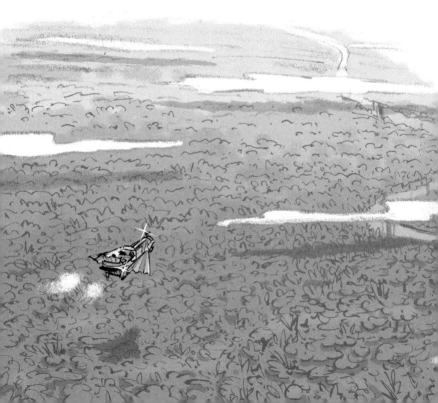

7

Where before they could hear nothing but the roar of Chitty's engine, now they could hear a skylark stitching its song into the blue afternoon.

Where before the air had been blowing round their heads like an ice-cold, turbo-charged hair dryer, now it was gently caressing their cheeks.

Where before the sky had been high over their heads, now the sky was nowhere in sight and what looked like the ground was hundreds of feet below them.

"Hey! What's the big idea?" snapped Red, who was holding on to the steering wheel, with his legs somehow dangling in the air.

"It seems," said Lucy, who—like all the Toot-ings—was sensibly wearing her seat belt, "that we

instance, and it will drop like a stone and smash into the ground. Chitty's brakes were different. When Dad pressed on them, she stopped and parked elegantly in the middle of the air.

"Shall we go back down, then?" asked Mum.

"Not sure," muttered Dad.

"Not sure what?"

"My foot is still on the brake. What if I take it off the brake and she starts falling? What if I take the hand brake off and the wings go in? What if—"

"Honestly," said Mum, "I think we should just trust Chitty."

Honestly, thought Jem, *I'm not sure we can.*

"We can't stay up here forever," said Mum, and reached across Dad for the hand brake.

"Wait!" said Dad. "Just let me think."

"Better not to," said Mum. "Whenever you think, it all goes wrong."

She slipped the hand brake. Chitty turned an elegant loop in the air, came the right way up, spread her wings, and began a long, lazy glide toward the ground. Of course, when her engine started up, so did the Chronojuster, and once again they felt the bubbles of time breezing through their bodies.

"What's going on? It tickles," said Red, as he sank back into the safety of his seat. "It tickles! And . . . whoa . . . what is that?"

Far below them, as far as any of them could see, stretched a forest. Long, wispy clouds flew like banners over the vast army of trees.

"That's rain forest," said Lucy.

"I'm setting a course for 1966," said Dad.

"Which way would that be?" asked Lucy.

"Well . . . forward . . . about forty years forward."

"We've moved in time since then," said Lucy. "And we don't know in which direction. Red just bashed the Chronojuster up and down. That forest could be a thousand years in the past. Or it could be in some strange future. We need to go down there and find out before we move."

"Where would we land?" said Jem. "There's no space."

"Yes, there is," said Red. "Over there. See that gap between the trees? It has to be a landing site."

"Well spotted, Red," said Dad, as he carefully adjusted the wing flaps and circled slowly toward the landing site.

Red shrugged. "You live on the street, you learn to notice stuff."

But it wasn't a landing site at all. It was a fat brown river. One of the switches on Chitty's dashboard flashed on and off as if the car herself was reminding Dad that she couldn't just land in the water.

"Mister! We're crashing! We're going to drown!" yelled Red.

"Don't worry," said Dad, flicking the illuminated switch.

Chitty withdrew her wheels and extended her floats. She skimmed the surface for a while, then slid onto the water like a duck landing on a pond. They chugged up a river that was so overhung with trees, they often had to duck or push them aside. Red and Jem climbed out onto Chitty's long, elegant bonnet, perching just behind Chitty's mascot—the Zborowski Lightning—and pushing the branches aside. The air was warm. Butterflies and dragonflies flashed in the shafts of dusty sunlight that filtered through the leaves.

"Maybe this is none of my business," said Red, "but where are we?"

"Judging by the density of the forest," said Lucy, "I would say Africa. Or maybe Amazonia."

"You mean . . . we're out of state? We're not in New York anymore?"

An alligator slid from the river's slippery banks into the water, speeding toward them without a ripple.

"No," said Lucy, "I don't think this is New York."

"Don't worry," said Mum, whacking the approaching alligator on the nose with her handbag. "We'll take you home as soon as we get our bearings."

"We gotta win that race, lady. There's twenty-five dollars riding on it."

"Yes, yes," said Mum. "Meanwhile, how about a game of I Spy? That usually helps pass the time on long car journeys."

"I'm no spy, lady. I did nothing wrong."

"I Spy is a game. You must have played it."

Red looked completely blank.

"But you must have played it. You just look around you. Pick an object and then tell us the first letter of its name, and we have to guess what it is."

"Do I get paid if you guess right?"

"No. It's just for fun."

Red looked blank again. It seemed like unpaid fun was a new idea to him.

"I ain't stupid, ma'am. I can give you the best shoe shine on the whole island of Manhattan. Ask anyone. Wanna know my secret? Well, it's a secret."

"But you don't know any games? Look. I say, 'I spy with my little eye something beginning with P.' Give it a try."

"Puma!" yelled Little Harry. There really was a puma following them along the riverbank.

"Very good, Little Harry. Now you try, Red."

"The secret of a great shoe shine is to spray water on the polish before you brush it off."

"I spy with my little eye something beginning with P," said Lucy.

The answer turned out to be a pangolin—a kind of armoured anteater—which was bowling along the muddy shore. Only Lucy had ever heard of it, so she won and gave her turn to Red.

"Does it have to be P every time?" said Red.

"No. It can be any letter you like."

"OK, then, P it is . . . for piranhas. Just there . . ."

Lucy had been dangling her hand in the water. She pulled it out hastily now. "You're supposed to let us guess," she said. "But on this occasion, I'm glad you didn't."

"Fish! Fish! Bitey fish!" yelled Little Harry, trying to reach into the water, to feed his own hand to the piranhas.

"No, Little Harry!" said Jem. He grabbed the strip of Cretaceous spider's web that was still stuck to Little Harry's wrist and yanked him back into his seat. "That was handy," said Jem. "Just what you need: a sticky and unbreakable leash."

They drifted upstream I-Spying otters and capybaras, macaws and rubber trees and waterfalls. When Red asked for "something beginning with F," no one guessed it and he said, "Folks!"

"What?"

"People."

"People begins with P."

"That's why I said 'folks.'"

"What folks?"

"Them folks there . . ." He pointed to the left bank.

"I can't see anyone," said Jem.

"Keep watching. See that tree? The one that hangs right over? Behind the root . . ."

Jem stared and stared. A branch twitched. There was a faint sound that could have been a whisper. "Is there someone there?" he asked.

"Ten someones," said Red.

"All I can see are leaves."

"When you live on the streets of New York City," said Red, "you learn to keep an eye out for trouble."

8

The people who were watching Chitty pass through the trees were hunters who had lived all their lives in the rain forest. They could pass through thick undergrowth without bending a leaf. They could run without breaking a twig. They painted their bodies in thick earthy paints for camouflage. Thanks to their ancient skills, they could pass, invisible and silent, through the forest. Once they'd had a look at Chitty, though, they couldn't be bothered with any of that.

When Chitty came chugging round the next bend, the Tootings found the banks lined with people. People who were not invisible or silent at all—people who were cheering and waving. Families leaped into canoes to follow the great car up the river. A group of young men paddled ahead of

them as if leading the way. By the time she hit the next bend, she was the flagship of a navy of excited canoes.

None of this was much of a surprise to the Tootings. Wherever they had gone in the world, people (as opposed to dinosaurs) had been thrilled to see Chitty—her gorgeous green paintwork, her gleaming exhausts. After all, Chitty was a work of art, and if you drive a work of art, people stop and look.

Beyond the bend, the river widened into a lagoon whose gently sloping gravel shores were crowded with more people, waving and pointing. Suddenly all the men on the bank raised their arms, shook their feathered bracelets, and yelled, "Chitty! Chitty!"

All the women raised their bows and arrows and replied, "Bang! Bang!"

They did it again.

"Chitty! Chitty!"

"Bang! Bang!"

One little girl said, "Bang!" a bit after everyone else, and everybody laughed happily at her mistake. Then they started to sing a song about Chitty Chitty Bang Bang.

"These people have a song about our car," said Lucy. "Doesn't that worry you?"

"They're just very excited to see us," said Mum.

"Maybe they don't get many visitors. Can you understand the words, Lucy?"

"They must be speaking one of the lost languages of Amazonia, which were all wiped out when the conquistadores arrived in the sixteenth century. So . . . no."

When Dad drove Chitty up onto the riverbank, children clambered onto her running-boards, her bonnet, and her bumpers. Teenage girls ran up and honked her horn. They greeted her like an old friend. Men came running from the trees with lianas and ropes and fastened them to Chitty's fenders and pulled her through the town, clapping and singing, "Bang! Bang!" and "Chitty! Chitty!" as they went. And what a town it was. The houses were all raised on wooden stilts ("for when the river rises," said Lucy). Children and strange, chickeny birds played in and out of the space between the stilts. All the houses were different—some had round windows, some had paintings on the outside, some had buckets of flowers hanging from every corner, some were covered in carvings—but none of them looked poor, and none of them looked grand. Everyone was dressed differently, but everyone's clothes were bright and new.

In the middle of the town was a market. There were piles of brilliantly coloured fruits and fat

vegetables and troughs full of fish. Unlike at the markets at home, people stopped and took things from the piles.

"Hey!" whispered Red. "Those people are just taking stuff and not paying for it."

"This seems to be a society that doesn't use money," said Lucy.

"You mean they're all robbers?" asked Red.

"No. They just don't need money. They share what they have."

"Wow," said Red. "We've got to get out of here."

"I think it's rather sweet," said Mum.

"Sure. Until they want us to share Chitty Chitty Bang Bang."

At the far end of the square was a house that looked completely different from all the others. It was not on stilts or covered in beautiful carvings. It sat square on the ground. Its garden was surrounded by a fence. There was a path leading to the front door. It had a pointy roof and four windows—though there was no glass in them. Where all the other houses had a platform you could climb onto, this one had a front door with a knocker on it. In other words, it was exactly the kind of house you might see in Basildon. Except it was in the middle of the jungle. Next to the house was a small, flat-roofed garage with an up-and-over door

that suddenly opened as they got nearer. Two big women strode out to meet them. Not big like your mum's friend who's too big for her dress, but big like boxers, or basketball players, or big, beautiful statues. Their hair flowed over their shoulders like shiny black waterfalls, decorated with clusters of jewel-bright feathers. The two women were so alike that at first Jem thought they weren't two women at all, but one woman twice. Their faces were identical. Their hair was identical. They were wearing identical clothes and identical feathers. When one of them raised her finger in the air, the other did the same. When one of them spoke, it was as though someone had pressed the mute button on the whole forest. Everything was quiet and listening, even the insects. This is what she said.

"Where on earth have you been? We've been waiting literally ages, haven't we, Imogen?"

"We really, really have, Eliza. We've been waiting for generations."

"Absolutely generations."

"You speak English?" asked Mum.

"Is that what you call it?" said Eliza. "We call it Chitty Talk, don't we, Imogen?"

"We do, Eliza. Can I say you're all certainly super-welcome here in Manau, but Chitty is the most especially welcome."

Imogen crouched down in front of Chitty's radiator and said, "Chitty Chitty Bang Bang, it's soooo wonderful that you've come back to us at last."

Eliza crouched down next to her sister. "We always hoped to see you," she said, patting Chitty on the fender. "Are you going to stay with us long?"

The whole crowd held its breath, waiting for the car to reply. The Tootings looked at one another. No one wanted to be the one to say that Chitty couldn't talk.

"Cars don't talk," said Red.

"Now, that," said Imogen, straightening up, "is very much a disappointment."

"How do you know her name?" asked Jem. "Have you seen her before?"

"Seen her?" said Imogen. "No. Heard of her? Yes. Waited for her? Double yes with bells on top."

"Some people said she was just a story, but now here she is. Real as rain and pretty as paint."

"I always believed in Chitty, but now that she's here . . . somehow I don't believe it! Can we touch her?"

"Of course."

All the people formed an orderly queue, and one by one they touched Chitty's bodywork. Some of them strewed flowers across her bonnet or twisted blossoms in between the spokes of her wheels.

"I think we're allowed to sit in her," said Imogen. "After all, we are the Queen."

"By all means," said Dad, opening Chitty's door so that the twins could climb in. "Are you both Queens, or is one of you the Queen and one of you . . . not?"

"We're both the Queen," said Eliza.

"It takes two people to be Queen," said Imogen.

"You can't be Queen unless there's two of you," explained Eliza.

"I must say," said Mum, "I love your bracelet."

"Really?" said Eliza. "Then, it's yours."

"Oh, I couldn't. Really . . ."

But Eliza held out her wrist to Mum and, as she did so, her splendid bracelet separated into six bright pieces, and those pieces flitted around her head. It wasn't a bracelet at all. It was a charm of tiny hummingbirds, trained to perch on her wrist or flit around her head like a living veil. Mum cooed in wonder as the hummingbirds flashed and thrummed around her.

"The garage is perfect, by the way," said Dad.

"You like it—it's yours," said Imogen.

"Oh, no, we couldn't."

"You like it, so it's yours," insisted Eliza, as though she were describing a law of physics.

"Do you like the house?" asked Eliza.

The only polite thing Mum could say was "yes," even though she knew what was coming next . . .

"Yours," said the twins together.

"The rule seems to be," said Lucy, "that if you say you like something, they give it to you."

"Oh, I love this one's hair." Eliza sighed.

"It's gorgeous, like gold," swooned Imogen.

"No!" gasped Red, clamping his hands on his head. "Don't let them take my hair!" But it seemed that all they wanted was to twiddle their fingers through his curls.

Inside the house was a long wooden table where baskets of luscious berries and shiny fruit snuggled up to sizzling slices of fish laid out on leaves the size of dinner plates. Wooden goblets brimmed with unfamiliar juices.

"I never saw this much food in all my life," said Red.

"It's all yours," said Eliza.

"Absolutely every crumb," said Imogen.

"Ever since the days of our great-grandmother, we've laid a feast out here each day, ready for the return of Chitty Chitty Bang Bang. And now she has returned. This is a great day. Please, eat . . ."

"What happened to all the food on all the thousands of days we never came?" asked Lucy.

"Every night the people came and ate it all. As they ate, they thanked Chitty Chitty Bang Bang. Even though she wasn't there. The feast was her present to them."

"Great-Grandmother's painting helped us think of her," said Imogen.

The wall was covered by a colourful painting. It showed a gorgeous old racing car with a handsome man at the wheel, an elegant woman next to him, and two pretty children in the backseat.

"She really caught Chitty perfectly," said Imogen.

"It's a super-perfect likeness. Every screw and every rivet."

"Every rivet and every screw."

"Of course, the people look nothing like you."

"No," agreed Mum, thinking to herself, *The woman is at least two dress sizes bigger than me.*

"Definitely not," said Dad, thinking, *I've got a lot more hair than him.*

"Nothing like us," said Lucy, who thought the girl looked revoltingly girlie.

"It's not us," said Jem, flicking through the log-book. "That is the Pott family—that's Commander Pott, the man who gave Chitty her green-striped wings."

"Never mind," said Imogen. "As long as Chitty is here, that's all that matters. Great-Grandmother said Chitty Chitty Bang Bang would return, which she has."

"And she said the car would solve all our problems. Which I'm sure she will."

"You have problems?" asked Dad, tucking into the biggest, juiciest mango he had ever seen in his life. "But this place seems so happy and wonderful."

"We have heaps of problems."

"Heaps on top of heaps."

"And heaps underneath heaps. Life is just stress and more stress here."

"With a break for stress."

"That's why we love Chitty Chitty Bang Bang," said Imogen, staring deep into Dad's eyes.

"We really, *really* love Chitty Chitty Bang Bang," added Eliza, staring pointedly into Mum's eyes.

All at once the room was filled with an awkward silence. Mum and Dad both understood that when the twins said they loved Chitty Chitty Bang Bang, the polite thing to say was, "OK, then, she's all yours." But how could they say that? Without Chitty to take them home, they would be trapped forever in sixteenth-century Amazonia. Because that's where they were. Mum looked at Dad. Dad looked at Mum. Parents looked at children. Everyone looked at the ground.

When they looked up, the twins and all the people of Manau had gone.

"Well, that was embarrassing," said Lucy.

"What else could we do? We can't stay in the Amazon forever. We haven't packed for it."

"Besides," said Jem, "we are actually on a mission to find the Potts and save the world from Tiny Jack."

"That's true," said Dad. "But honestly, you should try these mangoes first."

"I am really hungry," admitted Jem.

"Not surprising," said Lucy. "It's five centuries since supper and sixty-six million years since breakfast."

Maybe it was because all the food was strange and new, maybe it was because it was so fresh and juicy, but while they ate, they forgot about everything else. The fish was cooked in a sauce so surprising and complicated, their brains busied themselves trying to identify the ingredients. There were fruits the size of apples with hard spiky skin that, when opened, had flesh of different colours. They were bursting with a rich, sweet, sticky juice so delicious that all the thoughts that Jem might have been thinking—about how to save the world from Tiny Jack, how to repay the kindness of the twin Queens—dissolved.

"Gone!" said Little Harry. "Gone, gone, gone."

"No," soothed Mum, "there's plenty of everything left, Little Harry. Take as much as you like."

"Gone," said Little Harry again.

"Maybe he wants a drink," said Dad, picking up a steaming jug brimming with a dark, frothing

liquid. He poured some for each of them. It looked a bit like coffee but tasted like electricity and lit up your brain. Jem wondered what it was. Lucy said she believed it was chocolate.

"It doesn't taste a bit like chocolate."

"In the past, the people here didn't make chocolate into sugary bars; they made it into a hot spicy drink that was supposed to wake up your brain."

It must have woken up Jem's brain because the next time Little Harry said "Gone," he remembered with a sudden clarity that Little Harry is always right. If Little Harry said something was gone, then something was gone. Jem looked around the table to see what it might be. It was Red. Red had disappeared.

As soon as he got outside, Jem heard a frantic rattling noise coming from the garage door. Red was trying to tug it open.

"Red," said Jem. "It doesn't work like that. You pull it upward, and it kind of slides open. Here, I'll show you." But as he took hold of the handle, he thought, *Why is Red trying to open the garage?* So he said, "Red, why are you trying to open the garage?"

"Gonna take this car and win that race," announced Red with a shrug. "Lenny Man-Mountain said he'd give me twenty-five dollars to make sure Count Zborowski doesn't win the race. So I'm

going to go out there and win it myself. You can't stop me."

"Actually, I can stop you. You don't even know how to open the garage door."

"Come on, help me out here. Twenty-five dollars is riding on this!"

"You were really going to run off and abandon my whole family in the jungle for just twenty-five dollars?"

"What do you mean, *just* twenty-five dollars? Twenty-five dollars is a fortune. Do you know what I could do with twenty-five dollars?"

"Look around you. These people live in this amazing place and eat amazing food, and they don't have money at all."

"I *am* looking around," said Red, "and I am forced to conclude that this is not New York."

"I know this is hard to understand, but in our time, which is your future, the entire world is being threatened by a super-rich supervillain called Tiny Jack and his evil nanny. Only Chitty Chitty Bang Bang can save the world. Without her, everything is lost. That's what the Tooting family is doing here—we are on a mission to save the world. Do you think Dad would let twenty-five dollars get in the way of that?"

"What about thirty dollars?"

"No, I think he'd ask you to think about something more important, such as saving the world."

"What about twenty-nine dollars? Oh!"

He said "Oh!" because all the time he had been talking to Jem, he had been fiddling with the handle of the garage door, and now, quite suddenly, the door opened, sliding smoothly upward to reveal a cool, dark space lit by the busy, flickering glow of ten thousand fireflies.

"Wow," said Jem.

"I got to admit," said Red, "that is pretty. Hey, do you reckon if I took a few jars of those little bugs home, I could get cash for them?"

Jem said nothing. He wasn't looking at the fireflies. He was looking at the empty space in the middle of the garage. The space where the car should go. If there were a car.

Chitty had disappeared.

"I knew it," said Red. "They've been and gone and shared Chitty Chitty Bang Bang."

9

"The first thing we need to do," said Dad, "is ask the neighbours if they saw or heard anything suspicious, then we'll call the police."

"I'm not sure that early Amazonian societies had police forces," said Lucy. "Or phones."

"Let's ask the Queen, then. Go straight to the top."

A full moon hung above the square, silvering every corner of the town with its ghostly rays as they set out to look for the Queen. By that light they could see that it wasn't just Chitty Chitty Bang Bang that was missing.

It was everyone.

In all the village, there was not a flicker of light, not a whisper of conversation, not a single snore. The entire place was deserted.

"Marooned on the shores of the Amazon with no means of escape," said Mum. "What fun!"

"I don't think Chitty has marooned us," said Jem. "I think she's brought us here for a reason. Look." He showed them Chitty's logbook. The last place that the Pott family visited was Venezuela. "That's where we are. In 1966 they came here, and after that they disappeared. This is the last place they were ever seen. The painting of them in the house could be the last-ever picture of them."

"So the Pott family came here and suffered a terrible and mysterious fate. And now we are facing the same unspeakable doom."

"What exactly was the unspeakable doom?" asked Dad.

"I can't say," said Lucy, "because it was unspeakable."

"No," said Jem. "Chitty knows we need the Potts. She's brought us here so we can find them."

"Not only can't we find them," said Dad. "We can't find Chitty."

"It's strange," mused Mum. "The Queen seemed like such nice girls. You don't think this could just be some giant game of hide-and-seek?"

Red had never heard of hide-and-seek, and Lucy

had to explain the rules to him. "Can you play it for money?" he said. "Can we play it now?"

"Maybe we should wait till morning," said Jem. "It must be dangerous playing hide-and-seek in a forest in the dark."

"First clue!" yelled Red, running to a spot where a trail of deep, muddy ruts that could only have been made by a pair of wheels led into the forest. "The only wheels round here are on your automobile." He put back his head and yelled, "Coming! Ready or not!" and plunged into the jungle.

Following a jungle path is very different from sailing up a jungle river. On a jungle river, you have space to look around. You can see where you're going and where you have been. On the jungle floor, the trees crowd together so closely that every few paces you have to change direction, squeeze through a gap, clamber over a stump, wriggle round a knot of bushes. When you look back, there's nothing to see but a confusion of trunks and branches smothering the floor.

"How could they possibly have got Chitty through here?" asked Lucy.

"They did it, though," said Red. "Look. We got tracks here. Here. And here. Could be they can spot paths that we can't. Come on."

Red plunged happily in and out of the shadows. The others tried to keep up, but he vanished from view.

"Dinner!" shouted Little Harry.

"Oh, Little Harry, we've only just eaten," scolded Mum.

"Dinner!"

"Not now, Little Harry. We're looking for Red."

"Dinner!"

Only Jem noticed that Little Harry was pointing at something dangling from an overhanging branch. At first it was hard to figure out what the something was. It seemed as though part of the branch had been decorated with a colourful mosaic of tiny tiles, with an arm sticking out of the side. It was only after he'd looked at it from several different angles that Jem figured out what it was. Little Harry was right, of course. It was dinner. But it wasn't a little boy eating dinner. It was a little boy *being* dinner. A gigantic anaconda had trapped Red in its coils and wrapped itself around him.

"Mum!" gasped Jem.

Red's arm was waving frantically, so he must still be alive in there, somewhere among the glistening yards of hungry snake muscle.

"Hey!" yelled Mum. "Stop that right now!"

When Mum did her Furious Mum Yell at Lucy

or Jem, they always dropped what they were doing immediately. It didn't have the same effect on the anaconda. Possibly because snakes are deaf. Mum, however, was not used to being ignored. It gave her an amazing burst of strength. She leaped forward, grabbed the back end of the snake, and swung from it with all her weight.

"Careful, dearest," said Dad.

Mum's mighty swing brought snake and branch crashing down. The moment it hit the ground, the snake uncoiled and Red's head popped out.

"Help!" he gasped, wheezing.

"Never fear," said Mum. The snake was already tightening its grip again, but Mum had Red by the neck and was pulling him out from between the narrowing coils. She managed to get him almost clear when the snake rolled its eyes as though concentrating really hard, opened its mouth wider than you could ever have imagined possible, and swallowed Red up to his knees.

"Is this part of the game?" gasped Red. "Because if it is, can we stop playing now? I really don't like it."

Mum turned to Dad. "I'll hold on to Red," she said. "You wrench the anaconda's jaws open."

"My anaconda-fighting skills are limited," said Dad, "but the word today is *Don't worry, Red.*

Tootings to the rescue." Dad bravely tucked his hands in the anaconda's jaw and pulled it wider than ever. By now Red was thoroughly lubricated with snake spit, so he slid out easily when Mum pulled on him.

"Thanks, ma'am, you saved my life," breathed Red, as Mum wiped off the snake spit with a banana leaf. "Does that mean I have to give you money?"

"No, Red, don't be silly." Mum smiled.

"Help!" yelled Dad. No sooner had the snake lost its grip on Red than it had whipped its tail around Dad's waist and begun to squeeze. "Help! Help!"

"Help him, Mum!" pleaded Jem.

"He's just teasing." Mum smiled. "Of course your Dad knows how to escape from a hungry anaconda. Hasn't he escaped from dinosaurs and gangsters already today?"

"Actually I really do need help," gasped Dad, turning slightly blue.

"Your father knows how to escape from every difficult situation. He knows that all you have to do if you're attacked by a boa constrictor or an anaconda is make yourself as big as possible — by holding your breath or sticking your elbows out — and then suddenly make yourself as small as possible by breathing out and tucking your elbows in. Then the snake loses its grip, and you can just wriggle out. That's it. See? He's done it. He was teasing you."

Dad stood for a while, with one arm held in the air, saying, "I'm fine. Absolutely fine," over and over while trying to get his breath. "I really was teasing you."

"What did I tell you," said Mum. "Tease. Your father is a hero. He wouldn't let a snake defeat or even delay him. And now he's going to find Chitty for us."

Great spears of early-morning sunlight were stabbing through the branches. Butterflies with wings like sheets of wrapping paper unfolded themselves. The creaking of insects rolled across the forest floor like a wave. Now that it was daylight, they could see clearly that there was no path. Nothing to follow. No reason to go this way or that.

"This is probably that unspeakable fate you were talking about, Lucy," said Mum.

"Yes, the Pott family probably wandered aimlessly in the endless jungle, maddened by insects, weakened by thirst and fever, and finally eaten by snakes. Maybe their bones were in the stomach of the very snake that tried to eat Red."

"*Ga gooo ga!*"

"What was that?" exclaimed Lucy.

"*Ga gooo ga!*"

"Chitty Chitty Bang Bang!" said Little Harry—right as usual.

"It's coming from somewhere high up."

They could see now that one path slanted steeply upward, through the trees, toward the top of a hill. As they slogged up it, the sounds around them changed. The forest buzzed with the noise of insects, but as the path wound higher, the buzz turned to the chiming of birdsong. Higher still, the birdsong was drowned out by the booming of frogs and the natter of monkeys. Suddenly they could see air through the branches and for the first time realized how big the forest was. Clouds of leaves rolled by below like a separate green sky. There was even a low, constant roar, like the waves of the sea.

"Is that a motorway?" said Jem.

"It can't be."

"But what could it be?"

They climbed onward. All of them were thinking the same thoughts: *What if this is the wrong way? What if we get lost? How could they possibly have got Chitty up here?*

"Look!" yelled Red, pointing to a long, snake-like object glinting in the mud. "Another snake! Mrs. Tooting! Help me!"

"That's no snake," exclaimed Mum. "That's Chitty's exhaust pipe. We're getting warmer."

"On the one hand," said Dad, "that's good news. On the other, it does mean that bits are falling off Chitty. Keep an eye open, everyone. We can't afford to lose any of her parts."

The next few hundred yards of squeezing and scrambling took hours. On the way they gathered up one of Chitty's door handles, a spring from her upholstery, her toolbox, and her back bumper. All the time, the roaring got louder and louder. They came to a place where the ground rose almost vertically for twenty feet. The motorway noise was deafening now.

"We could climb up the tree and get onto the top of the bank this way," said Mum, shinnying up the nearest trunk. "It's not as hard as it looks," she called. "All you have to do is . . . Oh."

"Mum?"

"Mum?"

There was no answer. Dad went straight up the tree trunk after her, lugging bits of Chitty with him.

"Can you see her? Is she all right?" called Jem.

"She's . . . Oh," called Dad.

Then there was silence again.

Little Harry and Jem and then Lucy and Red swarmed up the trunk to see what had happened. But when they got to the top, they, too, could only think of one thing to say. Namely, "Oh."

The noise that they had heard rumbling down the hillside and through the jungle was not a motorway. It was a waterfall. The highest waterfall anyone on this planet has ever seen. So high that its top was lost in the clouds. Looking up at it, it seemed that heaven had sprung a leak. Water fell like a vertical river, fell so far that most of it spread into a curtain of mist on the way down. Then dropped into a wide, black chasm in the side of the mountain. Bridging that chasm, shrouded in mist from the thundering water, was something more amazing even than that amazing cascade. It was a town. A town of houses and streets and towers and gardens. A town that arched like a rainbow across the deep black cliffs. A town that shone like a sunset.

A town whose buildings were made entirely of gold.

10

"El Dorado—the city of gold," gasped Jem. "I thought it was just a story."

"The Queen thought Chitty was just a story," said Lucy. "But we turned out to be real. Now the lost city of El Dorado turns out to be not so lost after all."

"Your father is so clever." Mum smiled. "Some people can't even find their own lost car keys. Your father has found a legendary lost city of gold."

"Obviously it's quite exciting that we've found a legendary lost city of gold," said Jem. "But we must remember it's not what we were looking for."

"Isn't that always the way," said Mum. "You're looking for one thing, but you find something else altogether. It's the same when you lose your car keys and find your phone as it is when you lose a time-travelling car and find a legendary city of gold."

"This place must be worth a lot more than twenty-five dollars," said Red. "It's got to be worth a hundred dollars at least."

"A hundred million dollars would be nearer the mark," said Lucy.

"But what we really need is Chitty," said Jem.

A haze of tiny droplets from the waterfall wrapped the town in a mist, like tissue paper. Even though the street seemed to be deserted, it was full of movement. There were ghostly presences every-where—shadows dancing on the mist, reflections washing across the golden walls, hummingbirds flirting and whirring, and the waterfall roaring like an invisible football crowd. The first building they came to was a little domed house with a sign on the door that read:

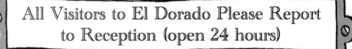

All Visitors to El Dorado Please Report to Reception (open 24 hours)

Dad pushed open the golden door, which was warm to the touch and which moved on its hinges as smoothly and silently as silk. He stepped inside. The rest crowded in after him, and the door swished shut. The dome was made of gold that was beaten as thin as paper. Sunlight poured through it,

making everything it touched glow golden. Mum and Dad looked like statues. The long, thick, curling things on the floor looked like golden pillows and cushions. Except that they were moving. Not to mention hissing.

"Oh, for heaven's sake," huffed Mum, "not MORE snakes!"

There were half a dozen hungry anacondas in there.

Dad put down the parts of Chitty

he was carrying and tried the door, but there was no handle on the inside. "Reception" wasn't reception at all. It was a trap.

"This must definitely be the unspeakable fate of the Pott family," said Lucy. "Digested in a walk-in snake pit. If we look around, we'll find their bones. Then we'll die." As she said this, one of the snakes tried to gulp down her arm.

"This is so annoying," said Mum, rolling up her sleeves. "Come on, everyone, lend a hand."

The Tooting family spent the next ten minutes anaconda-wrestling. Every now and then, Mum would coach them—shouting tips or showing them new grips. "Watch your dad," she'd say. "He's unbeatable."

It was Red who spotted the last undefeated snake trying to sneak off down a little tunnel. When he dragged it back into the pit by its tail, he found that it had a piece of rope clamped between its jaws. When Red pulled it, bells rang merrily somewhere overhead.

"It must be some sort of alarm," said Jem.

Within a few seconds, the door opened and in walked the Queen.

"How absolutely lovely of you to call," said Imogen, scooping up the last conscious snake and draping it round her neck.

"Welcome to El Dorado," said Eliza. "I see you have already met our pets."

"They tried to eat us," said Mum.

"You mustn't be cross with them. They're trained to eat visitors," said Eliza.

"Absolutely trained to. Trained them ourselves," said Imogen.

"We have to keep El Dorado a secret," explained Eliza, "and snakes seemed much the best way to do it."

"That doesn't work with us," said Mum. "No snake alive could defeat my husband."

"Please," said Dad, who was still trying to get his breath back. "You took our car. We need it back."

Imogen and Eliza looked shocked. "You can't

ask for a present back once you've given it. That's the height of rudeness, isn't it, Imogen?" said Eliza.

"Height *and* depth of it," said Imogen. "Don't be so rude."

"I think you'll find," said Mum, "that the height of rudeness is trying to feed your guests to snakes."

"Anyway," said Dad, "we didn't give you the car as a present. You just took it."

"Well, now, there's a reason for that, isn't there, Imogen?"

"There certainly is. When you came to us, we gave you all kinds of presents. Whatever you said you liked, we gave you."

"Which is only polite."

"If someone admires something, it's only polite to give it to them."

"And we admired Chitty Chitty Bang Bang like billy-o."

"We admired her twice."

"But you never gave her to us."

"Not so much as her spare tyre."

"That was rude."

"That was unusually rude."

"But our great-grandmother always said, 'When someone is rude, just ignore them.'"

"So we ignored your rudeness."

"And we took Chitty. Simple."

"It was simple till you tried to feed us to anacondas."

"We are a bit unpredictable at times."

"Would you like a tour of El Dorado? We're ever so proud of it."

"Ever so, ever so."

Everyone followed the unpredictable Queen out of the snake pit and into the streets of gold. Whenever they passed a house, windows would open and people would lean out and wave to the Queen. Or they would come running out of their front doors to tell them news. Or share problems. A couple of times, the Queen had to stop to examine a door that wouldn't shut properly or a dripping tap. Dad had brought Chitty's toolbox, so he was happy to help.

In the middle of the town square, mounted on a pedestal of gold, was a diamond as big as your head.

"What's that?" asked Red.

"That," said Imogen, "is a diamond as big as your head."

"We call it," said Eliza, "the Diamond As Big As Your Head. In the evening we come down here and watch the changing reflections of the sunset play in the depths of the diamond's heart."

"It's like a very early form of television," said

Lucy. "A very early, unbelievably expensive, and slightly abstract form of television."

"What's television?" asked Red.

The square led to a platform that jutted right out over the waterfall. From here they could see the whole rain forest and the great Orinoco River winding through it, as clearly as if it had been drawn on a map.

"This is where we were standing," said Imogen, "when we first saw Chitty heading upriver toward us."

"I had to dash off," said Eliza, "and get everyone to go back down to the village made of wood so we could pretend that we all lived there."

"Why?"

"People are always looking for El Dorado, City of Gold. If they find a perfectly nice city of wood where the City of Gold is supposed to be, it puts them off the scent."

"But it is so much stress."

"Such stress," agreed Imogen. "That's why you have to be two people to be Queen. Because El Dorado is two towns. One real and one pretend."

"But why?" asked Lucy. "A town made of gold should be one of the wonders of the world."

"If I had all this gold," said Red, "I wouldn't want anyone to see it. I'd keep it all to myself, too. Hats off to you, girls. You're doing the right thing."

"It's simple really," said Imogen. "El Dorado— City of Gold—used to be spread out all along the riverbank. But, as you know, people here love to give presents and get presents. People gave us all kinds of things—fish, pots, pigs, boats . . ."

"Those leaves that make your head feel funny when you chew them."

"They were fun. But all people wanted in return was gold. Everyone wanted gold."

ALL THE GOLD IN THE WORLD! (SO FAR DISCOVERED)

"We didn't mind giving them a bit of gold, of course, Eliza."

"No, of course not, but gold is so useful, you know, for plumbing and roofing. It's easy to cut. It's not too cold and best of all it doesn't go rusty."

"We'd just got the town how we liked it . . ."

". . . when people started taking it away, bit by bit. Imagine."

"Imagine people coming round taking your roof. Or your downspout."

"But we hated to offend anyone by saying, 'No, you can't have our golden downspout.'"

"Or our golden roof."

"So we moved the whole golden town up to the waterfall and pretended that all our gold had gone."

"It's nice that no one is offended."

"But it's a stress pretending to live in one place when you really live somewhere else."

"Double stress," agreed Eliza.

"Double stress multiplied by both of us," said Imogen.

"But now we've got Chitty. She will sort out all our problems."

"That's what our great-grandmother promised us. 'Chitty Chitty will come back,' she said, 'and solve all your problems.'"

"And she never lied."

"Well, well, pip-pip, must go and rule," said Imogen.

"Pip-pip, rule-rule," said Eliza. "A monarch's work is never done."

From the golden platform, the Tootings looked out over the unending jungle.

"What are we going to do?" said Jem.

"Search the city until we find Chitty," said Dad. "Then go straight back home, where no one tries to feed you to the snakes."

"We're in a legendary city of gold," said Mum. "The least we can do is take some photographs. Lucy . . ."

Lucy took out her jelly-baby phone, then almost dropped it. Staring at her from the screen was Nanny.

"Well, well, well." Nanny smiled. "Look where you are! The legendary Lost City of Gold. You know

what I think? I think the moment Tiny Jack gets his hands on Chitty, that will be the first place he'll go. He just loves gold, bless his heart. He'll go straight there, and he'll bring every scrap home."

"Home?" said Dad.

"That's what we call Zborowski Terrace now. We just love it here. It's so cosy!"

Lucy hung up.

"Don't answer it anymore," said Mum. "It upsets your father."

"I didn't answer it then," said Lucy. "Somehow she was there waiting for me when I picked it up."

"That was a good idea about taking the gold away," said Red. "We could take a truckload and whoop it up in Manhattan. Then when it's all gone, come back, get another truckload, and whoop it up again."

"Somehow I don't think the Queen is going to let us get away with that," said Lucy. "We have to do things their way."

"What do you mean?"

"We have to give them presents. If we give them good-enough presents, they just might give Chitty back."

"But we don't have any presents," said Mum.

"We're from the future," said Jem. "We must have something that they would think was amazing.

What about Little Harry's remote-control dinosaur? I bet they'd think that was worth a Chitty."

"Brilliant idea!" said Dad.

Little Harry knew straightaway what they were talking about. He clutched his little red backpack to his chest and said, "No, no, no."

"We'll find you another one," soothed Mum, "as soon as we get home. Two, in fact . . ." But when she got the backpack open, there was no dinosaur in there. "What happened? Did you leave it in Chitty? Did you lose it in New York?"

Little Harry was crying. Mum cuddled him while the others tried to think of presents.

"What about this sticky spider's web stuff?" said Jem. "It's so strong and thin at the same time."

"The rain forest is full of spiders," said Lucy. "They could pick as much of that stuff as they liked off the trees."

"It breaks my heart to say this," said Red, reaching into his pocket, "but do you think they'd sell it to us? I've got nearly ten dollars . . ."

"Oh, Red," said Mum, "that's the sweetest thing I ever heard." She kissed his cheek. He blushed. "But it won't work. They don't use money. They think it's silly."

"Yeah, but they're wrong. Money is the greatest. If we explained it to them . . ."

"No," said Dad, "that won't work. What we need is a shop or an all-night garage. Somewhere we could buy a big box of chocolates."

"We're in sixteenth-century Amazonia, Dad. There are no all-night garages," said Lucy, "but you've given me an idea. Jem, where's the log-book?"

Lucy flicked quickly through the pages of the logbook, which Jem had handed to her, until she came to "Monsieur Bon Bon's Secret Fooj Formula."

"I thought that was some kind of racing fuel," said Jem, "but Mum said it was . . ."

"Fudge," said Lucy. "It's a recipe for fudge. Follow me."

They followed her to the nearest house. A family was sitting around outside, playing a game with little glass balls.

"Are they diamonds?" gasped Red. "Can I see?"

Lucy said something to them in a language the others didn't understand.

"I thought you said that you didn't speak El Doradoan," said Dad.

"That was this morning," said Lucy. "I've had all day to learn."

"What did you tell them?"

"I told them I liked their stove. Also their pots and pans. They said we could have them."

"What do you want their stove for? You can't leave a family with no cooker."

"They can have it back in an hour."

The stove was in a courtyard, overhung with branches and blossom, around the back of the house. Lucy gathered the ingredients and pans she needed. The secret of Monsieur Bon Bon's secret fudge recipe is

TOP SECRET

This makes the fudge come out smooth and creamy instead of gritty and sugary. Lucy set to work.

"Lucy?" gasped Mum. "Are you cooking?" Lucy had never cooked anything before in her life.

"Think of it as an experiment in economics," said Lucy, "which just happens to be edible."

"It won't be edible if you let the pan bubble like that. It will be burned."

"I'm following the instructions."

"The instructions involve a certain amount of familiarity with the concept of not incinerating things."

The thick, black, tarry mixture in the bottom of the pan did look fairly unconvincing. Lucy started again. This time she read out the instructions and measured the quantities while Mum stirred and mixed and blended. Soon the pan was bubbling again, and soon after that faces began to appear, peeping over the courtyard wall. All over El Dorado people dropped what they were doing and drifted toward the smell. It was as if their brains had allowed their noses to take control of their bodies.

Dad opened the gate so that people could come in and see the fudge. For a while, they stood there, smelling it in silence, while Mum poured it onto a tray to cool. They had no idea it was something you could eat. It smelled so good that just smelling it was enough. No one even thought of eating it. As that lovely fudge fragrance floated out across the city in tattered wisps of steam, out across the tree-tops, all the squirrels, bats, and monkeys stopped what they were doing and sniffed the air. The whole forest fell silent.

When Lucy finally picked up a piece and popped it into her mouth, everyone lunged forward. She put up her hand and said, "Surely, your Queen eats first."

"Surely, the Queen eats last," said Imogen.

"Normally, yes," said Eliza, "but on this occasion . . ."

Hungrily, she reached for the fudge. Mum pulled it out of her way. "I think it probably needs to set," she said, "to bring out its true creaminess."

The waterfall itself seemed to wait with bated breath until the fudge had set to perfection. Then Mum said, "OK, it's ready," and with a great shout, the Great Amazonian Fudge stampede began. Elbows, knees, shins, and fists flew as everyone tussled to grab a piece. The city reverberated to the

sound of happy chewing and contented sucking. This is when Lucy announced her great idea.

"Your Majesty," she said, "and people of El Dorado. What you are eating not only tastes delicious—it is also the answer to all the problems of El Dorado. El Dorado is made of gold, but people from out of town like that gold and want to take it away. Because you are polite and lovely, you feel you have to give away your own doors and gutters and roofs as presents."

"Stress." Eliza sighed.

"Solid-gold stress," agreed Imogen.

"What El Dorado needs—what this whole beautiful forest needs—is something that its people will like more than gold. Ladies and gentlemen, Your Majesty, I give you . . . fudge."

"Oh!" said everyone. "Definitely."

"But," said Imogen, "what happens when we run out of fudge? There're already only"—she counted—"thirty-seven pieces left. And I want one."

"The magic of fudge," said Lucy, "is that you don't dig it out of the ground. You make it. You can make as much of it as you like. This is Monsieur Bon Bon's Secret Fooj Formula. With this recipe, you will have an infinite, inexhaustible supply of fudge . . ."

"Wait," said Eliza. "You mean we can eat this more than once in our lives?"

"You can eat this every day. You can share it with everyone who comes to visit."

"No one will ever want our gold again," said Eliza.

"Who would want gold when they could eat fudge?" said Imogen.

"Chitty Chitty Bang Bang, or at least her log-book," said Lucy, "has solved all your problems. She has moved you from a gold-based economy to a fudge-based economy. Which is loads better. In a fudge-based economy, no one ever has to be poor. In a gold-based economy, you can run out of gold. In the fudge-based economy, if you run out of fudge — make some more fudge. Your stress is at an end."

"You've solved all our social and economic problems," said Eliza.

"We must give her a present," whispered Imogen.

"We've got just the thing," said Eliza.

"Follow the monarch," said Imogen, leading the way down a wide avenue of trees. A troupe of little monkeys clattered through the branches above their heads.

"In there," said Imogen, pointing to what seemed to be a small golden garage.

"Look inside, look inside," said Eliza.

Dad was the first to open the door, the first to see — spread out on the earthy floor — a pile of

springs and wires and valves and lightbulbs, gaskets and bolts and nuts.

"What is it?" asked Mum.

"I know what it is," said Jem, who recognized every single nut, bolt, and clip.

"Me, too," said Dad.

"That," said Jem, "is Chitty Chitty Bang Bang."

"Well, this solves the mystery of how they got her through the jungle," said Lucy. "They took her completely to pieces, then left the pieces in a heap."

If you've ever come home to find that someone has taken your house apart piece by piece, leaving nothing but a neat pile of bricks and a stack of floorboards, you'll have some idea of how the Tootings felt looking at that heap of spare parts. For a long time, they didn't speak or move, but stood in silence, each thinking their private thoughts. Mum remembered the day they found the headlights on top of the Eiffel Tower. Now those headlights were lying on their side on the earth floor. Jem remembered the day he first saw Chitty's wings, carving through the sky above the cliffs of Dover. Now those wings lay against the carburettor like a pair of old deck chairs. Dad remembered where he had first seen that big, beautiful beast of an engine— stuck in a tree in a scrapyard. Now here was Chitty

in a thousand pieces, as though she had just fallen down from that tree, as though all the adventures they had had together were nothing but a dream.

"I must say," said Imogen, "I thought you'd be more pleased."

"We brought her all this way," said Eliza.

"But you took her to pieces," said Red. "How are we going to win the race now? It'll take years to put her back together again."

"Oh, we don't mind that," said Imogen.

"We waited years for her to come back."

"Years and years."

"We're happy for you to spend years fixing her."

"Well, well, must go and rule," said Imogen.

"A ruler's work is never done." Eliza sighed and off they went.

Dad and Jem surveyed Chitty's scattered components. "Here's the starter motor," whooped Dad, scooping it up from under Mum's feet.

"Don't bother," growled Red. "That car's not broken; it's destroyed."

"Dad will put her back together in no time," said Jem.

"What? With those fat fingers? I doubt it."

"Those fat fingers," snapped Mum, "rebuilt Chitty Chitty Bang Bang from scratch with no help from anyone."

"Actually I got a lot of help from Jem," admitted Dad. "Not to mention Professor Tuk-Tuk . . ."

"My husband took a rusty old engine stuck up a tree, and he turned it into the most beautiful car this world has ever seen."

"Stuck up a tree?" said Red.

"Stuck up a tree," repeated Mum, "in Basildon. That was just the engine. The headlights were in Paris. The bodywork was on the shores of the Indian Ocean. The wheels were in the Sahara Desert . . ."

"Why?" asked Red. "How did that happen?"

"That's a mystery I'm always trying to solve," said Jem. "You see, when you think about it . . ."

"I knew it!" said Dad, who'd been examining the starter motor all this time. "The carbon brushes and the end plates don't contact properly. If we can sort this out, we won't need to get champagne whenever she doesn't start. And there's the rear end seal. I've always had my doubts about that. We should strip out the transmission while we are here. You know, this could be the ideal opportunity for us to make Chitty better than ever."

"*Ga gooo ga!*" went Chitty's Klaxon, suddenly making everyone jump.

"Chitty agrees!" said Mum.

"What Chitty? There is no Chitty," growled Red. "There's a pile of parts."

"If there's one thing we've learned," said Jem, "it's that Chitty is a lot more than the sum of her parts."

Dad offered to let Red help him and Jem rebuild the most beautiful and technologically advanced vehicle ever made.

"How much will you give me?" said Red.

"Nothing," said Dad.

"Then, no," said Red.

So Dad and Jem spent days classifying nuts and bolts and cogs and screws. Days that reminded them of last summer — or of a summer five hundred years in the future, depending on how you look at it — when they had first rebuilt a camper van together. Back then they had sometimes spent a whole morning discussing where one piece of tubing should go, sometimes a day in silence, slotting this part into the other. Back then, Mum had brought them snacks and drinks whenever they looked tired. She did the same now. The snacks were slightly different, though: instead of cakes and tea, they were mostly baked snakes or pan-fried tarantulas that she'd caught while out trekking in the jungle with Imogen and Eliza.

"Food was so dull before Chitty came back," said Imogen.

"So very dull," agreed Eliza.

"Now we have baked snake in fudge sauce."

"And pan-fried tarantula in fudge sauce."

"And sometimes fudge in fudge sauce."

"And sometimes just fudge."

During the long misty days while Dad and Jem were rebuilding Chitty, Mum and Lucy (and Little Harry) questioned all the old people in town to see if they had any memory of where the Potts might have gone. They all said the same thing: "They went. They said they'd be back soon. But they never came back."

They searched the forest for some sign or clue. The Queen came with them to make sure they didn't disappear like the Potts. But it was hopeless. The forest was so vast. And also so full of distractions. Every time they saw an anaconda, Mum felt she had to wrestle it.

"I'm sorry, but I just had no idea I had such a natural talent for anaconda-wrestling."

"Don't apologize," said Eliza. "Nothing we like to watch more than a bit of anaconda-wrestling. Is there, Imogen?"

"Unless it's jaguar-punching," said Imogen. "We love jaguar-punching, too."

"I must say, now that we know how good you are at wrestling them, we don't feel so bad that we tried to kill you with anacondas."

"That does make it more forgivable," said Mum.

"Then, we are friends?"

"I suppose we are."

Those days spent high in the cloud forest were the most magical of all their adventures. Every morning they woke to the sound of the happiest, noisiest dawn chorus that they had ever heard. The sun lavished its warmth and light upon them, but thanks to the spray from the waterfall, it was never too hot. In the evening, they would join the people in the square and watch the colours of sunset dancing in the facets of the Diamond As Big As Your Head.

Red meanwhile taught all the children of El Dorado to play hide-and-seek.

"I'm not sure," said Lucy, "that a trackless equatorial wilderness on the brink of an unbelievably high waterfall is the best place for a game of hide-and-seek. People could get hurt. Or horribly maimed. Or go missing for years on end. Or be eaten by jaguars. Or piranhas. Or plunge to their doom."

"That's what makes it so good," said Red. "It kind of gives it an edge."

"As soon as Chitty is back to her old self," said Dad one evening when—yet again—Mum and Lucy had returned with no sign of the Potts, "we'll fly all over the forest until we find them. Then we'll go and deal with Tiny Jack and Nanny."

Next day, while Dad and Jem worked, Little Harry sat up on the seat in front of the steering wheel and pulled it this way and that. "Chitty Chitty Bang Bang!" he yelled.

He's right, thought Jem. *She is beginning to look like that unique Paragon Panther.*

"*Ga gooo ga!*" honked Chitty.

"There are a few bits and pieces I don't recognize," said Dad. "This glass dome, for instance. And this metal cone. Also there seem to be two extra engines. Or maybe they're not engines. They look more like atomic hair dryers. I never noticed them before. They must have been lodged under the back wheel arches, or maybe they're from the village, and they just got . . ."

"If only we could ask Chitty where they go," said Jem. "Sometimes, when you drive her, don't you feel like she's trying to tell you something? When you talk to her, do you sometimes feel like she's going to answer back?"

"No," said Dad. "Let's just stick these things in

wherever they fit and hope for the best. You know, I could live like this—just sitting around repairing classic motorcars in sixteenth-century El Dorado."

As the sun went down over the rain forest that evening, Dad and Jem fitted the last rivet. Jem cranked the engine, and Dad pressed the starter motor. Chitty started the first time.

"Tomorrow," he said, "we'll begin our aerial search for the Pott family. Now let's get some food."

Dad went to cook supper, but Jem sat for a while, leaning against Chitty's wheel arch as the bats skittered through the twilight. "Good night, Chitty," he whispered. The car did not speak, but Jem could hear the metal of her pipes cooling in the chill night air, the oil and the water settling down, and he knew that she was restless to go. As he walked through the moonlit golden streets, he thought he heard the softest good-bye snuffle from her Klaxon. But it could have been a pangolin looking for ants.

Next morning, when Jem woke up, Chitty had vanished.

"Not again!" groaned Mum.

"Don't worry," said Imogen, "it was us."

"It was you last time," said Mum.

"We thought she didn't quite fit in with the town . . ."

"All that green and silver—it clashed with the brickwork."

"So we sent her away . . ."

"Where to?"

"Oh. Not *away* away, just . . ."

From somewhere behind them they heard "*Ga gooo ga!*"

There was Chitty, a crowd of happy El Doradoan children pushing her toward them.

"What have you done to her?" gasped Dad.

"Can't you tell?" said Imogen.

"Isn't it obvious?" said Eliza.

Chitty did look different. Very different. Smarter. Shinier.

"We've had her covered with gold," said Imogen.

"*You gilded Chitty?*"

"What do you think?" asked Eliza.

"Do you like it?" said Imogen.

"It's very shiny," said Mum. "Sort of, Chitty Chitty Bling Bling."

"At least like this, you will be taking a little piece of El Dorado with you, wherever you go. Good-bye. It's very hard to say good-bye to such good friends."

"Oh, we're not leaving yet," said Dad. "We're going to search the river and the jungle for signs of the Pott family."

"We have to find them," said Mum. "We need

their help. The whole planet could be in incredible danger."

"What's wrong with incredible danger?" asked Imogen.

"We love incredible danger, don't we, Imogen?" said Eliza.

"Chitty always has somewhere to go." Imogen sighed.

"One day she will leave you, too."

"I think," gasped Jem, "she's trying to leave us right now. Run!" Somehow Chitty had slipped her hand brake and was rolling toward the edge of the cliff. The Tootings ran after her and jumped on board.

"Wait! Where's Red?" yelled Jem.

Just in time, Red came tearing out of the forest, flung himself into the back of the car, and yelled, "I won!" He looked back at the woods to see if anyone was behind him. He was so happy to have won his one hundred and seventh consecutive game of Extreme Hide-and-Seek (with jaguars) that he barely noticed that Chitty had leaped from the ledge and was soaring above the waterfall. He barely heard the cheers and whoops of the El Doradoans as they waved and shouted their good-byes and their thank-yous.

Chitty curved through the air above the abyss,

and came round in a wide, lazy circle, bringing them face-to-face with the full force of the waterfall as it fell. Everyone caught their breath—partly because it was so amazing, partly because the spray from the fall was so fresh and so cold.

"It looks like a lovely gold brooch," cried Red. "Where are we going?"

Hot air from the rain forest rises in great columns called thermals. Birds such as condors and vultures use these to lift them higher and higher into the air. Today—do as Dad might—Chitty rolled from thermal to thermal, like a huge mechanical condor, rising and rising in great circles as though she were climbing an invisible spiral staircase.

"Look," yelled Jem, as they finally rolled over the very top of the great waterfall. Below them was a vast, almost perfectly circular lake. There was nothing higher than it for miles around. It was like an eye looking straight into the sky.

"Where's El Dorado gone?" asked Red.

"Over that way somewhere. Under the clouds."

"You mean we're higher than the clouds?"

"Yes. A lot higher . . . Look."

A flock of puffy white clouds passed far beneath them. Through a gap they glimpsed a tiny flicker of light, like the flash of a camera. It was all that could be seen of El Dorado.

"I bet we're the first people ever to see that lake," said Lucy. "I bet no one will see it again for hundreds of years."

"We are way too high," said Red. "Take us down! Take us down!" He reached over the front seat for one of the handles.

"Red! Don't touch anything. You don't know which switch does what!"

Too late. He had already grabbed the Chronojuster. El Dorado disappeared in a flicker of nights and days and weeks and months.

No one who wasn't born in El Dorado ever saw the City of Gold again.

11

History rippled past the Tooting family like the pages in a flip book, until they found themselves gliding gently down into what seemed to be a waving green ocean.

"Grass?" gasped Dad. "It's grass. How can there be this much grass? Red, what have you done? This isn't Basildon."

"It wasn't Red's fault," said Jem.

"What? He pulled the Chronojuster."

Dad had brought Chitty down gently on a dusty road that ran across a prairie. Small brown islands looked up as he landed. These turned out to be grazing buffalo. They watched Chitty, then carried on chewing as Dad drove her forward.

"The Chronojuster was glowing," said Jem.

"Naturally, Red grabbed it. But who made it glow? Chitty did. Chitty brought us here. Why?"

The moment he asked the question, a massive old car thundered past them, whipping up clouds of dust and belching smoke from its gleaming exhausts. Jem looked behind just in time to see another car racing up behind them.

"That's the answer to your question," said Lucy. "The juxtaposition of fast cars and buffalo suggests to me that we are on the Kansas leg of the Prix d'Esmerelda's Birthday Cake. Fasten your seat belts, everyone!"

Chitty leaped forward and was soon alongside the car in front—a huge, royal-blue gondola with wheels that seemed to crush the stones beneath them. The driver scowled from behind a fabulously curly moustache as he pressed harder on the accelerator, trying to keep up with Chitty. But Chitty soon slipped past him and did what she often did when she overtook another car: cheekily waggled her back fender and gave him a triumphant blast of her deafening Klaxon.

"Honestly, she's so undignified." Lucy sighed.

The Kansas sunlight blazed off Chitty's golden bodywork, so that they felt like they were travelling inside a comet.

"What's that?" yelled Jem.

Far, far ahead they could just make out a tiny white dot in the middle of the road. No matter how fast Chitty went, the white dot did not seem to get any bigger. It was moving as fast as they were. It could only be one thing: Chitty the Second.

"The Count!" said Lucy. "Are we going to catch up with him?"

"Probably not," said Dad. "The brand-new Chitty seems to be faster than the dear old Chitty." As if in answer to this slight, Chitty's engine revved furiously and a switch on her dashboard glowed like an angry fairy light. "I've never noticed that switch before," said Dad. "I wonder what it is."

"Chitty is trying to tell us something," said Jem. "Shall I flip the switch?"

"What if it's that ejector-seat thing again?" asked Red.

But before anyone had time to consider this possibility, Dad flipped the switch. Everything happened so fast that at first everyone thought it really *was* the ejector seat.

The horizon rushed toward them. They felt like they were falling. Kansas was a blur of green. Sheer speed shoved all of them back into their seats. The tiny white dot became a white marble, then a white tennis ball, then a white football.

"I think we've just discovered what those funny

little extra engine things were for," said Dad, through gritted teeth.

Seconds later, the white football-size object had become a gleaming white racing car. They were slipping past the elegant, aerodynamic form of Chitty the Second. Chitty herself (the Original and Best Chitty) slowed right down, as though to allow her rival to get a good look at her new gleaming gold bodywork.

"I say!" yelled the Count. But before he could say anything specific, Chitty thundered past, waggled her fender, and sounded her victory Klaxon.

"So embarrassing." Lucy sighed.

On they raced toward the finishing line, leaving Chitty the Second far, far behind.

Fifty-six minutes and thirty-seven seconds later, Red was basking in the sunlight reflected in Chitty's bodywork. "Look at my arm," he said. "It's like I'm made of gold."

Then all at once, the sun was snuffed out. Jem looked up and saw the undercarriage of a plane, just a few feet above their heads, keeping perfect pace with Chitty, who had slowed down now that she had an insurmountable lead. As they watched, a ladder was lowered and down it came the elegant figure of Count Zborowski's butler, Crackitt. He hung from the ladder, just alongside Chitty, and,

with a smooth nod of the head, passed Mum a letter before climbing back up to the cockpit.

Mum opened the letter.

WHAT HO!
Jolly NICE TO SEE YOU AGAIN.
FEELING PECKISH? CRACKITT IS
GOING TO PUT UP ONE OF HIS
TERRIFIC SPREADS AT A PICNIC
SPOT WITH A CORKING VIEW
OF SOME FALLS.
WHY NOT PULL OVER AND TIE ON
THE OLD NOSEBAG WITH US?
        YOURS,
            the COUNT

"Stop for a picnic? Are you nuts?" cried Red. "We can win this race."

"Actually, I am quite hungry," admitted Dad.

"And a picnic could be really nice," said Lucy.

"Lucy, you hate picnics," said Mum. "You always say sunshine and laughter are the two most depressing things in the world."

But just after they drove through the next town, they saw Crackitt's lovely yellow biplane parked in the shade of a copse of trees. Crackitt was standing at attention, a crisp white cloth draped over his arm and, at his feet, a wide gingham tablecloth spread out over the grass. On it was the most fabulous picnic that any of them had ever seen. No one could have driven past a picnic like that. There was a pie almost a foot deep. Its pastry shone like glass. Steam drifted lazily from a hole in its crust. There were piles of crusty bread, huge chunks of cheese, jugs of lemonade, and a bucket full of grapes.

"His Lordship insists that you start without him," said Crackitt, as the Tootings clambered out of Chitty.

"Oh, we couldn't do that," said Mum. "We'll just enjoy the view until he comes."

The others all agreed. But the view that most interested them was not the one of the waterfall

but the one of that beautiful pie. It was a view that filled them with anxiety. What if someone stole it? What if there was an earthquake and the earth itself swallowed it?

"His Lordship really was most insistent that you start," said Crackitt.

"Oh, if he insists," said Dad. He dived on that pie, sliced it up, and passed it round so quickly that lightning itself would not have got a look in.

"Save some for the Count!" said Lucy.

But she needn't have worried. Each slice was so densely packed with meat, so bursting with flavour, that a mouthful was enough to keep their taste buds busy for hours. They savoured their slices while the sun slid over the horizon. Dusk was turning into night when Chitty the Second finally rolled up.

"I say," said the Count. "This is something! What a lovely spot. Pop a couple of tents up, Crackitt, and we'll pass the night here."

A yellow moon was high in the sky by the time they finished the picnic. The Count gave them all the news about the Prix d'Esmerelda.

"It's gone marvellously well. We're on for a record-breaking time."

"What's the current record?" asked Lucy.

"Six months."

"Six *months*?"

"Yes, but it looks like I'm going to do it in five months, three weeks, and four days."

"But these cars go so fast. How has it taken so long?"

"They do go very fast," said the Count. "But they will keep on running out of petrol. Then you have to find petrol, and sometimes there are no garages nearby. Sometimes there are no *people* nearby. In Texas we ended up having to dig for oil. Luckily I found quite a good oil field, so that's a few more bob in the bank. There were one or two other delays on the way. Kidnapped by bandits in New Mexico, for instance."

"Bandits!" whooped Little Harry, causing Jem to look around nervously.

"Were you in terrible danger?" gasped Lucy.

"Oh, they were frightfully nice chaps once I'd paid the old ransom. Then there was the whole business with the Grand Canyon."

"The Grand Canyon? What happened there?" asked Lucy.

"Well, the Grand Canyon is surprisingly large. And also quite a few feet deep. As holes in the road go, it must be one of the biggest. They say you can't miss it. But what if you *want* to miss it? A sign saying

> ## If You Go Any Further, You'll Fall In

might have been useful. Then there were tornadoes, too. Bears in Colorado. It's been quite a packed five months, three weeks, and four days. But now we're almost home. Tomorrow we should cross the finishing line. And it looks like we're the two front-runners. How on earth did you get ahead of me? I haven't seen you since the Catskill Mountains."

"We took a detour," said Dad.

"May the best man win tomorrow. Or the best girl of course. 'Night, all. Must get the old head down." He got up to stroll back to his tent, but before taking a step, he said, "I say! What's that?"

"That," said Lucy, "is the moon."

"Do you know, they've got a moon exactly like that one down in New Mexico."

"That's actually the same moon," said Lucy.

"You can see it here the same as you can in New Mexico."

"Are you absolutely sure about that? New Mexico is a dashed long way from here."

Lucy tried to explain lunar orbits to the Count, using a tangerine and an Edam cheese she picked up from the picnic.

The Count looked deep into her eyes and said, "Lucy, of all the girls I've met on all my travels, you are certainly the most . . . what's the word?"

Lucy tried to imagine what the word might be — "beautiful"? "mysterious"? "poetic"? "brilliant"?

"Informative," said the Count. "You're by far the most informative girl I've ever met. I say, do you fancy taking a spin with me tomorrow in Chitty the Second? With you in the passenger seat, we'd be sure to win the race."

"Yes, please," said Lucy straightaway.

"I thought," said the Count, "that you might need time to think about it."

"I'm a very quick thinker."

Next morning Lucy woke up to the sound of engines. Some of the other cars in the race had finally caught up with them and were thundering past the picnic site.

"We'd better wake the Count," she said.

"Lucy, wait . . ." It was Jem. He was crouched next to her sleeping bag, with Chitty's logbook open on his knee and a haggard, worried look on his face. He hadn't slept all night. "There's something I want to show you."

"We'll be late for the race."

"It's important. Don't wake the others. Not yet. I was going through the logbook, trying to figure out why Chitty had brought us here."

"It's obvious, isn't it? She wants to teach Chitty the Second a lesson. That's why we went to El Dorado, so she could have her golden makeover and then come back and win the race."

"That's what I thought. I was thinking how terrible it would be if we'd been through all these dangers just so that she could win a race. I was wondering if there was any way we could understand what she was thinking or make her understand what *we* are thinking, when I found this . . ."

A page from the *Encyclopaedia Britannica* had been glued into the logbook and folded over. Jem opened it. It was a page about Count Louis Zborowski.

"Commander Pott must have put it there. I think he

was trying to find out as much about the history of Chitty as he possibly good."

"It's Louis! That's a terrible photograph of him. Ha! His middle name was Elliot. Who knew?" She tried to take the book from him, but Jem nudged it away from her. "What else does it tell you?"

"It says here," he said, "that he died."

Lucy swallowed hard. Then she shrugged. "Well, of course he died. Everyone dies. If he'd lived until our time, he'd be . . ."

"A hundred and twenty," said Jem.

"Exactly. Who lives to be a hundred and twenty? Who'd want to live to a hundred and twenty? You know one thing I like to do while we're time travelling is look at all the people we meet and think about the fact they're all dead. That they're sort of ghosts. It's really melancholy, which is great. I look at the Count and think: You probably died in the war doing something heroic, or maybe you were killed in a duel or something."

"Or a race."

"Exactly. A high-speed collision as he broke a world speed record."

"A race like this one."

Lucy stared at Jem and then at the paper in his hand. Jem offered it to her, but she wouldn't take

it. Jem had to read it to her: "*Count Zborowski died tragically while competing in the final day of the Prix d'Esmerelda's Birthday Cake motor race in Chitty Chitty Bang Bang the Second. He lost control of his vehicle when his lucky cuff links got caught in the gear transmission.*"

"So you're saying . . . he dies today?"

"That's what it says here," said Jem, "but it's all right because we can save him. We can warn him not to wear his cuff links, or just tell him to take it a bit slower or . . ."

Lucy was quiet for a while, then she looked at her brother. "We can't," she said.

"Why not? Don't you want to save him?"

"Of course I want to save him. More than anything. But if we did, it would change the whole course of human history."

"But how? It's not like the Count is anyone important . . ."

"Everyone is important. Everyone is connected."

"But maybe if he'd lived, he'd've done something really amazing, like found a cure for global warming or something."

"Jem, we can't go round changing the course of history just because you think someone's got kind eyes."

"I never said anything about his eyes."

"It was a synecdoche. Look it up." She left the tent.

Outside, Dad was cranking Chitty's engine. "Come on, you Tootings!" he called. "Let's show that newfangled Chitty what the Original and Best can do!"

On the other side of the picnic site, Lucy saw the Count getting ready for the race, as Crackitt began loading everything into the biplane. As the Count pulled on his goggles, she saw the flash of his lucky cuff links.

"We've got to tell him," cried Jem, coming up behind her. "We can't just stand by and watch him be killed."

"You're right. So let's get going. Let's make sure we're miles ahead when it happens."

She and Jem climbed into Chitty, where Mum and Red and Little Harry were already waiting.

"Lucy!" called the Count. "Are you riding with me?"

Jem looked at her. He could see that she wanted to say yes. "Lucy, you'll be killed," he whispered.

"No, thank you, Count," called Lucy.

"But I thought . . . Oh. You changed your mind."

"That's right."

"Girls do that a lot. See? I'm learning about girls. See you at the finish."

"At the finish," agreed Lucy, sniffing back a tear.

"Couldn't we at least tell him not to wear his cuff links?" pleaded Jem.

But Dad had already slipped Chitty into reverse to get a better angle for joining the road. When Chitty was facing the right way, he slammed on her accelerator, and she tore off down the highway.

At the first bend, she came up behind the two cars that had rumbled past in the morning. The sun shone so fiercely on her golden bodywork that the drivers in front were dazzled by their own rear-view mirrors and had to pull over to let her pass. She bowled along the empty highway, her engine humming. So it was quite a surprise when, on the second bend, the shark-like silhouette of Chitty the Second sailed silently by.

"Ga gooo ga!" roared Chitty. The Count gave the Tootings a triumphant wave. And so did his passenger.

"Who's that riding with the Count?" said Mum.

"Oh, no!" shrieked Jem. "It's Lucy! She must have sneaked out of Chitty while Dad was reversing. Dad, you've got to catch up with them!"

"I realize that," said Dad. "This is a race, after all."

"It's a lot more serious than that," gasped Jem. He explained the terrible danger that Lucy was in.

But Chitty the Second was already disappearing into the distance.

"The booster engines. Remember the switch!" shouted Jem.

Dad tried to flip the switch that had made Chitty go so fast the day before, but now it wouldn't budge.

"What are we going to do?" sobbed Mum. "Can we make her fly?"

"We never really found out how to do it except by driving off something high."

"The falls. You could drive into the waterfall."

By now Chitty the Second had all but disappeared into the distance. Dad saw that there was no alternative but to try to get Chitty to fly. At the next bend there was a slip road that led straight to the lake and the waterfall.

"Hold on, everyone," called Dad, swinging the steering wheel to the left. But as quickly as he pulled it left, the wheel swung itself back to the right, keeping Chitty dead centre in the middle of the road, heading straight after her rival.

"She. Won't. Budge," gasped Dad, still using all his strength on the wheel. "We just have to drive after them."

"Maybe," said Mum, "Chitty doesn't want to catch up. Maybe she's worried that if we race too hard, we'll make the Count go faster and crash."

"But he's going to crash anyway. It's in the history books."

"I think we have to do what we can," said Mum. "And try to trust Chitty."

On they powered, through the lanes and woods. By late afternoon they could see the towers and skyscrapers reaching into the sky. Then the air was filled with the sound of sirens. Blue lights flashed in the road ahead.

"It looks like there's been an accident," said Dad. No one else spoke.

But there hadn't been an accident. Two police cars were blocking the road. One policeman was talking to the Count. Another flagged down the Tootings.

"Sorry, lady, you can't go no further. Take a look at the sign."

The sign said, "NEW YORK CLOSED DUE TO CATASTROPHE."

Mum jumped out of the car and hugged Lucy, who was standing at the side of the road. "Oh, Lucy, how could you do such a thing?" she sobbed.

"I'm sorry, Mum, I just couldn't bear to see him drive off to his doom like that."

The Count looked perfectly cheerful. "Sorry about the delay," he said. "Anyone fancy a glass of champagne?"

"That would be illegal, sir," said the policeman.

"So it would. You're quite right. Thanks for reminding me. Well, perhaps this obstruction is all for the best. No offence, Mrs. Tooting, but although your daughter may be very informative, she's not the ideal companion for a racing driver."

"Really? Why?"

"She doesn't appreciate the technical details of motor racing. For instance, she kept telling me to

slow down, which of course is exactly the wrong thing to do in a race. But which I had to do—what with her being a lady and asking politely. Also, she tried to get me to take off my lucky cuff links. I did try to explain that without my lucky cuff links, I wouldn't be lucky."

"Oh, dear. Perhaps she should finish the race in Chitty, then, instead of in Chitty the Second."

"I hate to disappoint a lady," said the Count, "but I'm afraid that seems the only way."

Red and Dad had meanwhile been asking the police about the roadblock.

"What kind of catastrophe is it, anyway?" asked Red.

"The catastrophic kind," grunted the first policeman.

"We can't give any details for fear of creating a national panic," said the second.

"Dad! Look out!" called Jem.

Chitty Chitty Bang Bang was somehow rolling backward down the hill. All the Tootings and Red ran after her. One by one they managed to clamber on board, while Dad struggled to gain control of the wheel.

"Deer!" yelled Little Harry.

"Where?" said Mum. "Oh, no!"

A pair of beautiful young deer were standing in the middle of the road, not moving, just staring as though hypnotized by the sight of Chitty rumbling toward them. Any minute now she would hit them. Dad snatched at the wheel, and Chitty bounced off the road and tumbled down an embankment. Seconds later she flicked out her wings and swooped over the trees. She banked and turned back toward the line of the road, flying low over the heads of the police and the Count.

"I say!" shouted the Count. "I hate to make a

fuss, but isn't that cheating? This is supposed to be a road race, not a sky race . . ."

Lucy waved down at him and watched him get smaller and smaller as they flew toward New York City. She felt in her heart that she would never see him again.

"Oh, if only he'd take off his cuff links," she said. "But I don't think he will."

The New York catastrophe certainly did seem to be catastrophic. As they flew toward the city, they saw below them crowds of people and columns of cars pouring down the highways, heading out of town. Little Harry kept leaning out and shouting, "Hello, people!" Jem was worried that he would lose his

balance and plummet to his doom, so he tied one end of the prehistoric spider's web around his wrist. Chitty sailed elegantly between the cliffs of glass and concrete along Wall Street and came in to land just outside the Bank of America.

"Well, at least you're safely home, Red," said Mum.

"Home?" said Red. "I don't want this to be home. I want to go back to El Dorado. We are going back to El Dorado, aren't we? That was the only place anyone ever played with me."

"But what about your mother?" asked Mum. "Won't she be missing you?"

"I ain't got no mother. Nor no father. And no grandmother now, neither. Nearest thing I ever had to family was you. We're going back, aren't we? Say we are. All I do here is work. All I did there was play."

"But this is your hometown."

"You sure?" said Red. "It's normally a lot busier than this."

Wall Street was completely deserted. Nothing was moving. Not a person. Not a car. They could hear water gushing from a fire hydrant a whole block away. The pavement glittered in the sunlight. They could hear birdsong—a flock of starlings tumbled past them just above their heads.

"Nice and peaceful," said Dad.

"Peaceful?" said Red. "Don't you ever notice anything? See that fire hydrant spouting water? Why isn't anyone doing anything about that? How did it get knocked over? See the way the pavement is shining? Can't you see why? Broken glass. Nearly every second-storey window here is broken."

"Oh," said Mum. "Goodness. Maybe there was a tornado."

"A tornado goes from air to ground, doing damage all along the way," said Lucy. "It would have messed up the cars and mailboxes, not just the second-storey windows."

"Some of the cars are messed up," said Jem. "Look at that one."

At the side of the road were three cars: a beautiful cream-coloured Buick, a gorgeous navy-blue Pierce-Arrow, and, in between these two, a twisted pile of scrap metal and shattered glass with some bent wheels sticking out of it.

"It looks like someone stood on it," said Jem.

"Something that could crush a car like a biscuit tin," said Lucy.

"And what," said Red, "was with the birds? What was their hurry? Like they were scared of something."

There was a sound like a giant foot crushing a half-ton biscuit tin.

"That sound reminds me of something," said Dad.

"Me, too," said Mum. "What is it?"

The sound came again.

"I've never heard anything like that in my life," said Red.

"But we have," said Jem. "I remember what it is now. I really think we should run."

"Is this a new game?" asked Red.

"Dinosaur!" cried Little Harry and—right on cue—the head of a very hungry-looking *Tyrannosaurus rex* swung around the corner. Its vast yellow eyes scanned Wall Street, searching for food.

"Now, this is what I call a game!" said Red. "What're the rules?"

There was no answer. Everyone had run.

They ran toward the Stock Exchange. It looked like the perfect hiding place. The doors were too small for a tyrannosaur. There were hardly any windows to poke its head through. The walls were too thick to smash down. Perfect but for one thing: the doors were locked. Dad rattled at them, but they wouldn't budge.

"We're trapped!" he gasped, turning round to see that the great beast was already trotting toward them, its huge tail balancing out its massive, swaying head.

"As a predator," said Lucy, "the tyrannosaur is incredibly sensitive to movement. We need to stay out of its sight line and stay very, very still. Quick, behind here! Where's Red?"

Red came running toward them. At the top of the steps was a statue of a fat man in a top hat. The Tootings crouched down behind it, hardly daring to breathe.

Something tugged at Jem's wrist. He looked down and saw the special sticky spider's web leash he had tied to Little Harry's wrist. It was stretched tight.

Oh no, thought Jem, *not again. Little Harry is out there somewhere. I'll pull him back in.*

He tugged at the web, trying to reel Little Harry in like a fish. Little Harry tugged back. Jem tugged harder but not too hard—he didn't want his younger brother to fall over. Little Harry came a bit nearer this time. He tugged again. Nearer again. It seemed to be working. Jem tugged one more time—a touch harder. Little Harry tugged back hard. Surprisingly hard. Shockingly hard. So hard that Jem was dragged out from behind the statue. Next thing he knew, he was being hauled down the steps. He tumbled and fell, but something—it couldn't be Little Harry, surely?—was dragging him across the pavement, and now it was hoisting him into the air.

Jem screamed.

High above him he could see the drooling mouth of the tyrannosaur like a hole in the sky. Below that were its fiddly claws . . . and in its claws was Little Harry. The leash that Jem had fastened to Little Harry's wrist was still there, tangled around one of the claws. When Jem had tugged on his end of the leash earlier, it wasn't Little Harry who had pulled back; it was the tyrannosaur. And now Jem was dangling from that leash, somewhere in the region of the dinosaur's scaly and surprisingly noisy belly.

That's a hungry dinosaur, thought Jem. *In a minute it will be less hungry. Which will be thanks to me. But not in a good way.*

He could have undone the leash. He could have dropped to the ground and run away.

But his brother was at the other end of the leash, so this is what Jem did. He gathered his courage and his strength. He took a handful of the leash and pulled himself upward. Hand over hand, he climbed up the leash to where his brother was trapped in the hellish claws of the infernal beast.

Gasping for breath, aching in every muscle, Jem hauled himself higher and higher until the moment came when he would have to touch the claw itself. He closed his eyes. He reached out. Cold

and hard as stone it was, but moving, like a living statue. He reached over with his other hand and touched something warm . . . Little Harry.

"Dinosaur!" yelled Little Harry, helpfully.

"I did notice," said Jem.

For someone who was trapped within the black claws and cold flesh of a dinosaur fist, Little Harry looked remarkably cheery.

"Dinosaur!" he reiterated.

"Honestly," said Jem, "I know." The jaws lurched forward and sideways and back. Jem felt seasick. But he tried to keep thinking. There must be some way to get Little Harry down.

The great jaws closed up, teeth grinding, breath steaming. The massive eyes swivelled and descended. The dinosaur was staring at Little Harry.

"Dinosaur!"

An oily rumble came from somewhere deep within the dark well of its throat.

"Shhh, Harry."

"Dinosaur!"

The same rumble from the same dark well.

"Dinosaur!"

There it was again.

Little Harry, thought Jem, *and the dinosaur . . . They're talking to each other.*

"Dinosaur!"

Rumble!

"Dinosaur!"

Rumble!

"Little Harry," said Jem, "do you know this dinosaur?"

"My dinosaur! My egg!"

"You do know him, don't you? Let me guess." It had suddenly all become very clear to Jem. "You stole this egg from the Cretaceous period, when it was still an egg. You carried it round with you for days in that little red bag. You hatched the dinosaur from an egg, didn't you, Harry? And then somehow left the baby dinosaur behind in New York when we went to El Dorado."

"Egg . . . all gone." Little Harry sighed.

"You hatched it from an egg," said Jem, "and now it thinks that you're its mother!"

"Mummy!" yelled Little Harry.

From far away Jem could hear his own mother howl, "Harrrrrrryyyy!"

But much nearer and much louder was the

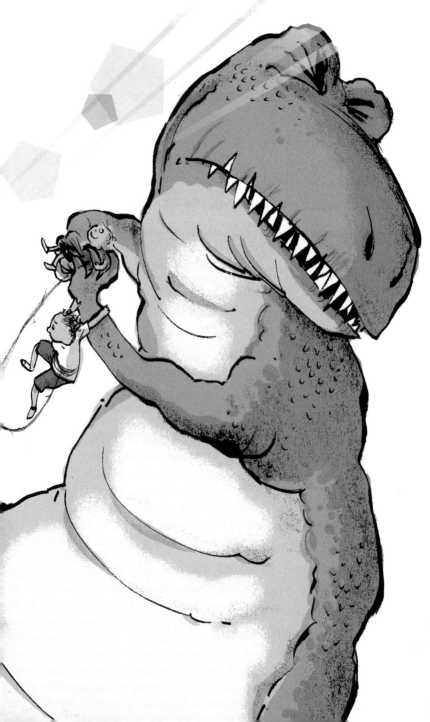

cheerful gurgle in the tyrannosaur's throat. A gurgle that clearly meant "Mummy yourself" in Tyranno-saurese.

"Oh," said Jem, "he's just a baby! A baby who thinks you're his mummy. A baby who'll follow his mummy wherever she goes."

Just at that moment, the dinosaur jerked its head away from them and groaned, as though it had been slapped. When it tried to turn back, it winced and groaned again, screwing up its eyes. Someone was flashing a light into them.

It was Red. Far below them, on the pavement of Wall Street, Red was holding something above his head, something that sent a brilliant light straight into the eyes of the dinosaur.

"Red!" said Mum. "Where on earth did you get that?"

"The main square in El Dorado," said Red. The object in his hand was the Diamond As Big As Your Head.

"You stole the Diamond As Big As Your Head!" gasped Mum.

"I didn't steal it. I was going to give it to you. As a present. For saving my life. It's lucky I did, too. Because this is going to save your kids' lives."

He flashed it one more time. The dinosaur growled and tried to shade its eye with its tiny

claw. As it did so, its claw opened, and Jem and Little Harry fell.

"Jem! Harry!" yelled Mum and Dad as their sons whistled downward past the scales and muscles of the tyrannosaur.

But just before they were smashed to pieces on the pavement, they were whipped back into the air again, then down again, and up again, and down again. They were still attached to the length of Cretaceous spider's web. One end was wrapped around the tyrannosaur's claw and the other around their bodies. They had completed history's only Tyrannosaurus Bungee Jump.

"OK, Little Harry," said Jem as they stopped bouncing and finally got their feet on the ground. "We have to get to Chitty. Go on. Go."

"Do walkings?"

"Yes, do walkings."

Little Harry toddled off across Wall Street, with the gigantic tyrannosaur obediently following behind, on the end of the leash.

"Into the car, Little Harry! Into the car!" said Jem. Then he called, "Mum! Dad! Everyone! To Chitty!"

Lucy was the first to realize what had happened. She explained everything. "It's called 'imprinting,'" she said. "When a bird or a reptile hatches from its egg, the first thing it sees, it calls Mummy.

This dinosaur thinks Little Harry is its mummy. Jem has attached it to Little Harry using his leash. All we have to do is pop Little Harry in Chitty, drive Chitty back to the Cretaceous period, towing the tyrannosaur after us, and turn it loose. Easy."

"Couldn't be easier," said Dad.

"Except," said Red, "for the plane."

"What plane?"

"The plane with all the guns and bombs and stuff."

A small red biplane, engine whining like a wasp, guns splattering the pavement with bullets, was heading down Wall Street straight for the dinosaur, which meant it was also heading straight for Chitty and Jem and Little Harry.

"The rest of you run," shouted Red. "I'll try to use the diamond to dazzle the pilot."

The others ran and leaped into Chitty while Red angled the diamond to catch the sun.

The plane kept coming.

The bullets kept firing. Red lifted the diamond higher and leaned back as far as he could. Suddenly the firing stopped.

Jem looked up to wave a thank-you to the pilot. Then he saw why the firing had stopped. It wasn't Red's doing at all. The pilot had stopped firing be-cause he was going to do something much, much

worse. As the plane turned overhead, flying so low that Jem could easily see its struts and wheels, the pilot leaned out and dropped a small black object over the side.

"Bomb!" said Little Harry gleefully.

"Bomb!" shrieked Jem.

"Bomb!" yelled Mum.

"Ga gooo ga!" (That was Chitty.)

"Gurgle!" said the tyrannosaur, which—as we know—translates roughly as "MUM!," by which he meant Little Harry. Little Harry was pointing up at the bomb as it fell. The tyrannosaur clearly took this as an order and, with an almighty swish of his tail, whacked the bomb back into the air, as if it had been a baseball and his tail a baseball bat.

The bomb exploded with a puff of harmless smoke just above Federal Hall. It wasn't much of a bomb really.

"Quick! To Chitty!" yelled Jem.

Little Harry climbed into the backseat, while Mum cranked her up and Dad started the engine. He drove slowly forward, giving Mum the chance to jump in. The dinosaur—still on the end of its leash, still thinking that Little Harry was its mummy—trotted along behind. Anyone who was looking out of a window that day would have seen a gold-plated vintage car carrying a family from

the future towing an obedient *Tyrannosaurus rex* by a lead.

"What's that noise?" said Jem. "It sounds like rain, but I don't feel anything."

No sooner had he said this than he *did* feel something. A long, thin strip of paper landed on his head. Another landed on Mum's, another on the windscreen. Strips of paper were flying everywhere.

"This is ticker tape," said Lucy. "It's what they used for information before computers . . ."

A storm of ticker tape was blowing all around them.

"Where's it coming from?"

"Look! Up there!" Every window higher than the second floor was packed with faces. When the dinosaur started its rampage on Wall Street, the people who had been out and about had fled to the subway or jumped into their cars. But everyone who was inside a building had simply run upstairs to get a better view. They guessed—rightly—that the dinosaur would not be able to manage the elevators and that they would be quite safe and

thoroughly entertained if they stayed at the windows. They had seen the whole drama. They had gasped in horror when the creature had picked up the toddler; cheered encouragement when Jem had climbed up to rescue him; howled in despair when the plane dropped its bomb; and cheered again when the dinosaur had batted away the bomb with its tail.

"A gold-plated car towing a tame dinosaur!" said one man. "I could wait a week and not see anything as surprising as this!"

"That kid who saved the toddler!" said one woman. "Do I know him from somewhere?"

"Sure you do. He's Jem Diamonds," said her friend, "the notorious getaway driver. He's the one who outdrove the whole police department before getting away in a boat. He's a notorious criminal."

"But also a hero. The way he rescued that boy. Made me wanna swoon! You got any more of that ticker tape?"

"This is a ticker-tape parade!" said Dad. "They're giving us a ticker-tape parade—one of the highest honours New York can bestow . . ."

"What are they shouting?"

"It sounds like 'Jem, Jem, Jem, Jem,'" said Lucy. "Why would they be shouting 'Jem'?"

"They can't be," said Jem. "You must have misheard them." But all the same, he stood up and waved. An almighty cheer rang up and down Wall Street.

"At the corner of Broadway," said Mum, "we'll turn left into the Cretaceous period. Hold on to your hats, everybody . . ."

So at the corner of Broadway, Chitty Chitty Bang Bang made a neat left turn and neither she nor the dinosaur was ever seen in New York again.

On the upper storeys of the Stock Exchange, the cheering crowds didn't notice the little redheaded boy running after the car, shouting, "Stop! Stop! Wait for me!"

12

When you turn left out of Wall Street onto Broadway, the first thing you see is Trinity Church. If you are the Tootings, the next thing you see is a wide water meadow where deer go bouncing from tussock to tussock. Drive straight across that meadow, and quite quickly you come to the Ice Age (you'll know that by the mammoths and sabre-toothed tigers). If you turn left there, you'll come to a thick forest where big shaggy mammals go shambling by. Keep going and you'll soon find the trees get taller and denser. After that you should see a primeval swamp with triceratops lolloping around in it.

That's where they stopped.

All was silent, save for the constant whir of giant dragonfly wings and the gurgling of the tyrannosaur.

Carefully, Jem undid the leash around Little

Harry's wrist. "Say good-bye, Little Harry," he whispered.

"Good-bye, Little Harry," said Little Harry, trying to climb out of the car. Clearly he was thinking of staying in the Cretaceous period with his dinosaur.

"No, say good-bye to the dinosaur."

Little Harry waved to the tyrannosaur. The tyrannosaur put its head to one side. It seemed to know that they were about to abandon it.

"All set?" said Dad.

"Couldn't we just wait a minute?" said Mum. "The poor thing looks a bit lost."

Even as she said this, the tyrannosaur's nostrils twitched. It turned its head. It had seen the lolloping great triceratops, and it had thought to itself, *Lunch*. Its tail swung over their heads. The ground shook. It thundered toward the water's edge. The triceratops turned slowly and saw it coming. They didn't move. They had seen the tyrannosaur, but their brains could only do one thing at a time. At the moment they were telling their jaws to chew leaves. If there was time a bit later, their brains might think, *Emergency: Better run*, but it would take that message so long to travel the hundred feet to their legs that really they might just as well concentrate on chewing.

The tyrannosaur got closer and closer.

"This is going to be really gory!" said Lucy.

"There's going to be blood and destruction every-where. Can we stay and watch?"

"I really think," said Dad, "that we should get out of here in case we end up as dessert."

He slammed Chitty into reverse, giving her a good run-up, and then zoomed toward the swamp, while tugging on the Chronojuster. Before they even reached it, the swamp was a frozen waste. By the time they had gone a mile across that, it was a wide prairie . . .

"Dinosaur!" sobbed Little Harry.

"He'll be all right," said Lucy, slipping an arm around her brother. "Just think about his big claws and surprisingly useful tail. He's a happy little dinosaur—he'll be back there now, killing and eating all kinds of other dinosaurs and having a great time . . ." But thinking about the abandoned dinosaur made her suddenly remember someone else. "Hey," she said, "what happened to Red?"

Millions of years in the future, Red had done his best to catch up with Chitty, but by the time he got to Broadway, she had vanished. He looked around. There was still not a soul on the streets. Alone in the middle of a vast, deserted city, hundreds of years away from the happiest time of his life, he felt lonelier than anyone has ever felt in the whole

history of this world. So it's no surprise that when, finally, someone did appear on the street, he almost ran over to them. They were a man and a woman. Almost like a mum and a dad. They seemed to be looking for something. Maybe they were even looking for a little boy. When he got closer, he recognized them. It was Lenny Man-Mountain and Bella Sposa. Bella had got rid of her wedding outfit and was now dressed all in red, wearing red sunglasses and with red-painted fingernails. Had the Tootings been there, they might have thought that she looked uncannily like Nanny. The very Nanny who, strangely unaged, was currently living in their house along with Tiny Jack.

Even though they had recently kidnapped his friends, tied them up, and left them in a barn, he was still pleased to see their familiar faces.

"Hi," said Red. "Remember me?"

"Of course I remember you." Nanny smiled. "The boy with the lovely red hair."

"You recently kidnapped my friends, tied them up, and left them in a barn."

"So we did," purred Nanny. "We apologize for any inconvenience we may have caused. Where are those friends now?"

"Well," said Red. "They sort of dumped me, I guess."

"Dumped you?" said Nanny. "What a pity. In that case, why not make the best of the situation and join us instead? We believe in making the best of a situation, don't we, Lenny?"

"We do," said Man-Mountain. "For instance, in the current situation, people see a big, mean lizard and run away. Many times in doing so they drop their wallet, or their cash, or even their shopping, which may contain diamond bracelets, for all I know. So we pick them up before people get wise to the fact that the dinosaur is gone."

"And if you ask me," said Nanny, "it is gone before it even came. Maybe it is not a real dinosaur at all, but just a hysterical illusion. The loot, however, is real, and we are grateful for your help in raking it in—as we are more than somewhat short of money at the present—thanks to this big lummox." She jerked her thumb at Man-Mountain. "Promised me he was going to rob all the gold in the Federal Reserve Bank just for me! Said he was going to make us rich. And now look at us, picking up nickels and dimes from wallets in the street. A girl has to get used to disappointment in this life."

Red looked up and down deserted Broadway. He thought how happy he had been with the Tootings and Chitty. How hard life had been before they came. How they had left without even saying

good-bye and forgotten all about him. Abandoned him in an empty city with no friends and no family. No one to play with. "So," he said, "you like gold?"

"Gold, diamonds, the secret of eternal youth— my tastes are simple," said Nanny. "Give me gold and diamonds, and I am yours to command."

"Would you really?" asked Red. "Be mine to command? Just for diamonds?"

"To be honest, it would depend on the quantity and also the size of the diamonds."

"What if it was a single diamond, but one as big as your head?"

Nanny stared. Red was holding up the Diamond As Big As Your Head.

"Kid," she said, "I'm all yours. Just hand that over."

"I will if you play with me."

"What?"

"I like to play games. And I've got no one to play with. If I give you the diamond, will you play with me?"

"Why, sure we will play with you. We will play all kinds of games. Did you ever play bank robbers? Or blackmailers? Hijackers? We can play all these games together, can't we, Lenny?"

"Sure we can, kid. What's your name?"

"He already tells you his name. His name is Red."

"Too hard. Can we call him Jack?"

"We are already confused on account of the number of Jacks we know. For instance, Jack the Dice, Jack the Hat, Hasty Jack, Two-Face Jack, Three-Face Jack, Halloween Jack . . ."

"But this Jack is different. He has a Diamond As Big As Your Head and also red hair. How can we confuse him with waste-of-time people such as those you mention? I vote we name him Tiny Jack."

"Tiny Jack," said Red. "I like that. Let's play bank robbers . . ."

Hundreds of years in the past, the Tootings were tootling through medieval Mexico on their way home from the Cretaceous period. They paused for a while to watch the Aztecs put the finishing touch to a giant pyramid. The Aztec pyramid rose up, then brambles and cacti grew all over it in the time that it took Chitty to slip into the air.

They flew across the Atlantic, which was mostly covered in ice, then not very covered in ice, then almost all covered in ice again. Soon Chitty was dipping toward the White Cliffs of Dover, bumping over the turf toward the A20. It was good to be breathing the fresh sea air (which was completely free of pterodactyls or bullets) and to look down on the bright blue bay (which contained neither

piranhas nor alligators). Soon they had landed on the dear familiar road with its helpful road signs, so different from the twisting and mysterious forest pathways of Amazonia. When passers-by tooted or waved, they all waved back. Chitty always made people stop and stare. More so than ever, now that she was covered in gold.

They stopped for petrol. It was the very service station they had stopped at on the day Jem realized that the little model plane he'd been given by the man in the scrapyard was Chitty's mascot: the magical Zborowski Lightning.

"We were just about here," said Jem, looking around nervously, "last time Tiny Jack tried to kill us."

They shuddered. They had all forgotten who was waiting for them in Zborowski Terrace.

"Of course! We can't go home!" cried Jem. "Tiny Jack is waiting for us. We have to go back to 1966 and get the Potts to help us."

"Why should we let Tiny Jack scare us out of our own home?" asked Mum.

"Because," explained Lucy, "he's very scary."

"But we are the Tooting family. We've faced dinosaurs and gangsters and anacondas. We're not scared of Tiny Jack. Or Tiny Anything Else. We can defeat Tiny Jack on our own. We don't need the Potts to help us. Time to go home."

13

It seemed no time at all before they had parked Chitty outside the house in the middle of Zborow-ski Terrace. They got out and lined up. They all held hands, ready to face whatever danger lay inside. They might have hesitated. They might have changed their minds. But before they had the chance, the front door opened itself and the kettle switched itself on.

"I'd forgotten all about the automatic welcome!" said Mum. "How lovely."

They went inside.

Everything looked just how they had left it the day they set out on holiday. There on the dining table were the sunglasses Dad had forgotten. Lean-ing against the wall was Jem's surfboard—which

they'd decided was too big to bring. There was a pile of newspapers ready for recycling. It was as though they had only just gone.

There was no sign of Tiny Jack. Or Nanny. Or anyone else.

"Are we sure they're not hiding upstairs?" said Jem.

"I'll go and see," said Mum.

"Careful!"

"I can wrestle anacondas. I'm not scared of a nanny."

There was nothing upstairs but their own dear bedrooms. The walls of the landing were covered with framed family photographs: pictures of Lucy holding Little Harry, of Mum and Dad getting married, of Jem in his first school uniform. Of everyone on the beach in Dorset.

"We used to think it was exciting going to Dorset," said Dad, who had come upstairs now that he knew it was safe. "But now that we've been to El Dorado . . ."

"It *was* exciting. It was lovely, too. Oh look!" said Mum, pointing at another photo. "That was the day you caught the fish!"

"It's nice to be home," said Dad.

"It's wonderful to be home."

"Tea's ready!" called Jem. "I'm going to go and

get some milk and biscuits from Mr. Ainsworth's shop."

Jem felt strangely happy walking round to Mr. Ainsworth's. He pushed his hands deep into his pockets, felt the sun on his face, and enjoyed the comfortable feeling of knowing exactly where he was going and what he was doing, without worrying about pumas or gangsters.

A bell rang at the door of the shop as he strolled in. Mr. Ainsworth came through from the back and said, "Hello, Jem."

"Hi, Mr. Ainsworth," replied Jem, thinking how nice it was when people knew your name. He put the milk on the counter along with the packet of ginger biscuits he'd picked out.

"Not seen you for a while. You want to start delivering the papers again?"

"Yes, I suppose so," said Jem, taking a paper.

"Been somewhere nice?"

"Just here and there."

"Home now, though. Best to be home for Christmas."

"Christmas?" gasped Jem.

"Don't say you've forgotten it's Christmas?" Mr. Ainsworth laughed.

Jem grabbed the milk, the paper, and the biscuits

and hurried home. He saw them now—the signs of Christmas all the way up Zborowski Terrace. On the lawn of number three stood a highly decorative plastic sleigh and six almost full-size plastic reindeer with lit-up antlers. A twinkly electric shooting star was parked above the door of number seven. On the roof of number nine, a giant inflatable Santa sat hunched over the chimney pot.

"Dad!" Jem shouted as he burst through the front door. "It's Christmas . . ."

"Christmas?" said Dad. "Did you hear that, everyone? It's Christmas. Come on, let's get the decorations up."

The Tooting family Christmas tree was a real tree—a blue spruce—growing in a pot outside on the patio. Every year they brought it in, and every year Dad played the game of pretending it was too big to bring inside the house. It never quite was, but this year it was close. The top of the tree just touched the ceiling when Jem and Dad moved it into its traditional position in front of the French windows. The Tooting family decorations were kept in a big box behind the water tank in the loft. Dad said that Lucy could climb up and get them since she liked dark, damp spider's-webby places so much. Lucy climbed up and sat for a while behind the water

tank, thinking about how quickly even the most exciting day turns into yesterday, then she brought the box of decorations down to the living room. She and Dad and Jem began to sort them. Mum stood staring out the window.

The decorations had been collected over many years. In a way, they were like a little history of the Tooting family. Here was the cardboard-and-glitter angel that Lucy had made at playgroup. Here was the robin made from Little Harry's handprint.

"And look," said Lucy. "Here's the crib that Jem made as a present to us all. Remember? The crib with five kings and no baby Jesus. Because he had silver plasticine for the crowns and forgot about Jesus completely."

"And here's the drawing Lucy did," said Jem, "of King Herod killing the innocent babies. And when Mum said it wasn't Christmassy, she said, 'Well, it must have been round Christmastime.'"

"Oh, yes," said Dad, "she really loved drawing pictures of severed limbs. And do you know what this is . . . ?"

"Yes, Dad, you tell us every year."

He was holding up a pair of delicate, sparkly little angels. "These," he said, "were the first decorations we ever bought. We didn't even have a tree. We just had these two angels—one each."

He sneaked up behind Mum and quietly hung the angels, one on each ear. She turned around, ready to tick him off, but then she saw the decorations the children had put up. Jem had already set the Advent candles on the table. Lucy had already strung red ribbons from the light fittings.

"Christmas." Mum sighed. "Christmas in our own house. Where else would we want it to be? Bring me the ladder, I'll put the angel on top of the tree."

"You know," said Dad, as he helped Mum down from the ladder. "We went to some amazing places and met some amazing people, but no one was as amazing as you are, and nowhere is as wonderful as this."

Mum leaned down and kissed him on the nose. Which was bad enough. But then he kissed her on the lips.

"OK, you've just ruined Christmas," said Lucy. "I'm going to my room. Call me in the New Year."

The moment she walked back into her room, though, Lucy's heart skipped a beat. Here were her books, her models, her drawings, her notebooks. Here were all the pieces of Lucy that Lucy had forgotten about. Plus there was a door. It had been a long time since Lucy had been able to close the door and loll about in a room of her own, just thinking and listening to the house stretch and rumble around her. She turned on her computer, her mind on all the Facebook updates that would be waiting for her—all the bits of news and gossip, everything that had happened while she was away. How lovely it was going to be to catch up with all that. How strange it was to have had so many adventures but be back in their own house, with hardly any time gone.

She thought about how nearly they had changed the whole course of human history by accidentally taking a dinosaur to New York. But the dinosaur did change the course of the race. The race in which the Count was killed. Maybe he didn't die after all? She turned on her computer. All she had to do was look him up on Wikipedia, then she'd know his final fate. What if it was something worse? What if he was still alive? While the computer booted up, she knelt upon her bed and looked out the window. Snow was falling through the streetlights.

That's strange, thought Lucy. *I didn't notice that it was snowing.* She pressed her face against the window to get a better view. "Oh!" she said. "It's not real snow at all." Moving down Zborowski Terrace was a machine like a kind of grit-spreader—but it wasn't spreading grit. It was spreading snow. A thick carpet of perfect white snow. Moving along that carpet, just behind the snow-spreader, was a beautiful, enchanting sight. A sleigh—a real sleigh—pulled by a dozen very real reindeer. In the driver's seat was a woman dressed like the Snow Queen, and next to her was someone dressed as an elf. Children came running out of all the houses to get a closer look.

"Mum! Dad!" shouted Lucy. "Look out the window."

"What?"

"Look. Just look."

Lucy settled down at her desk, and as her computer went online, she listened to the excited voices discussing whether they really were real reindeer, and how many there were, and what were they doing there, and . . . were those other children getting a ride on it?

She listened as the front door opened and Mum led Little Harry out into the street. She watched as Mum carried Little Harry right up to the sleigh.

*

The Snow Queen lady smiled from under her fur-trimmed hood and asked Mum if Little Harry would like to sit up alongside her.

"He's just a bit nervous," said Mum. "Maybe I could get up there with him."

"I'm afraid we have a height limit," said the lady. "It's a health-and-safety thing."

"I'll go with him," said Jem. "Unless I'm too tall, also."

"No, you're just right. Is it OK with Mum? If big brother looks after Little Harry?"

"I think so," said Mum.

So Jem boosted Little Harry up onto the beautiful sleigh.

"Well, isn't this exciting?" said the lady with the hood. She raised her whip and cracked it over the backs of the reindeer. The reindeer leaped in their harnesses and galloped off down the street.

"Doesn't that look incredibly dangerous?" said Dad, who had come out to see what was happening.

"Nothing wrong with a bit of incredible danger," said Mum.

"But isn't it a bit odd?" said Dad.

The neighbours were leading their children back indoors. The children tugged at them, wanting to

follow the sleigh. Lucy came out into the artificial snow.

"There's something very strange happening," she said. "According to Facebook, it's the fifteenth of June."

"There's something wrong with your computer," said Mum. "Everyone knows that Christmas is the twenty-fifth of December."

"That's what I thought. Then I looked at the newspaper Jem bought earlier. That says the fifteenth of June, too."

Just then, Mr. Ainsworth from the shop went by on his bicycle. "Happy Christmas!" he called.

"Happy Christmas!" said Mum. "See, Lucy? Of course it's Christmas. Little Harry and Jem just went for a ride on Santa's sleigh."

"Mr. Ainsworth," said Lucy, "how many shopping days to go till Christmas Day?"

Without a second's hesitation and with a merry chuckle in his voice, Mr. Ainsworth replied, "Just a hundred and ninety-one shopping days to go."

"A hundred and ninety-one? Isn't that quite a lot? Doesn't that mean it's . . ."

"June the fifteenth," said Lucy. "It's not Christmas at all."

"It didn't used to be Christmas," agreed Mr. Ainsworth, stopping his bicycle. "But ever since

Tiny Jack came to live here, there's no such thing as Not Christmas. He wants it to be Christmas every day. Always Christmas, that's his motto. Always Christmas and never winter."

"Did you just say," said Dad, looking down the street to where the sleigh was careering round the corner and out of sight, "did you just say 'Tiny Jack'?"

"The very same. Why, he's the living spirit of Christmas. Well. Must go. Ho, ho, ho."

Mr. Ainsworth pedalled off.

"To Chitty!" shouted Dad. "We have to follow that sleigh."

The sleigh bounced down Zborowski Terrace and onto the main road. Cars pulled over to let it past. Drivers leaned out to take photographs with their phones. They didn't hear Jem shouting, "Call the police! Call my mum!"

Soon the sleigh was at a slip road to the motorway, where it stopped. Jem grabbed Little Harry and tried to jump free, but with amazing dexterity, the woman in the cloak cracked her whip, and it wound itself around Jem's feet. Holding him by the shoulder, she pulled Santa's sack from the back of the sleigh and pushed it over Jem's head, then stuffed Little Harry in after him.

Plunged into darkness, the two boys could not see what the drivers could see: a large helicopter made of Legos dropping out of the sky toward them, and the woman whipping off her hood to reveal a mass of gorgeous red hair. It was Nanny.

Seconds later, a winch descended from the helicopter. Nanny grabbed it and, with the two boys in a bag over her shoulder, she was hauled skywards. Once she was aboard the helicopter, it soared off over the Downs toward Dover.

Inside the sack, Jem and Little Harry could hear Nanny laughing. "Look behind us, Tiny Jack," she trilled. "Somebody wants to play . . ."

Chitty Chitty Bang Bang flew through the night, hard on the tail of the chopper. Into and out of the moonlit clouds, over the White Cliffs of Dover, and out to sea, skimming the waves. Until up ahead they saw what looked like a small town rising out of the waves.

"Château Bateau!" cried Lucy. "Look! They're landing on the main deck."

"Tiny Jack's evil lair. We can't land there—he'll feed us to the piranhas."

"I'd like to see him try," snapped Mum. She grabbed the steering wheel and brought Chitty

skimming in to land between two great chunks of standing stone.

"Crikey," said Lucy, as she stepped onto the deck. "Look! He's stolen Stonehenge."

"Yes, that was a bit naughty," came a voice from behind them.

Nanny.

At the same moment, they were all struck by how strangely like Bella Sposa she looked. But how was that possible?

"How nice of you to bring the car," she purred, "and to polish her bodywork so brightly. Why, she almost looks as if she's made of gold. Tiny Jack will be pleased. He does love gold. He's tucked up safe in bed just now, the little darling. I'll wake him. I can't wait to see his face. This is quite the nicest thank-you present ever. You really shouldn't have."

"Thank you for what?" snapped Dad.

"Thank you for giving you back your children." Nanny smiled.

She pointed to the Santa's sack, which was dangling from a wire, hanging over the piranha pool. The water in the pool boiled with hungry fish.

"I have to admit that in the past we have thought of trying to steal Chitty from you, but really you're all so clever, we found we couldn't

do it. And, besides, it's so much nicer to get things as a present, don't you think? Tiny Jack loves it when people just give us things. For instance, you could give us Chitty Chitty Bang Bang. And we could give you Little Harry and Jem."

The Tootings stepped away from Chitty. Nanny pressed a button on a small remote she took from her pocket, and the water drained from the piranha pool, leaving the fish gasping and flopping. "Looks like it's fish for tea again tonight." She sighed. When the fish had stopped flopping, she let Little Harry and Jem out of the sack.

"Mummy!" yelled Little Harry, running back to Mum.

"That's right," said Mum. "Mummy is here."

"And so, finally, is Tiny Jack." Nanny smiled.

A little figure had appeared at Nanny's side. The Tootings stared. At last they were face-to-face with their nemesis, their evil archenemy. All the Tootings gasped.

"But Tiny Jack," stammered Dad, "you're Red. Our little friend Red. The boy we . . ."

"The boy," snarled Tiny Jack, "that you abandoned in New York all those years ago."

"Don't feel too bad about it." Nanny smiled. "After all, you did leave him with a Diamond As

Big As Your Head and two hardened criminals to take care of him. Really a very good start in life."

"You look well," said Mum. "You haven't changed a bit." It was true that Tiny Jack seemed not to have grown an inch. He still had a mop of thick curly red hair, even though he must be one hundred twenty years old by now. "What's your secret?"

"Tiny Jack is fabulously wealthy," said Nanny. "Money can buy you anything, even youth."

When Jem looked closer though, he could see that Tiny Jack had changed really. His eyes were dull and mean and weary. His fingernails were bitten to the quick. His hands were old.

"You all forgot about me. And all I wanted was to play a few games."

"He just wants to play." Nanny sighed. "He really does love to play."

"Dear Red . . ." said Mum.

"It's Tiny Jack," said Tiny Jack. "Not Red."

"We didn't just leave you behind," said Lucy. "We would have liked to take you with us. But we thought if we did, that would change the course of history. We were always trying not to change history. We even let poor Count Louis drive to his doom in the end."

"History," sneered Tiny Jack. "I OWN history." He pointed to Stonehenge and to the Sphinx and all the other great treasures he had stolen.

"We could play a game now," said Dad. "We've got Travel Scrabble in the car."

"Too late!" roared Tiny Jack. "Soon I will play a different kind of game. A game called Destruction. Cities will be my pieces. Death will be my dice."

"What about hide-and-seek?" said Mum.

"Take them away!" roared Tiny Jack. "Take them for one last ride in Chitty Chitty Bang Bang. One last ride in my car."

When Nanny cranked the engine and climbed into the driver's seat, a great hope arose in Jem's heart. Even as the Tootings got in behind her, he thought that Chitty wouldn't start: not for her; only for them.

Chitty started the first time. Nanny drove her straight to the edge of the cliff and over it.

Of course! It was a trap! Chitty would surely crash into the sea and rid the world once and for all of that terrible supervillain and his nanny.

But Chitty floated lazily over the sea on her gorgeous wings.

Soon they were all lost in their individual memories of their Chitty adventures. Lucy thought about

her last sight of the Count; Jem of the City of Gold; Mum and Dad of the breathless nights of party-ing in Manhattan. *Dinosaurs,* thought Little Harry. They were all so lost in their daydreams, they were all surprised to find that Nanny had parked on a busy London street.

"Everyone out," she said.

Obediently they stepped out onto the pavement while she settled once more into the driver's seat.

"You'll never get away with this," said Dad.

"Chitty won't let you," said Mum. "She likes us. She'll never let you take her away."

"I'm the only one who understands her," said Jem. "We're not going to let you keep her. We'll get her back somehow."

"Somehow I don't think so," said Nanny. "I've come up with a simple but brilliant way to stop you from stealing her back." She slipped the hand brake and readied the clutch.

"Oh, really?" sneered Jem defiantly.

"Oh, really, really, really, really, really." Nanny smiled before adding, "Really."

She drove off. A few minutes later, they saw a small shape with powerful headlamps soaring high over the rooftops.

It was only when she had gone that they real-ized that the people around them looked different

from the normal London crowd. They were mostly men, and nearly all of them were wearing hats. Mostly woollen hats with matching scarfs. Some of them were wearing rosettes and carrying wooden rattles.

"Football!" shouted Little Harry.

"He's right," said Jem. "She's put us down outside a football match."

"Oh!" said Dad, looking up at the white domed building across the road. "That's the old Wembley Stadium. She might have left us a bit nearer to home."

"You mean," said Lucy, "the old Wembley Stadium with its iconic two towers built in 1923 and described by Pelé as the Cathedral of Football . . ."

"That's right," said Dad, "dear old Wembley."

"The Wembley Stadium that was demolished in 2003?"

"Ah," said Dad.

"Oh," said Jem. "Nanny hasn't just left us in London. She's left us in the past."

"But how long ago in the past?"

Dad stopped a passing family—a mum, a dad, and two children—and asked them who was playing.

"Who's playing?" said the father, a distinguished-looking man in a Navy uniform.

"Who's playing?" The little boy laughed.

"Why, England, of course!" said the girl.

"England and Germany," said the mother.

Jem was staring at this family. He seemed to have seen them somewhere before.

"It's the World Cup Final," said the man in the Navy uniform. "And after that, fish and chips. Good afternoon." He marched briskly toward the turn-stiles, taking his family with him.

"England in the World Cup Final!" said Dad.

"How unbelievably exciting," said Mum, squeez-ing his hand.

"The Potts!" said Jem. "That's who they were. The man in the Navy uniform was Commander Pott, and the children were Jeremy and Jemima. We searched the Amazon for them, and now we've found them in north London."

"How lovely!" said Mum. "We'll have so much to talk to them about."

"Doesn't anyone understand what's happening here?" spluttered Lucy. "When was the last time England was in a World Cup Final?"

"1966, of course," said Dad. "Everyone knows that."

"So where are we now?"

"We are in 19 . . . Oh," said Dad.

"Exactly. Nanny and Tiny Jack are worried that

we'll try to get Chitty back. So they've solved that problem by dumping us in the past."

"Perfect," said Jem.

"How is that perfect?" said Lucy, "We're in London over thirty years before we were even born. With no way of getting back to our own time, and now an evil supervillain and his nanny have got the means to travel back and forth in time doing whatever evil things they please."

"We're in the same time and the same city as the Potts. If we join forces with them, we know we can defeat Tiny Jack once and for all. And maybe even get Chitty back for good."

"You're so right," said Mum. "Quick, everyone! After them!"